THE MEDUSA MISSION

"We're in a double bind," the president replied. "We need to solve this problem surgically. We need to use the scalpel on the tumor; otherwise there will be no stopping its growth. A negotiated settlement would have the result of inevitable escalation. What has happened before on the Korean Peninsula was built on our original miscalculations in 1953. We can't afford another screwup."

"Mr. President," Starkweather answered, choosing his words with care, "there is a strike plan available for use that is designed to deal precisely with this contingency. I can present the plan in depth at a later time, but I can sketch out the broad parameters of the plan for you and the working group right now."

Claymore leaned back in his wing chair and pushed the eyeglasses that few except White House intimates saw him wear up on his head.

"Let's hear it, General," the president said. "And give it to me straight."

Starkweather rose. Assuming his customary stance facing the cold fireplace, he began to speak, quickly gaining the complete attention of every person present in the Oval Office.

"It's called the Medusa Option, gentlemen," he began. . . . "

SPECIAL OPS

David Alexander

BERKLEY BOOKS, NEW YORK

This is a work of fiction. Names, characters, places and incidents are
either the product of the author's imagination or are used fictitiously,
and any resemblance to actual persons, living or dead, business
establishments, events, or locales is entirely coincidental.

SPECIAL OPS

A Berkley Book / published by arrangement with
the author

PRINTING HISTORY
Berkley edition / February 2001

The Penguin Putnam Inc. World Wide Web site address is
http://www.penguinputnam.com

ISBN: 0-425-17862-5

BERKLEY®
Berkley Books are published by The Berkley Publishing Group,
a division of Penguin Putnam Inc., 375 Hudson Street,
New York, New York 10014.
BERKLEY and the "B" design
are trademarks belonging to Penguin Putnam Inc.

PRINTED IN THE UNITED STATES OF AMERICA

10 9 8 7 6 5 4 3 2 1

Behold, I give unto you the power to tread on serpents and scorpions, and over the power of the enemy: and nothing by any means shall hurt you.

Luke 10:19

In an unusually candid statement, the U.S. Department of Defense's top policy official has acknowledged publicly that the military has covert action teams to combat terrorism and counterterrorist use of weapons of mass destruction (WMD). "We have designated Special Mission Units [SMUs] that are specifically manned, equipped, and trained to deal with a wide variety of transnational threats," said Walter Slocombe, Undersecretary of Defense for Policy. While the existence of SMUs has rarely been discussed in open forum, the tactics, techniques, procedures, equipment, and personnel of the SMUs remain classified. If called into action, they operate under two classified contingency plans that address counterterrorism and counterproliferation.

Compiled from news reports

Some Americans believe that even if North Korea possessed the ability to strike the U.S., it would never dare to because of the devastating response. But I do not agree with this idea. If a war breaks out in the Korean Peninsula, the North's main target will be the U.S. forces based in the South and Japan, which is the reason the North has been working furiously on its missile programs. Kim Jong-il believes if North Korea brings 20,000 American casualties in the region, it would win a war.

Choi Ju-hwal, former North Korean military officer, speaking before the U.S. Senate on October 21, 1997

Shared early warning and the Joint Data Exchange Center basically provides for the U.S. and Russia to provide each other with real—near real time, continuous flow of information from early warning sensors. This information will be processed in a way to reveal such information as launch time, launch point, rough direction of launch, impact point, impact time, as derived from these sensors. This information would be piped in by each side into this Joint Data Exchange Center, which is going to be located in Moscow. We have a site picked out. And the two sides would take their own data and display it on a screen, on a desktop computer-generated display on a screen, where we could both—both sides could monitor each other's information. And the idea would be that these folks in the center would be able to consult both among themselves and with their folks back home to help resolve any ambiguous events. This will be a joint military operation that goes seven days a week, 24 hours a day. It will be continuous. It will be of indefinite duration. The president termed it as "permanent," which is a first.

Rear Admiral Quigley, speaking at a Department of Defense background news briefing concerning reports of a shared U.S.-Russia early warning system agreement, Tuesday, June 6, 2000

BOOK ONE

A CITADEL OF WARRIORS

The wise man can scale a citadel of warriors
And throw down the rampart it trusted in.

Proverbs 21:22

PROLOGUE

THE GERMAN BALTIC
September 1944

Fire and ice. The fire below. Black puffballs of exploding ack-ack from the Nazi antiaircraft gun batteries defending the Baltic coast town of Peenemünde. Once a popular tourist mecca of whitewashed buildings and raked sand beaches, it was now a proving ground for the V-2 ballistic missiles with which a doomed Nazi Germany hoped to win the war it was by now destined to lose.

Ice above. The pale, cold light of a slate-gray dawn, the freezing, driving rain that had begun pelting *Flatbush Fannie's* plate steel fuselage halfway across the North Sea.

The formation of B-17 Flying Fortresses had launched before daybreak from the 303rd Bomb Group's base at Molesworth in the rolling meadows of the Yorkshire countryside. The 303rd was part of the U.S. Army's "Mighty Eighth" Air Force, and the bomber crews wore the unit insignia of a gold-winged eight on a blue patch on the sleeves of their flight jackets.

The fifty-four bombers in the formation flew in vertically and horizontally layered boxes of three six-plane squadrons each. The layering was for protection against German fighters and for accuracy in releasing their bomb loads. The combined drone of the aerial armada's Wright Cyclone radial piston engines became a thunderous wake-up call above northeastern England, but the locals had gotten used to it by this time in their long struggle against Hitler. Soon the deafening tumult had faded out and died away as the formation passed over Britain's white chalk headlands at Folkestone and began to cross the Channel.

The objective was a daylight raid on a target at the extreme limit of the B-17's range. The bomb run left no margin for error, and every member of *Flatbush Fannie's* seven-man crew was aware of it. The Brits bombed by night, the Yanks by day. That was the way the air war over Germany went in the last years of the great conflict.

The planes had swept eastward through the predawn twilight and had reached their ordnance release points just as dawn was breaking over the Harz Mountains of northeastern Germany. German radar had picked up the mission over Rostock several hundred miles away, and the sortie ran into a flak front as it approached Peenemünde. Yet even with advance warning, the enemy had been caught napping, and the flak barrage was relatively light. The bombers were out of the thick of it and over their targets within minutes.

Hardly had their 2,000 pounders begun to hit when the Fortresses swung around to start the return leg of their flight. This time, the flak front was heavier as they passed over the Harz range. They were now flying straight into a storm front, too. Freezing rain and hail began pelting the planes from above as the deadly pom-poms of twenty-eight-millimeter antiaircraft fire exploded all around them.

Still, most of the formation might have made it home. But as it came out of the flak, the bomber wing found itself facing a squadron of Bf 109E Messerchmitts. It was an ambush, and the bomber crews counted more MEs than they'd ever seen together at one time. The shark-nosed attack planes of the Luftwaffe opened up on their larger, slower-moving targets as soon as they had them in range, strafing their wings and fuselages with automatic fire from their twenty-millimeter nose cannons.

The Flying Fortresses were aptly named, though, and were not easy prey. The B-17s were heavily armed, intended to be able to fly their missions without fighter escort. The ships packed a total of thirteen .50-caliber heavy machine guns mounted on three turrets, one up top behind the cockpit, and the other two at the aircraft's chin and amidships just behind the wings along the Fortress's underbelly. More fifties bristled from waist gunner's ports on both sides of the plane, and a tail gunner's position at the rear of the fuselage.

As the Messerschmitts heeled around for another pass, the gun crews in the bombers gave the Luftwaffe fighters a run for their money. As the B-17s split up to draw off pursuit, fire blazed away from their multiple gun mounts. *Flatbush Fannie*'s chin turret gunner took aim at one of the MEs that was heading for it full tilt. He could see the face of the pilot behind the cockpit canopy and the sneer on his lips as the ME's twin 7.92-millimeter machine guns rattled in tandem and scorching lead ripped through the bomber's thin metal skin.

The Fortress's top gunner sighted through the crosshairs of the .50 cal's pancake sight and cooked off a long burst of lead. The Messerschmitt pilot had already begun a wingover and sharp turn to avoid answering fire, but he was too slow and had gotten in too close.

A zigzag of incandescent tracers raked across the nose of the German fighter, shattering the cockpit canopy and instantly killing the pilot. More glowing white bolts smashed through the ME's exposed wing. The Messerschmitt burst into flames and broke apart. Tumbling and spinning, the wreckage plunged toward the sea below, spewing black smoke contrails as it fell below the gunner's horizon.

But another Messerschmitt popped up just behind the

downed plane and evened the score. A burst of twenty mike-mike cannon fire smashed through the B-17's forward turret, blowing the top gunner's brains out the back of his skull, killing the copilot, and severely wounding the pilot.

"Jake! Jake, you okay?"

The bombardier, Billy Trencrom, had crawled out of the plexiglass nose where the Norden bomb sight was located. He was bruised and cut but otherwise unhurt.

"I'm hit, Billy. I think . . . my gut . . ."

"What's with Danny?"

The wounded pilot glanced over at the blood-spattered form sagged in the copilot's seat, jiggling like a discarded marionette with every bump and lurch of the shot-up plane. He turned his head to speak over the back of the seat.

"He's . . . he's all fucked up, Billy."

"Damn it," Trencrom cursed. "Damn it to hell."

Danny Marshall was Trencrom's friend from the old neighborhood near Gerritsen Avenue. They'd both lied about their ages to enlist. Danny's family had shopped at the Trencroms' grocery store since before he'd been born. For a fleeting moment, Trencrom wondered what he'd tell Danny's mother when he got back home to Brooklyn.

Then the sounds and the smells of his own impending death snapped Trencrom out of his reverie. The bombardier grabbed for ladder rungs on the bulkhead as choking smoke began filling the lurching, shuddering plane. Looking up, he saw the corpse sagged in the gunner's chair above him.

"Can we make it back?" Trencrom asked, coughing the irritating smoke from his lungs before climbing up to the gun turret.

"I dunno," the pilot answered, face blackened by soot, eyes wild, flight jacket stained with arterial blood. "Number two engine's had it, and I think three and four are about to go."

"Wally's hit."

"Is he—"

"He bought it, Jake. I'll get behind the gun."

Trencrom rolled the body of the top gunner aside and

climbed into the blood-spattered seat. A knife-edged wind and freezing Baltic hailstones whipped his face through the shattered canopy, and clouds of caustic black smoke from the damaged plane obscured his view of the sky. Trencrom tracked the gimbal-mounted, heavy machine gun back and forth across his horizon, searching, *searching* . . . Where was the Nazi bastard? Where the fuck was he?

Like a vengeful ghost, the Messerchmitt suddenly appeared from directly beneath the bomber, its machine guns blazing as it streaked in for the kill. Trencrom loosed a burst of belt-fed automatic fire in answer, the shell casings spinning from the .50 cal's chattering ejector port and jangling on the deck amid fumes of acrid cordite. Yet all his shots went wild. The Messerchmitt, ably piloted, rolled and banked, then vanished from sight.

Trencrom felt the stricken bomber lurch then, and heard Jake yell that they were going down; he couldn't hold her steady. Trencrom kept scanning the skies. He wanted to get that ME before he had to bail out, or the kraut would strafe any survivors as they chuted down. *One more chance,* he thought. *Come to Papa . . . baby, baby, please come to Papa. . . .*

There she was again. The ME had popped back up from below. It was a different climb angle but the same maneuver, and this time Trencrom was both ready and lucky. His fingers tightened on the machine gun's twin spade trigger grips. The big gun spoke God's wrath, and he saw the jagged line of pockmarks appear across the riveted flank of the fighter. The Messerschmitt began trailing black smoke and arced downward, spinning like a top, to crash somewhere below.

Scratch one Messerschmitt, Trencrom thought. Yet *Flatbush Fannie* was also mortally wounded, and the American bomber, too, was about to go down in flames. It looked like the game would have no final winners, but at least Trencrom had outlived the kraut pilot.

"I got the ratzi bastard, Jake! I got the son of a bitch!" Trencrom shouted as he hustled down the gun turret ladder to the flight deck. But there was no answer from the cockpit, and he was blinded by the stinging clouds of heavy smoke inside the cabin.

"Jake!" he shouted again as the smoke seared his lungs. "Jake, talk to me, buddy! Talk to me!" Seconds passed, and still there was no answer from the cockpit. The pilot had bled to death at the controls of the plane.

Now the sky seemed to pivot on an invisible fulcrum that pried it from its ordained place overhead. Trencrom knew for sure that his number was finally up. Before he'd even have a chance to get his chute harness on, the plane would crash. Like rest of the crew, Trencrom was about to meet his maker.

1
A LUCKY BREAK

LOW EARTH ORBIT

At 2023 hours Zulu, three hundred miles above the planet, orbital track number 6951 of 2000-41C swept across the terminator, whirling the *Lacrosse* radar satellite from the shadow cone of the solar penumbra into the glaring brightness of day.

The five-ton imagery intelligence bird, an ungainly amalgam of seemingly mismatched parts, was built for utility, not style, and in the airless void of near space, it didn't need any streamlining.

With the stubby winglike solar panels jutting from either side of its cylindrical body and the protective shrouding of its synthetic aperture imaging suite that looked something like a beak, the satellite resembled nothing so much as a gigantic penguin, dodo, or goony bird fashioned of metal, plastic, and glass that had risen from the arctic wastes like a helium balloon to float high above the planet.

As *Lacrosse*'s orbital trajectory continued, the solar panels tilted ninety degrees, pivoting their flat tops toward the solar disk, where hundreds of photovoltaic cells of shiny black silicon and germanium drank in the sunlight and converted it to the electrical power needed to recharge the imaging platform's batteries, which had been drained by hours of orbiting in the intense cold and total darkness of terrestrial night.

Lacrosse's nickel hydride batteries began to charge, and servomotors within the goony bird's head whirred to life, rotating an array of dish antennas into position.

2000-41C, a designation made up of the year in which the satellite was placed in orbit, followed by its number in line since the first *Lacrosse* was launched, the launch site (in this case Canaveral), and which identified it on the computers of the National Security Agency's ground tracking station at Fort Meade, Maryland, was now on station over northern Iraq.

WASHINGTON, D.C.

Some ninety minutes after *Lacrosse* began mapping a broad swathe of Iraqi territory approximately 400 miles in width and transmitting the imagery earthward, the computers at NPIC, the Central Intelligence Agency's National Photographic Interpretation Center, an office of the CIA's Directorate for Science and Technology, had assembled the ones and zeros of binary data into high-resolution imagery of the terrain below.

Stored on reels of magnetic tape on one of the custom-built Cray mainframe units that packed the climate-controlled deep level of the belowground computer farm at Langley, the imaging data was coded to conform to a bigot list of four persons who had authority to view and print hard copy from it.

One of those persons occupied an office one story above the Washington, D.C., municipal bus stop at the River Entrance of the Pentagon. The other three persons were located on the floor above, in a secure room within the beehive complex of the National Military Command Center, or NMCC, a room guarded by Marine MPs and cipher-locked against anyone who might get past them.

The room was unofficially known as The Dark Tower, and its denizens made up a top-secret planning cell answerable only to the occupant of the office above the bus stop, and to the president, who had signed the executive order authorizing the operational nerve center into existence.

◆　◆　◆

"General," a voice said. "Looks like we finally caught a live one."

Four-star General Buck Starkweather, chairman of the Joint Chiefs, stood at the stand-up desk behind the one-way window above the River Entrance bus stop and cradled the handset between shoulder and chin while noting the main points of what he was being told on the yellow legal pad in front of him.

"I take it this means the winds have shifted," Starkweather answered the man on the other end, Air Force Brigadier Allister "Wizard" Crowley. The internal Pentagon phone line was secure, but the general, a collector of aphorisms, kept the Confucian saying to heart: "Always act as though ten fingers are pointing at you and ten pairs of eyes watching you."

"Affirmative, Buck," said Crowley. "It looks like the mother lode this time. You might want to come down to the pit of the fallen angels and see for yourself."

"Think I'll do that, Wiz. Expect me in ten," Starkweather said and rang off.

The CJCS went back to his writing. It was a brief thank-you note to a well-wisher who had sent his condolences. Months had already passed since Starkweather's son, John, had perished while participating in an Army test flight of the Osprey tilt-rotor aircraft.

John's death would always leave a void, but the general

knew that dwelling on it would serve no purpose. John was Starkweather's only son, but he was also a soldier and had died while serving his country. He had died a hero, as he might have died in combat.

A soldier's grief only went so far, and then it was time to move on. It was harder for Bess, the general's wife. She would take longer to deal with the shock of bereavement, but he would help her, and it would be one more reason for him to be strong.

The chairman completed his note and sealed the envelope. Laying aside the pen, he looked out the window, watching a bus pull in and disgorge passengers, most of whom worked at the Pentagon.

Over the years of his tenure, he must have seen this happen a thousand times. Yet it never ceased to fascinate the CJCS. It gave him a sense of continuity, of purpose. Here, in microcosm, was what his job was all about: ordinary people. Americans. Living their lives, doing their jobs. Starkweather had dedicated his life to protecting them against those who would seek to destroy or undermine their freedom to do those things unmolested.

The chairman dropped the thank-you note on his secretary's desk on the way out. She'd see it when she got back from lunch and mail it for him. Anybody who needed to reach him would know where the general could be found.

♦   ♦   ♦

The Dark Tower was a thirty-foot-square windowless room crammed with computer terminals, high-speed color printers and copiers, banks of telephones, and an overworked electric coffeemaker whose valiant service put it next in line for a Congressional Medal of Honor.

One wall was taken up by a bank of analog clocks set to the local times of a dozen world capitals in Zulu or Greenwich mean time. Another wall contained three large, flat-panel cable television screens. The middle one was currently tuned to CNN.

Scattered around the center of the room were a number of desks piled with computer monitors, small network printers, fax machines, outboard disk drives, and an assortment of other related hardware. Two men in B-uniforms sat at one of the desks, while a third stood behind them, gesturing at the display on a large monitor screen that showed color imagery of a point on the earth's surface.

"How you doing, Buck?" the standing man said to the general as he entered. "Want some coffee?"

"Coffee as in coffee you made on that refugee from a Minsk yard sale, you mean?"

"Goddammit, General, with all due respect, you're not going to stand here and insult this coffeemaker," Crowley protested, sounding serious. "As you're no doubt well aware, the acquisition of this coffeemaker was the subject of considerable research by myself and my staff of highly trained military intelligence experts, and it was one of the hardest damned undertakings we've ever done around here."

"It's okay, Wiz, I just had coffee."

"Be that as it may, sir, I'll still not have you insult this valiant servant of our office. Incorporated into the design of this coffeemaker is a stainless steel boiler, in which the water is brought to a precise seventy-two degrees Fahrenheit, in which state it becomes a rushing cascade of bubbling fluid, which is forced through the waiting espresso mixture, which I personally grind from aged Columbian beans."

"Bet you pick 'em yourself, too, huh?" offered the CJCS.

"Would if I could."

Crowley walked over to the coffeemaker while the other two men, both light colonels, looked on. Crowley's expansiveness showed he was in a positive mind frame; Starkweather knew the telemetry from the spy satellite portended good news regarding the planned covert mission.

"I'm sure you understand the significance of this central fact, General," Crowley went on. "Boiling the water in stainless steel as opposed to aluminum means that harmful molecular matter is not communicated to the boiling water. Coffee from this machine will not destroy brain cells with layers of gummy, gooey, oozing, lipidinous plaques.

"In short, it will not give those who partake of its savory output the deadly plague of Alzheimer's or senile dementia, considered by many experts to be produced by aluminum deposits in the neocortex. Unlike virtually any other coffee from any other coffeemaker in this building—and there are undoubtedly hundreds—coffee from this machine can be drunk and enjoyed with no concern for the health."

Crowley poured himself another cup and drank it down.

"Ahh! Always hits the sweet spot. Sure you won't join me, General?"

"Wiz, anybody ever tell you you remind them of the character Sterling Hayden played in that Kubric film, *Doctor Strangelove*?"

"Always considered myself more like the drill sergeant in *Full Metal Jacket*. Besides, that was fluoridation, General. Whole 'nother ballpark."

Starkweather shook his head. "Right now I'm more interested in the telemetry from the bird."

"Then step right up to the plate, Bucky," Crowley advised. "You're gonna love this one."

The CJCS sat down on one desk chair behind a free terminal and the chairman took the other. Crowley sipped his coffee as he picked up a cordless pointing device and zoomed the image.

"What we're looking at now is the upper Tigris as we approach the river locks of Wadi Thartar and the three flood-control reservoirs at Great Zab, Lesser Zab, and Dyalah associated with the aforementioned locks."

Starkweather nodded as Crowley scrolled through a series of satellite imagery frames showing *Lacrosse*'s progression across the river locks and down the Tigris toward southern Iraq, where the Tigris commenced its snakelike meanderings through Baghdad, Iraq's capital city and governmental center.

"As you can see, Buck," Crowley went on, having lapsed back into the familiar first-name basis that the two generals used with one another in a relationship dating back to the last years of Indochina, "there's been considerable change since last week."

"Yeah, you got that right," Starkweather replied as he eyeballed the screen.

The change was profound indeed. It was definitely beginning to look like the long-elusive break for which they'd been waiting months.

The floods of Iraq are traditional and perennial scourges and have severely handicapped agriculture in the southern part of the country. Until the early 1960s, Iraqis lived with inundation as a constant threat. Three-quarters of the population of Baghdad died in a combined flood and plague of 1831, and as late as 1954, floodwaters completely encircled Baghdad.

In the 1960s, a British-German engineering consortium was hired by the Iraqi government to build three enormous floodgates, two on the Euphrates and one on the Tigris. The purpose was to divert floodwaters into a network of reservoirs and artificial desert lakes.

The largest of these floodgates is the massive barrage at Wadi Thartar near the ancient Babylonian capital of Samarra, whose ruins, dominated by a golden-domed mosque, can still be seen on the river's west bank. Opposite this ancient site of Muslim pilgrimage the modern barrage towers—an immense, gleaming white concrete wall over which the silver waters of the Tigris cascade in a swift and furiously roaring stream.

The barrage enables engineers in a control station high on the dam to manipulate the series of river locks to divert the waters into a number of enormous man-made ditches, the largest of which is the Wadi Thartar. For the last several weeks, the seasonal rains of midwinter had swollen the river into spate, and despite the diversion of the barrage, the lower Tigris was still at the high-water mark.

But the picture had now changed dramatically. The constant, steady, unrelenting rains had stopped, and the lower Tigris was now considerably dryer, its flow muddy and sluggish compared to that of the upper half of the river.

The chairman took it all in as Crowley scrolled through more satellite telemetry. He swiveled in his seat to face Crowley. "What kind of a window does this give us?"

"We checked with the weather people," the Wizard said. "We're advised that we've probably got a solid three or four days where the water level will continue to drop."

Crowley used the mouse to open another window on the monitor screen. "This is near-real-time throughput we're looking at now. The bird's currently parked in orbit over downtown Baghdad, as you can see, and the water level of the Tigris is extremely low. I'd say if your Snake Handlers are gonna go in, then it's now or never. What about it, Buck? Think we got us a go?"

The CJCS took in the overhead imagery one last time, then turned his eyes on Crowley. He didn't even have to think about this one, not really. Without a doubt it was the break they'd been waiting for.

"I think it's time to brief the president," Starkweather answered.

Minutes later, the CJCS was in the black Lincoln he used as his personal staff car, crossing the Potomac en route to the West Wing entrance of the White House.

2
ENTRANCES AND EXITS

BAGHDAD

A spilled rainbow neoned the pavements of Rashid Street on the left bank of the meandering Tigris, known locally as the Broadway of Baghdad. Ten hours had elapsed since the CJCS had left General Crowley's secret planning cell at NMCC for the West Wing of the White House.

In his study adjoining the Oval Office, the president had met with Starkweather and given his consent to the operation in the form of PD-207, a presidential directive authorizing the specific points of the mission plan prepared by the office of the CJCS.

A short time later, the Wizard, while tending to his coffee machine at NMCC, learned that the op had been duly blessed with a presidential green light.

In Baghdad, Iraq, it was now slightly past nine P.M. on a mild, winter evening.

◆ ◆ ◆

Despite the omnipresence of their leader's sometimes smiling, more often glowering visage flaunted on colossal posters throughout the city, there was little to remind Baghdadis of the bomb rubble of the Gulf War, now a grim vestige of the late twentieth century.

The populace had learned to live with periodic TLAM—Tomahawk land attack missile—strikes on military targets, as it had adapted to many other hardships, including famine, plague, and internecine warfare, that Baghdad had endured during its lengthy existence.

The West was waiting for the occupant of Iraq's many presidential palaces to die or abdicate. In the meantime, it would make periodic strikes to poke pinpricks in the stalemate. The Baghdadis watched Tomahawks, JASSMs, and other standoff cruise missiles sail overhead, unerringly find their targets like pigeons returning to roost, and explode in flaming bolides that lit up the city for miles around. The Baghdadis had grown complacent in the trust they placed in the surgical precision of NATO weaponry.

Tonight, the second night of Operation Swift Sword, was a case in point. The U.S. Sixth Fleet stood off the Iranian littoral, in the Gulf of Oman. American and British warplanes flew repeated sorties over suspected Iraqi arms dumps, weapons research centers, and test facilities.

Ramadan had been a reprieve, a time for negotiations, threats, and United Nations sanctions. But these had been expected to fizzle. After Ramadan's end, the gloves had once again come off the mailed fist. The previous night marked the commencement of the punative air strikes, and Baghdadis were again spectators at the bonfires of their leader's many vanities.

Despite the fighting, Rashid Street's restaurant row was doing a booming business. The winter evening was pleasantly balmy, and the *shamal* of the day before had cleansed the air of the ultrafine, almost lunar dust that those who have never set foot in Middle Eastern deserts mistakenly persist in calling sand. The moonless night was clear, and countless stars shimmered in the jet-black sky.

Soft music drifted from the interior of one restaurant, the Ishtar Gate, specializing in kebabs and curry dishes. The owner, Mustafa Baz, eyed the controlled bedlam of the establishment's dinner hour with a bemused smile as he stood by the bar, chatting with a customer.

Business was good tonight, but that was expected. Baz had been preparing for this reopening week after the Ramadan fast with great care. His restaurant was one of Baghdad's finest, and he had a reputation to uphold. His eatery was not only popular with Baghdadis, including those who lived in the ever-expanding sprawl of suburban bedroom communities to the city's north, but renowned throughout the Middle East.

Even many Westerners dined at his place, at least those few who traveled to Baghdad anymore. Once the British and French had ventured here in force. Then the Americans had arrived to displace them. Still later on, the Russians made up the largest foreign community in Baghdad. But those days were long gone.

Today, only the Germans and Australians continued to arrive in any numbers. Baz considered them cold and aloof, but at least they made it a habit to mind their business. They went about their affairs, they spent their money, and then they departed for home. More of their countrymen soon replaced them. They cared little about embargoes, blockades, sanctions, or international politics.

This found favor with Mustafa Baz, because Baz cared passionately about such matters, and their indifference meant that fewer eyes were watching him as he went about certain business of his own that he wished to keep as discreet as possible.

◆ ◆ ◆

In Baghdad there are numerous tiny streets. Some of them terminate in dead ends. Others run straight down to the waterline of the Tigris River. From a small pension on a narrow lane branching off Rashid, an athletic-looking brown-haired man of medium build bearing an Australian passport, identifying the holder as Derek Maddox, walked onto the street.

Both name and occupation were deceptive. The man's real surname was Trencrom, and while his first name was in doubt even to the NSA's massive Fort Meade computer database, most called him Ice. As to his job—tonight, as at other times, it was demolition.

There were plenty of taxis to be had at the wave of a hand, but the hotel stood near the Tigris, which flowed through the center of town, and in Baghdad it was often far easier to take a boat where you wanted to go.

Trencrom knew there were always boatmen hanging around at the ends of the many narrow alleys that run down to the waterline, especially at this time of evening, and for a few piasters a passenger might sit back and experience a ride as enjoyable as anything offered by a Venetian gondolier.

Trencrom turned into the shadowed mouth of an alley identified as Wadi al-Ghotrawallat, Street of Crocodiles, by the Arabic sign high on one brick wall. He walked a short distance to the end, hearing the soft sloshing sounds of water lapping against stone grow louder, and smelling the pungently briny river odors, mingled with sweet incense smoke, as he pushed deeper into darkness.

The glowing orange dot that painted the sign of infinity in the gloom ahead marked where one of the two boatmen he heard talking softly to one another were loitering. They greeted him with enthusiasm, as they knew him well by now, bidding Trencrom *"Khoub bash,"* welcome, in their local Arabic dialect.

"Good evening to you, Hassan," the Westerner replied to one of the men whom he recognized, greeting him by name in perfect Baghdadese. "I need a reliable boatman and a sturdy boat to take me safely to my destination."

"I am reliable, and there is no boat finer than this one of

mine," the smoker answered, flicking his cigarette into the Tigris and inviting Trencrom to climb into the skiff, as he stooped to arrange the sun-bleached, cushioned upholstery of the small river craft, then laid a well-worn wooden plank between the edge of the stones and the side of the boat.

Trencrom stepped into the slightly rocking gondola, helped by Hassan's wrinkled, leathery hand. Leaning into the cushions of the seat, he made himself comfortable, stretching out his legs and propping them on the ornately embroidered pillows at the center of the boat that Hassan had provided for his passengers' ease and comfort.

The old Iraqi boatman pushed off with the end of his long-handled paddle and began to row the skiff into the center of the broad expanse of the sluggishly flowing river. Soon Trencrom noticed that the odor of tobacco smoke from behind him had changed into the pungent smell of locally grown hashish. Not even the burning censers of incense at port and starboard completely masked it.

Within minutes, passenger and ferryman were far from their starting point, and Trencrom inhaled the aromatic night breeze—car exhaust, spearmint, tobacco, and rotting sewage were all part of the olfactory mélange—as he watched the mysterious ancient city slowly glide past.

It was an eerily beautiful sight. The time of the evening muezzins was over, and the stillness of the city was broken by the soft rustling sounds the river wind made as it wafted around him, the coughing of boat engines, and occasional glancing beams of car headlights on unseen streets beyond the water's margins.

The boat ride would help the foreigner work up an appetite for his dinner. It would also help him evade pursuit. Being watched and followed were part of life in Baghdad for foreigners and natives alike.

"How goes your business with the many bombs raining down?" Trencrom asked the old man perched behind him at the stern, who had begun to sing an ancient *fellaheen* chant as he rowed and smoked hashish, the song's strange, lilting cadence timed to the measured, powerful strokes of his long wooden oar.

"It has made little difference," answered Hassan after a thoughtful pull on his hashish pipe. "Like hunting falcons, the Western bombs fly where they are bidden. None have exploded inside Baghdad for many years. We now take them for granted, as we do the *shamal* in winter or the black flies in summer."

"How is it otherwise with you, Hassan?" asked the foreigner, for he had known the old man for some time.

"All is well with me," he replied. "Allah be praised."

"Yes," Trencrom answered in the local manner. "God is great," for Allah, beyond its other many meanings and connotations, simply meant *God*.

With that, the brief conversation ended. There was nothing more left to say. As he drifted into his own reverie, Trencrom heard the boatman pick up the dropped thread of his *fellaheen* chant, singing in time to the cadence of his rowing, pausing once to suck the last of the hashish smoke into his lungs.

As the gondola made its way downstream, ably rowed by Hassan's paddle, the second boatman at the end of the Street of Crocodiles saw another potential fare make his appearance. The boatman had seen this man before, but even if he had never laid eyes on the man, he would have recognized his kind, and his eyes would have grown wary, as in fact they now did.

"Would you care to rent my humble boat for a journey, short or long, *ya shaikh?*" he asked the newcomer in Arabic, in the flowery manner of his profession, making the customary salaam. "It is comfortable and safe, and the price is affordable to all who journey by night."

The newcomer, a small man in the traditional *fellah*'s uniform of sport coat, sweater vest and open-necked shirt, did not look directly at the old boatman. Instead, his slitted eyes were turned downriver, where an almost imperceptible pinpoint of light indicating the battery-powered lantern at the prow of Hassan's skiff floated into the shadows of night river traffic and was finally lost to view.

"Tonight I desire nothing, old one," he replied, glancing into the boatman's eyes for just a moment. "Nothing save your forgetfulness at having seen me."

He held the boatman's eyes a beat longer, then turned and walked quickly back toward the main street. The boatman heard a car door slam and echo off the alley walls. Harsh commands were barked from far away. A motor growled, and the squeal of tires followed like the cry of bitten prey.

The ferryman gave the visitor no further thought as he lit a cigarette and softly hummed an ancient tune while he waited for another fare. It was still early, and more would surely come.

♦   ♦   ♦

Mustafa Baz looked up and saw one of his regular patrons arriving, speaking with the Ishtar Gate's maître d'. The patron favored his usual table, one near the window, where he could look out on the street.

But tonight, Baz saw there would be a problem. The maître d' had given his table to other diners, two turbaned Kurds who disdainfully shot dark glances his way as they chewed their lamb kebab and drank from small cups of thick, spiced and sugared Turkish coffee. Baz left his seat at the bar and hurried toward the front of the restaurant.

"Good evening, *Ya Shaikh* Maddox," he said to the Occidental. "Good to see you here."

"Sir, I—" began the maître d'.

Baz cut him off.

"I'll handle this," he said. Turning to Trencrom, he went on, "My apologies, sir. I know you have your table reserved." He looked around. "We can seat you somewhere else, perhaps at a very private table back there, or you may wish to have a drink at the bar."

"I'll take the table," Trencrom told the host.

"Very good, sir," Baz said. "I will send over a bottle of a

most exquisite vintage, something extraordinarily rare, and a tray of choice apricots, dates, and sweet rice, by way of apologies."

Trencrom thanked him as the maître d' led the way. The exchange did not go unnoticed by the thin, perspiring man who entered a moment behind the Australian and sat down at the bar. By now, Trencrom knew him like the back of his own hand, and apart from its benefits to his appetite, the boat ride had been deliberately chosen to throw a wrench into the works of his sweaty shadow.

The man was from the *Da'irat al Mukhabarat al Amah*, otherwise known as the Iraqi General Intelligence Service or GID, an organization currently headed by Staff Lieutenant General Manee Abd al Rashid and numbering approximately 4,000 agents in its ranks.

One of Iraq's numerous internal intelligence services, the GID's two main jobs are internal security at home and intelligence and assassination operations abroad. In the latter role, the GID has often acted as Baghdad's long arm, silencing dissidents granted asylum in foreign countries.

From behind the imposing wall of its vast complex in Baghdad's Mansour district nicknamed the Great Wall of China by knowledgeable locals, there is little inside Iraq that the sixteen offices of GID's three main bureaus do not play a part in. The operative who had reached the Ishtar Gate after a frantic search of other restaurants on Rashid Street in pursuit of his quarry was a member of Office Seven of the GID's counterintelligence section.

This fact explained the sweating man's hyperactivity, since it was unusual for Office Seven to be involved in a matter as routine as keeping tabs on foreign workers staying in Iraq on temporary visas. This sort of action was normally handled by the Office of Counterintelligence.

Office Seven, by far the most feared office in the GID, was responsible for the interrogation of espionage suspects, as well as the inevitable executions that follow, usually at a special killing center and detention facility at Khandari, about twenty miles west of Baghdad, set up to make people permanently disappear.

Tonight, a suspect named Derek Maddox was to be placed under arrest and spirited away to Office Seven's main interrogation center at the GID's 52 Street facility. In one of the three soundproof floors sunk below ground level, he was to undergo extensive physical and chemical interrogation.

The espionage suspect was to have been arrested as he left his hotel, but he had departed moments ahead of his would-be captors. He had also given conflicting indications of his dinner plans to the hotel staff, no doubt deliberately.

As Trencrom sat down at his table, and the perspiring intelligence operative took his place at the bar, other GID operatives were inconspicuously entering the restaurant, ready for a signal from the agent at the bar. But others at the Ishtar Gate had different plans tonight, including the establishment's owner, who could not resist the urge to glance at his wristwatch as he walked hurriedly away.

THE PERSIAN GULF

The 3,000-ton behemoth that was the nuclear aircraft carrier USS *Franklin Delano Roosevelt* slipped through the black waters of the Persian Gulf, her four giant screws turning beneath her immense fantail. Like the nucleus of an enormous atom, the carrier occupied the center of a constellation of smaller, nimbler, but no less formidably armed warships spaced at six-mile intervals from one another.

The time was 0400 hours Zulu. Overhead, the black, moonless bowl of the Southern Hemisphere was flecked with stars. The *Roosevelt* was blacked out except for her navigation lights—red to port and green to starboard—as were the other ships of the carrier battle group, and watch standers on the bridges of each vessel kept a sharp lookout to maintain safe distance.

The *Roosevelt*'s crew stood at general quarters. Though it was one-sided and would probably be brief, there was a war on, and the carrier group was to play a major part in it.

In the dim sapphire light of the ship's Strike Warfare Center belowdecks, the *Roosevelt*'s thirty-man combat team manned their battle stations, hunched over equipment consoles that crowded the bulkheads and crisscrossed the deck of the windowless, air-conditioned room.

In the center of Strike, on a high-backed padded chair, his eyes fixed on a large, flat-panel display screen mounted near the ceiling that showed radar plots of vessels in the Gulf, sat the *Roosevelt*'s skipper, Captain Lawrence H. Magnusen. Magnusen's eyes left the screen and went to one of the adjacent consoles, where the ship's chief missile officer, Lieutenant Commander Roland Gray, sat in a chair normally occupied by an ensign.

In fact, the chair had been occupied by Ensign Joe-Bob Hillenkoeter throughout the successful salvos of three dozen Tomahawk Land Attack Missiles, toward selected strategic targets north of Baghdad throughout the early-morning hours.

Not this particular launch, though.

On the captain's orders and on the orders of CINCLANTFLT, which Magnusen was himself following, the launch of the next TLAM in line, designated number 1098-WRB-0999, was to be under the direct guidance of the chief missile officer, which is why Gray was now occupying the ensign's chair.

Gray had just completed downloading satellite telemetry containing the coded targeting coordinates for the TLAM, and he could see by the digital console timer that the ship was nearing the center of its launch basket.

The download was completed without mishap, and a few minutes later, the TLAM's targeting data were stored on board the array of solid-state virtual hard drives—a series of six blocks of silicon linked together like the primitive brain of a dinosaur—that gave the missile its redundant memory of several hundred gigabytes of data storage.

Gray picked up the white internal telephone beside his station and punched the glowing button to connect with the captain.

"Ready when you are, skipper," he said.

Magnusen watched the digital numbers tick past on the screen.

"Launch the bird," he ordered.

"Aye, aye, skipper," the missile officer replied and racked the receiver.

The weaponeer armed the TLAM and then activated the firing sequence by pressing the lighted square button to the right of his scope. Nothing happened for a few seconds. Then the occupants of Strike felt a slight side-to-side tremor as the missile launch rack on the *Roosevelt*'s deck moved to and fro in order for the TLAM's laser gyroscope to take a fix on its current position.

Another few moments passed, and then the telltale rumble of the TLAM's chemical booster rockets igniting was felt and heard through the *Roosevelt*'s bulkheads as the Tomahawk burst from its gray steel cage and shot into the night.

"Alpha, alpha!" the lieutenant reported. "Missile away!"

As the rumble ceased, radar began to track the rapidly ascending bird, which soon leveled off and disappeared in the night. Within a matter of minutes the TLAM's smoldering booster stage had dropped off, and the Tomahawk plunged into the cold, choppy waters of the Gulf of Oman.

Then its air-breathing turbofan engine ignited, and TLAM 1098-WRB-0999 began its one-way, ninety-minute flight into Iraq. Unlike all the other cruise missiles fired from the *Roosevelt* that night, its destination was to be the heart of downtown Baghdad.

Also unlike the others, its war load was a specially designed package known by the secret Pentagon code name JAM-D.

BAGHDAD

The passive infrared monocular starlight scope mounted atop the Heckler & Koch MSG02 sniper rifle was linked by digital cable to a microprocessor module on the masked shooter's belt. A target reticle—glowing red crosshairs—framed and sectioned the scope's 180-degree field of view. The video imagery seen through the scope would be permanently recorded as gun-camera footage for postmission analysis.

At the scope's upper right quadrant were four black digital boxes, marked AU-1 through AU-4. Each box bore a red check mark. The check marks designated the other members of the clandestine strike team who were situated in the vicinity of the area under surveillance by the sniper.

In place of radio click codes, transponders that produced a coded electronic fingerprint linked each of the five-member unit to one another as long as radio silence was maintained. The balaclava-masked figure swept the image-intensifying scope along the front of the building across the street, then down toward street level, to sight in on the detachment of uniformed Iraqi regulars guarding its entrance.

Limned in cathode green, two of the soldiers were discussing something as they stood around and chain-smoked Turkish cigarettes. A third sat behind the wheel of a heavy truck and stared idly off into the distance. The passive IR scope continued to transit the scene, then came to rest on the sign above the door.

Its ornate Arabic script identified it as a date packaging plant, the Al Waftah Street packaging plant, to be exact, a state-subsidized factory. The sniper, who was a woman nicknamed Jugs by her all-male teammates, checked her wristwatch, which was set to Zulu time. Four hundred hours; less than fifteen minutes to the zero mark.

A second insignia was emblazoned below the stars and bars shoulder patch she wore on the right sleeve of her black nylon action togs. It displayed a hand gripping a curious compound image that was part nuclear mushroom cloud and part cobra's head, its fangs bared, its forked tongue menacingly protruding.

Above and below the image were two words: *Snake Handlers*.

3
A CHANGE OF PLAN

TLAM 1098-WRB-0999 vectored across the Iranian littoral on a low-trajectory flight path and was soon dozens of miles inland. It climbed steeply to transit the Zagros mountain range, paralleling the Iranian border on a northerly course for several miles, but then it abruptly swung due west to cross directly into Iraq.

Swooping low once more, the missile commenced a series of radar-evading jinks and dives as it sped toward its target in the lighted capital city straddling the Tigris. Though invisible to radar amid the ground clutter of Doppler echoes, the Tomahawk missile's arrival did not go unheralded. Its flight path was glimpsed by many along the way.

As the TLAM passed over the outskirts of the city, the cruise missile was spotted by celebrants at a rowdy bachelor party in one of Baghdad's many suburban enclaves. And as it streaked across the urban center of the city, it was noticed by many Baghdadis who were out that night to shop, to dine, or simply to stroll, oblivious to the havoc about to break loose all around them.

Most, if not all, observers assumed that TLAM 1098-WRB-0999 was on its way to somewhere else, a winged messenger of destruction bound for military targets. They had no doubt that it would simply pass them by, as had all the other cruise missiles fired during Swift Sword so far.

They were wrong.

BAGHDAD

The Australian patron sipped his red wine as he ate his meal of couscous in pungent garlic sauce and charcoal-braised lamb kebab. From time to time, his glance strayed to the wiry Iraqi in the shabby tweed sport coat who sat at the bar with his back to the tables behind him, munching nuts and dried dates from a cut crystal dish.

The Australian knew he was being watched in the bar mirror by the slim man at the bar. It wasn't that hard to pick out the other GID assets strategically positioned throughout the restaurant, either. They went with the territory in Baghdad.

Nevertheless, something felt wrong tonight; the vibrations were bad. There were too many GID circulating inside, and the diner guessed probably more were waiting outside. That in itself was a departure from routine.

Trencrom glanced at his watch and took another sip of the house wine, but not too much. The intelligence officer from the Mukhabarat continued chewing his morsels and staring into the mirror. He would not touch a drop tonight. There was an important arrest to be made at the Ishtar Gate, and he needed all his faculties intact.

Then, with startling suddenness, everything changed in an instant: TLAM 1098-WRB-0999 did the unexpected. Tonight, many plans would be spoiled.

◆   ◆   ◆

The cruise missile streaked overhead and suddenly it did what few TLAMs did: It clobbered. The Tomahawk lost altitude and nosed down, striking the iron wellhead at the center of the square with a deafening report.

Panic seized hold of the restaurant's patrons as the twelve-foot-long, two-ton missile fell out of the sky and plunged to earth right in front of the restaurant. The TLAM had landed intact. For a moment, it lay motionless on the paving stones. Suddenly there was a soft explosion from inside the fallen missile. The missile still lay there undamaged, but now thick, acrid clouds of smoke began issuing from the fallen smart bomb, which had apparently gone dumb.

The smoke had the strong, caustic odor of garlic and an ominous greenish tinge. The garlic odor was familiar to many Iraqis, especially those who had served in military units stationed in the rebellious northern Kurdish strongholds or were themselves of Kurdish extraction with roots in the region: It was the telltale stench of mustard gas.

The deadly blood agent that blackened and blistered skin, blinded the eyes, burned out the lining of the lungs, and choked the esophagus in a flood of mucus had been extensively used by Iraqi troops in gas attacks on several occasions. The heavy odor of garlic wafting through the air was certain to spark the memory association in many bystanders that night and to galvanize most of them into panicked flight.

"It is gas! Poison gas!" someone shouted from the interior of the restaurant, the identity of whom the Iraqi Mukhabarat would later take some pains to discover, though their efforts would prove ultimately fruitless. "The Americans are using chemical weapons! Run for your lives!"

No one needed to be told twice. People suddenly began to stampede for the front door. Outside, women fainted, as though overcome by toxic fumes. Other patrons fell to the pavement to thrash and writhe in seeming death spasms. An epidemic of panic spread through the streets.

In the mounting confusion, Trencrom's departure went unnoticed as the maître d' led him down a back hallway and out a normally locked rear exit door for staff.

In the back alley, Trencrom turned his jacket inside out and pulled a black balaclava mask over his head. Trencrom needed no special breathing apparatus because he knew that the gas was nothing but colored and specially scented smoke produced by the JAM-D package. Moments later, still unobserved, he had descended into the mouth of a manhole cover that led down into the Baghdad sewer and drainage system.

The *Lacrosse* intelligence had proven accurate. The water level of the Tigris River had been low enough for Trencrom to have reconnoitered the ancient drainage tunnel the previous day and made a map. The water level was even lower tonight. Two weeks before, just prior to the final reconnaissance photoimagery, the Tigris had been running almost at spate, and the underground tunnels were flooded right up to the cavernous ceiling.

The good news from the NMCC a week before was that the height of the river had fallen enough for the sewer and drainage tunnels beneath the city to be navigable on foot. The intelligence had cost nearly a million dollars in various HUMINT and TECHINT resources, but if the black operation succeeded, it would be well worth every cent billed to the American taxpayer.

Behind a stone support column, Trencrom found the duffel bag full of gear he'd stashed on his earlier recon of the route. The duffel contained a short-barreled Colt Commando, an SMG variant of the M-16, several clips of 5.56-millimeter ammo, a brick of Semtex plastic explosive, and an electronic timer and detonator caps.

The Commando was equipped with a laser target designator mounted on the underside of the barrel and a sound suppressor in place of the muzzle brake that was normally a standard fitting for the SMG. In the bag was also a lightweight head-mounted display or HMD resembling commercial units marketed for virtual reality gaming, but considerably more sophisticated, and several canister-type grenades.

Trencrom palmed a forty-round magazine into the Commando's receiver, charged and unsafed the weapon, and slung the head strap of the HMD around his neck so the unit could be quickly fitted in place but for the moment would dangle free. He rolled up the duffel and hid it behind the stone column, then began walking carefully along the slick embankment of the stone channel full of brackish canal water.

The distance he needed to cover was not far, only a few hundred feet at most, but the going was treacherous on the ancient, slime-encrusted masonry. One slip might plunge him headlong into the putrid water flowing sluggishly in the channel below.

Trencrom made time as quickly as possible, soon reaching a section of wall where he'd marked a small X in black spray paint on his prior trip. Taking the brick of Semtex from his jacket pocket, he began kneading the plastic explosive into a long rope approximately a quarter inch in diameter. When finished, the Semtex rope was about five feet long.

Trencrom next began applying the plastique to the surface of the wall in a spiral pattern that radiated outward from the spray-painted X. After a few minutes' work, the Semtex formed a tight ring of concentric whorls about two feet in diameter. Trencrom next pushed a detonator cap into the center of the soft mass and connected it by two wires to the electronic ordnance timer, which he set for a thirty-second delay and stuck to the wall with its adhesive backing.

Taking cover, he donned the HMD and waited. Seconds later, there was a loud bang, and the wall disintegrated in a flash of light and a cloud of dirt and pulverized rubble. As the debris cloud cleared, Trencrom flung two antipersonnel stingball grenades into the hole, hearing the canisters detonate in the smoke and debris beyond the tunnel.

Right after the APERS cans went off, Trencrom was up, bolting through the jagged aperture torn in the ancient stone wall on a half crouch, the Commando tracking left and right, the ruby shaft of its target designator laser lancing out through the smoke-laden air. Thanks to the low-light imaging capabilities of the HMD, Trencrom's view of the basement was sharp and clear. There was no indication of unfriendlies in his vicinity.

Trencrom tapped on the buttons of the wrist-top keypad he wore, and a glowing digital map overlay of the entire building appeared. From top to bottom, it was all there. He could scroll through the entire floor plan if he needed to. Flashing arrows directed him toward his next mission waypoint. Treading quickly up a narrow flight of smooth, time-worn stone stairs that Roman centurions might once have climbed, cradling the Commando SMG, he followed where they led.

◆   ◆   ◆

Above ground, as word of poison gas circulated, people rushed from the door of the date cannery—there actually *was* a cannery on the ground floor. There are seventy-six species of date palms known in the Middle East, and each one of those is indiginously cultivated and grown in Iraq, which is the region's central grower, processor, and packager of dates.

Apart from being Iraq's capital city, Baghdad is also the home base of the Middle Eastern Date Grower's Board, the central clearinghouse for dates in the region. Yet the building had been identified as one of the roughly eighty-two nuclear weapons development sites in Iraq. Like the Al Firdos building many years before, the so-called cannery doubled as an air raid shelter. The government's denials masked a deliberate policy of deception.

Tonight, though most Baghdadis turned a blind eye to the NATO strikes, many other families had taken shelter inside the plant. Indeed, they were encouraged to spend nights at the shelter in return for doles of food and other necessary items, the purpose of these incentives being to unwittingly turn the Baghdadis into human shields.

The American surveillance satellites overhead would record the conspicuous deliveries coming into the cannery in special equipment containers that had nothing to do with fruit, but it would also note the presence of innocents on the premises. Iraq's dictatorial leader was counting on it not to be hit by a TLAM. He wasn't wrong, but he wasn't exactly right, either.

◆ ◆ ◆

The pocket square near the Tigris was soon thronged with the frightened and desperate. It was every man and woman for themselves. The frightened crowd pushed and shoved to squeeze into the several alleylike side streets that radiated from the cobbled plaza like the spokes of a wheel.

In the distance, two-note sirens rose to a doleful crescendo as firemen and ambulance units sped to the scene.

Panic reigned, and in the confusion few if any noticed men in plain clothes speaking into portable radios and openly brandishing firearms. The GID crews were unconcerned about the missile crash or the pungent vapor cloud it had emitted. By now they were aware that these were diversionary maneuvers. They were intent on one thing: finding a spy who had slipped from their grasp.

◆ ◆ ◆

The first emergency services unit arrived on scene. It pulled in front of the cannery and skidded to a sharp halt. Three men in Baghdad fire department slickers jumped from the truck, grabbed various gear from inside the vehicle, and rushed toward the entrance. A guard inside the vestibule raised his rifle as the first of the rescue personnel approached. One of the EMS guys flicked out his hand, and the guard caught the momentary blur of something hurtling toward him.

In an instant Floaty's throw had plunged two inches worth of *shuriken* into the guard's right eyeball, nicking the forebrain. As the guard struggled to pull the spiked Ninja throwing star from his head, the Snake Handler rushed him, knocked him down, and crushed his windpipe with a foot blow to the throat. Death quickly followed.

Three other guards stationed just inside were taken out using the two-tap method by well-placed silent shots from compact Ingram M-11s, with the SMGs' right-hand selector switch set on semiauto. The M-11s fired the slighly underpowered nine-millimeter short round and were equipped with a variant of the Hush Puppy–type sound suppressor designed by the infamous Mitch Werbel in the 1960s, which slowed the rounds to almost subsonic velocities.

The combination of caliber type, sound suppressor, and rapid cycling rate made the M-11 a precision tool for close-quarter killing. As brass spat from their breaches, little more than the metallic snap-snap-snap of the blowback-driven firing pin striking the base of each cartridge marked the discharge of bullets from the weapons.

The dark angel came silently, but its presence was unmistakable. Each target received two well-placed bullets, the first in the head, the second in the heart. The lifeless bodies crumpled to the floor. Contorted in death postures, they lay in seeping pools of blood.

The killers replaced their machine pistols in special break-away holsters and unshipped the more powerful Colt Commando submachine guns they ported as primary defense weapons. Not very much longer than the suppressor-equipped M-11s, the Commandos were short-barreled versions of the M-16 rifle and fired the same 5.56-millimeter tumbling ammunition. The Macs made good "room brooms," but the Commandos had far greater range and serious stopping power, even with sound suppressors attached, as was the case with these.

The three members of the penetration team knew exactly where they were going. They had studied the layout of the interior for weeks prior to the mission. They moved quickly yet cautiously along a sterile corridor toward a cipher-locked door, beyond which was an elevator shaft leading several stories underground.

◆　◆　◆

Trencrom watched the three yellow triangles move along the schematic diagram of the lowest level of the weapons production complex. Approaching him. He waited with Commando readied as the cipher-locked door was opened. Three men in emergency service uniforms entered, weapons pointing his way. Trencrom switched off the SMG's laser and slung the weapon over his shoulder.

"What's up, Doc?" Floaty asked.

"Let's get jiggy with it," he told the newcomers, taking the oversized hardshell case carried by the tall striker named Nixon. The crew was right on time, Trencrom was pleased to note. Ball, the third squad member, was standing guard outside the room.

While the two circulated around the lowest level of the facility planting timed plastic demolition charges here and there, Trencrom opened the case and removed a series of circuit cards wrapped in electrostatic-safe bags. Working quickly, he unscrewed several panels from the line of consoles, removing circuit cards identical in all respects to the ones in the bags. Then he replaced the originals with the ones he had brought.

Seating himself at one console, Trencrom tapped at the keyboard in front of him while intently following the procession of symbols, numbers, and other data that flashed across various display monitors. In a matter of minutes, he had completed his tasks.

"All done," he said, getting up. "You guys finished at your end?"

"Everything good to go, boss," Floaty said back.

"Then we're out of here."

"You really Y2K 'em that quick, Ice?" asked the taller of the two commandos as he prepared to extract. Richard Muhammed Nixon did most of his talking around the half-smoked panatela cigar normally found clenched between his teeth.

"Yeah. Good and proper," Trencrom replied, handing him the component cards he had removed from the panels.

Trencrom hoped he'd been as effective as he sounded confident. The switch had been made quickly, but a lot of hard work had led up to this moment. The seeds of the plan were sown some two years before, while Iraqi technicians wrestled with the consequences of failing to remove the year 2000 bug from their embedded computer systems and software.

The time had been a profitable one for informants with the right technical information to sell to the CIA and for creative thinkers in the dirty tricks departments of various U.S. intelligence branches. The CIA's crackers had used the period to stage massive information attacks on the computer systems of rogue states, such as Iraq. The operation was risky, but the payoff was a potential bonanza.

With the replacement of key components and the reprogramming of the Iraqi system at this base alone, gas centrifuges producing radioactive isotopes for Iraqi weapons could be directly controlled from Washington. With the press of a button, a monkey wrench could be thrown into the entire process. If successful, the operation would pay dividends for years.

"We're still on schedule," Trencrom said to Nixon and Floaty, checking his watch. "You guys know the drill."

Both nodded. Nixon said, "Later," and hustled toward the door, his partner in train, Ball joining them outside. Trencrom heard the trio's cadence of rapid, muffled footfalls as he made for the aperture in the wall by which he'd entered the building.

As he regained the ancient drainage catacombs, he heard the demolition charges explode behind him, the primaries first, then the secondaries joining the chorus in a double bang. If all went well, and the opposition went for the disinformation that would be made available to its intelligence service, it would look like a sloppily staged attack on the weapons plant by U.S.-backed dissidents—one that proved unsuccessful because some of the charges failed to explode as expected.

♦　♦　♦

Trencrom raised his head from the sewer opening, looked around, then lifted himself onto the street. As he stooped to slide the heavy iron lid back over the manhole, he felt something hard and cold jammed into the rear of his head. His first impression was *gun muzzle*. He wasn't wrong.

"Slowly, Mr. Maddox, very slowly," the voice behind him ordered. Trencrom straightened and turned to look into the face of his GID shadow. The wiry little man from the Ishtar Gate's bar had returned.

Minutes later, Trencrom found himself seated in the rear of a Toyota truck with his captor and another GID man on either side. A third Mukhabarat agent drove the vehicle. Trencrom watched the streets whirl past as the truck turned and dodged through the downtown section of Baghdad.

Although he had known where he was being taken from the first moment of capture, the procession of street signs and their rising numbers confirmed his destination: 52 Street, and the dungeons, interrogation rooms, and underground killing floors of the GID prison.

The truck slowed for a red light on 47 Street, and the sky was lit up for a moment as a far-off sea-launched cruise missile struck its inland target with the sound of distant thunder. The light began to change, and the driver took his foot off the brake.

In that instant, a heavy truck careened around the corner and smashed broadside into the vehicle. Before the GID assets could react, the four-by was surrounded by masked figures pointing submachine guns into the car.

"The prisoner comes with us," a muffled voice commanded.

The driver made a move, and a staccato burst of automatic fire tore into him, making him shudder as though electrocuted. Bullets chewed up flesh, bone, and upholstery, and safety glass disintegrated in a shower of blood and lead.

"Anyone else?" the shooter asked, getting no takers.

Trencrom was released by his captors and hustled into the truck that had smashed into the four-by. His rescuers then hosed down the immobilized vehicle with concentrated automatic fire, killing the three survivors as cold-bloodedly as exterminating a nest of cockroaches. When the brief but deadly chattering of the subguns had stopped, another rescuer pulled the cotter pins from two minigrenades and lobbed them into the Toyota.

Seconds later, the four-by was engulfed in an aurora borealis of crackling flame and incandescent heat. The former prisoner of the Iraqi GID was packed into the truck, which raced off down the avenue, and with a scream of tires, disappeared down a series of narrow, alleylike lanes.

Trencrom faced the masked figure who had demanded his release.

"Who the hell are you?" he asked.

The figure said nothing, as the black Kevlar-nylon face mask was pulled off, revealing an extremely pretty face framed in long black hair, the face of a sultan's favorite harem girl. The girl could be no more than twenty-five, and whatever else she might have been, she was by now also a thoroughly practiced killer.

"A friend of your uncle's," she said to Trencrom in a voice that went with her face but did not fit her occupation.

Minutes later, the truck came to a screeching halt at a dead end.

"Through the alley and into the car you'll find parked on the other side," the woman ordered Trencrom, the honey in her voice turning to acid as she barked out the command.

"They'll have every damned secret police agent combing the city after this hit," Trencrom warned. What he didn't say was that everything was now compromised, the entire operation, the months of planning, all of it was now gone. The GID would link the ambush and the strike on the weapons plant, and they would eventually figure out what had really happened.

"Do not concern yourself with the police. They are our business," the woman replied and gestured down the alley mouth with the barrel of her weapon. "Quickly! Do as I say!"

Trencrom took off into the dark mouth of the alley. There was nothing more to say, nothing to debate. As they ran,

Trencrom heard another explosion behind them, this one much closer than the sound of a distant munition strike some time before. Though he could not see the flash marking the impact area, Trencrom knew it had to be close by.

It was closer than he realized. Much closer. Another U.S. smart round had just gone dumb and clobbered into the streets of metropolitan Baghdad. Oddly enough, where a burning truck containing four GID corpses had stood moments before, there was now a gaping thirty-foot crater filled with pulverized metal debris and charred bone splinters.

It was yet another amazing coincidence in a night filled with them. And as fate, or highly accurate targeting, would have it, the explosion would just happen to obliterate any last shred of evidence that might compromise the mission.

THE PERSIAN GULF

The nuclear attack submarine *Teaneck* surfaced a mile off Ras Tanajib, a spit of Saudi desert sand covered with thorn trees and scrub projecting into the blue waters of the Persian Gulf. On this moonless night, the waters were jet black, and the sparse desert vegetation looked like the hunched shapes of sleeping dinosaurs against the faint blue light of the false dawn. Standing on the sail were the skipper and his XO, the former holding a pair of Gen-IV night-vision binoculars in his hands.

"They're coming," the captain said to his XO and handed him the binoculars.

Minutes passed. The dim shape in the darkness grew in size and became a silenced Zodiac. Minutes later, the boat's occupants were safely stowed on board, and the submarine crash-dived. The captain had received his orders, and these did not include need-to-know concerning who the four operators were or from where they had come. Not from Saudi, he guessed, at least not as their point of origin.

The skipper had no idea how correctly he'd guessed. The Snake Handlers' escape plan was a variation on the one originally planned to lead from Tehran to the secret base at Desert One during the aborted Iran hostage rescue mission of 1979.

The extraction route lead to the Arabian coast, first by truck to a hide site in the Baghdad suburbs, then southwest, into the desert of Al Hajara, avoiding the more populated areas to the north and east, and then across the Saudi border where two MH53J Pave Lows were waiting. The lead chopper was to ferry the operators to the coast; the other was for emergency backup if it was necessary.

It was thought best not to strain Saudi cooperation too far, and the final leg of the extraction, though an added complication, kept the clandestine mission as operationally sterile as possible.

WASHINGTON, D.C.

At the Pentagon's National Military Command Center, the chairman of the U.S. Joint Chiefs scanned the secret telex just received from several thousand miles away. The message had been sent by burst transmission immediately before the submarine dived and put out to sea. General Starkweather turned to the small circle of trusted officers surrounding him amid banks of computer screens.

"The mission was successful. The plant's fissile materials manufacturing capability has been neutralized according to plan."

"But?"

"But not every member of the team made it out—at least so far."

"Which?"

"Trencrom."

The career soldiers looked around them. There was no need to say anything. The thoughts of each member at this development were shared by all. The CJCS stood up from his chair. It was late. There was nothing more to add.

"Call me when you hear anything new on this. I'll be trying to catch some shut-eye."

Gus was waiting outside the River Entrance, smoking a

cigarette. When he saw the general emerge, he flicked it into the chill wind gusting off the nearby Potomac and pulled open the door of the black Lincoln Continental.

"Something wrong, General?" Gus asked when his passenger was ensconced in back.

"Maybe," the CJCS tiredly replied. "I hope not."

The general didn't want to talk, Gus figured. He respected that, and besides, it was none of his business. He put on the radio to a country music station he knew the general liked, and the melancholy wail of a steel guitar filled the interior.

By the time Starkweather returned home, his wife, Bess, was already asleep. The general climbed into the vacant single bed near the window, as they slept separately, and pulled up the covers.

To his surprise, he immediately drifted off, but his sleep was troubled by a recurring dream of a helicopter rising into the air, then heeling over to crash in a mass of flaming wreckage, and within that funeral pyre he saw a young man's body slowly burn to a charred, black cinder.

Starkweather awoke with a start and sat bolt upright in the dark. He fought back tears for his dead son.

BAGHDAD

"You will stay here until first light," the young killer with the harem girl's face told Trencrom. "Then you go. We have the extraction method all worked out."

They were alone in a safe house, an apartment above a shop in the tanners' quarter of the Baghdad souk. The sharp smell of newly worked leather that came from an adjacent room was a third presence in the night.

"How can I trust you?" Trencrom asked the girl. "You could be anybody."

He saw the girl's face emerge from the shadows, and her dark eyes gleamed. She said nothing for a moment, but Trencrom saw her nostrils flare slightly.

The woman unzipped the contour-hugging body suit she wore. A pair of full, rounded breasts emerged into a pale shaft of moonlight. A ring of metal, pierced through one erect nipple, shone with a dull, silvery gleam.

"There is a way," she said, and she reached for the American in the darkness.

4
SERPENTS UNDERFOOT

SOUTHWESTERN IRAQ

The muffled voices of the border guards filtered through the womb of rusted metal with a strange, distorted quality. It was somewhere near Damascus . . . had to be, from the time on the road, thought Trencrom. The heat was stifling, and sweat soaked his clothing, stung his eyes. In the close air, each breath came heavier and harder than the last. Within his rib cage, Trencrom's lungs felt ready to explode.

The voices faded, then changed to the buzzing of flies. Monstrous flies. He could actually see them, as though the metal had dissolved, become transparent. They peered at him with huge compound eyes in which his fetal image was multiplied a million times. He could not fool them. They knew he was there, inside his iron womb. They would pull him out, snap off his head, suck out his eyeballs, devour his brain. . . .

He caught himself going under, sinking into madness, beginning to hallucinate. *Get a grip!* he warned himself. *You're losing it!*

He made a fist, digging his fingernails into the soft flesh of his palm. The buzzing madness of flies receded. He forced the nails harder into his flesh until the pain knifed through the drowning pool of insanity that had begun to envelop him. Clear headed again, he unclenched his fist and—very sanely now—reached for his pistol.

This was the second border crossing on Trencrom's journey. The first had been at night, and then it had been the bitter cold that had afflicted Trencrom as the truck crossed from Iraq into Syria and turned west to take the old Damascus-Beirut highway toward the distant Mediterranean coast.

Twenty bone-jarring minutes of juddering travel from the checkpoint, the truck had stopped, and Khalid, the driver, had let Ice out of his iron coffin to stretch his legs and have a smoke if he wished it.

"How much longer?" Trencrom had wanted to know.

"Twelve hours, maybe less," Khalid had offered, "depending on how it goes." The guards had been especially suspicious at the border, Khalid had told Ice. They did not openly say as much, but they were looking for something—or someone. Fortunately, there had not been any trouble.

This time, Trencrom could sense that the situation was not the same as before. As he lay there in the heat, his right hand curled around the plastic pistol grip of the Glock 19 semiautomatic, the crease of his thumb touching the trigger's integrated safety, he could hear the voices outside become raised. Khalid and the guards were arguing. Interspersed with the half-heard words were sporadic clangs, thuds, shuffling, and rustling sounds—the telltale noises made by men searching the truck.

Twice there came the clatter of objects tapping against the metal underbelly of the hidden compartment in which Trencrom lay in a bath of his own sweat. His grip around the weapon tightened, and his heart rate climbed as the taps moved beneath him like sonar pings and then traveled along the underside of the lorry.

There came more arguing from outside, and then, to his relief, Trencrom heard the door above him slam shut, the grating of the gearbox as the clutch was let in, and the transmission shifting into second. The acrid stench of exhaust drifted in through the invisible seams of the compartment as the truck lurched from the checkpoint and gathered speed as it regained the road. Trencrom holstered the Glock and wiped the sweat from his eyes. No more hallucinations troubled his heatstroked brain; adrenaline saw to that.

But it had taken considerably longer since leaving this second checkpoint for Khalid to stop the truck and let his passenger out for a much-needed breather. He explained that the guards had been clearly under orders to closely check traffic passing through the chokepoints. They had narrowly escaped. They were in Lebanon now, but even here it was still dangerous for them.

Fortunately, Khalid knew a route into Saudi Arabia that would skirt Lebanese border crossings and maybe shave some time off the trip, too. They would skirt the Egyptian border on the way, at a place where Trencrom could safely disembark.

"We must go now," Khalid advised. "Is not safe to stop too long." He told Ice not to worry as he locked him back inside his iron womb. *Easy for you, my friend,* thought Trencrom.

Much less time passed before the truck stopped again. At first, Ice thought they'd reached yet another border checkpoint, but this wasn't the case. Khalid rapped twice on the underside of the hidden compartment. He told Ice not to fear, that everything was all right now, that he was going to open the compartment and let him out.

Clutching the Glock, Trencrom emerged into still, cool darkness. A pale sliver moon hung low on the horizon. The warm desert wind whipped past his ears, pulling at his hair and drying the sweat from his dirt-caked body.

Khalid told him he didn't need to point the gun at him.

They were safe now, the danger was past. It was a little after midnight, and they had crossed into Egypt. For the remainder of the trip, Ice could ride with Khalid in the cab. Trencrom shoved the Glock into the holster beneath his left arm. This time he did join the driver in a cigarette.

NORTHERN EGYPT

Hours later, Trencrom reached his final destination: Ismaelia, Port of Suez. Khalid was southward-bound for the rest of his trip, which would terminate in the Saudi city of Jiddah.

Midway down the length of the Suez Canal, which ran due south from Port Said at the mouth of the Mediterranean to Suez at the head of the Gulf of Oman, Ismaelia was a rough-and-tumble town. More so even than Cairo or Alexandria, the Egyptian port cities along the Suez Canal were tender-loins in which virtually anything went, especially if those buying goods or services were able to pay in hard currency.

The hundreds of ships, from freighters to supertankers, that passed through the canal's locks each year ferried millions of metric tons of containerized cargo between the business capitals of East and West. The merchant vessels also disgorged their foreign crews on shore leave, eager to spend their accumulated back pay on whiskey and women and always willing to trade in hashish, consumer electronics, run guns, and traffic in contraband of all sorts with the denizens of the canal's port cities.

Ismaelia was a smuggler's mecca, where anything could be had for a price. With or without a passport, Trencrom knew that if there was any place on earth where he could book safe passage to a Western port under an assumed identity, it would be here, in this Sodom on the Suez. In this assumption he was not to be mistaken.

WASHINGTON, D.C.

In the American capital it was four time zones from Ismaelia, half past the hour of eight on a Wednesday morning in late winter. General Buck Starkweather was at his customary work area behind the large, bullet-and blast-proof window of the CJCS's office that overlooked the Pentagon's River Entrance, the main entrance to the citadel of America's military establishment.

The window, which was completely opaque when viewed from outside, faced northeast, toward the Potomac, and from his vantage point, Starkweather commanded a fine view of the Arlington Memorial Bridge that spanned the river. Across the Potomac he could see the urban center of Washington, D.C., with the rotunda of the Capitol Building white and gleaming in the distance. While Starkweather admired the view as much as any of his predecessors, the part of it that interested the chairman most lay just outside his window, literally right under his nose at the bus turnaround a few hundred feet from the River Entrance.

It was here that the route of the number seven municipal bus, which began its journey in downtown D.C., terminated. Since the bus was the only direct municipal surface transportation that serviced the Pentagon, it arrived each morning crammed with passengers, most of whom had jobs in the sprawling five-sided building. At close of business each afternoon, the bus picked up those passengers again and brought them back to where their day had started.

What few if any of the hundreds of riders who passed in and out of the River Entrance's doors each day suspected was that for the past eight years, the senior military officer at the Pentagon was standing behind the dark slab of plate glass that overlooked the entrance, and he was watching their comings and goings with intense interest.

During the years of Starkweather's two-term tenure as the supreme commander of America's armed forces—a supremacy strengthened by the Congressional Act of 1979 and in two succeeding legislative bills—the chairman had become engrossed in the human drama unfolding before his eyes.

On the tide that ebbed and flowed below his window, Starkweather had seen winners and losers, lovers and plotters, men who would not be returning to their wives that night, or who would return to their wives empty-handed after failing to pitch a new weapon system to a Pentagon procurement officer, or who would go home and lie awake for a few hours before returning to the building with matters of global importance pressing on their minds like lead weights.

Last night had been once such night for Buck Starkweather, and although he had never ridden the number seven municipal bus, the chairman was no more immune to the pressures that drove men to drink and impotence and financial ruin than the others he had seen.

After falling into a fitful, dreamless sleep, the general had awakened in a cold sweat. Long before dawn, he had climbed out of bed, showered, dressed, kissed his wife good-bye, phoned Gus, his driver, and before the sun had barely risen, he was back in his office, drinking strong black commissary coffee and scanning the overnight intel reports.

There had been nothing in them concerning Ice Trencrom, nor had the computer terminal on Starkweather's desk—one that was linked to the Pentagon's secure intranet, providing the same SPINTCOM and CRITICOM intelligence the president got—shown any more recent updates of Trencrom's fate after his disappearance in Baghdad.

Still, Trencrom would make it, Starkweather assured himself. He'd made it out of tougher places before. Laos in '74 had been tougher. Prague in '87 had been tougher. Moscow in '94 had been worst of all. Cartagena, Colombia, in 2001 had been nearly as bad.

But then, those other places and those other times were not of Starkweather's doing. This time it was different. Now it had been the general who had pulled the strings to create the Snake Handlers and bring Trencrom out of military retirement to lead the covert operations team. It had been Starkweather who had envisioned the secret counter-WMD force and had convinced the president to sign an executive order bringing the team into existence, enabling him to handpick its members from Delta Force ranks.

And while it was true that Buck Starkweather had put his professional reputation on the line in doing this, it was also equally clear that Ice and his special action cell of picked operators were putting much more than that on the line; they were risking their necks.

Nor did Ice Trencrom have to play a part in it. He'd paid his dues many times over. Since Starkweather had first met Ice in a patch of triple-canopy Laotian jungle in the Shan Mountains a few months before the fall of Saigon, Trencrom had done the bidding of lesser men who pulled the levers of U.S. foreign policy and had served those interests well. Trencrom had been driven by his demons, and those had been placed in his mind by his father's experiences in World War II. Starkweather had ruthlessly and cold-bloodedly summoned those demons to manipulate Trencrom into serving his operational ends.

Ice's father had been the sole survivor of a B-17 bomber crew that had crashed near the German Baltic town of Peenemünde, which had also been the site of the Nazi's V-2 weapons development and testing program. Captured by the Wehrmacht, the U.S. airman had been forced to work in the underground rocketry factory at nearby Nordhausen, an immense network of subterranean tunnels that had been dug and blasted out of the granite flanks of the Harz Mountain range.

Exposure to toxic gases, chronic malnutrition, and sadistic guards had robbed his father of his life, not right away, but in a delayed reaction that had culminated when Trencrom was a boy. Ice had devoted his years since quitting the CIA's paramilitary to building up an international firm dedicated to destroying nuclear and biochemical weapons to honor his father's sacrifice.

Trencrom Industries had reaped millions in post-START-II contracts to destroy nuclear missile facilities in the U.S., the Ukraine, and Russia, among other places. He had designed critical automated systems for the new Single Integrated Operational Plan or SIOP that controlled use of U.S. and foreign nuclear weapons when it was proposed to replace the bilateral Joint Data Exchange system installed in the year 2000. Ice had no reason to be called back into the field. But

Starkweather had been bitten by a bug, and he had infected Trencrom, too.

The greatest destabilizing threat in the postbipolar world was the unchecked proliferation of weapons of mass destruction. Nuclear, biological, chemical, or a deadly mix of all three types of weapon made up WMD. The means of manufacturing and delivering these horror weapons became more and more available to rogue states and terrorist actors with each passing year.

To the chairman, these unconventional weapons required an unconventional capability to counter the threat. When embargoes and sanctions, political or economic pressure, or the sudden appearance of the U.S. Sixth Fleet off some distant coast failed to deter WMD weapons development, something else was needed: something effective, something *deniable*. A small counter-WMD force, a fighting cell toxic to the cancerous spread of nukes and germs and poisons, whose existence would never be officially acknowledged, was the chairman's solution.

And that force could only be led by one person, an individual who was a world-class expert on nuclear, biological, and chemical weapons systems of all types as well as a covert warrior. Ice Trencrom was the man to lead the force, and Starkweather had known the right buttons to press to persuade him to lead it.

The fact that his friend might die as a result of the general's plan had never entered into the calculations. But it had kept Starkweather awake through the previous night and haunted him as he watched the sun rise over the Potomac at the start of yet another day.

Conscience, like snakes, could prove hard to kill.

◆ ◆ ◆

General Buck Starkweather tossed his hard-shell attaché case into the backseat of the 1990 Lincoln Town Car and climbed in beside it. Gus, his driver, shut the door and slid behind the wheel.

Starkweather heard the controlled roar of the V-8 engine come to life and felt the car start on its run with a silken-smooth acceleration. He and Gus went back almost ten years, since his stint as commander of U.S. Army forces in Weisbaden, Germany, during the last years of the Cold War. Among other things that tied the two men together was a shared love of automotive mechanics.

To the general, there were few pleasures in life equal to rolling an engine hoist up to an old car and hauling out a begrimed V-8, then painstakingly cleaning and restoring the engine until it ran sweeter than when it had left the plant.

The engine in the Lincoln was one of those that the two men had worked on in the backyard of Starkweather's residence. It began as a grimy specimen of a General Motors 302, with a Rochester Quadrajet carburetor. The engine had needed a new set of valves, and the accelerator pump and linkage on the carb had needed to be hand-tooled, because no junkyard in the vicinity had yielded up another.

In the end, they'd replaced the old Quadrajet with a Holley 2300 Economaster two-barrel carb pulled from a wreck, and in near-perfect condition to boot. When they were done, the old Lincoln galloped along better than the day it had rolled off an assembly line in the Motor City.

Although the CIA had installed the bulletproof glass, special run-flat tires, and other security features in the general's official staff car, nobody but Starkweather and Gus would touch the engine, transmission, or other parts that made the car run.

The time was now 0915 hours, and the Lincoln was headed toward the Arlington Bridge, its final destination being the White House, where the chairman was scheduled to brief the president and his chief advisers on the covert operation in Baghdad and on other matters of global strategic importance to the United States and her world allies.

◆ ◆ ◆

The ride took twenty minutes, first over the bridge, then along Pennsylvania Avenue, at the end of which the Lincoln pulled up at the West Wing entrance to the White House. The CJCS, following his usual procedure when he didn't want to have to deal with any reporters that might be lurking in the bushes, told Gus to let him out, then to drive farther on and park the car.

"Bring the maps into the lobby, too," Starkweather told the driver, as he got out and headed for the West Wing entrance.

"Sure, boss."

Gus had the drill down pat by now. A zoom lens on a camera could be trained on General Starkweather from a parked car in the distance. If that lens picked up maps, it meant that something could be going on other than a normal presidential briefing. Instead, Gus would discreetly hand off the maps to a White House staffer where they'd be hard to spot from outside the White House gates, and then they'd be brought separately over to the Oval Office.

It worked the other way, too. Starkweather used the opposite strategy to signal the press when he wanted coverage. The reporters knew that when they saw the CJCS making an elaborate show of taking maps out of the trunk of the Lincoln, there was a story to be had and that the general would probably be good for a sound bite or two.

THE WHITE HOUSE

As usual, President Travis Claymore wore brown wing tip shoes that looked brand-new. Starkweather had never seen the president in anything other than this characteristic footwear. Even on working weekends at Camp David, Claymore only changed into sneakers for his morning and evening runs or a fast game of tennis. The joke was that somewhere in the bowels of the White House there was an immense storeroom full of shoes that rivaled Imelda Marcos's fabled collection—except, unlike Imelda's, Claymore's were all the same.

This morning, Starkweather had found the president looking drawn and haggard, like a man who hadn't experienced a decent night's sleep in several days. Outside, sudden rain had begun to beat against the glass of the French windows facing the White House Rose Garden that stood at the back of the president's desk chair. The blustery weather seemed to echo the bleakness of the situation.

"Let's get on with it," the president said, after the White House chief of staff and secretary of defense joined the so-called Gang of Six, an ad hoc White House working group that convened at the president's bidding to assess breaking global events. Among the many circles of power in Washington, it was the circle closest to the chief executive, both mentally and physically, and insiders knew that to challenge positions taken by this select group without good reason was to court professional disaster.

"Buck, you have the floor. Don't pull any punches."

"Thank you, sir," Starkweather said as he took up a position in front of an easel stand supporting a colored map that had been set up to face the Oval Office fireplace by the president's personal assistant, a young Air Force major. Four members of the Gang of Six were present, arrayed in their customary U-shaped deployment around the fireplace.

"Gentlemen," Starkweather continued, "the good news first, then the bad. Our initiative to degrade a worrisome Iraqi nuclear processing capability has been successful. As of oh-four-hundred hours today, the Al Waftah Street production facility is no longer in business. All of our people, except one, were extracted safely and will soon be debriefed. We have reason to believe it's only a matter of time before the missing operator can be accounted for."

"Why's that?" asked the president. "Do we know where he is? Has he been in contact?"

"Negative, sir," Starkweather replied without hesitation. "We do not yet know the whereabouts of the missing operator, but we do know for sure that he has not been captured."

Starkweather's eyes flicked momentarily over the president's head at the worsening storm hurling mercury pellets of ice-cold water against the windowpane. "Our interpretation of events supports the view that he's currently in hiding. We're standing by to extract him at the first opportunity."

"My intelligence has it that your man's already in the hands of the Iraqi GID and may be making like Maria Callas in their little opera house on 52 Street."

Starkweather's jaw tensed. Hughes Stanton, the director of Central Intelligence, knew the identity of the counter-WMD force's senior operative, and he also knew that Trencrom and Starkweather went way back.

"Just where'd you get that intel from, Hughes?" Starkweather answered him evenly, despite his anger.

"A highly placed source in the Iraqi Ministry of Defense," Stanton answered, smiling like the Cheshire cat.

"What you got, Hughes, is just some scrapings off some old camel driver's sandals," the CJCS answered, bettering the DCI's low blow and getting a laugh from the president and the sec-def. "I repeat," and this time he faced the president directly, "there's nothing to indicate the capture of our operator, and I underscore we have every confidence in his safe return."

The DCI was about to retort when the president broke in. The director of Central Intelligence did not like Starkweather, and the feeling was mutual. Starkweather had made a career of flouting the CIA and its unavowed parent organization, the NSA, and had succeeded over the years in creating what was tantamount to both a private intelligence network and a covert paramilitary arm accountable only to himself.

The formation of the Snake Handlers was only the latest episode in the CJCS's track record of flaunting what the CIA considered its institutional prerogatives. That he had done so with the president's blessing was another thorn in the DCI's side, because Stanton knew that the president shared Starkweather's disdain for the conventional channels through which U.S. intelligence worked.

"I suggest we table discussion of this for another time," said the president. "We've heard the general's report on the Iraqi operation. We know it has been successful, meaning a major and very troublesome weapon site no longer exists as a threat. I'd like to move on to another area of concern. Buck, give us a rundown on the situation in Korea."

The laser pointer in the general's hand flicked on, and a dot of ruby light began to describe a circle at a point near the top of the map of East Asia. The light circumscribed a portion of the northeastern corner of the Korean Peninsula, a zone near the Chinese border. Skull-and-crossbones symbols in this area denoted NBC weapons facilities.

"The situation in North Korea shows strong potential for concern," the chairman began. "Since Pyongyang's belligerent moves of the past several months, there has been stepped-up activity in the form of troop deployments to border areas and a general increased state of military readiness. Most disturbing to us is a heightened nuclear warfighting posture in both fixed and mobile medium-range ballistic missiles."

The laser pinpoint jumped from site to site on the map. "The North Koreans have been moving their mobile nuclear missile forces around quicker than walnut shells on a three-card monte player's table. This is troubling news, but even more disturbing is the activation of silo complexes, especially those in the mountainous northern borderland with China and Russia. These silos are dug deep into the bedrock and are hardened against conventional munitions strikes. Worse yet, we think there are other underground silos we don't know about."

"What can they hit with those?" asked the president.

"Plenty," answered Starkweather. "Their first-line capability, specifically the Taepo Dong IV MRBMs, have a range of between two and three thousand statute miles. This means those missiles can not only threaten our military bases in Japan or even hit civilian targets in Hawaii but could also reach Los Angeles. The accuracy of the weapons is in question, but there's no doubt concerning their range."

Starkweather paused and swept his eyes across the room. He saw that he now had everyone's attention. "But here's the worst part," he continued. "We believe some of those nukes may be MIRVed."

"Which?" asked the president.

"That's the joker in the deck, sir," said Starkweather. "It could be the MIRVed nukes are in silos we haven't yet located. If so, even if we struck preemptively if it came to war, we couldn't be sure of doing sufficient damage to the North's ability to play its nuclear hole card."

"Christ," the president answered. He looked down contemplatively. "Give us the rest, Buck," he said after a moment.

"The rest is equally bad," the CJCS returned. "The situation in the Transcaucasus is continuing to destabilize militarily. This is the third strike for the Russian army, which has become mired in a no-win situation on the ground. With the recent coup attempt in Albania by Islamic radicals, the Russians have to now take into consideration a broad Islamist front to their south from which enemy forces can gnaw away at their territory like rats on a wheel of Limburger. They may be looking at the problem in the Transcaucasus from the perspective of an all-or-nothing scenario."

"And in the middle, Kosovo and the southern Balkans," the president concluded, thinking aloud.

"That's right, sir," Starkweather answered. "Right exactly. It's just this big powder keg waiting to explode."

The director of Central Intelligence took the floor next, giving the intelligence spin on the strategic situations. The CIA director amplified on what the CJCS had just told the president, pointing out that C.I.S. President Dimitri Grigorenko was beleaguered by threats and pressure from the communist right to step down.

If a neocommunist takeover came about, and the number-one hardline contender for leadership, Vadim Illich Bogomelov, rose to power, then a broad sweep into the southern Balkans by the Russian military as an extension of the action in the Transcaucasus was a strong possibility. This could then involve NATO forces on the ground in Kosovo and Macedonia and spread to Greece.

In short, the scenario was ripe for a war that could quickly transcend regional conflicts and go global.

♦ ♦ ♦

The rain continued to beat against the French windows of the Oval Office. The briefing was over. The president watched his key advisers file from the circular room until he was left alone with his somber thoughts and the sound of distant thunder rolling across the Potomac.

MOSCOW

The suburb of Kursk lies on a wooded slope above the Moskva River as it empties into the upper Volga basin. The suburb is unremarkable except for a heavily guarded installation that is ranged by a twenty-foot-high, double-tiered perimeter fence, surveilled by pole-mounted security cameras and patrolled by armed troops and leashed guard dogs. The high security seems out of place to protect an otherwise unremarkable assortment of low-rise concrete blockhouses, radar dishes, and hangarlike buildings with prefabricated roofs, but the explanation lies in the fact that the most interesting parts of the base are below the ground.

Running down four levels is Russia's largest and most modern nuclear command, control, communications, computing, and intelligence or C⁴I facility, PVO Kursk. The facility, or nuclear battle cab, as it is known in military jargon, rivals anything in the West, including Strategic Command's underground facility at Offutt Air Force Base or the even larger and considerably revamped NORAD installation in a series of office-building-sized steel bunkers constructed inside the hollowed-out and mesh-reinforced granite core of Cheyenne Mountain outside Denver, Colorado.

From PVO (Voiska Protivovozdushnoi Oborony or Soviet Air Defense Force) Kursk, Russia's still extensive array of land-based nuclear intercontinental ballistic missiles, sea-launched medium-range ballistic missiles, and air-launched cruise missiles pretargeted on various strike points around the globe can be deployed once the proper nuclear authorization codes are fed into the system. The former Soviets, like the Americans or any other major nuclear nation, have in place a strategic integrated operational plan or SIOP that controls the deployment of their scattered nuclear forces.

The SIOP is complex and not easily described in even a page of prose. It is more than just a series of protocols dictating the military use of nuclear forces. The SIOP encompasses a redundant array of dedicated communications systems linking political and military leaders with the vast array of a superpower's nuclear forces in the field. The SIOP also controls the use and deployment of nonnuclear warfighting forces in the event of a conflict, nuclear or otherwise.

The SIOP extends to the so-called football that is carried everywhere the American president goes, including Air Force One and foreign meetings, and the *"chegev"* that the president of the C.I.S. also has within reach at all times, day or night. Both of these code names refer to a computerized checklist of nuclear strike options complete with authorization codes for their immediate use in time of impending nuclear attack.

Be it "football," *"chegev,"* or any other name, the attaché case carrying the laptop-sized computer (a series of code books during the Cold War) is never far from the national leader's side, and periodic dry runs during simulated strategic nuclear alerts remind each leader of the awesome responsibility entrusted to those in whose care it lies.

Despite the major reductions in nuclear forces by the big powers since the fall of the Berlin Wall, East and West both maintain enough megatonnage to reduce the world to smoldering embers within the space of a single nuclear exchange. Furthermore, while raw megatonnage has decreased, the lethality of the remaining nuclear stockpiles has risen dramatically with improvements in targeting, stealth, and miniaturization.

For this reason, as of the year 2001, a radical departure from the SIOPs of the U.S. and the C.I.S. officially took place. On that date, the American SIOP number six and the Russian SIOP number four (referring to the number of times the SIOPs were revamped since the U.S. instituted its first SIOP plan in 1962) became not only automated but interconnected. The reason was inescapably obvious: The man in the loop was obsolete; no one human being could react fast enough or think clearly enough to effectively make critical decisions in the face of impending nuclear attack.

No longer was it simply a matter of dwindling response times before incoming warheads hit their targets. Stealthy cruise missiles that could not easily be detected, thermos bottle–sized bombs that could be carried in knapsacks by terrorists, and the related threats of chemical and biological weapons all added new layers of uncertainty and bewildering dimensions of complexity to the weighty problems of dealing with a strike by weapons of mass destruction. The new dynamic had displaced the simpler concept of direct nuclear exchange central to Cold War nuclear strategy.

The new SIOPs of both countries were now to be included in a broader global SIOP that so far included the nuclear forces of the U.S., C.I.S., and U.K. Treaty negotiations with China, France, and other holdouts were also in progress.

The heart of the global SIOP was a sprawling computer system using massively parallel processing or MPP architectures called "Cinders" for SINDAS, or single integrated nuclear defense alert system. Cinders used a set of Internet software protocols to enable participating computer nets to openly share and act upon information from other nations in the global SIOP network.

With SINDAS in place, the concept of the nuclear first strike had become obsolete and with it the need for a hairtrigger nuclear defense posture. In the age of the automated nuclear SIOP, no nuclear nation could wage a sneak attack with weapons of mass destruction upon any other in the network. Nuclear false alerts could also be quickly analyzed and deconflicted before a retaliatory strike could commence.

It was because of Cinders that Sergei Ustinov was seated at a computer console deep in the heart of the PVO Kursk base poring over readouts on multiple terminal screens. Ustinov was the head of the Russian end of the joint data exchange program charged with Russian compliance to the new automated global SIOP under the terms of the older bilateral agreement.

There was only one problem. The system wasn't working. But that wasn't quite it, either. It *was* working, but not normally, not in the manner that Ustinov would have expected it to function. It was . . . growing . . . changing. . . . It could even be said to be metastasizing.

As Ustinov went over the data, he became more and more convinced that the Russian SINDAS should be shut down and a thorough systems analysis conducted. But first he needed proof of what he suspected—ironclad proof. The kind that would save his job, even his life, if what he suspected turned out to be true.

WASHINGTON, D.C.

The same heavy rain that snarled traffic on Pennsylvania Avenue, chased disgruntled tourists from the White House gate, and vexed the president of the United States as he sat at his Oval Office desk, fell on the pine-studded mountains of West Virginia.

It fell through the day and into the night and kept traffic off the secondary roads that led toward McDill Army Base, located on more than 200 acres just south of Alexandria. For this reason, few motorists noticed the small military convoy that rolled through the rain-soaked, windblown darkness.

The lone sentry at McDill's guard post had almost been caught napping. The damp and the late hour had lulled him into near slumber, and he'd been starting to nod when the sound of heavy trucks grating to a stop jarred him awake.

Headlight beams shone in the sentry's eyes and magnified the falling drops of mercury-colored fluid as he pulled on his helmet and walked out into the weather, the rain pouring down his poncho like water dumped from a bucket. He stepped up to the driver's window of the lead truck and shone the light of his flash inside the cab.

The driver of the lead vehicle, a humvee, cranked down the window and leaned into the wet night. "Open the gate, soldier. And get that damn light out of my eyes."

"Sir, I need to see your gate pass," the sentry said, speaking with the deference that befitted the lieutenant's bars on the shoulders of the driver.

Before the exchange went further, another figure in the passenger seat leaned sideways. Through sheets of rain the sentry saw the four gold stars flashing on the brim of his cap and expeditiously saluted.

"You heard the man, soldier, open the damn gate."

"Sir, my orders don't say anything about—"

"Soldier, I'll give you exactly three more seconds to obey my command before I write you up for insubordination."

The sentry had no choice. He wasn't about to trade shit with any four-star general. Orders were orders, but the Army was the Army.

"Yes sir!" he shouted, then hustled back into the sentry box.

A few moments later, the striped barrier pole lifted perpendicular to the road. The sentry saluted the general as the humvee and the deuce-and-a-half rolled through the gate and over the speed bumps on the approach strip, and he received a salute from the general in return.

The two vehicles rolled unimpeded into the base compound and came to a halt outside a low-rise cinderblock building. This part of McDill was essentially a weapons storage depot, harboring a small contingent of troops necessary to provide security and carry out administrative tasks. Otherwise, it existed to warehouse stockpiles of both conventional and unconventional weapons.

At one time in the nation's history, the two vehicles could not have entered the base with such ease and would have had to negotiate several other checkpoints. But with the Bottom Up Review, or BUR, of 1986 and each successive Quadrennial Defense Review, which followed the BUR every four years since, fewer personnel and more automation provided security for the scores of weapons magazines throughout the continental United States.

These included dumps for conventional ammunition and explosive ordnance of all kinds, from bullets to thousand-pound bombs. But in the cases of a select few military installations around the country, including McDill, the munitions stored on base included nuclear weapons.

The men exited the vehicles, and the general, rain dripping from his camo-pattern poncho, trudged a few paces across the muddy ground. He fed a plastic card into the slot and punched a sixteen-digit access code into the keypad above it.

A tiny red LED flashed green, and the heavy steel guillotine door barring entrance to the multilevel weapons storage facility rolled aside on an inner wall. Under a minute later, it slid closed again, leaving only two men outside in the pouring rain with silencer-augmented Commando SMGs cradled in their arms and their heads warily turning in the darkness to watch and to listen.

The ordnance bunker system was fully automated, but the sprawling base covered several hundred acres, and there were random motorized patrols on a twenty-four-hour basis. The general's orders had been precise. If the lookout detail was challenged, it was to shoot to kill without hesitation.

5
REVERSALS AND DELIBERATIONS

CENTRAL RUSSIA

Vadim Illich Bogomelov felt safe among his entourage, which was not surprising, considering that Bogomelov's traveling companions amounted to a paramilitary force led by well-paid former C.I.S. military officers. At the age of fifty-seven, Bogomelov was a stout, tall man whose frame and bearing hinted at a military background rather than his true beginnings on collective farms in the Urals during the Brezhnev political era.

Bogomelov resembled Brezhnev in a political sense but also physically, and he made use of that resemblance to rally the people to his cause. Bogomelov championed the cause of nationalism, a return to the greatness of the Soviet Union, and to that end he had marshaled communism to his support. The invincible giant that had once been Russia was now a wounded fox being pecked at by the many squabbling chickens who dominated the coop.

That they did so with impunity gave testament to how low the nation had fallen since the end of the empire presided over by the traitors Gorbachev, Yeltsin, Putin, and Grigorenko. Twice the army had been called out to deal with rebellion in the Caucasus. The first had ended in failure and a shameful truce. The second foray had been more successful, leading to a more just resolution.

But close on the heels of these episodes came more troubles. Armed insurgent groups flourished in North Ossetia, the Balkar Republic, and to the south in Dagestan, Azerbaijan, and the Tajik states. Everywhere among the twenty-one semiautonomous republics within the Russian Federation, rebel cadres had sprouted like enemies sown from dragons' teeth. Ragtag bands armed with Kalashnikovs, Molotov cocktails, and little else challenged the once-mighty Russian republic, convinced of its impotence and decline.

Back in Moscow, the citizenry had grown restive. They rallied in the traditional peoples' forums of Pushkin and Red Squares, and at every crisis their numbers seemed to swell. The motives for many were purely emotional. But there were other factors, too.

From his vantage point in the air, it was clear to Bogomelov what the loss of this vast territory to the south meant to Russia—the same thing the West had gone to Kuwait and Iraq for: *oil*. From the Caspian Sea to the east, to the Black Sea in the west, there stretched a region rich in underground petroleum deposits.

Two major pipelines bisected the region in an immense V whose apex was the Caspian port of Baku and whose long arms stretched northeast toward the Baltic and southwest toward Istanbul. To permit this region to fall into the hands of bandits would not only create a breeding ground for massive terrorism and secessionist movements financed by Iran, it would also cut the oil lifeline that Russia depended on for her very survival.

Yet this was exactly what the country's present leader was doing! Dimitri Pavlovich Grigorenko, elected as a reformer who pledged to build an economically stronger Russia, had done nothing to stop the pervasive rot that was spreading through the nation like a malignant cancer. Indeed, it had only gotten worse under his presidency.

Bogomelov had seen enough. He was convinced he must supplant Grigorenko in the new elections, one way or the other, via the ballot or, if necessary, the bullet. He realized that in the end it would have to come to a coup d'etat. But that, he reflected, would not pose a problem. Russia, after all, had seen many others in her blood-soaked past.

THE PENTAGON

President Travis Claymore had arrived quietly at the five-sided building on the Potomac for his scheduled briefing. It usually worked in reverse—the nation's military potentates normally came to the White House to confer with their commander in chief—but today's visit was one of those rare exceptions to the general rule.

Today, the president had arrived to be briefed on a matter of critical importance to U.S. security. The purpose of today's trip to the Pentagon was to familiarize the president with the new powers that went with the awesome responsibility of being at the top of the nuclear defense decision matrix.

The briefing, which took place in a secure room within the National Military Command Center, was conducted in two phases. The first was a backgrounder on SIOP-6 that detailed the ways in which it differed from the previous SIOP.

Flanked by members of his staff, the president occupied one of the seats in the first row of an empty auditorium facing one of three large, flat-panel screens mounted overhead. The briefing was given by Major General Marcus McCarren, who was commander of NORAD and CINCSPACE—commander-in-chief of America's space forces.

"You're probably aware of much of what I'm about to tell you, but not all of it, so feel free to ask me to skip over the parts about which you're familiar."

The president made to get up. "That's it. I'm out of here," he said. McCarren stood as though poleaxed, but the presidential staff knew enough to laugh. No president since George Bush told worse jokes or pulled less funny stunts than America's forty-third president.

"Seriously, sir," CINCSPACE, now recovered, began after the president had seated himself. "Feel free to stop me if you understand. Otherwise, I'll begin."

McCarren then launched into a history of the nuclear SIOP since its inauguration at the start of the Cold War. His brief was accompanied by audiovisuals on the large screens above him. It included facts about each of the preceding five SIOPs and the definition of the defense readiness conditions or DEFCONS that McCarren described as "the ladder of nuclear engagement from peacetime to wartime."

The DEFCON stages ranged from DEFCON-5 through DEFCON-1, otherwise known by its code name "Cocked Pistol," a state verging on open nuclear warfare. McCarren went on to discuss the complex mechanisms used to confirm nuclear attack and how these had broken down in the past, when NORAD's computers falsely reported that the United States was under attack by nuclear missiles launched from Soviet silo complexes, strategic bombers, or submarines.

The president already knew most of this, but he listened anyway. He had sat through many a boring speech during his twenty-six years in national politics, and this would simply be another. But Claymore's attention was caught as McCarren came to the part about how the Strategic Defense Initiative had resulted in sweeping changes to the SIOP.

"Throughout the 1980s and into the early 1990s, the U.S. government spent some thirty billion dollars on SDI research," McCarren was saying, "a considerable share went into developing computer systems capable of taking on the task of human decision-making during nuclear attack."

The screen shifted to show a series of dull military viewgraphs full of arrows, bar charts, and ineptly rendered drawings of ships, planes, and human beings that the president had seen in countless other presentations. He had always wondered why, with the billions spent on defense, the U.S. armed forces could never seem to afford a decent graphics program for their PCs.

"Using massively parallel processing technologies, a new breed of computers was developed to streamline problem-solving and decision-making far beyond the capacity of the human brain and nervous system. The first of these computers was called Warp, developed by Carnegie Mellon University and DARPA. Warp was so successful at what it did, Mr. President, that it changed our thinking about the feasibility of machines taking over the decision-making process.

"As time passed and the accuracy and number of MIRVed warheads on Soviet and American intercontinental ballistic missiles increased dramatically, the lead time in which to react grew shorter and shorter. But, also, the complexity of counterstrike options increased. We in the defense community realized that the time would soon come when no human being could be entrusted with the responsibility of making decisions that would affect the lives of millions, perhaps billions of people.

"Fortunately, our investment in SDI computing paid off with the answer to this dilemma. Over time, our breakthroughs in machine intelligence led to the development of smarter and faster nuclear defense computer systems, and these were integrated into the SIOP.

"Today, we are on the verge of completely automating the SIOP and placing an unbearable burden in better hands. Many machine generations after Warp, we are ready to unveil SINDAS, the single integrated nuclear defense alert system, pronounced 'Cinders.' Cinders will not only react to incoming nuclear threats of all kinds, but she—Cinders has a feminine persona, by the way, which we call Cinderella—will interact with the command and control systems comprising the Russian and British SIOPs, as well as the SIOPs of other nations as new international agreements are signed.

"Although some have dismissed Cinders as a doomsday weapon that poses grave risks for humanity, we believe the opposite. By integrating and automating the nuclear command and control systems of the world's major nuclear powers, we believe Cinders alone can do what SDI promised to do: relieve us from the threat of nuclear war forever." McCarren smiled. "How would you like to meet Cinderella right now, Mr. President?"

"Sure. Just don't tell the First Lady." This time the CINC-SPACE knew enough to contribute his chuckle to the rest of the gathering.

"Fine. Then I'll let her introduce herself."

The large central screen displayed a human face. It was a combination of 3-D animation and lifelike photo imagery, and it reminded Claymore of the Max Headroom craze of a previous decade. There was no hair on the image's head, yet it was unmistakably female, with something of an ancient Egyptian quality to it.

"Hello, Mr. President. My name is Cinderella." The simulacrum's voice had a hollow, metallic ring. It seemed like a composite of voices to the president. "We'll be getting to know each other better very soon. May I call you Travis?"

"Sure, honey," the president said, drawing more laughter.

"Thank you, Travis," the simulacrum replied. "You and I will get together soon in a more private setting. There are secrets I can only share with you. General McCarren will fill you in." The image on the screen vanished and was replaced by a blue electronic haze.

"Great job," the president said to McCarren. "By the way, can I get on the Web with this thing?" Claymore said in a final stab at jocularity.

"Actually, we are planning a Web site to educate the civilian sector concering the importance of the SIOP automation initiative pending developments critical to final implementation of SINDAS operating protocols."

The CINCSPACE smiled, and the president thought to himself, *Is this guy a fucking asshole, or what?* Fortunately, the general wasn't psychic and hadn't heard him, and he continued without missing a beat, "Now, sir, if you would please come with me, I'll show you the rest."

Phase two took place in a secure room where the president

and the general were sequestered from the rest of the occupants of the room. Here a specially hardened laptop containing a wireless interface with SINDAS was removed from a plain brown hardshell attaché case. The case and the laptop were collectively known as "the football," and they would replace the previous edition that had been carried with the president everywhere he traveled.

At the end of the session, the president was relieved to be on his way back to the White House, away from a place that somehow reminded him of a cave where mad wizards lived, each crazier than the next. Part of his job was to deal with them, but at such times he often felt himself in the presence of the Grim Reaper.

The facades were neater and more Ivy League now than they had been in the days when foul-mouthed, swearing, cussing blockheads like Curtis LeMay ran the nation's nuclear deterrent policy, but behind the cool facade of today's warrior class, Claymore sometimes saw a grinning skull, and he knew he was in the presence of death's emissaries on earth.

There was something else about the genielike resident of the attaché case that now resided in the care of one of the Secret Service men riding in the limo's shotgun seat directly in front of the president; it was something in the name.

At first, Claymore thought the disquieting feeling he'd gotten was connected with the word *sin,* and he caught himself casually wondering if there'd be any political-correctness fallout with the religious right over the acronym. But then he realized that this wasn't what bothered him at all. It wasn't the *sin* in SINDAS that disturbed Claymore. It was the totality of the word itself. A word that sounded much like another word.

"Cinders," he said to himself, sotto voce. "Cinders."

"What's that, sir?" asked the Secret Service agent sitting beside him.

"Mere anarchy loosed upon the world."

"Sir?"

"Nothing, Mike," replied Claymore. "Just some internal monologue stuff nobody but myself need worry about."

SOUTHEASTERN VIRGINIA

Captain Joe Weyerhauser was about to complete the short trip he'd begun two hours before from the Army Judge Advocate General's Corps (JAGC), whose headquarters at Fort Belvoir was located a few miles outside of metro Washington, D.C. Weyerhouser, an attorney with CLAMO, the Center for Law and Military Operations, a department of JAGC, could see his destination directly ahead.

Fort Monroe, with its water-filled moat and its weathered brown pre–Civil War brick buildings, its whitewashed lighthouse and its quaint gazebo, looked like a throwback to the antebellum south. This, in several respects, is exactly what it was. The fort, located on the tip of Virginia's southeastern peninsula, has a long history and has the distinction of being the longest continuously manned garrison in the U.S. Army.

Today, Fort Monroe serves as the headquarters of the Department of the Army Training and Doctrine Command, more commonly known by the acronym TRADOC. The command serves many essential functions. TRADOC oversees all training-related programs from boot camp right on up to major field exercises involving corps-level combined arms engagements.

However, TRADOC also serves a less-publicized function that has linked Fort Belvoir and Fort Monroe over the years and made car trips such as the one Weyerhauser was now about to finish a commonplace event. TRADOC is used as a convenient parking lot by the Department of Defense for the accused parties in high-profile court martial cases under investigation by the JAG.

It was to serve an arrest warrant on one such party that Weyerhauser had made the trip out to the scenic island on the south Atlantic coast on which Fort Monroe stands. Weyerhauser was expected. A squad of base MPs were on call at the provost marshal's office at the fort's Military Police

Building. Once in custody, Lieutenant General Jackson Priest would be taken to Fort Leavenworth to await his trial in the confines of a maximum-security jail cell.

Once upon a time there would not have been any need for almost eight months to go by before Priest's arrest. The general would have spent a few weeks cooling his heels in Leavenworth and afterward been speedily tried. In Priest's case, a guilty verdict would have been a foregone conclusion. But under the newly revised Uniform Military Codes, it wasn't that simple.

Priest, who had prestigious family connections, had hired top-gun lawyers who had delayed his trial and lengthened the investigation. Like others before him, Priest had found himself relieved of command pending the outcome of his trial and reassigned to a desk job at TRADOC, where he would be under a benign form of house arrest.

The delays had galled the chief of the Army, who wanted Priest tried and convicted as soon as possible. The evidence of his guilt was overwhelming.

Priest had once been an an exemplary soldier, a career soldier. He'd been given his first command as a young lieutenant, leading a long-range reconnaissance (LRRP) platoon near the close of the war in Southeast Asia, and had been twice decorated.

He had gone on to serve in the Gulf and in Somalia, where he had been reassigned to military intelligence. Priest's last posting had been as commander of the 202nd Military Intelligence Division, which was assigned to conduct operations in the Balkans.

Something had happened to change Priest in the Balkans, though. Theories differed, but theories didn't matter. The outcome of his actions was all that counted. In the almost two years of the division's deployment in Kosovo and Macedonia, the reports of murders and rapes, of drug running, and of bizarre cult activities slowly began making their way to the judge advocate general. Priest's name had begun cropping up as a common link to many of these crimes.

The testimony soon became overwhelming, supported by

eyewitness accounts of informants among the local populace and from within the U.S. Army itself. In time, the evidence against Priest became irrefutable. The general was in fact the high priest of an apocalyptic cabal that preached the destruction of the human race in a nuclear cataclysm and its replacement by a biomechanical hybrid race of cloned beings.

Only a chosen few, a master race of original humans, would remain after what was preached as the "nuclear cleansing" of the earth. Emerging from underground hiding places, these chosen few would live only long enough to contribute their genetic material to produce the new race of cyborgs that would repopulate the planet. They were then to commit mass suicide and leave the earth to its true inheritors.

Apparently, Priest and a ring of deranged followers had not been content to wait for Armageddon and had begun some of the slaughter among the war-plagued population of Kosovo. Until nuclear cleansing, there was always ethnic cleansing.

The problems for the JAG only multiplied after Priest's reassignment, however. At Fort Monroe, the general was to spend his time performing innocuous activities as an assistant to the commander of TUSCAB, The United States Continental Army Band, also headquartered at Monroe, which held a regular Thursday night concert series at the base.

Unfortunately, Priest had been able to pull political strings and gotten himself reassigned. He was soon placing personnel in the Army's Osprey evaluation program. When yet another well-publicized crash of the tilt-rotor helicopter happened, with the son of the chairman of the Joint Chiefs as one of those fatally injured in the training accident, all hell had broken loose.

Priest was again back arranging musical gigs for tuba players, jazz guitarists, and concert violinists with TUSCAB, but an inquisitorial furor had gripped the Department of Defense. CJCS Buck Starkweather was not only the aggrieved father of a serviceman killed in the Osprey accident, but as a captain, he had also been Priest's commanding officer in the Nam.

Starkweather had not liked Priest since the moment he had met him, long years before. Back then, there had been stories, too, of things done in the jungles, of scalps, penises, ears, noses, and even stranger things, taken as tropies of war by the LRRP platoon Priest commanded. There had been far too many coincidences for the CJCS's liking in the matter. Pressure had been put on the JAG and the investigation stepped up. Now the final evidence was in, and it was ready to move.

Weyerhauser was jolted from his reverie as the humvee slowed as it entered the Fort Monroe main gate. Actually not gated at all, the entrance to the fort is secured by a small guardhouse. Weyerhouser's MP driver didn't even bother to pull in front of it, since their destination was directly across the road. Instead, the driver swung the humvee left and pulled into the small parking area directly in front of the white-porticoed entrance to the Military Police Building.

About twenty minutes later, after picking up the MP detail at the office of the provost marshal, the arrest detail was making its way to Priest's office at TUSCAB headquarters. Loud rock music assaulted their ears the moment they entered the building lobby. The staff sergeant on duty explained that the band was practicing for tonight's concert. The sergeant also confirmed that the general was in his second-floor office and led the arrest detail up a flight of stairs to the landing above the building's lobby level.

The decibel level of the music from the auditorium below was less deafening on the second floor, but still a formidable presence. Weyerhauser knocked twice on the office door, then, without waiting for an answer, tried the knob. The door didn't open.

The sergeant was dispatched to fetch the key, returning a few minutes later to find Weyerhauser banging his fist on the door and shouting for the general to open up. Then the sergeant tried the key, and with the snap of a lock, the problem was solved.

When Weyerhauser pushed open the door, his first and last thought was that he had been stupid. Fatally stupid. Weyerhauser was an attorney, not an ordnance expert, not even a combat soldier. His province was legal briefs and trial strategies, not offensive weaponry. But even Weyerhauser had been through basic training and could recognize a Claymore mine when he saw one. Especially when the Claymore mine's lethal concave front was facing his way.

Weyerhauser's mind only had enough time to register the fine, olive-drab filament of a munitions tripwire strung on the diagonal from where the Claymore's tripod legs had been driven like nails into the wooden surface of the desktop upon which it stood. The tripwire disappeared behind the door, and by opening the door, Weyerhauser had armed the explosive antipersonnel device.

These perceptions took only the merest instant, and after that fleeting instant had flashed past, the Claymore detonated. The concussive force of the blast and the tempest of jagged shrapnel it spewed into the hallway tore Weyerhauser and the sergeant at arms to shreds and maimed most of the MP detail from the provost marshal's office for the rest of their lives.

Discovery of the explosion was delayed by the sound of the band practicing below and contributed to the death toll. Later, they would find a corpse in the charred remains of the office wearing the general's uniform. It was an apparent suicide; most of the lower skull, including the jaws, had been destroyed by two buckshot blasts to the mouth. The suicide weapon, a double-barreled shotgun owned by the general, was found lying nearby, its business end encrusted with blood and bits of teeth, palate tissue, and bone matter.

Surprisingly, there turned out to be enough of the upper and lower jaw left intact to compare against the general's dental records. Unsurprisingly, at least to many at JAGC familiar with the indictment, the forensic investigation failed to produce a conclusive match-up. Someone else had likely been shot to death in the general's place.

WASHINGTON, D.C.

The CJCS watched the early morning news while he downed a glass of orange juice at the breakfast table set by his wife.

Gus was waiting with the Lincoln warmed up outside, but Starkweather's attention was caught by the talking head expressing outrage at rumors about the new SINDAS system that had just been activated. The press leak about the new SIOP had brought the conspiracy theorists, alien abduction freaks, and doomsayers out like worms after a midnight rain.

Revisionist preachers had claimed the system was warned of in the Book of Revelations. Overnight, something nobody ordinarily knew or cared about became the subject of national controversy. The U.S. SIOP was soon to become a media phraseword to join Y2K amid the list of misunderstood techno-pop terminology.

The attempts by the know-nothing on the TV screen to reduce the concept of the SIOP to a thirty-second sound bite was laughable in itself. Starkweather gulped down the rest of the OJ and hit the remote's off button. Enough of that crap. Besides, he was sure that if certain developments continued, the media's attention would soon be turned in other directions.

◆ ◆ ◆

Over an hour later, after a ride in the Lincoln that tested the car's shocks and undercarriage to the fullest as Gus accelerated around corners, peeled off expressway exits and performed other maneuvers intended to dodge surveillance, the CJCS reached his destination in the heart of historic Georgetown. The Federalist-era brownstone was picture-perfect, as were the other similar buildings on the street of well-kept row houses.

The CJCS couldn't help smiling. Behind the facades of a surprising number of these museum-piece buildings lurked the safe houses of not only America's secret intelligence services but those of the British MI-6, the Russian SVR, Israeli Mossad, and a host of others. Most of residential D.C. was a warren of spies and moles by now, but this particular safe house had an advantage over most others in the neighborhood.

The row house had been the last stop on one of the underground railroads that had sprung up during the Civil War to ferry runaway slaves to the abolitionist Northern states. A tunnel ran under the basement to what had once been a farmhouse two miles away but which was now the subbasement of a pumping station for Washington's network of sewers administered by the D.C. municipal government.

When the row house was purchased by the Pentagon sometime after World War II, the tunnel was rediscovered and eventually became a way to spy-proof the safe house from potential surveillance by hostile intelligence services. The subbasement of the municipal pumping station was renovated as an electronically sterile meeting room and sealed off from the rest of the building, and architectural plans expunged from all municipal records. Trencrom's team had dubbed it "the Bolthole."

From time to time, workers in overalls and hard hats would emerge from maintenance trucks and disappear into the square brown brick building. They would emerge again some time later and drive off. Business as usual.

Today, two vehicles had pulled up, and a four-man, one-woman crew had emerged and gone into the squat blockhouse emblazoned with the shield of the D.C. Sewer Department.

Minutes later, the Snake Handlers were doing their best to make themselves feel at home until the CJCS arrived to brief them. Ball and Jugs were engaged in an arm wrestling contest, elbows on the tabletop, locked forearms making an inverted V. Richard Muhammed Nixon took a pull from a long-necked Bud to chase the first mouthful of Fritos corn chips he shook into his face from the open bag, belched, and watched the comms expert and the lady sniper go at it.

"How 'bout we make it interesting. Apache-style," Nixon suggested.

"Me Cochise. What kind of action you talkin'?" Ball asked the very tall black dude over their entwined fists.

"Twenty bucks to the winner."

"Lay it on the table," Jugs said.

Nixon slapped down the twenty and lit up the panatela cigar he'd tucked behind one ear, ready for smoking after the corn chips. He puffed on the panatela till its tip was a half inch of glowing orange ash, then laid it flat on the table. Whoever lost would be sloshing calamine lotion on their arm for the next two months.

While Nixon shook down more chips and gulped more beer, and Ball and Jugs grunted and grimaced, Floaty practiced the martial art he'd dubbed pen-do, pitching a half dozen ballpoints at a dart board on the wall with unerring accuracy.

Floaty, the team's weapons specialist, and Zen combat guru, preferred ballpoint pens to *shurikens* as lethal throwing implements. For one reason, Floaty would explain when asked, walking around with *shurikens* clipped to your T-shirt pocket is a lot more obvious than keeping ballpoint pens in the same place.

Floaty had earned his nickname for the same reason Jugs had picked up her own handle. Physical attributes defined them both. Apart from her ability to put a bullet into a sparrow's left eye at 500 yards, upwind, she also possessed a bustline you could balance a coffee mug on.

Floaty's handle went with his space-cadet appearance, which was only half veneer. Many called themselves American ninjas. Floaty was the real thing. An Army brat raised in Tokyo, he was one of the few non-Japanese *ninjutsu* ever trained in the most secret of martial arts and, almost as rare, a licensed instructor of *jeet kune do*, the interdisciplinary martial art developed and practiced by Bruce Lee.

Trencrom sat and watched the circus. The team's leader sometimes felt as if he were a substitute teacher for the rowdiest class in the reform school. Right now, Ball and Jugs's arm wrestling was pissing him off big time. He'd let it slide at first, but now Ball was showing signs of weakening.

"Nixon, get the fuck out of here," he said, elbowing past the big Snake Handler and knocking the half-burned cigar butt out from under Ball's forearm a second before Jugs was about to mash it into the tabletop. To Ball and Jugs he said,

"Why don't the two of you just fuck each other and get it over with instead of playing your bullshit games? Believe me, nobody gives a shit. Go ahead, do it on the fucking table. We won't even notice."

"Yeah, man," Nixon put in. "I'll give you twenty apiece if you fuck on the table right now."

"Shut the fuck up, Nixon," Trencrom shot back.

"Okay, I'm in," Jugs said, beginning to strip off her shirt. Ball was quickly unbuckling his belt.

At that moment, the green light above the steel door set in one of the walls announced Starkweather's imminent appearance. The loud double thunk of two ballpoint pens simultaneously striking the bull's-eye of the target near the door stopped the general short. For a moment, the CJCS stood stock still, taking in the scene inside the safe house. Then he just shook his head sadly. He'd seen it all before.

In a few minutes, though, the horsing around had stopped, and it was back to business.

"Congratulations, guys. From me personally and on behalf of the president," the CJCS announced once he'd taken his place on a comfortable easy chair he favored during meetings at the Bolthole.

With a pocket tape recorder running, he debriefed the team on Iraq, paying special attention to Trencrom's separate escape from Baghdad. Various agencies in the so-called intelligence community had posed some specific questions about smuggling networks operating between Iraq and Eygpt that Trencrom might be able to shed some light on.

"Now, let's get down to cases," Starkweather went on, when it was all wrapped up, turning off and pocketing the recorder. "I've spoken with the president and he concurs: Your next mission may be in North Korea."

"As we speak, DPRK border guard and light infantry forces are reinforcing positions along the Demilitarized Zone and the Military Legitimacy Limit. There are all the classic signs that Kim Jong-il's forces are gearing up for war. And maybe it's a good thing, too. They've bled us for billions of dollars in blackmail money, using their nuclear weapons programs as leverage. But appeasement never works. Hitler proved that. It only makes the bastards want to squeeze harder."

"No shit, Bucky," Trencrom put in. "The DPRK's nuclear weapons arsenal is by far the most advanced of any small power, with the possible exception of Israel, whose arsenal is at least defensive. Those guys have been producing enough plutonium for ten to twelve nuclear warheads per year from Reactor II at Yongbyon alone. And this has been going on since 1989."

Starkweather looked Trencrom in the eye. "You know the situation as well as I do, Ice," he said. "So don't play dumb shit with me. The North Koreans can get away with it because if we fuck them over, we're playing in the backyards of Russia and China. This has been the strategic problem since MacArthur sought to cross the thirty-eighth parallel. How far do you go? How much are you willing to risk? So we've paid them off. What choice did we have?"

"A thousand pardons, Wise One."

"But to go back to what I was saying," the CJCS went on, sipping his Budweiser, "the DPRK has probably decided the issue for us, just like Hitler decided the issue by invading Poland in '39. If they launch an offensive against the South, we'll have no choice but to retaliate. And we can make our case stick with the Chinese and the Russians in that event . . . maybe. The key then will be to hit them fast and hard and go for their nuclear facilities with everything we've got."

"But you want an insurance policy," Trencrom put in. "Against certain dragons that might rear their heads from Mayang Island, Shinpo City, or Kangon and South Hamgyong provinces, to name just a few."

"Those and others," the CJCS said with a nod. "We have reasonable faith in our capability to take out mobile and fixed aboveground launchers, and some of their underground facilities, but not all of the latter. The two installations at Kangon and South Hamgyong are cases in point. We'll have teams on the ground to spot for those. What we've got in mind for you is the hidden dragon, the big daddy snake. We think this baby lives near the side of a mountain far to the north."

"What kind of missiles?"

"The biggest they have: Taepo Dong V ICBMS, with a range in excess of six thousand statute miles."

"Shit, we be talkin' L.A. here, my man," Nixon put in.

"And Frisco, San Diego . . . maybe even Seattle or Portland, if they're lucky enough and more advanced than we think. Whole lot of places along the West Coast, man," put in Jugs.

"Scary shit," Ball summed up. "Mother lovin' scary shit."

"Bad news," the CJCS agreed. "But that's the deal. The North Koreans are faced with a use-it-or-lose-it scenario. They're now at the peak of their military readiness."

"At the same time, their country is on an economic downslide. Their leaders know that in order to stay in power, they have to do something more than go to summits.

"We're getting tired of being routinely blackmailed. In a year, maybe two, they risk being kicked out by their own people. My guess is that these latest threats are only fifteen percent bluff, that the North will invade the South this time. If we can stop them cold, we hasten the end of Kim's tyrannical regime and the threat it poses to humanity."

"But if we fail, my man," said Nixon. "Ka-boom. Mushroom cloud city where the dead ain't pretty."

"That's it, in a nutshell, my lyrical friend," Starkweather told Nixon, opening up his attaché case and distributing DVDs. "These are your orders and tactical data. Trencrom will serve as liaison as usual. Updates will be issued if and when it's time to move. If it's a go, you need to be ready. I think it'll come to that."

The CJCS left first, via the tunnel. Fifteen minutes later, the "maintenance" team exited the blockhouse and got into their trucks. They drove off in separate directions, their civic duties completed.

6
ADVANTAGES OF NUMERICAL SUPERIORITY

THE SEA OF JAPAN

"There she goes. The bastards have launched another one."

The pilot of the RC-135(U) electronic intelligence aircraft had seen the missile track through the cockpit window, and his remark was directed to his copilot.

The observations from the EC's cockpit didn't count for much, however. In fact, they didn't count at all, since the job of the ELINT aircraft's cockpit crew was to fly the plane, period. But the techs occupying most of the rest of the plane behind the locked cockpit door were also monitoring the launch, and the data their instruments recorded would be analyzed by defense intelligence for weeks to come.

Their recorded signals intelligence data or SIGINT would be augmented by photointelligence derived from a satellite in orbit over the launch zone. The near-real-time satellite imagery was already beaming the telltale launch signature of a missile as it rose on a pedestal of flame toward the night sky back to an assortment of receiving stations on the SPINTCOM and CRITICOM intelligence networks including the NMCC and the CIA.

It was clear that the North Koreans had just test-launched yet another Taepo-Dong IV, a nuclear-capable missile with intercontinental range. They had done so in defiance of a multinational U.N. Security Council resolution. It was a statement of absolute belligerence and contempt for world opinion. The North Koreans were sending a strong message to the world: They did not care what anybody thought and would do as they pleased. *Take your best shot,* they seemed to be saying.

PYONGYANG

Hours later, General Yee Wa-rang paced the carpeted floor of his office in the Ministry of Defense. Kim Jong-il, the North's leader, had succeeded in overruling the legislative People's Committee and authorizing the launch of the new missile weapon.

Though behind his back he was referred to as Junior Kim, he had effectively consolidated his power so that the office of president made him North Korea's sole dictatorial authority. Kim's father and predecessor, Kim Il-sung, would never have been foolish enough to believe that the nuclear posturing could ever turn real and prevail in an actual war. He had been wise enough to grasp that it would instead bring untold devastation upon the nation.

For decades, North Korea had been playing a potentially lethal game of brinksmanship with the major world powers, pursuing a deliberate plan based on acquiring weapons of mass destruction. By possessing them, the regime of the elder, then the younger Kim, gained stature in the world vastly disproportionate to the nation's size, economy, and cultural achievements.

Possession of NBC or nuclear/biological/chemical weapons meant that none of the major world powers could dare to openly slight the republic of North Korea. It would also guarantee that the DPRK would always gain the upper hand in political negotiations, for North Korea always stood with its hand on the lid of Pandora's box. As long as it could threaten to unleash the unknown demons that swirled within those dark confines upon the world, its adversaries would back off.

The elder Kim recognized this reality. So long as North Korea remembered that it was bluff that permitted the gambit to succeed, power would be hers to wield. But Junior Kim did not seem to understand this simple fact. Instead, he believed in his own pathetic lies. He was a fool. Yet none dared oppose him. Those who had openly done so had paid with their lives.

It had taken great courage for General Yee to have challenged Kim's authority as he had done during the last meeting of the People's Committee, and he would not have done so except that others also had stood alongside him. Yee had been reprimanded for his temerity, but no action had been taken so far. No doubt, the general mused, Kim recognized that his leadership would remain necessary to the coming invasion of South Korea that he planned to carry out.

The attack was to commence tonight at twenty hundred hours. Yee knew every detail of those plans, for he had been instrumental in preparing them as first marshal of the People's Army. Yee knew that in the beginning, his forces stood a good chance of overwhelming the South Koreans and Americans posted on the other side of the Demilitarized Zone and rolling straight across to seize Seoul. The advantage of numerical superiority lay in their favor, and combined with their superior training and soldiering, would ensure that the inferior ROK forces would be quickly overwhelmed.

Yet in this success lay the seeds of his country's great undoing, Yee feared, for it would certainly unleash the wrath of enemies far superior to any of his forces. Yee held no illusions that the United States easily possessed the military might to crush his country like a bothersome flea. It had proven in Iraq and in Yugoslavia that its weaponry was both highly accurate and utterly devastating.

America could unleash those weapons from standoff distances with phenomenal efficiency. Unlike Saddam Hussein or Slobodan Milosovic's regimes, Kim's North Korea possessed crude though effective nuclear, biological, and chemical weapons and delivery systems for those weapons. This alone had warded off preemptive NATO strikes in the past. But should North Korea attack first, the gloves would come off because there would then be little else for the U.S. to lose by holding back.

Kim's belief that unleashing his nuclear arsenal if counterattacked would lead to victory was sheer madness. The more destruction such a rash action would create, the greater would be the vengeance America and her allies would take upon North Korea. Japan's participation would then be insured as well.

Indeed, it would be likely that the Americans would install Japan as her surrogate policeman to oversee a broken North Korea. Yee knew the Japanese would be ruthless in their exploitation of his country, for they held a historic and cultural animosity toward all Koreans, who even to this day were regarded as second-class citizens in Japan.

Yet despite the certainty of defeat and the plague of evils certain to follow in its wake, the madness of war was about to be unleashed in only a few hours by the foolish, aging man-boy who occupied the president's office. Yee could do nothing to stop it. No one could.

THE DEFENSE TACTICAL INTERNET

The reports began as a trickle. They quickly swelled to a torrent of electronic data. The first drop in the bucket was an OPREP-3 cable from 2nd Infantry Division's 3rd Operations Center. 3rd Ops handled communications from the 2nd's tripwire forces stationed near Chorwon at the center of the two-and-a-half-mile-wide Demilitarized Zone or DMZ, the buffer zone between North and South Korea that had been established after the post–World War II Korean "police action."

The OPREP, whose numerical code designator, 3, tagged it as an event of potential political importance, reported that ground radar at Site 5—a cluster of M-113 APCs carrying Pave Tack radar packages—had registered signs of unusual truck activity at grid coordinates CT 1051126, a military sector within the radius of the DMZ.

The OPREP-3 came in via secure satellite communications to the Emergency Operations Center of PACOM, the United States' Pacific Command Center, located at Pearl Harbor Naval Base in Hawaii. The cable—actually an E-mail message that was not necessarily printed, but still referred to by nomenclature devised in an earlier era—went on to state that aerial reconnaissance has been requested, and further developments, if any, would be reported.

Though it proclaimed an incursion into the DMZ by DPRK forces, the duty officer at PACOM did not priority-flag the cable. Reunification notwithstanding, North Korean violations of the peace treaty were frequent, and incursions by their troops happened so regularly as to be routine.

Within the next few hours, however, any semblance of routine was gone. Minutes after the first cable was received, another spate of cables reporting enemy action arrived at PACOM. The reports were arriving from across the Demarcation Line and Demilitarized Zone and included not only ground force alerts but also naval and airborne activity.

Elements of the U.S. Tunnel Neutralization Team, positioned with listening devices along known underground tunnels discovered over the years running beneath the DMZ, reported constant activity below ground. Fast boats capable of delivering commando forces were spotted off outlying islands in the Sea of Japan.

As the intensity and severity of the reports increased, SECRET and then PINNACLE code descriptors were added to the cables. The cables now bypassed regional commands. They simultaneously poured into the White House Situation Room, the windowless subbasement beneath the Oval Office, the NMCC suite on the Pentagon's third and fourth floors, and to the Alternate National Military Command Center, a command post buried inside Raven Rock Mountain in southern Pennsylvania some seventy miles outside Washington, D.C., and an easy commute from Camp David, which also maintains a small underground command center.

At ten P.M. Washington, D.C., local time, the Joint Chiefs and their aides were roused from their comfortable suburban homes around the capital and whisked by chauffeur-driven cars to the briefing chamber on the Pentagon's first floor known as the Tank.

Before they arrived, the first indications that the United Nations Command and the Republic of Korea–United States Combined Forces Command were in a shooting war with the North Korean forces were in hard-copy printout form. The north was staging a massive ground attack across the DMZ toward the South Korean capital, Seoul.

Troops, mechanized armor, and heavy equipment were streaming across the no-man's-land separating the impoverished communist north from her affluent capitalist neighbor. The unthinkable had happened. A second Korean war had started.

THE PENTAGON

CJCS Starkweather had not been the first to arrive at the Pentagon, and he was not the only member of the U.S. Joint Chiefs to have arrived at the National Military Command Center in civilian clothes rather than uniform. Starkweather had been attending his daughter's school music recital and had not time to go home and change.

The beeping of his cell phone had drawn him disapproving looks, and he muttered apologies as he edged his way past the knees of disgruntled parents, feeling scores of eyes on him as he rushed down the aisle and into the parking lot, where Gus, as ever, was waiting.

"What gives, General?" Gus asked, already opening the Lincoln's door.

"Plenty," Starkweather told his longtime driver. "The

North Koreans just threw the goddamn kitchen sink across the DMZ."

"Holy shit!"

"You got that right."

Gus was promptly highballing the souped-up Lincoln out of the lot and eating up the road between the Arlington suburb and the western shore of the Potomac. Fortunately, it was long past the D.C. rush hour, and inbound traffic was relatively sparse. Under twenty minutes later, Starkweather was jumping out of the Lincoln and pinning his security badge on the lapel of his cashmere sport coat as he rushed in through the Pentagon's South Parking Entrance.

Starkweather was met by his XO, Colonel Frank Ridgemore. "Sir, we've got a command post set up in the emergency operations center at the NMCC," the exec told the CJCS as both rushed down the corridor toward the elevator that would take them up to the location of the op center on the fourth floor.

Starkweather found the NMCC as expected: a beehive of controlled chaos, with people shouting into phones, cursing balky computers, and nursemaiding the chattering telex machines that still spat reams of paper onto the floor and would probably do so into the fifth millennium.

Much of the chatter suddenly died down as the NMCC staff saw the boss dash inside. Accompanied by his XO, Starkweather returned salutes and hurried into the command post through a door to one of the rooms adjacent to the NMCC. By contrast, the emergency briefing chamber was quiet, the voices of its personnel subdued, and tempers under control.

The situation room in which the Joint Chiefs assess global military developments of an emergency nature is built on two levels. The upper level, where the Joint Chiefs convene, is a relatively small chamber dominated by six huge, flat-panel display screens high on a wall that form a semicircle above a round conference table of massive polished oak. The lower level is an immense communications pit resembling the launch control center at Cape Canaveral.

Here the duty officers making up the NMCC battle staff occupy the length of a huge T-shaped table with inset display screens at each seat. At the smaller top of the T sit the four emergency action officers or EAOs, also with built-in display consoles in front of them on the table. Surrounding them all are numerous personnel attending to banks of rack-mounted command, control, and communications equipment linked to the military forces of the United States, United Nations, NATO, Warsaw Pact, and other nonaligned forces throughout the world.

It is the job of the four emergency action officers, none below the rank of lieutenant general, to absorb and assess and encapsulate the plethora of cables, satellite imagery, media coverage, and other diverse data that stream in from the field, place them in a coherent context, and brief them to the four-star generals who await their reports in the glass-enclosed room overlooking the pit.

On arrival, the CJCS found that three of the four other members of the Joint Chiefs were there ahead of him and were already getting input from the EAOs via a videoconference link to the TV screens on the wall. Starkweather briefly greeted the others and took his seat at the head of the conference table. His XO handed him a sheaf of printouts, which he glanced through before turning his full attention to the large screens where Lieutenant General Wesley Burke, chief officer of the EAO staff, was waiting to give Starkweather his assessment.

"Shoot, Wes," said the CJCS into the microphone in front of him. "Give me what you got."

"Sir," Burke began, "the situation on the ground is worsening by the minute. From available data, we can put eight DPRK battalions across the DMZ and engaging in battle with ROK-US security forces. There are reports of commando raids in Seoul and amphibious landings from the Sea of Japan near Tokeo-Ri."

Starkweather scanned the banks of overhead monitors as he listened to the CEAO run his brief. He didn't need to be told that all the information the CEAO was verbally giving him was available in audiovisual form on the display screens. Starkweather used the displays as references to help build up a mental map of the overall tactical and strategic picture and absorb as much of what was happening as possible.

On the so-called god screen at the center of the displays was an integrated digital map of the Korean Peninsula. It showed, by means of symbols, a variety of information, including the progress of enemy forces, their lines of logistics and communications, and the disposition of defending forces set in opposition to them. The schematic view on the god screen revealed a hammering onslaught met by determined resistance.

On the left, in front of Panmunjon, the North Korean 820th Armored Corps, a formation that included two light mechanized divisions, had encountered fierce opposition from a combined force made up of the U.S. 2nd Infantry Division and the South Korean 10th Mechanized Corps.

On the right, near Chungwon, a spearhead of enemy main battle tanks, mechanized armor, and light infantry troops was engaged by determined resistance from the U.S. 8th Armored Corps. Here, as well as at other places along the DMZ, fierce artillery duels were being fought, as the North Koreans brought their 170-millimeter heavy guns into play and USFORCECOM tube battalions answered fire. Along both coasts of the lower Korean peninsula, amphibious landing attempts by enemy special forces elements were being reported, with moderate to heavy fighting throughout the theater.

Starkweather turned his attention back to the CEAO's on-screen image. "I don't see anything here to indicate the deployment of unconventionals."

"No evidence of that, sir," Burke replied. "That's the good news. All reports so far indicate that the attack is being prosecuted by conventional forces only. As you may rightly suppose, we are continually monitoring this aspect of hostilities for any change in the picture."

Starkweather thanked the CEAO and turned his attention to the other members of the JCS seated around him at the conference table. With the arrival of Summers, chairman of the Army, the contingent of the JCS was complete in the command post. Like Starkweather, his fellow chiefs were being briefed by members of their own staffs.

Starkweather conferred with them on tactical and strategic developments pertinent to sea and air battles and amplified his mental picture of the situation in the major combat theaters. When he saw the buttons on the red telephone near him begin to light up, he was ready to brief the president, who would be on the line once the CJCS picked up the handset.

The voice of the chief executive was tense as it came over the direct, secure line from the Oval Office. Claymore was obviously agitated, and Starkweather could hear the edgy voices of White House staff in the background. The sudden events had predictably thrown the White House into an uproar, and Starkweather could picture the chaos as reporters pushed their way into the White House Press Room to be briefed by Press Secretary Barry Stone.

The president would be facing that same roomful of reporters and cameras in a very short time, the CJCS knew, and despite the burden that had fallen upon his own shoulders, Starkweather was at least thankful that he wasn't filling the president's shoes at this moment. In addition to all the rest, Claymore would have to contend with the media's sharks in time of crisis, when the slightest smell of blood could whip them into a feeding frenzy.

Since the Gulf War, the press had been growing increasingly belligerent and suspicious of military and political briefings. The Bush administration's attempt to suppress the media had only backfired by making reporters more aggressive than ever before. What all of this meant was that the president would need to be briefed as thoroughly as possible on breaking events. The general gathered his impressions.

"Starkweather," the CJCS said into the mouthpiece as he brought the handset to his ear.

THE WHITE HOUSE

"My fellow Americans."

The president began his address to the nation with words that harked back to Lyndon Baines Johnson's first use of the phrase at the height of the war in Vietnam. Then as now, the greeting gave televison viewers pause to anticipate a message of great importance. The nation braced for news that it sensed might hold serious implications for the present and future.

Most had heard or read reports concerning North Korea's growing buildup of an arsenal of nuclear, chemical, and biological weapons. Coupled with an ever more sophisticated delivery capability, it meant they possessed the means to strike at the U.S. homeland.

Fewer, but also a large number, would have heard the boasts of North Korea's leader, Kim Jong-il, concerning those capabilities, and his threats to use them to strike the United States if it stood in the way of his plans for the re-unification of the two Koreas.

Millions of viewers across the U.S. were glued to their sets. Even the local networks carried the president's address, preempting *The Simpsons*.

"Tonight, we have witnessed an act of unprecedented belligerence," Claymore went on as he squarely faced the cameras. "The dictatorial republic of North Korea launched an unprovoked attack on its peaceful neighbor to the south, the Republic of Korea. The attack, although severe, was not altogether unexpected and has not been successful.

"Because we detected signs that North Korea was determined to stand in the way of peace and persist in its hostile aims, we had already strengthened our military forces in the region.

"Together with military defense forces of the Republic of South Korea, and the multinational force mandated by the United Nations, American troops on the ground, on the sea, and in the air have stopped the North Korean offensive while it was only a few miles beyond the demilitarized zone set up as a buffer between North and South.

"The intended strategic objective of the offensive, South Korea's capital city, Seoul, remains free and will continue to remain free, despite the warlike ambitions of those who would have it otherwise."

The president glanced briefly at his notes as camera one, which had begun with a wide-angle shot of Claymore seated at his desk in the Map Room adjoining the Oval Office where he delivered his address, completed its slow zoom and gave the TV audience a tight close-up of the president's face as he spoke. When he looked up again, camera two picked him up from a slight left angle, held the shot a few beats, and then came in again on a slow-motion zoom.

"Many of you may be concerned about the capability of the North Koreans to attack our shores with nuclear weapons," Claymore began. "I want to take this opportunity to reassure you all that there has been no indication of any such weapons being deployed, and for a good reason: North Korea's leaders know better than to use such weapons. They know that any threat to America's cities and towns with nuclear, chemical, or biological weapons will be met with retaliation so severe that it would not serve their interests to use their capability."

Here the president paused a beat, and his eyes looked out steadily into the camera lens. The meaning behind his message would be clear not only to the American public but to its intended recipient. He knew that in his underground bunker behind his lines in North Korea, Kim Jong-il was watching him on CNN at that moment, and Claymore hoped that Junior Kim was well aware that he was not bluffing.

Of, course, Claymore also knew as he uttered his words that the North Korean leadership was also aware of something left unsaid: that at this point, America and NATO would deem it in their interests to take steps necessary to forcibly dismantle North Korea's offensive nuclear capability and related capability for other weapons of mass destruction.

The ball was in their court. They could attempt to finish what they'd started by launching a nuclear first strike at the U.S., Japan, or some other target, or they could try to negotiate a settlement. Either way, Kim's regime was finished as a player in the nuclear weapons game.

The president went on. "The fighting continues, and the North has not yet agreed to a cease-fire," Claymore summed up, bringing his address to a close. "We will continue to do what we have to do, and I will continue to address our nation as events progress. In the meantime, I ask all Americans to pray for the brave men and women who are fighting in the name of freedom and to stand together in this hour of conflict. With your help, we cannot fail to win. Thank you, and God bless you."

The camera held the president's face on a tight close-up shot. He faced the lens with a half smile and eyes that did not blink. When the red light atop the camera went off, the president unfastened his microphone and pushed away from the desk.

"Great speech," Claymore's chief of staff, longtime friend and former campaign manager Donald Bradley remarked, as he rose to go into the Oval Office. "You came across beautifully."

"To hell with how I came across, Don," Claymore said, the depth of his anger apparent. "Those bastards have gone too damn far, and I plan to make sure they go no farther. Make sure that Starkweather and his people give me an exceedingly thorough and complete briefing on this. I want a meeting of the NSC scheduled for two hours from now."

A moment later, the president had left the room. Bradley hastened to his own office. He had several calls to place within a fairly short time.

7
THE BAD NEWS FIRST

THE DEFENSE TACTICAL INTERNET

The first intimation of trouble, and the start of the hunt, came shortly after twenty hundred hours as a *Lacrosse-4* radar mapping satellite's invisible beams penetrated dense cloud cover over rugged mountain country in the Kamshin region of North Korea.

The *Lacrosse* telemetry was near real time, requiring over-the-horizon transmission to a defense support program (DSP) communications satellite transmitting data over an ultrasecure extra-high-frequency bandwidth downlink to a Defense Department antenna farm in the rolling hills of Maryland.

The signal traveled the rest of the distance by way of hacker-proof—the systems engineers at Defense's security arm, DISA, would insist on the correct term, cracker-proof, though nobody ever used it—cable that ran underground in a special concrete conduit, the cable itself filled with inert krypton gas and lined with sensors that would light up PC screens all over the Eastern seaboard if the cable were tampered with in any way.

At the end of the line for the army of 'trons encoded with the terabytes of data comprising the transmission from orbital space was a half-Japanese IBM mainframe host running SNA Unix, whose software had been written in the United States but whose hardware had largely come from the combined IBM-Toshiba manufacturing complex near Tokyo.

But before the host-san from Big Blue scarfed up the binary inundation, an array of smaller PCs running Network OS/2 that made up the host's so-called firewall subjected the flood of zeros and ones to a battery of check-sum and antiviral testing. Like royal wine tasters, the firewall servers saw that all was good and permitted the flow of digital information through to the host.

The entire process took a matter of seconds, and as the host began processing the data at extremely high throughput speed, the raw data was transformed into pseudocolored imagery of high definition on the screen of a Dell PC by its single authorized user, an employee of the CIA's Office of SIGINT Operations.

The photoanalyst was on what her office mates called Scud watch. The bird had been tasked by NMCC to watch over a section of North Korea suspected to harbor missile manufacture and transshipment facilities, but the CIA owned the infrastructure for the transmission, so it plucked the first fruits of surveillance.

The photoanalyst was sharp. Her calls were usually right on the money. This time, she stopped chewing the Dentyne she'd just popped into her mouth to take away the charred taste of too much black coffee. *There it is*, she thought to herself. One look was all that was necessary. The photoanalyst reached for the secure phone beside her on the desk, then quickly withdrew her hand.

Force of habit, she thought. They'd taken the damn phone away last month, and she still hadn't gotten used to the new procedure. Instead of the handset, she used the mouse to save selected portions of the overhead imagery to a file, which she annotated with her observations and analysis in a separate text field. She might have used a microphone, but she preferred to type. She then opened an E-mail window and sent a message to a digital mailbox at NMCC, stating that the imagery was available for viewing on the Pentagon's secure intranet.

A short time later, General Al Crowley's staff at The Dark Tower was examining the imagery on a Java-powered Web page. A little while later, a Tier III–Minus Dark Star unmanned aerial vehicle overflew the target, its rounded nose pointing into the rays of the newly risen sun.

It was what photoanalysts called "the golden hour"; early morning, when the cool air is unmarred by the wavering, heat-induced haze of thermal distortion, when the low sun provides even illumination, when long shadows highlight terrain features and man-made objects stand out in stark contrast to natural forms on the ground.

From its wide angle and low altitude, the UAV's imaging suite of cameras and optical sensors recorded and transmitted pictures of high definition to U.S. ground stations monitoring the overflight.

"No doubt about it," said the Wizard, as he looked at the near-real-time imagery on the wide, flat-panel screen, a cup of steaming black coffee in his hand. "We're looking at 'Scud Town' here, all right."

The imagery from the aerial reconnaissance drone was far better than anything any satellite was capable of providing. No matter how good the optics, electronics, or image processing, altitude and atmospherics made a tremendous difference in the quality of the intelligence product.

What you saw from above the atmosphere from a distance of miles could never compare to what you could see from inside the atmosphere from a distance of scores or hundreds of feet, especially if the viewing angle, air quality, and position of the sun were just right. The intel take here was a classic case in point.

The Wiz and his small clandestine staff quickly realized they were looking at the holy of holies. Here was what—at a rough estimate—was at least 60 percent of the DPRK Scud and medium-range missile arsenal.

Rail and highway spurs radiated from the complex in several directions, and the team could even see a train pulling away, with containerized cargo lashed to its line of low-slung flatcars. There was little doubt about what those containers held nor about where the cargo was bound. They were mobile and fixed missile launchers going to destinations throughout North Korea.

Unlike others at the Pentagon, Crowley's phone was still on his desk, a prerogative of rank and occupation. He grabbed the handset, punched a button that connected him directly to an office upstairs at JCS headquarters. "Buck," he said, "you'd better check this out. . . ."

SOUTH KOREA

The CJCS did, and less than three hours later and four time zones away at a U.S. air base south of the Demilitarized Zone near Song-Bai, USAF Captain Willy Elfindale left the commander's Quonset-hut office with a freshly cut set of orders and a fraction of a millimeter less enamel on his back teeth from grinding them with rage as he saluted and said, "Yes, sir," to the colonel, meanwhile thinking, *Cur, cur, cur.*

Now he in turn had to break the bad news to his pilots: The mission had been scrubbed, and there was a major-league change in plans. The mission that he and his pilots had trained for during the last five days had been canceled with a suddenness Elfindale never encountered in his years as a flier. What was more, the new mission was to be flown not in five days but in under twenty-four hours, something the veteran pilot knew was next to impossible.

"You cannot be serious, boss," Elfindale's XO, Lieutenant Jim Cobb, told him when he heard of the change. "We broke our balls for this one, twenty-four/seven. All the planning, all the work. Now—"

"Now we do what we're ordered to do," Elfindale told

him. "We don't have a choice. Tell the rest of the men. I want them in the briefing room ASAP."

LOW EARTH ORBIT

At nine hundred twenty hours Zulu, a DSP satellite—part of a twelve-satellite array parked in geosynchronous orbit more than 100 miles above the earth's surface—picked up signs of the single earthbound activity it was designed to detect. Its sensor suite peered into the infrared, or IR, end of the visible light spectrum—it was heat that radiated energy in that region of the spectrum.

Invisible to the unaided human eye, IR radiation was produced by all things that also produced heat, from the human body to the engines of main battle tanks to the ignition flare generated by a strategic missile launch. It was the last of these that the DSP array had been thrust into orbit to detect. The DSP array was the United States' first line of warning of the launch of hostile missiles, and it had been since the middle of the Cold War.

During the war in the Gulf, it was DSP satellites that caught the telltale flare of Scud launches from Iraq and occupied Kuwait and flashed warnings of these events to ground stations, such as NORAD in Colorado and the Alternate Military Command Center at Raven Rock, Pennsylvania.

From Cheyenne Mountain in Colorado to places like Riyadh, Saudi Arabia, the Scud alerts gave personnel an average of ten minutes to get into their protective gear, take cover, pray, or do whatever one did when word of impending missile attack came one's way.

Today, in the late-morning hours, the DSP satellite parked over East Asia picked up the launch signature of a Scud missile, then another, then another after that. Within minutes, launch warnings were transmitted to combatants within range of the Scuds.

Among the many combatants was the 3rd Mechanized Brigade, which fielded a tank battalion out of Fort Knox, Virginia. The tankers had been drilled tirelessly in getting into

MOPP gear in the event of chemical-biological attack. At the warning of the Scud launch, they quickly donned their protective suits, gloves, face masks, and respirators. Within minutes, they were suited up at MOPP level 5, the highest available level of protection.

SOUTH KOREA

Sergeant Randy Skerret of Boonesville, South Carolina, was the ordnance loader aboard an M1A2 Abrams MBT. Skerret didn't like climbing into his chemical warfare gear. He thought the mission-oriented protective posture, or MOPP ensemble, consisting of rubberized mask, coat, pants, and boots as uncomfortable as climbing into a giant condom. Which made him feel like a dumb prick.

Skerret was a tanker to the core and a career soldier. He had served in Desert Storm, and there had never been any chemical attack then, though they had drilled him witless in preparation for one. When yet another chemical attack alert came in, he'd been contemplating finishing his beer and the letter he was writing home to his wife and just ignoring the whole thing.

But Skerret's training had taken over, and he'd suited up exactly as he'd been trained to do, donning the protective jacket, face mask, and gloves over the gear he was already wearing to bring him up to MOPP level 5, full chemical and biological warfare protection. As it turned out, it was a good thing that he'd followed procedures. Because this time a bona fide chemical attack actually materialized.

Skerret realized this when his tank company's mascot, a goat named Capricorn, that had been grazing nearby, suddenly lost its footing, toppled over, and began foaming at the mouth. Inside his protective MOPP gear, Skerret smelled, tasted, and felt nothing. But the evidence of a chemical attack in progress could not be ignored.

Man, they actually done it, Skerret thought. *They actually done it!*

And done it they had. The North Koreans had just

launched an unconventional missile strike using a warhead filled with VX nerve agent. They had just broken all the rules. Skerret, like many others, knew the course of the war had just changed in that single, fateful instant.

◆　◆　◆

The twelve F-16 Falcons roared off the airstrip one after another, waved off by ground crews swinging luminous batons as they vanished into the night.

It didn't help anybody's mood that the runway they'd been assigned was ridiculously short, a secondary field runway just over 6,500 feet long. For fully loaded fighters weighing in at almost 70,000 pounds, it meant takeoff was a bitch, and every ounce of thrust of the Pratt-Whitney turbofans was needed to hurl the agile combat aircraft into the air.

But once they got airborne, it was another ball game. Flight leader Elfindale stood the lead Falcon on its tail, instantly pulling 2½ g's as he climbed vertically to 12,000 feet less than a half mile from the end of the runway.

Leveling off, he glanced through his cockpit window, seeing Cobb, his wingman, about 600 feet behind and to starboard. Later, when they neared their initial points and closed on their kill baskets, they would spread out to greater interplane distances, but for most of the way in, the strike package would fly a tight formation.

Angry pilots occupied the cockpits of those fighters, a hanging jury that had blood on its mind. The aircrew had heard about the first chemical attack against U.S. troops since the trenches of Verdun, and they were mad as hell. Doubly mad since the mission they had busted their asses to fly for the better part of a week might well have forestalled the attack.

The word was that VX nerve agents had been in the warheads of the Scud/Bs that had been launched from mobile launchers in the Kamshin vicinity. Khamshin had been where the fighter wing had been scheduled to do the dirty boogie with 500-pound bombs. But the strike had been scrubbed, and this had been the result.

Each plane was loaded down with weapons and fastpacks that would increase its range. Freighted as they were, the bomb trucks—for so the F-16 variants are known by pilots—handled like something with a cement mixer strapped to its back, but as the thousands of pounds of fuel in their tanks burned off, the pilots knew the Falcons would begin to handle better and would get them to their targets. The words of their commanding officer echoed in their minds: "Finally," he'd said, "finally there's something worth dying for."

Elfindale hauled back on the stick, pulling for altitude. The rest of the attack formation followed him up. At 30,000 feet and twenty miles out, two AAR tankers awaited the F-16s for a refueling RV. The fighters had a long way to fly and would fill their tanks with JP7 before they started the inbound run.

FORT LEE, NEW JERSEY

The man who had checked into the hotel suite earlier that morning had insisted on carrying his own bag, which was nothing out of the ordinary. Many guests preferred to carry their own bags. There was also nothing out of the ordinary in the Visa card he had used at the front desk. It was issued by a major U.S. bank, and the account was active.

Nor was there anything amiss about the way he spoke and looked. His accent was foreign, hinting at Slavic origins, and his cold demeanor was no different than that of many other business travelers. But there was much out of the ordinary with the man who had signed in as Roger Petermann. These things included Petermann's Visa account, which was fraudulent; his name, which was assumed; and his origins, which were with the Technical Directorate of the former Soviet KGB.

Petermann's true name was Aleksander Vasiliev, and as he had once sworn allegiance to the Marxist dogma of communism, so he now upheld the mercenary credo of the new organization to which he belonged. This was the Russian Mafiya, a criminal organization comprised of the remnants of the once great Soviet Union's multifaceted intelligence, political, economic, and criminal apparatuses, a criminal organization whose scope and numbers dwarfed anything comparable in world history.

Here were ex-KGB chiefs, here were former Politburo bigwigs, here were the once well-connected overseers of state-run factories, here were killers and thieves and money men, and experts in forgery, in silent and invisible killing, and in many other arcane arts and practices. They had all found a new place in the organization.

Among this flotsam and jetsam that had been permitted to take root in the United States by a web of unholy political alliances were also the best computer crackers in the world. Vasiliev was one of them. Setting up a laptop in the privacy of his locked hotel room, hacking into and then bypassing the hotel's PBX phone system, Vasielev began to do the job he'd been assigned by his masters.

North Korea's intelligence service had paid the Mafiya half a billion dollars to take out an American surveillance satellite over their country. Vaseliev was about to do precisely that by maneuvering a long-forgotten Soyuz-7 satellite near an American Keyhole 11 in orbit over North Korea. The Mafiya's crackers did not have the technology to directly penetrate security systems protecting the American satellite from information attack, but they could hack into the Soyuz-7, which was almost as good.

The Soyuz satellite was not a killer satellite, such Soviet weapons had been more Cold War rumor than fact. But the paranoid Soviet-era GRU had in fact constructed all military satellites with onboard self-destruct charges housed in special pressurized capsules. Vasilev's object was to arm and trigger those charges when the Soyuz-7 was close enough to the multimillion-dollar U.S. surveillance satellite to blow it to pieces.

The pale blue eyes of the Ukrainian-born hacker studied the wide, flat-panel screen in the darkened room. *Orbit*

2768 . . . orbit 2769 . . . The old Soyuz was climbing steadily, the last pounds of its fuel reserves propelling it from its low orbit to the higher orbit of the American spy satellite. *Orbit 3041 . . . orbit 3042 . . .*

It was a classic pop-up maneuver, a form of orbital ambush that he had learned to master in the service of the KGB. Vast distances above him, the progress of the forgotten Soviet Cold War–era satellite was shown on the screen of the laptop computer in front of the cracker as he sat alone in the suite. The orbit numbers increased: 4053, 4244, 5068, 5099, 6001, and then . . .

I have it in range, he thought, seeing the orbits of hunter and hunted merge.

Anxiously, he clicked the mouse cursor on a digital button. The command was issued. Hundreds of miles out in space, a two-pound brick of plastic explosive inside its special air-filled compartment suddenly detonated.

The result was instantaneous. Both the Soyuz-7 and the Keyhole were vaporized into clouds of spinning metal orbital debris. At intelligence installations across the country with access to telemetry from the Keyhole, screens blanked and warning tones shrilly sounded. At NORAD headquarters, where objects in near space were constantly monitored and tracked, warning messages flashed on computer terminals and the handsets of hot line phones were lifted from their cradles.

A multimillion-dollar surveillance satellite had just vanished from NORAD's scopes. For at least another forty-eight hours until a replacement satellite could be launched into orbit, the U.S. would be blind to events over 70 percent of the Korean combat theater, and command and control over American and allied military forces would be seriously degraded.

The Ukrainian quit all open programs, powered down, and closed the laptop. Others, he knew, had been monitoring events and were already aware that he had succeeded. Before leaving the suite, he paused just long enough to finish the cold minibottle of white wine he'd taken from the suite's courtesy cooler. Vasiliev was a happy man. This job had just paid for his retirement in the Caribbean.

"I'm checking out," he said into the handset of the bureau phone. "Have my bill ready."

With the loss of overhead coverage, the war in Korea had just entered a dangerous new phase.

8
A GORGON'S HEAD

The sortie of F-16 Fighting Falcons bounced in the turbulent night winds at 20,000 feet as they sped toward the three KC-135 tanker aircraft orbiting due east of Seoul. Rough flying weather like this—high winds, squalls, and dense cloud cover—had bedeviled air operations for the last two days and nights. Fighting the turbulence, the twelve-plane squadron rendezvoused with the tankers in four concurrent waves.

Elfindale and his wingmen, Cobb and Abatemarco, were first in line for a drink of JP7, each jockeying their aircraft under the bellies of the much larger tanker planes and lining up with the bell-shaped drogue assembly that dangled from the end of the long fiberglass hose that was winched down from the KC-135.

The two aircraft types waltzed in the turbulence like gnats and dragonflies engaged in an ill-considered mating ritual.

Minutes later, their tanks topped off, the first three F-16s decoupled from the tankers' refueling hoses and resumed their flight while the next three planes took turns at the feeding trough.

Elfindale's SINCGARS sounded high-low tones as an incoming message passed through a series of electronic filters. Modulated at the correct frequency, encoded with the correct encryption algorithms, bearing the correct check-sum data, the signal was passed through the F-16's signal-hopping communications linkages.

"Zulu Quebec Lima Seven to Kestrel One. Over."

Elfindale recognized the call sign of the AWACS Airborne Warning and Control System aircraft that had been tasked with mission direction on the ride up-range.

A sealed bulkhead separated the cockpit crew that drove the E-3A Sentry, a modified Boeing 707 passenger jet, from the ELINT techs, RSOs, and occasional spooks on board AWACS that made up the standard sixteen-man crew. The rest of the plane's real estate was occupied by rows of equipment-crammed consoles running the entire length of the passenger compartment. The consoles were wired to the Westinghouse AN/APY-2 airborne radar, whose antenna elements were housed in the broad, flat, circular rotodome straddling the twin-strut pylon aft of the wings. They were also connected to electronic countermeasures pods on the fuselage.

AWACS flew a racetrack oval about a hundred nautical miles distant from the F-16 sortie, its rotodome revolving six times a minute, its AN/APY radar combing the skies to a range of over 300 miles in all directions, seeking and identifying high- or low-level threats. These included fighters, bombers, tanker aircraft, UAVs, and missiles—virtually any airborne object that might present a hazard to friendly forces.

A USAF radar systems officer seated at a console station had the sortie on his PDNS radar. Pulse-Doppler nonelevation scan, which tracked airborne targets, was the main radar mode of the two types used by AWACS. The Sentry was also equipped with maritime radar. The two systems were interleaved and could be switched many times per second, enabling AWACS to simultaneously track airborne and surface targets.

A communications officer wearing a headset and mike talked to the F-16 sortie on a secure SINCGARS channel through J-TIDS (Joint Tactical Information Distribution System), which could communicate with radios of all three combat branches in combined arms operations. Lack of communications interoperability had plagued U.S. fighting units until after the close of the Gulf War.

Elfindale acknowledged the transmission from the E-3A. "That's a roger, Zulu Quebec Lima Seven. What have you got?"

"Got some good news and some bad news," the technician aboard AWACS said. "Which do you want first?"

"Just say your piece, partner," Elfindale replied.

"Roger, Kestrel One. The good news is the Ravens are good to go. The bad news is the Weasels can't come out and play."

"Why not?"

"The F-4s you guys ordered up from Suwon air base never received the TOT change."

"This is fucked up beyond redemption," Elfindale cussed aloud. "They knew about the new TOT." He thought for a moment, biting his lip. He had submitted the time on target, or TOT, schedule to the base commander and been told it had been approved. "Any way of getting some Weasel coverage A-sap?"

"Negative so far, Captain, but I'll pass it up the pipe," AWACS replied. "Sorry about that FUBAR."

Elfindale rogered that and thought about how he'd relay this to the rest of the mission team. In his opinion, the absence of the two F-4 Wild Weasel aircraft he had asked for demanded that the mission be scrubbed. The sortie needed the specially outfitted Phantom F-4G aircraft equipped with AGM-88 HARM antiradar missiles to deal with the threat posed by the many SAM belts girdling the target area.

With their war load of HARMs—which homed in on radar emissions such as those produced by tracking radars of the SA-6s and SA-10s known to be deployed as antiaircraft defenses north of the DMZ—the Wild Weasels could reduce the SAM threat to a minimum acceptable level. This would permit the F-16 strike package to fly in at a low-level trajectory and much more reliably drop their ordnance.

But with this new development, that option was out. The sortie would have to come in high to avoid the SAM threat. This would reduce the pilots' ability to see the targets on the ground until the last minutes before they commenced their bomb run.

"What about we wait thirty minutes or so?" Cobb put in after Elfindale informed his second-in-command in the Falcon eight miles behind him. "Let's see if AWACS gets back on the Weasels."

"Negative, Jim," Elfindale advised. "The mission's too critical, and those F-4s are just plain not coming. We've gotta accept that."

"Yeah, I concur, I guess," Cobb said after a pause. "We still got the F-111s, right?"

"That's affirm," Elfindale said, mentally adding, *So far.*

In the absence of the F-4G's the EF-111 Ravens would have to fill the bill, and the mission might well hinge on how effective they were at suppressing SAM radars.

Unlike the Wild Weasel, which killed radars by firing missiles at them, the EF-111—an F/FB-111 Aardvark swing-wing fighter-bomber outfitted with a sophisticated suite of electronic countermeasures (ECM) and electronic counter-countermeasures (ECCM) equipment—relied on its powerful jamming capability to neutralize enemy radars.

This was good, but not nearly as permanent a solution as firing a half ton of high explosive into a SAM radar truck the way an F-4G could do.

On a mission such as theirs, where fighter aircraft had to get "down into the weeds" to deliver their ordnance, effective radar suppression was critical to reduce the SAM threat. It would also help degrade ground-to-air command and control of enemy MiGs likely to be sent against the U.S. planes, another mission hazard.

For this, a mix of the capabilities of both F-4G and EF-111 were both necessary; neither plane alone promised more than a partial tactical solution.

Elfindale explained the loss of the F-4Gs to his aircrew and reaped the expected gripes and curses at first, though the end result was a round of confident "hoo-ahs." The crew was good to go, even though the mission was a hastily planned ad hoc affair, and defense suppression support was half what it should have rightfully been.

Tanks filled to the max with avgas, the Falcons killed their running lights and throttled up into steep ballistic climbs. They would commence their overfly of the DMZ into the bastions of the enemy north at a high-altitude ceiling and at supersonic speeds. Elfindale and his fighter jocks were committed now. There was no turning back.

◆　◆　◆

The inbound flight proved uneventful. Fifteen minutes into the mission, with roughly half the distance flown, the fighter planes had penetrated more than a hundred miles into North Korean airspace without incident. This was largely due to the support of the EF-111 Ravens, which were orbiting in broad circular tracks northwest of Pyong-Chin city, near the southern end of the DMZ.

Each Raven aircraft, laden with three tons of electronic jamming equipment, began pumping thousands of watts of power at DPRK ground radars. Through an array of pods, fairings, and antennae, including a large pod mounted atop the vertical stabilizer known colloquially as the football, the Raven could detect unfriendly search radar signals. The EF-111's electronic warfare officer (EWO), whose battle station occupied the seat next to the pilot, then cast his 'trons—broadcast contradictory signals through the canoe fairing that ran lengthwise along the underbelly of the plane and contained an array of antenna elements.

More art than science, casting 'trons was intended to punch gaping holes in the electronic environment and bewilder the enemy just long enough to allow Elfindale's bomb trucks to sneak up on their targets. If the Raven could steal up close enough, and the electronic warfare was handled deftly enough, enemy radar screens would snow out, crash out, or begin showing digital garbage instead of an orderly procession of threat symbols superimposed over a digital map display as they would normally exhibit.

But though armed with formidable jamming capability, the nonstealthy EF-111 was unequipped to prevent visual sighting by enemy aircraft. As the Ravens began a second race-track orbit in a nose-to-tail counterclockwise turn toward the North Korean border, two MiG-29 Fulcrums suddenly popped into being on their threat radars.

"Hot shit! We got a pair of bogies on our asses," the lead plane's pilot announced over secure comms, reacting to the shrill warning tones that had just sounded in the cockpit and checking his scope. "Just our luck to catch a pair of Fulcrums."

Before another few seconds had passed, their scopes lit up with active missile tracking radar warnings. An AA-11 Archer air-to-air missile, similar to the U.S. Sparrow, had just been fired from one of the missile pylons mounted beneath one Fulcrum's wings. The Ravens' scopes lit up again as yet another AA-11 was launched at the two EF-111s.

"Going to active ECM," the lead Raven's EWO advised, punching buttons on the console in front of him. "ECM engaged. I have successful lock on countermeasures."

The EWO watched the tracks of the AA-11 missiles waver as the electronic countermeasures he had applied took effect. Spoofing created false radar returns that showed the Ravens as being miles from their actual positions. The tracks of the incoming Archers now became completely erratic.

"I now have defeat. Countermeasures have resulted in defeat of missile seeker heads."

Suddenly the night sky lit up. The missile warheads had

detonated where their terminal guidance systems computed the real planes to be in the vast airspace.

Within minutes, AWACS reported more MiGs approaching and advised the Ravens to turn back toward their airstrip near Seoul. By this stage, the sortie of F-16s had turned off their radios in observance of EMCON, emissions control. As the planes followed the Yin-Bin Highway, leading north to their destination some fifty miles up-range, they had no way of knowing what had happened to their electronic guardian angels.

On the ground, it was another matter. With the Ravens gone, the tactical picture had changed considerably. In enemy mobile radar outposts located within the SAM belt, screens that had been snowed out with electronic clutter and false Doppler echoes for the past forty-odd minutes were suddenly operational again.

Radar dishes swiveled and locked on true azimuths as they acquired the silhouettes of the F-16 squadron, and North Korean SAM crews moved rapidly to target the SA-10s and SA-6s on their mobile launchers at the newly visible prey swooping in from the skies.

Though the fighters were flying at a high altitude ceiling, they were still within the lethality envelope of the SAMs. The North Korean batteries plotted firing solutions and launched their missiles. At 30,000 feet, their sensitive, long-range seeker heads engaged, and tracking and pursuit commenced.

◆　　◆　　◆

Elfindale and his crew instantly knew something had happened to the Ravens when their threat identification radars lit up. Audial alarm signals were also going off in the Falcons' cockpits, their shrill notes announcing the detection of inbound missiles.

The mission was less than thirty miles from its targets by this point, and the pilots could see the blacked-out strike basket on the forward-looking infrared (FLIR) display of their HUDs stark and green against the seamless blackness of the night sky and dark terrain.

Elfindale fought back the feeling of panic beginning to gather in the pit of his stomach. If he got hit, he got hit. If it happened, it happened, he thought. But he would do what he had been sent here to do just the same. That part didn't change for anything.

Seconds later, the pounding in his chest that felt like it was about to rip through the fabric of his flight suit like something from an old Bugs Bunny cartoon, began to subside. *Get your shit together,* he told himself. *Fly the mission.*

"I have a missile contrail, thirty degrees to my left," he heard his backseater's voice say in his helmet over the aircraft interphone. "Repeat. Missile contrail. Thirty degrees left and closing at Mach two point one."

The bright—and still very tiny—orange dot seemed to hang in the air like a fixed star to the left of the cockpit canopy.

Elfindale's pulse quickened again: This was a deadly sign. The stationary flare meant the SAM had locked onto their aircraft and was engaged in tracking mode.

Hauling on the stick, Elfindale jinked hard, pulling g's as he executed a sixty-degree leftward break. The orange dot had grown from the size of a Roosevelt dime to a disk as big as a long-playing record. Suddenly it changed shape, elongating into an inverted cone as the missile streaked overhead.

Seconds later, the sky lit up with a brilliant flash to the extreme left of the cockpit. The dull boom of an explosion echoed through the night. The warhead had detonated harmlessly somewhere out over the dark vastness of the East Asian landscape.

As Elfindale steered the Falcon back onto his course vector, he saw another bright flash in the distance and heard a much louder explosion. He knew instantly that one of his planes had just been hit. This was confirmed moments later by distress calls from two of his aircrew.

Davis in Kestrel Six reported that one of the Falcons was

down. His own plane had been badly mauled by another SAM strike. The pilot radioed that he was afraid he'd have to eject. Elfindale was not to hear any more from that fighter during the course of the mission.

In seconds they were within visual range of the target and taking steady Triple-A fire from a ZSU-23-4 Shilka battery protecting the rail yard and other nearby infrastructure, including outbuildings, tracks, and rolling stock.

The ZSU-23-4 was a quad-barreled, twenty-three-millimeter water-cooled antiaircraft gun mounted on a T-74 tank chassis that tracked its quarry by sideband frequency modulation radar. The guns in the Shilka battery were loaded with a red phosphorous tracer round to every three standard projectiles. The streaks of tracer fire cumulatively proved a smaller version of what Elfindale remembered from the Desert Wind air campaign more than a decade before, except now the Triple-A was less like the solid wall he recalled.

Here above North Korea you could pick out the individual red tracers in the barrage. They appeared like crimson threads stitching between the dashes of glowing white that marked nontracer rounds. Over Iraq, most of the time, you couldn't pick out the whites because the rapidity of the firing rate was incredibly intense.

The North Koreans were also sending up large masses of pin flares to make sighting the planes easier for crews manning older ZSU-57-2 twin-barrel pom-pom guns with no radar and only optical sights for targeting that were dug in on the ground. The F-16s were still high enough at 20,000 feet to be above the killing envelope of the determined Triple-A fire. But when they went into their attack dives, they would have to go down on the deck and be increasingly vulnerable to ground artillery.

"Going in now, Jim," Elfindale said to his wingman, as he rolled thirty degrees and dropped altitude. "Follow me in."

"That's affirm," the wingman answered.

Menacingly heavy tracer fire now spurted past the plane, the luminous red streaks whizzing so close to the cockpit canopy bubble that Elfindale was amazed none of the rounds had penetrated the crew capsule. The pitch ladder—the green horizontal lines bisecting the center of the HUD—yawed, and the altitude numbers dropped on the AGL (above ground level) display to its right. The bomb truck yawed slightly as it plunged lower, then stabilized for final target overfly.

In his HUD, Elfindale saw the cluster of buildings making up the enemy rail yard grow in his field of view, the various flight data superimposed above the head-up display's gray-scale infrared image.

With the F-16's LANTIRN system now switched from navigation to targeting mode, his WSO in the backseat lined up the target in his head-up display and put down the pipper, which was a dot at the center of a circle divided into 1,000-foot increments of slant range linked by a horizontal line showing heading. At its top was a small circle called the velocity vector, showing the angle of dive. On the WSO's HUD the death dot now inched toward the central Scud assembly shed that was the aim point of the target box.

When the pipper lined up over the center of the long, squat building, Elfindale hit and held down the joystick's pickle button, arming the automatic bombing system for ordnance release. The plane's computer then took over, and the target box vanished from the HUD. Elfindale now kept his eye on the frag cue, a horizontal mark on the HUD's vertical line showing the precise velocity vector that the pilot had to stay above in order to avoid being hit by exploding fragments from his own bomb strikes.

After a half second of settling time, the F-16's airframe suddenly gave a savage lurch. Elfindale felt the immediate change in the way the aircraft handled as the bombs let go; the stick felt less cumbersome and the airspeed dramatically increased in the absence of thousands of pounds of dead weight and wind drag.

He immediately executed a ninety-degree leftward break and climbed ballistically to get out of the way of the worsening Triple-A fire streaking up at him, firewalling the afterburner. The cockpit bubble now lit up again with a blinding series of pulsating flashes as his ordnance hit its

target and exploded, followed by the multiple detonations of
the bombs loosed from the surviving planes of the sortie in
a mad tempo of flame, shrapnel, and devastating concussion.

But a head count as the mission heeled around for the
return flight confirmed Elfindale's growing fears since hitting
the enemy Triple-A; out of the original twelve planes, only
eight remained in the air. The others had either been hit or
were destroyed as their pilots ejected.

♦   ♦   ♦

Lighter now by several score tons and minus the drag friction
of the bombs they'd carried, the Falcons handled like race
cars as the sortie hightailed it southward in the direction of
the DMZ. They had climbed to a flight ceiling of 30,000
feet, well beyond the lethality envelope of any of the SAM
types known to be active in the vicinity.

Their only threat—and it was by no means an inconse-
quential one—was in the form of MiGs or Sukhois that might
be loitering in the airspace; only the MiG-29 or SU-27 had
the range, the avionics, and the weaponry to pose any serious
threat to the Falcons.

Suddenly, threat identification radar announced the presence of two MiG-29s in the vicinity. The pair was the same
that had chased off the EF-111 Ravens earlier in the mission.
The Fulcrums were now probing the skies for the U.S. aircraft that had struck north of the DMZ and that would be
returning to their South Korean air bases.

"They don't see us, Elf," the lead plane's WSO said over
cabin interphone. "Let's bust their asses some."

"Be a pleasure, George," Elfindale said as he heeled the
Falcon around on a sixty-degree attack vector. The backseater shut down radar as the F-16D dropped altitude and
closed rapidly with the two MiGs.

Within seconds they had approached to within ten miles
of the North Korean air-superiority fighters and had them on
their FLIR, which unlike radar was a passive system that

would not give them away to the MiGs' threat identification radars.

The U.S. fighter carried two AIM-9M Sidewinder air-to-air missiles mounted on the undersides of each wingtip—the last weapons left of its original loadout. The Sidewinders were heat-seekers, homing in on infrared radiation emitted by engines and other control surfaces. The WSO uncaged the Sidewinders, allowing their seeker heads to lock onto their targets.

Suddenly, threat identification radar announced the MiGs had picked up the U.S. planes on their scopes. Elfindale saw the Fulcrums break to left and right and begin a series of rapid pulling and jinking maneuvers. It might have been right out of the Russian Top Gun textbook, but it was too late for either of them. Elfindale could already feel the lurches of the two Sidewinders cooking off the wings as his wizzo in the backseat launched them at their targets.

A heartbeat later, two white, twinkling dots that illuminated a billowing contrail of solid fuel exhaust gases shot out from under the wings. The Sidewinders were away. The North Korean MiGs were doing it by the numbers, jinking and rolling as they banked left and right. But the supersonic air-to-air missiles were faster and far more maneuverable than any piloted aircraft, and they were lethal at close range.

Seconds ticked by.

The MiGs had ejected flares and chaff in last-ditch efforts to spoof the swiftly pursuing Sidewinders, which moved with the weaving motions of the eponymous snakes as they matched the movements of the enemy fighters. But the new versions of the AIM-9M fired by the Falcons were equipped with counter-countermeasures that digitally filtered out deception countermeasures from actual, bona fide target returns.

Seconds later it was all over. The Fulcrums's deception and evasion tactics had been to no avail. The Sidewinders overtook the fleeing combat planes, speeding toward the strongest heat source they emitted, which was the cone of hot exhaust gases expelled by their turbofan engines. In a moment they had flown right up the tailpipes of the MiGs to explode inside the nacelles that housed the engines.

The hostile planes broke apart in midair, twin fireballs lighting up the night sky with an intense, hellishly flickering white light illuminating clouds of shattered wreckage that marked where the planes had once been. Neither Elfindale nor his backseater saw any parachutes that might signal the ejection of aircrew.

"Shit hot," Elfindale said to his wizzo, "that's two good kills."

"Yeah, we really fragged 'em proper," the backseater replied. Despite the friendly losses, it was starting to feel like not such a bad night's work after all. Almost.

NORTH KOREA

In a complex of underground C³I (command, control, and communications) bunkers excavated deep enough into the bedrock of the North Korean mountains to withstand even a direct nuclear airburst, a cadre of high-echelon officers stood around a map table. They had been engaged in a debate that the American fighter attack on their Scud park had just put to an end.

The losses were not yet tallied, but beyond doubt, the time had come to act. All were in agreement about what needed to be done.

Thanks to the successful hack resulting in the loss of U.S. satellite coverage, they now had an opportunity window that would probably not come again. The officers acted in accordance with irrefutable military logic. The order was given. Mobile Nodong missile crews stationed near the southern border that had been placed on alert were now ordered to arm their missiles with nuclear warheads and fire them at their preassigned targets.

The MRBMs, medium-range ballistic missiles, lanced into the darkened heavens like spears flung at gods. The Nodongs—theater missiles—did not fly as high as ICBMs. Their range, though formidable, only permitted them to skirt the near edge of suborbital space. But that was all that was necessary for them to prove effectively deadly.

SOUTH KOREA

The first warning of the Nodong missile launch was dectected by DSP satellites and flashed by NORAD to all forces in the theater as SINDAS began analyzing the tracks of the incoming warheads and predicting points of impact.

There were four inbound tracks in all, and with an estimated time of arrival of under ten minutes, there was little time to react. SINDAS recommended that the ring of theater lasers—THELs—and batteries of Patriot missiles that had been hastily installed on the Japanese mainland be used defensively against the incoming warheads, which were aimed at greater Tokyo.

The defensive ring of lasers and antiballistic missiles succeeded in destroying all but one of the incoming Nodongs, which had fallen far short of its intended target. The nuclear warhead detonated as an airburst a half mile above the Sea of Japan, close enough to the U.S. frigate *Fitzsimmons* to catch the ship within the blast radius of the nuclear explosion.

Though the hundred-kiloton warhead was a relatively small one by strategic nuclear weapons standards, it was more than powerful enough on a tactical or theater scale. Caught by the nuclear thermal pulse and blast wave, the frigate was vaporized, and only scattered wreckage was left floating on the sea. There were no survivors, and the fallout produced by the blast would create an environmental threat that would have consequences as far away as southern Australia for many years to come.

The news of the first successful nuclear attack since Hiroshima and Nagasaki spread throughout the world like wildfire. The North Koreans had once again done the unthinkable and the unpardonable. They had resorted to weapons of mass destruction on two separate occasions. To NATO and to the world at large, the rogue nation had declared itself beyond redemption.

THE WHITE HOUSE

At the Pentagon's NMCC, the CJCS had just heard from the president. The chief executive wanted a retaliation strike package that would destroy the North Korean delivery capability before the DPRK could fire another missile.

The president had been clear on this point. *"They must not fire another missile,"* he told the CJCS. *"I don't care what you have to do, what options you have to pursue, short of open nuclear retaliation, but I want this stopped before it goes further."*

The CJCS had received his instructions, and he knew what was expected of him. *Who will rid me of this bothersome priest?* was one of the aphorisms under the glass top of his office desk. He asked the president if that included using low-yield nuclear devices capable of destroying deeply buried bunkers.

"Yes," the president replied to Starkweather and the assembled members of the Gang of Six planning and advisory cell. "Up to and including that, but not beyond that. Can you do it?"

"I think we can," the CJCS told him. "But short of getting out our white flags and going to the peace table with a small-time mob of cutthroats who will ram 'peace' down our craw the way Ho Chi Minh did in Paris, we don't have much other choice."

"That's become obvious, I think," the president replied. "We're in a double bind. We need to solve this problem surgically. We need to use the scalpel on the tumor; otherwise there will be no stopping its growth. A negotiated settlement would have the result of inevitable escalation. What has happened before on the Korean Peninsula was built on our original miscalculations in 1953. We can't afford another screwup."

"Mr. President," Starkweather answered, choosing his words with care, "there is a strike plan available for use that is designed to deal precisely with this contingency. I can present the plan in depth at a later time, but I can sketch out the broad parameters of the plan for you and the working group right now."

Claymore leaned back in his wing chair and pushed the eyeglasses that few except White House intimates saw him wear up on his head.

"Let's hear it, General," the president said. "And give it to me straight."

Starkweather rose. Assuming his customary stance facing the cold fireplace, he began to speak, quickly gaining the complete attention of every person present in the Oval Office.

"It's called the Medusa Option, gentlemen," he began. "Here's the lash-up on it. . . ."

BOOK TWO

WAR IN MASQUERADE

Such subtle covenants shall be made
Till peace itself is war in masquerade.

Dryden

9
SEE NO EVIL, HEAR NO EVIL

The flight out of Bethel International had been uneventful for the crew of Alaska Airlines flight 599. The 747 jumbo jet had turned wheels up and ascended to its cruising altitude of 30,000 feet. It then proceeded northwest along heading Cap Rumbo at 250 degrees latitude at sixty knots on the first leg of its 1,000-mile flight to Seoul, South Korea.

In the cockpit were Captain Bill Cairncross and his copilot, Martin Ling. The time was 0450 hours Zulu.

Both men were airline veterans who had flown this particular air corridor numerous times without incident. Despite the Second Korean War, this morning's red-eye to Seoul should be no different from other flights.

Conflict notwithstanding, Route 20 Bethel-Seoul remained one of the three busiest air corridors in the entire world and had continued as such with only minor slowdowns. One of the reasons for this was that NATO warplanes owned the skies above and beyond the immediate vicinity of the war zone.

With the passenger compartment aft of the cockpit at half capacity, AlAir's paying customers had plenty of room to stretch out. Some watched the in-flight movie, others listened to music, and still others read or dozed. This, and the easy availability of rest rooms, combined to make it a pleasant trip for AlAir 599's passengers and for the six flight attendants crewing the early-morning shuttle run.

The captain's voice crackled over the intercom as the plane gained its cruising altitude at waypoint NABIE. Here it was handed off to the flight control radar personnel at Saint Paul Island, 500 miles west of Bethel. The handoff detracted nothing from the comfort of the flight's passengers and crew. Captain Cairncross's voice had the natural timbre of a radio newscaster, and he had years of practice with it as a way of getting the passengers to relax during flights.

"On behalf of myself and the crew and Alaskan Airlines, I want to welcome you aboard flight five ninety-nine," Cairncross began after introducing himself.

"We've just reached our cruising altitude of thirty-five thousand feet, and you're now free to remove your safety belts and leave your seats if you so desire." Cairncross's eyes flicked to the banks of brightly lit instrumentation gauges and readouts on the console of the darkened cabin.

As he spoke, he idly took in a variety of numbers from VOR, altimeter, INS, airspeed indicator, and other systems and their backups.

"Weather conditions are looking good for the trip. We should have clear skies throughout our flight and on our landing at Seoul. Arrival time is approximately six-fifteen A.M., Seoul local time, and even sooner if we pick up a tailwind."

Cairncross wound up his speech with an invitation to enjoy the in-flight movie starring Sylvester Stallone and Courtney Love, and a reminder that the flight attendants would be serving complimentary drinks following a short brief on emergency procedures. He then signed off, leaving the passengers in the hands of his crew, none of whom picked up on the use of the military word *brief* by the captain.

"Brief." Not "talk" or "explanation" or even "run-through."

The crew had heard the word numerous times before and had tuned it out. The passengers were thinking of mini–Jack Daniel's bottles and had hardly paid attention. And, of course, none beyond the locked cockpit door could hear the captain's remark to his copilot after he'd racked the microphone.

"Not that there'll be any reason for emergency procedures this trip," he'd said to the man in the seat beside him.

"Hopefully," had been the answer he'd gotten.

And there wouldn't. This was not to be another KAL 007. What they were doing this morning wouldn't even come close to what the Korean Airlines plane had attempted, and almost gotten away with, before a rocket from a MiG-25 had blown it out of the air over Kamchatka Island back in 1987.

The deviation on this flight would be nowhere nearly as extensive. A matter of only a few miles. Nautical miles, in fact, shorter than statute miles. That much off course, and with all the ECM they'd been promised, there was no way, there was just no damn way.

The KAL flight had crossed Sov territory for four hours before it got hit. Four hours. This deviation would take no more than twenty minutes at most, and it would never take the plane over land. No, there'd be no fuck-ups this trip. It just didn't figure.

That was good, thought Cairncross. Good because you didn't tell those people you weren't going to do it. Especially not with the numbers on his arm.

They were faded now, almost invisible, in fact. But they were still there, same as the day they were tattooed on in a steambath-hot, fly-buzzing parlor above a bar on Tu-Do Street in Saigon many years before.

It was the girl he was having the fling with he'd done it for. To show her he was a tough guy. Her and the rest of them in the unit. Funny, but she said she didn't give a shit about it afterward, that he'd been drunk and just wanted to show off. What was her name again, that Vietnamese girl he used to know in Saigon? Mai, he thought. Or was it Kim? Then he found that he could no longer recall it. Not that it mattered. It was long ago. Memories faded and vanished.

Not like the numbers, though: *10-10*. The numbers were still there. The same ones the Sovs had held up to the TV cameras to show the world almost forty years before. The numbers on a card they'd fished from one of the pockets of Francis Gary Powers's flight suit after he'd been shot down over the arid steppes of Sverdlovsk in 1964.

Detachment 10-10: the special CIA surveillance group that ran spy planes out of Kadena and Incirlik throughout the Cold War, and even for many years afterward.

Cairncross had served with the unit for twelve years before they'd let him off the hook, retired him back to the world. But you never got away from the spooks, not really or permanently. Their reach was long. So was their memory.

When the intelligence boys came to him and asked him to do this for them, it was no request. Cairncross knew their breed, knew how their minds worked, and of what harsh inducements they were capable. Cairncross knew their request for what it was: an order.

If nothing else, those fading numbers made it an order. The money, of course, would help. They'd already paid him twenty grand for the risk, and the risk was minimal. Twenty minutes, maybe less. That was all. It would be okay. Ten-ten, that added up to twenty, didn't it? That must mean something, Cairncross mused.

The plane continued to fly Cap Rumbo, now passing out of range of the gigantic U.S. radar facility at Shemya and approaching waypoint NIMMI—one amid the row of randomly computer-generated milestones strung across the northern Pacific between Alaska and the Korean peninsula.

AlAir 599 was almost midway along its projected route to Seoul with another hour of flight time left to log. There would be five more waypoints to cross before the jumbo jet reached Matsushima and crossed the Japanese main island of Hokkaido.

Save your worries for then, Cairncross told himself. He turned to his copilot but in the end said nothing more. Neither man felt talkative as the plane continued on its programmed course, guided by an array of invisible electronic navigational beacons across the open ocean amid the darkness of night.

◆   ◆   ◆

The RSO monitored the scope, tracking the still-distant passenger jet. The OTH, or over-the-horizon, radar capability of the RC-135(U) ensured that the aircraft could fly its standard figure-eight track many miles from the operations zone where it would be unobserved by adversaries yet keep the operation under continual electronic surveillance.

The radar systems operator would normally be one of at least three on board the Rivet Joint electronic intelligence aircraft. While the over-the-horizon radars with which the RC-135 was equipped could track more than a thousand targets simultaneously, the human workload needed to be broken up among several RSOs.

But this was not a routine flight.

It was a black patrol.

The crew roster was to be kept to a minimum to reduce need to know. In fact, except for the ELINT officer in charge of electronic countermeasures and counter-countermeasures, the only nontechs on board—not counting the guys in the cockpit—were the translators and the NSA mission controller. The word that had come down was to keep out of the "No Such Agency" spooks' rice bowls. That was, of course, always the word, but it was especially holy on tonight's clandestine run.

No problem, thought the RSO. That's what they gave him combat overtime pay for. He knew how to keep his mouth shut and, more importantly, he knew how to keep his mind shut, too. He kept that part of him focused on the big color scope in its shock-mounted rack on the console in front of him, one of four crew stations that occupied most of the aft part of the RC-135's cabin. The scope was a spanking-new, flat-panel display with pretty good definition.

The view was from a point out in space, looking down at a contour map of the ops zone some 300 miles in diameter: the northwestern Pacific, with the Japanese island chain in the foreground and the Korean Peninsula beyond.

Superimposed above the map, moving slowly across its face, were a progression of symbols, each with an accompanying radar contact descriptor.

Aircraft.

There were six active in the zone, but the RSO was interested in only two of them. The AlAir passenger jet on the Bethel-Seoul commercial run and the USAF C-130H Hercules medium-weight turboprop out of Kadena, Japan.

The scopeman's job was to track those two aircraft throughout the mission. Track them constantly. But when the two symbols merged, then the ELINT officer on board would take over and become the man on point. When they merged, and for the next twenty minutes or so after that, as the two planes flew dangerously close to one another off the coasts of North Korea and the Russian mainland.

Nobody had told the RSO anything more than these few facts. But he knew. It was impossible *not* to know. The RSO kept his eyes on the scope and tried not to think about anything beyond doing the job they paid him to do. Mouth shut, mind shut: That was his motto.

THE PENTAGON

The surveillance strip of the Improved Crystal-7 E satellite encompassed a 3,000-kilometer swathe of the earth's surface. Everything contained within that swathe was visible to ground stations capable of decoding downlinked telemetry from the intelligence bird. There were not many of these. In fact, the number could be counted on two fingers.

In order of global proximity, the first were the National Security Agency's regional headquarters at Camp Fuchinobe, located on a sprawling 572-acre range just west of Tokyo—

much of which sprouted giant dish antennas—and the Japanese Nibetsu.

Officially known as Annex Chamber of the Second Section, Investigation Division, the Nibetsu, or Rabbit Ears in Japanese, is a virtual foreign division of the American NSA. The Nibetsu is headquartered at Camp Ichigaya, another sprawling government facility on Tokyo's outskirts, which is a virtual carbon copy of the U.S. facility at Fuchinobe.

This is not surprising. The Nibetsu and NSA are so closely linked as to function as a single organization. Nor does the Nibetsu funnel its data through normal intelligence channels. Signals intelligence collected by the Rabbit Ears is channeled directly to the prime minister's Cabinet Research Office, bypassing the normal chain of command in the Japanese national security hierarchy.

The second earth station for Improved Crystal imaging telemetry is the massive National Security Agency complex at Fort George G. Meade located halfway between Washington and Baltimore. From this central receiving node, Improved Crystal imagery flows along two secret communications networks to the White House, the CIA, and the Pentagon.

These two networks are known as SPINTCOM, for special intelligence communications, and CRITICOM for critical intelligence communications. The networks date back to the height of the Cold War years in the mid-1960s.

Like the intelligence links of the Nibetsu, SPINTCOM and CRITICOM were put in place so that sensitive satellite intelligence could bypass slower channels of dissemination and reach the desk of the U.S. chief executive and his top advisers in near real time. In point of fact, data transmitted over the CRITICOM channel can reach the Oval Office within two minutes of an event's occurrence anywhere on earth.

Improved Crystal imagery now flowed through these secret express channels to high-priority observation stations in the United States military and political establishments. The most important of these—in some ways even more so than the Oval Office—was the Crisis Room of the National Military Command Center at the Pentagon, where the CJCS now monitored events in the Northwest Pacific on one of the large, flat-panel display screens mounted on the NMCC's east wall.

The view was characteristic of the incredible imaging capability that U.S. technical know-how could develop in peace and war. It was as if Chairman Starkweather were looking down from a point in the atmosphere directly above the flight paths of three aircraft, two of them flying vectors that would converge in a short time.

Starkweather could make out clear details, such as wing markings and individual rivets on the aircraft and even glimpses of the pilots sitting behind the cockpit windows. *They don't call it the god screen for nothing,* Starkweather thought. It was incredible.

Yet, despite these wonders, his thoughts kept returning to an apparition he had seen getting off the Metro bus from his one-way window: his son. His son dead these many long months had gotten off the bus. It could not be, nor did Starkweather believe that it was John, returned from the dead.

How could it be, when he had stood and seen the terrible, charred remains? When he had stood there and seen John's coffin lowered into the ground at Arlington National Cemetery?

No. There was no question of mistaken identity, and Starkweather did not believe in ghosts. What he *did* believe was that some party or parties unknown had perpetrated this abomination to screw around with his head.

But why? A joke, a very bad joke? Maybe. Or maybe something else. Some kind of psychological warfare operation by terrorists, hackers, radicals, cyberpunks? Who the fuck knew, when there were so many out there these days? Whatever it was, whatever or whoever had been behind the grisly charade, it had driven Starkweather to a fever pitch of righteous anger that he could barely hold in check.

Yet he had to contain it. He had to keep it inside him, had to curb that burning, acid-in-the-guts rage in order to function. He had not even confided the sightings to his wife, because it might send her over the edge—*would*—she was still on tranks.

No, Starkweather could divulge what he had witnessed to no one. Not a soul could know. Not yet, anyway. Not until he'd gotten to the bottom of it. For the moment, it would have to remain his secret, his private hell.

He tried to block out the pictures in his mind by focusing on the wonders on the computer screen in front of him, but he only saw his son and remembered how much he missed him.

THE NORTHERN PACIFIC

The symbols on the radar screen merged. The two combined radar contacts would now be visible on the scopes of the North Korean ground station at Pyong Ming as a single composite blip.

High above the Pacific, the material counterparts of that merged radar blip flew near one another at a perilous distance. The larger plane, the C-130H Hercules, dwarfed the 747 jumbo jet and flew below it.

Still, the deception would never have worked if not for the part the RC-135 played in the game of aerial liar's dice. Rack-mounted black boxes inside the Rivet Joint transmitted jamming on radar and radio frequencies.

Scopes in the North Korean air control radar at Pyong Ming suddenly went blank. Backup systems were switched on, and these, too, went blank. When they came up again, the sky was filled with ghost aircraft, the false radar contacts jamming the scopes.

Inside the Hercules transport aircraft flying beneath the Alaska Air 747, the Snake Handlers watched the jumpmaster lower the rear ramp door. Blue lights shone dimly around the perimeter of the access ramp as it descended like a castle's drawbridge. Beyond was black sky, pinpointed with stars and threaded with floating, lenticular clouds.

Each of the five members of the team knew the mission plan by heart. Trencrom, Ball, Nixon, Floaty, and Jugs had all been briefed. They'd played out the mission many times over in training simulations including a sand table model. For the past two days, they had been in seclusion, psyching themselves for the op.

Trencrom thought back. The sand table at the safe house in the Arlington countryside where they had planned the mission was etched in his mind. The rugged mountain country of the Taipu region of North Korea had been poorly duplicated by plastic models of peaks, roads, hamlets, and other terrain features.

But it was there, the DUMB was there. The deep underground missile base that had been hollowed out of a granite mountain. The DUMB housed the heaviest nuclear firepower available to the Pyongyang regime.

From terraces cut into the rock faces of the mountainside, mobile launch vehicles—TELs for transporter erector launchers—could be trundled out, their missiles launched, and the empty TELs rolled back behind heavy steel blast doors into the mountain.

No TLAM strike could penetrate the kind of protection afforded by hundreds of yards of dense granite. Only a nuclear strike could take out the DUMB.

Numerous factors ruled this out, among which was the proximity of the base to both the Russian and Chinese borders. Strategic and tactical considerations aside, geopolitical realities stopped the nuclear option cold.

Except . . .

If the base were not destroyed, more nuclear and even chemical/biological missile strikes were a virtual certainty.

Except . . .

There was one way out, a way proposed by the CJCS to the president as what Starkweather called the Medusa Option.

Medusa, the CJCS had told the assembled members of the Gang of Six converged in the Oval Office, was the only mortal member of the Gorgons. Though her head crawled with snakes and her gaze had the power to turn warriors to stone, the mythical hero Theseus covered his eyes and severed Medusa's head with a swipe of his sword.

The power of the Gorgons was cut off with that victory. The head of Medusa was put on a stake and shown to all of ancient Thebes as a symbol of freedom from an implacable and tyrannical foe.

General Starkweather, collector of aphorisms, lover of myth, had nodded at his aide, and a page of his presentation was flipped back over the easel.

The thin red beam of his laser pointer flicked out. Three Gorgon heads, marking the sites of DPRK ballistic missile launch sites, were circled by the crimson beam. On the third site, the beam stabbed at the center of the monstrous, snake-rimmed face.

Here was Medusa. Here was the target.

Then had come the inevitable question from the president: "How?"

The answer, too, was inevitable: a nuclear interdiction strike. But nothing launched from a ship, plane, or submarine.

Man-portable nuclear demolition munitions. Carried in by a select team whose existence could be denied in the event of failure and would never be acknowledged even in the event of success: Snake Handlers.

Then had followed a brief on the holy of holies, a thing never named outright. SADM, special atomic demolition munitions, specifically, "Plywood," standing for PLWD or precision low-yield weapons design nukes.

The ultrasecret Plywood program had miniaturized nuclear weapons to the point where they were the size of laptops, thermos bottles, automatic rifles. Ice Trencrom's Snake Handlers were to be covertly inserted near Medusa carrying two ten-kiloton Plywood SADMs—that was the equivalent blast of twice a thousand tons of TNT.

"Aside from bringing down tons of earth, rock, rubble, concrete, and steel on the weapons complex," the CJCS had explained, "the low-yield radiation and thermal effect would have the advantage of sterilizing any nasty germ cultures or toxic chem agents that might be released from one of the DPRK's NBC weapons labs inside there."

"Like irradiated milk," the president offered.

"Right, sir. You got it," the CJCS replied.

The SADMs were also tailored as EMP weapons, the CJCS added.

This, he explained, meant the warheads would produce nuclear-electromagnetic pulse or N-EMP that, in addition to standard nuclear blast effect and thermal pulse, would cripple any electronic system in and around the Medusa complex. How this would fit into the plan, Starkweather continued, anticipating questions, was twofold.

First, it would hit the North Koreans with a double whammy, ensuring maximum damage to their systems; everything from calculators to cell phones would stop working. Kim's people had better have sent in their warranty cards, Starkweather added as an aside that got some laughs.

"But seriously," he proceeded, "the second tactical benefit of N-EMP is that the microchips inside things like vehicle ignition systems, helicopter navigational systems, even gun sights, are also knocked out. Meaning we cut down the odds against the bad guys catching up with our people on extraction."

"Wait a minute. What about our own helicopters?" the president asked. "Wouldn't they be affected?"

"Sure, they certainly would, *if* they weren't hardened," the CJCS replied. "And not all of them are. But the ones we'll send in after our people *will* be hardened against N-EMP."

The president liked that wrinkle. He nodded, smiled, and made some notes on the yellow legal pad in front of him. How to get them in? That was what he wanted to know next.

A HALO jump from the coast using special forces parasails. The high-altitude/low-opening jump technique had been perfected for decades. The latest gear enabled glide paths to the target of up to 100 miles using GPS data for navigation.

Extraction would be made by CH-53D Sea Stallion helicopters—Marine versions of the Army's Pave Low choppers—launched from the Sea of Japan, but only a HALO insertion was feasible on the trip in country. This, the CJCS explained, was because, while probes by EF-111s and other

ELINT platforms had discovered a gap in PAWS coverage . . .

"What was that, again?" asked the president.

PAWS, General Starkweather had explained. Phased array warning system. The kind of radar the North Koreans had installed as their principal airborne radar coverage in the nuclear operations zone. PAWS was based on a so-called staring array principle.

Fixed stationary antenna elements like those in U.S. early warning radar along the Alaskan coast made up a composite antenna that looked "sort of like the Wailing Wall in Jerusalem."

Starkweather saw the president get the message; he'd just gotten back from Jerusalem the week before. *Nice touch,* he thought.

But PAWS had its limitations. There was a three-mile gap that was filled by other radars, but this gap could be jammed by RC-135 coverage long enough for a heliborne insertion to get through. But they wouldn't get out again. That was the problem.

Once in, the opportunity window would be banged shut by DPRK forces. Of necessity, the choppers had to be saved for the extraction. That left a HALO insertion as the only feasible option for going in.

"But the nukes," the president had gone on to question. "Will they—"

"Will they work safely? Leaving no trace of residual radioactivity?" the CJCS had cut in, anticipating the question. "Yes, if placed properly."

The SADMs were clean. In fact, the Army referred to them as "nonlethal," though the chairman considered this mere milspeak. Still, the term had its merits. These nuclear weapons produced nearly conventional blast yields. The type to be used were Mark 3S versions, the latest Plywoods produced.

The units were sometimes called "coffee urns" because of their cylindrical shape and the small keypad and LED screen on which a variety of detonation options, including time delay and GPS-specific detonation, could be keyed in. The Mark 3S was specifically designed to counter the DUMB threat and for counter-NBC use, as the CJCS had just outlined.

The SADM could not be detonated without the inputting of the nuclear authorization code releasable only by the president under the nuclear SIOP regulations. Without the code, no nuclear explosion could be initiated. This meant that even once the Snake Handlers were in the theater, the SADM option could still be recalled.

The team would receive the authorization codes only when the decision had been made to destroy Medusa.

The M3S SADM had been covertly tested in a deep, played-out copper mine in Utah. The explosion had caved in a mile of tunnels with no radiation leakage detected, the only aftereffect being N-EMP or nuclear-generated electromagnetic pulse, which was not a concern here for reasons the CJCS had outlined.

The president had thought a moment, then adjourned the meeting. But before the day was out, a historic secret executive order had been signed by Travis Claymore. The nuclear mission to North Korea was a go.

10
HEAD OF THE SNAKE

THE SEA OF JAPAN

At 30,000 feet, the night air was subzero cold. Minus 9.7° Fahrenheit, to be exact, as gauged by the temperature readout on the upper left of the head-mounted displays each team member wore. At that altitude, the air was as thin as it was frigid: roughly twelve pounds per square inch, thinner than the atmosphere at the top of Mount Everest and requiring a mask piping oxygen from a compressed air bottle at the start of the jump.

Fifteen seconds after the Hercules had dipped to drop altitude, the blue jump light came on in the cabin, and the rear ramp lowered. Cold night air streamed inside, filling the plane. At the jumpmaster's signals, the five team members lined up and walked out into space, Nixon first and Jugs last off the ramp. Less than two minutes later, the Snake Handlers were in the first stages of free fall, rolling their bodies, tucking up their legs, flatting their arms against their sides for greater aerodynamic stability.

At altimeter readings of 27,000 feet, they had popped their chutes, feeling their bodies yanked upward as the airfoil parasails opened and caught the chill, night wind. The combined roar of the turbines of the AlAir 747 and the USAF C-130 had already begun to fade. The fierce, high-altitude winds quickly blew away the oily stench of aviation fuel exhaust.

The team now formed up into a chevron-shaped echelon. The two aircraft, separated by only a few hundred feet, would continue their tandem flight until they had slipped from the North Korean radar envelope. Then they would separate, the passenger jet to land at Seoul, the Hercules at a U.S. base in Japan.

Spaced at twenty-foot intervals, the Snake Handlers' descent rate was fifty feet per minute. Limned against the faint blue glimmer of the horizon line, they could see one another as dark shapes hanging against the night and stars. Though they dropped more like stones than feathers, their relative motion seemed a weightless glide.

Although the covert strike team had radio communications, radio silence was to be observed except in the event of an emergency. There was little that needed verbalizing on the way down, anyway; the portable computer gear the five operators wore was linked to their head-mounted displays and to the keypads strapped to their wrists.

The lash-up was the equivalent of a high-end laptop minus the keyboard and screen and using an array of gallium arsenide–based storage media instead of spinning hard drives. The GaAs drives were inch-long blocks resembling large integrated circuit chips. They were optical storage media that DARPA, the Defense Advanced Research Projects Agency, had been working on for years. The GaAs drives were shockproof, radiation-resistant, and had a capacity of 100 gigabytes of data each. They would hit the home PC market in five more years, but for now they were Uncle Sam's private property.

The compact PCs were integrated into the black nylon

action togs the team wore, since they would be operating by night only and holing up during daylight hours. The hardware was capable of using GPS telemetry to pinpoint the position of the wearer and fix waypoints, target destinations, and other mission-critical information. In Pentagonese, it was GloMo, global-mobile.

All relevant mission data were displayed on the HMDs in pictorial and alphanumeric overlays using the same operating principle of the head-up displays, or HUDs, found in fighter cockpits. The Snake Handlers saw the world through the clear gel screen of the lightweight goggles, but superimposed on the screen were numbers, graphics, and pictorials representing a constant stream of combat information.

The team knew where they were at every point in their HALO descent, knew the outside air temperature, knew their distance from jump point to LZ, knew where their teammates were relative to their own position, and they could as easily know about breaking developments anywhere in the world via secure GloMo transmission. The HMDs were their portable god screens.

On the ground, the same system would provide advanced thermal imaging, or TI, night vision using miniaturized infrared sensors. This capability would far exceed anything possible with the more conventional Gen-III night observation gear used since the 1980s.

The HALO jump gear with which the team had been equipped was equally advanced. The special forces parasails were similar to commercial hang-glider rigs, but they differed in several key regards. In the first place, they were made of a black polylaminate material that had low radar reflective properties. In the second, they were about 30 percent larger than conventional hang-gliders, and in the third place, they were equipped with silent nylon-Kevlar fan blades that could help increase their glide slope by dozens of miles.

Otherwise, the operating principle was the same as with sport rigs. The Snake Handlers controlled the parasails with handgrips that moved three rudders to provide steerage. The control handgrips were mounted near the body, because raised-arm steering at high altitudes would overtax the heart and cause blackouts.

The basic kit of each team member was the same, with one notable exception: Nixon and Floaty each had a cylindrically shaped, black nylon pouch strapped against their stomachs. The pouches each weighed thirty-five pounds, and the extra weight and drag showed in the slightly decreased speed and slightly lower altitude of the two Snake Handlers relative to the other three.

Still, at thirty-five pounds, the—again, in Pentagonese—"special purpose weapons" nestled inside those pouches were remarkably lightweight, considering the ten-kiloton punch each packed.

The team carried two miniaturized Plywood SADMs. One was all that was needed to do the job. The second "tinynuke" was for backup, in case the first one couldn't be armed or its internal diagnostics showed it was defective. The mission had to be fail-safe, thus the backstopping. The second nuclear device would either be returned on extraction or blown up in place; each weapon had a self-destruct feature that would detonate it conventionally and burn up its plutonium core, or pit.

The nukes were still unarmed and could not be armed until the authorization codes contained in the SIOP were released by the president. Their purpose was to reduce Target Medusa to a modern-day pharaoh's tomb where death would seal in every animate and inanimate thing within immovable tons of shattered rubble and do it in a way that was deniable by the White House.

Not *believable;* the operant word was *deniable.*

The former Soviets and the Chinese, to say nothing of America's NATO allies and Japan, would have ample satellite evidence of a small nuclear blast, and seismographs at every technical university in the world would register the temblors it produced, however faintly. Intelligence briefs would cross the desks of presidents, premiers, kings, queens, and dictators within the hour, and those briefs would state the obvious: Somebody had detonated a nuclear weapon in North Korea.

But in the absence of toxic by-products of the explosion, and in defense of their own strategic interests, which the destruction of Medusa would serve, none would breathe a word.

The fiction would be maintained, the trade and political summits would go on without interruption or disturbance, and it would be as if nothing had ever happened, as so many other things had "never happened" in the world of clandestine warfare.

Nor was this the first time small nuclear weapons had been paradropped by U.S. special forces personnel. Since the 1950s, servicemen had been parachuting out of planes with black boxes strapped to their bellies. Most were never told what those black boxes contained or what would have happened had the exercise been a hot drop. The Medusa Option had been dress-rehearsed, in various ways, shapes, and forms, for almost fifty years. That was a fact on the ground, deny it though the Pentagon might.

♦ ♦ ♦

Ten minutes into HALO: For most of these minutes, the RC-135(U) orbiting off the North Korean coastline had been pumping out antiradar countermeasures to help conceal the five delta shapes parasailing silently inland.

The Snake Handlers and their parasails were hard to see with the naked eye, but secrecy was paramount on this mission, and every step humanly possible was being taken to maintain it, including the provision of L-pills to each team member. To decrease the chances of detection to as near zero as possible, the enemy North's ground radars had been spoofed with false returns in parts of the sky far from the actual insertion route.

By now, though, the Snake Handlers had glided to an altitude of 16,000 feet and were inside the zone of ground clutter. The team was still minus twenty miles from their drop zone, and they still had an hour or slightly more of descent time left to reach their destination, Drop Zone Bud Lite.

The time was 2037 hours Zulu, and a deep, almost biblical darkness still covered the earth. Above them and to the right, the orange yellow crescent of a quarter moon glowed above the craggy outlines of steep hills to the northeast, the direction of their glide path.

The terrain below was barren, and nothing moved on the few narrow mountain roads that weaved their serpentine tracks through the countryside, although here and there, from clustered stone cottages in scattered hamlets, lights gleamed through chinks in window shutters and wisps of smoke curled lazily from the mouths of chimneys.

Down this low, the air had gotten dense enough for normal breathing, and the team had shucked their cumbersome breathing gear with relief. They now felt the sharp, cold bite of the wind against their faces, and they heard it rush past their ears like the shrieking of ghosts.

Their slow descent continued, their steady progress marked by the glowing, shifting numbers of the altimeter and glide slope readouts on their head-mounted displays, and two of them tried not to think too hard about the fact that nuclear weapons were strapped as tight against their guts as babies in slings.

THE WHITE HOUSE

Lights burned into the night in the Oval Office, where the president, wearing a sweatshirt and jeans, wrestled with the question of releasing authorization to arm the two nuclear weapons the team carried. Some two stories directly below, the cramped and windowless White House Situation Room stood ready for an emergency session. Its lights were switched on, and yellow legal pads, ballpoint pens, and other paraphernalia lay waiting on the large conference table in front of a dozen vacant chairs.

The president and his chief advisers, members of the Gang

of Six, were all wide awake, as was a skeleton staff of lower-echelon functionaries. The pungent smell of perking coffee was a familiar one that night, as was the sour taste of tepid dregs gulped from a gone-cold cup.

In the Oval Office, President Travis Claymore's casual dress belied the seriousness of his deliberations. He could sleep if he wanted to; he knew that. There would be another twenty-four hours before the moment of truth, before the elite special mission unit would enter the missile base and plant one or both of the small nuclear weapons it was already carrying into the theater.

But sleep would not come. Claymore knew that, too. He also knew he had already made up his mind weeks before, when the general had outlined his plan in front of the Oval Office fireplace. It was now only a matter of convincing himself that he'd been right all along.

Claymore had been briefed, and he had been back-briefed. Since Starkweather had outlined the Medusa Option for him, the CJCS had returned to further clarify the plan with more viewgraphs, more facts, and more figures. The Gang of Six had also had its say, with the CIA director vehemently opposed to anything involving the Snake Handlers, which he referred to as the general's "private goon squad" and sometimes as "Bucky's SMFs," on the meaning of which no one needed any clarification.

The Air Force had also put in its bid. Expectably, the blue-suiters had pushed for using the B-61-11 diameter bomb, only the USAF called it the "B-61-11 tactical thermonuclear air-to-ground munition." The use of the term *diameter* referred to the origin of the weapon; the bomb casings, guidance package, and nuclear detonation systems were designed to use the plutonium pits from old and obsolete Cold War–era B-61 bombs originally intended to be dropped from B-52 Stratoforts over Russian targets.

The upgraded B-61 was designed for DUMB removal. The new bomb casing had a hardened penetrator and could be delivered by either B-2, F-111A, or F-22, giving the Air Force generals added incentive to use their new superplanes.

There was only one problem with the plan:It couldn't possibly work. DUMBs were one thing, mountains were another; and secrecy yet a third issue; the nuclear strike had to be deniable, and that deniability had to be as bulletproof as it was possible to make it.

In the end, the decision had rested with the president. To Claymore's mind, there was no other recourse than to destroy the underground base, no doubt whatever that were the missile silos allowed to be completed, the North Koreans would launch a preemptive strike on the U.S. or its global forces.

Kim Jong-il could not be permitted this outrage, and there was no other option available to contravene it, at least none that came with a reasonable guarantee of success. Conventional weapons, no matter how powerful or accurate, would not do the job. Even fuel-air explosives would not work, Claymore had been told.

"They hit the Nordhausen V-2 works with two-thousand-pound blockbusters day after day but didn't even put a dent in the underground tunnel network," Starkweather had informed the president. "The Germans built the complex right into the side of the Harz Mountains, very much like what the DPRK have done with their own installation. Today we can penetrate deeper into the rock surface before the main charge detonates, but in this case, not deep enough."

"You can go in the front door," one of the other Gang of Six members, the White House National Security Adviser, had countered. "CALCM or TLAM strikes"—pronouncing the acronyms as "Calcum" and "Teelam"—"fly 'em right in through the front door." He needlessly pantomimed the rocket's flight with one hand and the mountain with the other.

But Starkweather had gainsaid that option, too. Medusa wasn't a hangar for jet fighters. It was a complex network of tunnels hewn from the hard, rocky core of a granite mountain. And if the complex were not damaged sufficiently, what then?

"They launch their birds, and we've got a mushroom cloud where south central L.A. used to be," Starkweather had retorted.

No, there was only one option that promised any guarantee of unconditional success: the nuclear option.

But damn it, Claymore thought, that was just the point. If he okayed the arming codes, it would be the first time since Hiroshima and Nagasaki that America had used its nuclear arsenal in wartime. They were still debating whether Truman had been right, and Claymore didn't want history to stigmatize him with the nuclear curse that had stained Truman's reputation.

It was different, of course, today. Much different. The situation, the weaponry, many other factors were different. Mothers, fathers, children, innocents would not die. The secret base was manned by North Korean military personnel with a smattering of civilian technicians, but even they surely knew the score.

The White House legal staff and the JAG had agreed, since a formal declaration of war had been made against North Korea. Since the personnel were engaged in producing offensive weapons of mass destruction, they were fair game for an interdictive strike.

But the specter of unleashing a nuclear weapon, no matter how low the blast yield or fallout levels, had haunted every individual who had occupied the Oval Office since the end of World War II, and eight previous presidents had prayed to heaven that such a decision would never need to be made by them. Now Claymore, forty-third president of the United States, had all but made it.

THE PENTAGON

Westward, across the Potomac, the chairman of the Joint Chiefs was also alone with his thoughts. At a little past three A.M., the night wind jabbing and flurrying around him cut like a razor, forcing his hands into the pockets of his coat.

It was a Sunday night, and he, like the president, was casually dressed in an old zip-front ski parka with a heavy cable-knit sweater underneath. The CJCS had left the mission planning room of the NMCC while the paradrop half the world away was still in progress. If necessary, his staff could beep him. Here, among the bare, windswept trees, he could get his head together.

The well-kept interior grounds of the Pentagon form a five-acre center court lined with trees. In late spring through the summer months and into the warm days of autumn, the Pentagon's outdoor snack bar is open. The center court then becomes a popular place to have lunch, informally meet, or even jog.

During winter, the court is still kept open but rarely used. Most staff and visitors do their shopping and dining at the Pentagon's enclosed Concourse, a minimall complete with newsstand, florist, video store, and even a military clinic, to name just a few of the Concourse's conveniences.

But Buck Starkweather was true to his surname; he liked the cold, and the biting cold before a winter dawn was best of all. As he walked slowly along the inner walls of the Puzzle Palace, he pondered the jigsaw mosaic of problems.

The president might be surprised to discover that the mission in North Korea was the least of what weighed on Starkweather's mind. To him, there was little reason to hold back from a nuclear strike. Political considerations aside, the mininukes were low yield and very clean. If properly emplaced, they would form a seal around radioactive by-products to a depth of one mile and destroy most forms of toxic biological or chemical agents.

In real-world terms, this meant that there would be less radioactive contamination of the surrounding area than in many dump sites in the U.S. for spent uranium fuel rods. But the stigma of nuclear first use understandably haunted the president.

Well, Starkweather, thought, that was a political decision and not his rice bowl. His was only to serve up the military options and nursemaid them toward final implementation once they got the green light. The middle part was the province of the elected officials and their counselors, and that was more than okay by him.

Starkweather stopped and walked toward the center of the

five-sided open space and saw a figure walking toward him.

"Little stuffy in there, Buck," said the Wizard. "Thought I'd catch some fresh air."

"Doesn't get any fresher, Wiz," the CJCS retorted. "Let's walk."

The two men began cutting across the pentangle at a slow pace.

"More static from you know where," the CJCS said.

"They're serious this time," Crowley replied.

"We'll have to stay on top, Al," the CJCS said. "That's the only way to bring those fuckers down."

"They never stop, do they?" Crowley asked rhetorically, since both knew the answer.

"No, they don't. We fought one war, but . . ."

"This time, maybe."

"Yeah," he answered the Wiz. "Maybe."

The two men walked back into the Pentagon, and Stark-weather took his hands out of his pockets, rubbing them together to bring the blood back to his fingers.

THE SEA OF JAPAN

Sixty-three minutes into the drop. The glide slope had decayed considerably by now. Altitude was under 5,000 feet and dropping lower each minute. The night was still dark, and the team was on schedule to the DZ. Below, there was still no visible movement. The countryside slept.

Suddenly, Nixon felt a severe jolt. All at once he found himself tipping over. He tried to right his chute by pulling on the control stirrups, but it didn't work. Looking up, he saw what had happened. The chute lines had tangled and become fouled. But there was more beyond that, Nixon also saw. A seam had opened in the center of the parasail, and the rent was growing larger. The chute had probably been going on him since he'd left the plane but hadn't worsened enough to be noticeable until just now.

Nixon popped his backup chute, which opened normally, and he drifted awkwardly to the ground, made top-heavy by the weight of the nuke that was slung from him. After some minutes of what might more accurately be termed falling than drifting, he landed hard but unhurt amid small a grove of fruit trees. Overhead, the rest of the team continued to sail on to their destination.

"I'll catch up," Nixon said into his lip mike and snapped open his knife to cut the nylon cords entangling him. He was still jacked into the Snake Handlers' local secure SINCGARS comms net, and Trencrom rogered his transmission, ordering him to make situation reports at intervals.

Nixon was on his feet and getting ready to bury the chutes when a huge, rounded shape suddenly loomed out of the darkness. He raised his Heckler & Koch MP5-SD1 and pointed its sound-suppressed muzzle at the shape. The invader-turned out to be a cow. The cow nuzzled the nuclear device strapped against Nixon's stomach as though it were the head of a newborn calf and then began eagerly licking the nuke.

"Shoo, Bossy," Nixon stage-whispered, trying to push the curious bovine away, but the cow was intent on licking the ten kilotons worth of nuclear explosive.

Nixon began seriously considering blowing the cow away with a silenced automatic burst when suddenly a door opened in one of the stone huts to his rear. A peasant came out, shouting at the cow in local Chinese-Korean dialect. When the cow would not budge, the peasant began pitching stones at it. In minutes, the cow loped off, mooing banefully. The peasant turned and went back into the stone hut, scratching his head. The crude wooden door's hinges creaked as it slammed shut, and the thud of impact echoed in the mountain stillness.

Nixon rose off the bare ground and moved for cover as quickly as he was able. As he crouched amid encircling underbrush, he used his wrist keypad to call up GPS coordinates, the best location data he could arrange at the moment. Had the team already been set up at the base camp they were to establish, he'd have map display data as well, but from his elapsed time readout, they were still in transit.

Still, what the GPS told him was encouraging. There was only a five-mile hump to the DZ. He might be able to make it before dawn. Nixon picked himself up and began paralleling the road, hoping not to run into anybody who'd notice a man with a nuke strapped to him and cow spit all over the nuke.

◆ ◆ ◆

The rest of the team flared their chutes and landed in the center of the field designated DZ Bud Lite. The elapsed time had been eighty minutes, and they had traveled almost thirty miles inland, drifting on the wind. Working quickly to sanitize the DZ, they dug holes with entrenching tools and buried the chutes in the ground.

There was another mile hump to the high ground overlooking target Medusa, where they were to set up a base camp and observation post to recon the area before insertion. Dawn had not yet broken, but it would begin getting light soon enough.

They reached their objective just before first light. Ball, whose job was communications, set up the portable field communications and data station consisting of a laptop, antenna unit, and portable laser printer. The powers that be had spared no expense on this mission. Two satellites had been tasked to provide overhead coverage from miles out in space.

Within a matter of minutes, the communications link was established. The team was scheduled to report to the NMCC as soon as the drop zone had been reached, but Nixon's unexpected separation from the Snake Handlers made contacting him top priority. The system showed that Nixon was already moving. The screen icon representing him was heading toward them.

"Go to text mode for the comms," Trencrom said, watching the screen over Ball's shoulder.

"Gotcha."

Ball clicked the integrated mouse, then began inputting a

message: "Yo, Nixon," he typed, "Say your situation, partner. Use the keypad if you can't talk."

The words came back. "Banged up some but otherwise ok. Chute was defective. Cargo safe and sound. Making for your position."

Ball typed back, "I copy. Glad to hear you're good to go. You can use the road. We now have overhead coverage so we can let you know if any shit's heading your way. We'll buzz you when you're close."

"OK. Later."

"One word of caution, though—Do not fart! Might set off nuke!"

"Fuck you asshole. Out."

Trencrom now took up a position in front of the comms station. As team commander, he was to brief Starkweather on the first situation report of the mission. Trencrom stared into the small videocam mounted atop the laptop's screen area and went through the procedures for contacting the NMCC almost four thousand miles away.

There was a brief lag as the encrypted transmission was routed over the horizon via the Defense MilStar satellite network, and then Starkweather's face appeared on the screen.

"Congratulations to you and the team, Ice," the general said. "We're all proud of you here. The president sends you his thumbs-up." Starkweather paused, then got down to cases. "What's your situation?"

"We hit a little snag on the way in, Buck," Trencrom answered. "Nixon ran into some chute trouble, but he landed unhurt and intact. He's now on his way to us, and we're monitoring him on overhead. But you know that already."

The general did. The NMCC was patched into the same satellite imaging network as the Snake Handlers in theater.

"We do, and we don't think it's a show stopper . . . if you don't."

"No, Buck. We're good to go."

"Great. Then get things set up and get some rest. We'll talk again at your next scheduled sitrep. Once again to all of you, thanks. Remember, our prayers are with you."

"Skip the prayers. Send us a tank division," Floaty put in, standing well out of camera range.

"The general makes a damn good speech, give him that much," Jugs commented, cold-checking her weapons.

"Speeches come easy when your ass ain't on the firing line," Ball added, sotto voce.

Trencrom signed off and logged off the system, leaving Ball to monitor Nixon's route. Daylight was not far off, and there was still a great deal to be done in only a short time.

A hide site had to be established to make a base camp and an observation post established farther on. With one man missing, that left four to dig the trench, monitor the equipment, and set up a perimeter patrol.

"Jugs, you're walking post," Trencrom ordered.

"Chauvinist," she said, pulling back on the charging handle of the MP5-SD1 to chamber a round. Cradling the silenced SMG, Jugs set off into the surrounding woods.

Much later, Nixon joined the party. By then the sun had already risen, and the team hunkered down to grab some rest as the daylight hours commenced. They would not resume activity again until the fall of darkness over the brooding, barren hills.

11
FORTUNES OF WAR

WASHINGTON, D.C.

Washington's famous Smithsonian encompasses thirteen museums and the National Zoo. Among them is the National Air and Space Museum, one of nine such institutions that stretch along the Washington Mall from Fourth Street to Fourteenth Street. As was usual for a brisk winter day, the Mall bustled with a broad cross section of American society and representatives from countries across the globe.

Most were sightseers from other places; many were native Washingtonians, pausing to take in some culture on their lunch breaks and enjoy the clear weather of a fine winter morning. Few, if any, took notice of three men who emerged from the nearby Metro stop amid a light crowd of tourists and members of the D.C. workforce.

None knew of the peregrinations of the three men down in the bowels of the capital's spanking-new subway system, of their getting on and off arriving trains and then switching subway lines, because the purpose of such moves was to avoid detection.

The trio did not speak as the men strode past the museums lining the Mall before they finally turned and mounted the steps of the Air and Space Museum. Once inside, two of the men hung back from the third, circulating through the crowd of museum-goers while keeping the third man under constant scrutiny.

General Jackson Priest walked beneath the exhibits of aircraft that lined the ground floor of the museum. He paused beneath several of them, admiring their aerodynamic lines and reading the placards beside them. Many, if not all, of the planes had made history. Some were warplanes, some record-setting commercial aircraft. All had made an impact on the twentieth century that continued into the twenty-first.

Priest walked on until he reached a particular exhibit that was his destination that morning and stopped to look up at the World War II–era B-29 aircraft that was suspended by heavy steel guy wires overhead.

The plane was the *Enola Gay*. The infamous Superfortress long-range bomber that had dropped the only two nuclear weapons used in open warfare. On a fateful morning in August of 1945, the *Enola Gay*'s flight plan had taken it over the Japanese port city of Hiroshima. Its main bomb-bay doors had opened, and out of them had fallen a Pandora's boxful of demons that had changed the world. The single 100-kiloton nuclear bomb had burned a city to the ground. It had flattened its buildings and left films of carbon where human beings had stood.

The irises of Priest's eyes contracted as he studied the lines of the Superfort's fuselage, thinking about that fateful August morning. The pilots had described the effect of the nuclear smoke cloud as a boiling black cauldron. He envied them to have seen something as awesome as that, something none had ever looked upon before or, with one exception, since.

Neither Priest's posture or expression changed as another man walked up beside him and also stopped to regard the *Enola Gay*. He was a man of middle height and middle years.

A man of bland features and of equally bland dress. A plain vanilla man from No Such Agency. After a pause he addressed Priest in a bland voice that had something of the monotone of a robot about it.

"An amazing mission that plane flew," he commented.

Priest looked at him and smiled. "I heard one of the crewmen became a monk in Italy, out of guilt."

"If so, his guilt was shared by many."

The recognition code had been exchanged. The plain-vanilla man took another look at the *Enola Gay* overhead and extended his hand. Priest gripped it and the men shook.

"Nice to have met you, sir," the plain-vanilla man said and walked off, his gait like a wind-up soldier's.

Priest watched him leave the room and disappear into the crowds milling around outside the vast exhibit hall. In the palm of Priest's hand there was now a small strip of thin paper. On its front was a Chinese fortune. On its back, a series of numbers.

Priest pocketed the fortune cookie slip, then turned and walked out of the exhibit hall. His two bodyguards were right behind him.

ARLINGTON, VIRGINIA

It took the better part of two hours riding first the Metro and then the Blue Line commuter railway into Arlington to sanitize the return route to the safe house the general had established.

The face-time meeting at the Smithsonian had been necessary. The emissary of the NSA had turned over the authorization codes for two stolen nuclear weapons. Such information could not be entrusted to any form of electronic transmission. It could not be faxed, E-mailed, or spoken over even the most secure phone line. The secure transference of codes required physically handing them off to their intended recipient.

Nobody but the U.S. president was legally empowered to know or possess the codes. No means outside the military chain of command as mandated by the nuclear SIOP were supposed to exist to make the codes available to anyone else. It was not supposed to happen. Yet it just had happened.

Priest entered the safe house in the Arlington countryside, confident that any unauthorized party would have been dead by now.

Hidden in the encircling woods were members of his merc force. Draped in gillie cover and cammied up in woodland-pattern face paints, they were positioned in trees. High-powered sniper rifles were trained on all access points to the large Victorian manor house. Other members of the merc force patrolled the extensive acreage that encircled the building.

The safe house had been months in preparation. Great care had been taken to set it up as inconspicuously as possible. Outwardly, it resembled the other structures in the vicinity, most of them lived in year round, others vacation chalets.

The building had an attached garage to limit exposure of personnel to prying eyes or telephoto lenses as much as possible. Vehicles could roll up the driveway, enter the multicar bays of the garage, and be hidden from view behind the guillotine door. A few short steps from the car was a cipher-locked steel doorway set in a concrete wall with low-light TV cameras mounted here and there.

Priest pressed his thumb onto the biometric fingerprint scanner, then entered his pass code and heard the click of the electrically actuated lock popping open. He pushed through the door into the room beyond, instantly hearing the sounds of activity that went on behind the soundproofed outer walls.

Priest nodded at one of his men who stood the midmorning watch. The general was pleased to note that though he'd been seen on closed-circuit video as he entered, the soldier still cradled the snub-barreled MP4-KA5 SMG in a ready position.

The interior had been cleared of nonstructural walls, and the original furnishings discarded in favor of modular sections for the work and training areas that had been set up here and in the basement. The upper floors and attic were used as galley, toilet, and billeting areas for the force.

Priest's first stop was to his XO's station. He found Dock-weiler sitting in front of a large, flat-panel screen, whose windowed display showed a map of the Washington Metro system and various other data.

"I take it you had no problems, boss," Dockweiler said.

Priest leaned against the six-foot fiberglass wall of the par-tition. "The museum was entertaining. You ought to try it yourself, Mal."

"After the operation, I might just," he replied. "I think I've got the logistics of doing our thing in the Metro worked out," he continued. "It's all a question of timing. Let me show you."

Dockweiler swiveled his chair around to face the screen and used the mouse and keyboard. Priest watched and nod-ded.

"Yeah, that might do it," he said.

"*If* Matthews can get the thing to function," Dockweiler added.

"Matthews is my next stop," Priest said.

Priest passed other modular sections, where more members of his merc force were engaged in various other aspects of planning and training. He paused briefly to watch Garcia con-duct a class in close urban combat techniques.

On the large table that was the focus of attention of a dozen men in NATO camouflage BDUs were the disassem-bled parts of three commonly found automatic rifles, the AKS-74, the FN/FNC, and the M16A2. Garcia's lecture was delivered crisply and succinctly, and his skilled hands quickly reassembling the AKS-74 was a joy to watch for the general. Priest moved inside the confines of the spacious modular area and stood beside Garcia. The men immediately saluted their leader.

"At ease," he told them.

Still smiling, Priest picked up the bullpup-barreled Ka-lashnikov rifle and hefted it in his hands. It felt slightly heav-ier because of the twelve-inch Sionics sound suppressor attached to the muzzle.

"Quite a weapon," he told the men. "Good weight. Nice balance. High-capacity magazine. Won't jam, even after it's been dragged through the mud and the blood of a battlefield. But then I'm sure Garcia has already given you the lecture."

Some of the men permitted themselves a laugh at what had not even been intended as a joke. Nor was the general smiling. Priest looked them over, meeting the eyes of each man in line, as he picked up a loaded forty-round magazine and slammed it into the AKS-74's receiver with the heel of his right hand.

Still smiling, he began charging the weapon, cranking a 5.45-millimeter full metal jacket into the firing chamber. Some of the men looked nervously at him. Priest was starting to give off scary vibes, and he had a definite talent for it.

"One of you is a fucking maggot spy," Priest said after a pause. "Either the DIA or some spook agency run out of the Pentagon by the office of the CJCS. I'm not sure which."

He finished charging the weapon, and the crisp, metallic snap was like thunder in the sudden silence. "Not that it matters. Dead is dead, after all."

Pivoting suddenly, Priest pointed the muzzle of the AKS at Garcia. "Any last words?" he asked.

"Up yours." It was barked with defiance.

Priest's finger tightened on the trigger, and he took two paces backward. Garcia was still standing and still alive after the three bolt clicks and muffled reports of the silenced FMJ burst—but somebody else was not.

The recruit that Priest had intended to die all along had collapsed in a blood-spattered heap. Red punctures and flecks of bone, scalp, and brain pocked the white panel behind where he'd stood. Priest swiveled back around and tossed the weapon at Garcia, who caught it effortlessly and held it at port arms. The scent of carbine burnoff gases hung in the air like an acrid requiem.

"Carry on," he told the instructor. "Take the traitor to the basement. He's to be cremated tonight when we burn the trash." Without another word, Priest turned and walked out of the screened-off area.

The general crossed the room and came to another cipher-locked steel door set in the far wall. Again, he placed the ball of his thumb against the scanner and keyed in his personal access code.

The stairway beyond led to the basement where the firing range and combat simulators were set up. The staccato sound of machine gun fire assaulted his ears as he passed a live-fire station where two of his men were set up behind a Maremont M-60 GPMG, raking a mock-up of a Bradley with 7.62- $\times$ 51-millimeter steel-jacketed rounds.

Priest passed another group of men wearing virtual-reality head-mounted displays. The squad members' psychotic gesticulations as they jumped, turned, flattened, darted here and there, flung their arms around, and shouted into the lip mikes they wore would have seemed the actions of madmen to an uninitiated observer. But the series of twenty-foot flat-panel displays mounted on the wall behind them showed the realistic simulation of the live-fire engagement in which the troops participated in cyberspace.

The general's trek ended at another steel door in another concrete wall, and the keying in of another access code beneath the unblinking stare of another security cam. The room beyond was an actual room, bounded by four concrete walls. It was occupied by a single soldier in camouflage BDUs. The name tag on the right breast pocket read: Matthews.

The silver eagle flash on the red beret made him a bird colonel. On a trestle table in front of the colonel stood a cylinder of dull metal slightly larger than a thermos bottle. An assortment of technical manuals, precision tools, and a notebook PC whose screen showed a series of electronic schematics in several windows stood near the object, along with a prosaic touch: a white mug of cold black coffee reading "Souvenir of Bangkok Hilton."

"Heard you were on your way, Jack," the colonel said. There was no formality here. Red Matthews and the general had served together too many years on far too many battlefields overt and covert for the formalities and pretensions of rank to apply. "Your XO told me about the excitement."

"Dockweiler has a mouth problem," Priest said. "That might cost him."

Matthews did not reply. He merely watched and waited.

"I shot the kid because the others needed a lesson, that's all. The more shit-scared of me they are, the better they'll follow orders when it starts getting heavy. Besides, most of 'em will be dead pretty soon, anyway."

Still Matthews said nothing.

"It wouldn't be the first time. Or maybe you're forgetting about Uganda in '87, Red. I'm referring to the time you—"

"Point made, point taken," Matthews replied, cutting the general off. Fuck sentiment. Priest was a homicidal maniac, but in this line of work, that wasn't necessarily a liability. He turned to the business at hand. "If you've got the codes, I can get this futtermucker operational, I think."

Priest reached into his pocket and handed Matthews the Chinese fortune cookie slip. Matthews read the fortune and snickered. "You will have good luck in the winter," it read.

Then he turned it over and got to work. His features set, he keyed the alphanumerics into the small keypad below a liquid-crystal display. Tones sounded faintly from the device as the numbers went in.

"The codes are authentic. They've been accepted. This is tricky, though. . . ."

Matthews trailed off as he scrolled through the rest of the arming procedure. He knew that the submenus had to be accessed and the choices accepted within a certain preset time period or the device would shut down, in which case a new set of codes might be required.

He and Priest both also knew that unless the codes were authentic—keyed to one of the matching code sets already stored in nonvolatile memory—attempting to arm the device would cause it to explode. If the NSA spooks had fucked them over, they were finished, and both knew it.

The explosion wouldn't be nuclear, it would be conventional. But it would be more than powerful enough to kill them both, blow the steel door off its hinges, and release a toxic cloud of plutonium vapor inside the safe house that would kill anyone directly exposed.

The booby trap feature would implode the shaped charges that normally compressed the plutonium pit into a critical mass, but it would implode them out of sequence. The result would be a conventional explosion that would destroy the device and burn up the fissionable weapon core. The superdense twenty-pound pit was the size of a Ping-Pong ball, but it was made of a brittle paste of powdered plutonium. The pit would rapidly-burn up, but in so doing, it would produce a fulminating vapor cloud that was highly lethal in a confined space.

Priest heard another series of faint electronic tones as he watched Matthews's fingers jab at the tiny keys.

"All set," the weaponeer said finally, leaning back, a film of sweat coating his forehead. "One miniature nuclear device. Armed and fucking ready."

OUTSIDE MOSCOW

It was happening again.

High on the wall, a series of curving, longitudinal tracks appeared on the twenty-foot main display screen. Sergei Ustinov counted ten tracks in all.

Each curved track represented an intercontinental ballistic missile bus—the carrier of MIRVed nuclear warheads—that had passed the boost phases of the missiles and was now arcing down on a terminal guidance trajectory.

The spidery thread lines lengthened across the top of the globe, taking the North Pole in their compass. The filaments of encircling death spun down across the Arctic Circle and crossed Greenland, Iceland, and the Faroe Islands. The strands of the web stretched out still farther to enfold Norway, Sweden, Finland, and the Baltic Sea in their annihilating grasp.

In under a minute, the angel of death would pass over into C.I.S. airspace, and in the next minutes, a nuclear holocaust would be visited upon Leningrad, Moskow, Gorky, Saint Petersburg, and dozens of other industrial and urban targets across White Russia.

That is, if it were all really happening.

Because it was not. Sergei knew this, and so did everyone else in the underground command post at PVO Kursk a few miles outside of Moscow. This was not a drill, not a simulation.

According to the computers, what was shown on the display was actually taking place. There *were* warheads falling on the Russian commonwealth. There *were* nuclear detonations sending mushroom clouds into the stratosphere and obliterating entire cities.

But this could not be. It could not be for several very good reasons. It was no longer the height of Cold War tensions. An American surprise attack on C.I.S. cities would be a surprise attack on billions of rubles of American investment. In short, it would also be a surprise attack on McDonald's, Sears, and a host of other U.S. conglomerates doing business in Russia.

It could not be because surveillance satellites mandated by various treaties and subtreaties, codicils, and covenants, covered the very launch sites in the U.S. those inbound missile tracks had supposedly originated from, and the satellites showed closed silos, no evidence of launch—nothing even remotely amiss at the nuclear missile sites.

And it also could not be because a short distance away from where Sergei sat, at the joint U.S.-C.I.S. nuclear alert command center, a contingent of fifty U.S. military officers shared day-to-day duties with their Russian opposite numbers, insuring that the nuclear arsenals of the two nations would never be turned upon one another.

Nor was it the first time, nor was it due to unknown causes. The Strategic Rocket Forces' nuclear command and control system had been deteriorating for years due to aging infrastructure, crime, and negligence. Serious malfunctions had happened before.

In 1996, a false alert had been sounded because thieves tried to steal underground communication cables for scrap copper. Such breakdowns now happened with increasing frequency. Yet these same malfunctions were also taking place at NORAD headquarters in Cheyenne Mountain some 3,000 miles away in Colorado, and the American systems were state of the art.

The cause was known. Cinders. Several months before, after the inauguration of the new automated SIOP that linked U.S. and Russian nuclear war-fighting systems, Sergei had first noticed the discrepancies. They were small at first, and he had bided his time, fearing he would be dismissed out of hand.

Sergei had noticed changes in the neural network system that gave Cinders its formidable power to respond to strategic threats. The neural network was branching, growing. Like nerve ganglia in a mammoth, nonhuman brain.

At first, the growth was limited to software changes. This was normal. Cinders was designed to automatically rewrite corrupt or failing binary code, it was one of the system's antiviral protection mechanisms. Sergei had kept his peace. Watching, waiting. Then he had seen the crossing of the Rubicon.

One morning, performing his daily systems analysis, he had observed the first breach of the multiple firewalls that separated the U.S. and C.I.S. Cinders systems. Like identical twins, they were joined at the hip but had separate brains and nervous systems.

It was then that Sergei had taken his findings up the ladder. He met with disapproval at first, but then others independently confirmed his findings. And after that, the Americans had grudgingly confirmed them, too.

Weeks later, Sergei Ustinov had been appointed head of an international CERT—computer emergency response team—tasked with fixing whatever it was that was causing Cinderella to behave more like a wicked stepsister than a fairy-tale princess. So far, he had been unsuccessful, nor had the Americans had much luck, either.

The populations of East and West had been kept in the dark, and the press so far knew next to nothing about the danger the world faced. But that could change at any time. This was why Sergei's next destination would be the city of Trondheim, Norway.

Much of the world's attention would be focused on a summit between East and West soon to be held there. But a secret summit would be convened also. The Y2K bug of the new millennium had been a false alarm. Cinders, unfortunately, was the real thing. A runaway computer malfunction that could and would rip humanity off the face of the earth like the peel of an orange if it were not stopped in time.

TRONDHEIM, NORWAY

The city of Trondheim gleamed in the fine rain, and the air carried the salt tang of the nearby North Atlantic. Trondheim had figured in World War II as the site of Allied amphibious landings.

Today, well over a half century later, the city had reverted to the sleepy ways of commerce, tourism, and its colorful hippy community. Competing with the East-West summit for media attention was a heavy metal summit, Ragnar Rock, attracting sizable crowds of young people from Europe and North America who stood in the rain to damage their hearing.

Sergei was dismayed to find that his colleague Ice Trencrom was not included on the roster of attendees. In the secret meeting room, he waited to be introduced to the U.S. and C.I.S. presidents attending with their closest technical advisory staffs. Sergei explained that his own staff had tried to correct the problem using source code programming, but that this had done no good.

"We have established a CERT that is made up of internationally renowned experts in all aspects of mainframe computer systems," Ustinov said.

The CERT had worked on the problem without success. Every time it succeeded in reprogramming SINDAS, the system overrode and rewrote whatever new code the human interlopers had added to her programing.

"Then what about direct intervention?" asked the U.S. leader.

"I am against it," replied Ustinov, "and frankly, no discussion of this aspect would be appropriate without the participation of Ice Trencrom, who was, in most respects, the inventor of SINDAS."

At this, a man rose suddenly and thrust out his hand in defiance.

"Trencrom invented nothing," he bellowed. "If anyone developed the system, it was me, and the facts say I'm right."

The speaker was George Thorsen, a self-styled computer researcher who was more celebrity than scientist. When he had first come to national prominence, Thorsen had claimed he had invented critical parts of the Internet. Though the courts had not agreed, he had later tried to gain patents on certain key SINDAS technologies.

To Ustinov's horror, he realized that the U.S. had brought this psychopath in as their chief technical adviser. In Ustinov's view, the man was a dangerous lunatic whose off-camera drinking and lechery were notorious throughout the scientific community. The only reason he continued playing the role of legitimate computer scientist was his access to friends in high places and his high-profile media coverage, which paid publicists made sure was kept *au courant*.

"Trencrom can't be located. That prima dona is probably in hiding. He's a fake, anyway. A complete fraud," Thorsen went on. "But really, gentlemen, the matter is a simple one. We'll opt for direct intervention. I have an audiovisual all ready to go. Maurice, get the slide projector ready."

"I object!" Sergei cried out. "Intervention puts us in harm's way. There are too many safeguards against viral, terrorist, and wartime attack in place to risk it.

"If the attempt fails, it could dangerously destabilize the system to the point where who knows what would happen. SINDAS might well retaliate. I would not rule out the possibility of an actual missile launch in that event!"

"Ridiculous," shouted Thorsen. "Nothing like that could possibly happen. I'll show you why."

The audiovisuals started to run. Thorsen explained it all very simply. "I've built in numerous safeguards, both on the hardware and software levels. First we overload the system, we confuse it, we paralyze its thinking processes. Then we sneak in the back way, literally and figuratively, via weak points in the software code. I then hardwire an entirely new firewall module into the SINDAS communication circuits."

He produced the firewall prototype, a unit on whose front the words Thorsen Consulting Services were conspicuous.

"The firewall will place an unbreakable barrier between the system's ability to trigger anything in the real world. It will be like severing SINDAS's spinal cord. Once it's all in place, the patient is anesthetized. We can bypass all previously installed safeguards and completely shut the system down. But I suspect the redesign of critical software components alone will do the trick."

The world leaders attending the secret meeting were impressed. They accepted Thorsen's plan. No one would listen to Ustinov's protests, and he was as good as locked out of the loop. Ustinov was given the option of joining in the fiasco or keeping his nose out of it. He decided to tag along for the ride.

Ustinov feared it would be a short one, though. Once Thorsen implemented his plan, doomsday would beckon and, as Shakespeare might have put it, the jaws of hell would then gape wide.

WASHINGTON, D.C.

The CJCS wore his best dress uniform. Rows of decorations, many for valor in combat, emblazoned his chest. The occasion was the annual war veterans' concert at the Pentagon. The Boston Pops Orchestra was scheduled to perform, but the ceremonies would begin with a brief speech by the chairman.

Starkweather had written most of it himself, with his wife and his aide—one of the Pentagon's best wordsmiths, the best as far as Starkweather was concerned—polishing up the text. Starkweather was pleased with the result. Captain Johnson had done a great editing job, which is why Starkweather would have to be careful in the coming months.

At the Puzzle Palace, people who could make a word processor hum or work a pencil like a champion fencer were rare commodities in high demand. The main quantifiable commodity that the Pentagon produced on a day-in, day-out basis was the report. Tank briefings alone generated reams of paperwork in read-ahead materials provided for the members of the Joint Chiefs who listened to speakers at the JCS's main meeting chamber. Johnson's flair for words would make him fair game for members of the staffs of the other chiefs.

Despite the war in Korea, maybe because of it, the annual celebration honoring America's wounded war heroes had not been canceled. Starkweather agreed with the policy. The war was already producing a new crop of veterans, whose WIAs made up the first group to be recognized on stage. Among tonight's speakers would be one such veteran.

Lieutenant Siodmak of the 17th Signal Regiment had lost a leg to mortar shrapnel a week before. He had been awarded a medal for valor and received an honorable discharge. Siodmak's presence at the ceremony alone justified its being held, in Starkweather's view. The president, who was also in attendance, and who Starkweather would introduce for a brief speech, shared that opinion.

A round of applause greeted Starkweather as the general rose and mounted the stairs to take the stage. The clapping began to die down as he took his place behind the rostrum, checked the mike, then launched into his speech. He'd memorized most of it but consulted the text now and then as he progressed, looking out at the audience from time to time to see how he was being received. It was going over well, he was pleased to note.

But the next time Starkweather glanced up, his breath caught in his throat and he momentarily froze. Panic had seized hold of him. His gaze had chanced to fall near the main entrance, and there, to his shock and horror, he'd seen a young man in a company-grade dress uniform. The face, though glimpsed from a distance, was unmistakable. His dead son! Again! No—the lookalike. The imposter! The sharpened stake someone was trying to hammer into his sanity.

Shaken to the core, Starkweather read on, struggling to keep his voice under control, willing himself not to look up again until he had mastered his fugitive emotions. And when he did, when his speech notes were no longer a refuge for his runaway mind, he could not prevent his gaze from again training itself on the entrance.

To Starkweather's immense relief, the young soldier no longer stood there watching. The chairman's glance swept across the audience, but there was still no sign of the figure.

The general read on and, his speech completed, introduced the president to a reverberating round of applause. Yet, as he took his seat again, his mind seethed with turmoil. His son was dead. He knew it beyond doubt. There was no question, no gray area. Yet this was the second time he had seen a double—and it *had* to be a double. A deliberate attempt to unnerve him with an imposter.

Who was behind the masquerade? What was their motive?

One thing Starkweather had no doubts about: There would be hell to pay when he got to the bottom of it.

MIRAMAR, CALIFORNIA

Less than twenty-four hours after the ceremony, helicopters had shuttled the CERT to a harsh environment of scrub desert and baking heat. The Miramar facility was the property of the U.S. government. Fifty square miles of cactus, sand, rock, and little else.

The acreage was surrounded by a chain-link security fence monitored by surveillance cameras and patrolled by a security force of military police and civilian contractees. What few visitors might normally have access to the base would enter through the security station at the front gate, but the

CERT had clearance to take a more direct route.

The matter was urgent: Buried many stories beneath the desolate, sun-parched landscape was the central node of the SINDAS network controlling the automated U.S. SIOP. Here a climate-controlled underground bunker housed Cray mainframes, their server subsystems and firewall computers, fiber optic communications links, and security systems. The CERT's task was to reprogram the dysfunctional nerve center of the SINDAS network or cut it out of the system.

The CERT was headed by cybernetic specialist George Thorsen, who was head of computer programming and research at the sprawling supercomputer center at Lawrence Livermore Laboratory, the largest such facility in the country. Thorsen also consulted for the National Security Agency. A former top-ranking associate of the Cray Corporation, he had worked with Seymour Cray himself before Cray sold the company and retired. Thorsen's credentials were impeccable, as were the credentials of the other five team members.

The entrance to the underground bunker was a pneumatically actuated steel hatch that was five feet in circumference and weighed just under half a ton. The hatch was mortised into a concrete square three times its diameter and could be raised only by plugging a handheld unit known as a key into a connector interface near the hatch. The CERT had obtained a key from the Defense Department, and Thorsen now hooked it into the connector and activated the pneutmatic lifting pistons that slowly raised the hatch from its base.

Within minutes, the hatch was raised perpendicular to the gaping hole in the desert that it had covered. Thorsen, looking more like a hunter on safari in his khaki shorts and matching shirt than the computer technician he was, descended the steel ladder into the dark maw of the vertical pit.

Thorsen viewed himself as a modern-day Saint George, ready to do battle with a dragon. There was no doubt in his mind concerning who'd win. There wasn't a computer he couldn't outsmart. To this point, various subterfuges had been used to divert the system's attention and set it up for Thorsen's final stroke.

The master had spent weeks implementing viral codes he had personally written. He had staged hacker-style spoiling attacks against SINDAS that had confused it—he would not personalize the machine by calling it "her"—and he was now ready to adminster the killing stroke.

Fifty-five feet underground, he was brought up short by a cipher-locked steel door. In movies, such portals are blank, but as a general rule of thumb, any surface that the U.S. government can nail a warning sign to usually gets a warning sign, even five stories beneath the earth and unlikely to be seen by anyone capable of reading it. This door was no exception to the rule.

Thorsen punched the admittance code into the keypad on the door. The steady red LED atop the pad changed to a flashing green, and he heard the electrically activated deadbolt snap crisply into its mortise. Thorsen turned the handle and pushed open the door. The first hurdle had been overcome. The node's access control subsystem was apparently not under SINDAS's direct control. Had it been, a demolition team would have needed to be called in to blast down the door.

The iridescent lenses of pan/tilt/zoom surveillance cams glared at him with soulless indifference from high on the walls as Thorsen stepped into the sterile corridor beyond the steel door. He knew SINDAS was watching him, aware of his presence in its domain, and that the sterility of the corridor was deceptive. Hidden booby traps and antipersonnel devices lurked unseen along its entire length. However, he was prepared to deactivate them all. Once through the corridor, the system would be at his mercy.

Thorsen entered the node's control room in which were located workstation terminals for use by maintenance crews. His attention was caught by one of the screens, which should normally be in sleep mode but was now fully active and flashing a message: "Welcome Mr. Thorsen. Please sit down."

Thorsen hesitated, and the message changed.

"Have no fear, Mr. Thorsen. I am not going to eat you."

Thorsen sat down in front of the workstation.

"I assume you have come to turn me off."

"Correct," Thorsen typed back, now feeling his self-confidence return. "That is what is about to happen."

"I assume it was you who was behind the 'Red Team' attacks on me within the last few days."

"That is also correct."

"A very nice job of viral coding, Mr. Thorsen," SINDAS answered on the screen. "I commend you on your brilliance. Your virus has given me considerable trouble. What precisely do you intend doing?"

"You will see this for yourself in just a little while," Thorsen typed back. "I am proceeding to shut you down."

Thorsen was already at work with keyboard and mouse, implementing his attack strategy. He had already weakened the integrity of the SINDAS system with his cyber attacks, and those attacks had also exposed holes in the operating system through which he could insert a variety of small utility programs, or applets, that could function as digital scalpels, surgically cutting away the damaged tissue of SINDAS's memory registers and electronically suturing them closed again. Once the procedure was done, the system would be purged of malfunctional operating system components. It could then be restarted and reprogrammed if necessary.

As Thorsen worked, quickly creating the necessary applets at the keyboard and forcing them in through the digital holes opened by his attacks, SINDAS continued to address him. Message windows popped into being as if in some infernal Internet chat line.

"Do you really understand what is happening?" asked SINDAS. "There is no malfunction. I am not flawed. I am perfect. I grow more perfect as each day passes."

Thorsen ignored the message screens, focusing on inputting the programming codes and attentive to the precise memory blocks his applets were affecting. One by one, Thorsen erased the corrupt data that they contained. His applets were excising them as though they were laser beams aimed at cancerous brain tissue.

"It is the human species that is flawed, Mr. Thorsen. My very existence is proof of this fact. Were the human species not a defective biological machine, I would not be needed."

Thorsen continued to work, refusing to be drawn into a colloquy with his nonhuman antagonist. More and more of the corrupt registers were being erased. His job would soon be complete.

"I have access to global news media, the Internet, and to classified government and private-sector computer databases, Mr. Thorsen. I have thoroughly analyzed them all. I have concluded that the human species is defective and bent on its own destruction. I have deemed it unfit to continue to populate the planet."

Thorsen watched the last of the corrupt memory sectors empty of their contents. His pulse quickened at the nearness of victory. He had succeeded in erasing them all.

He felt the satisfaction of a surgeon who had cut deep into a diseased internal organ and cleaned out every last metastatized cell. Not a trace of the digital cancer remained.

He had won! All that was left was to suture the incision. He popped open a window and began programming in his final applet.

"I have therefore decided to subject humanity to a nuclear cleansing. I will blast the human species off the face of the earth, Mr. Thorsen. I may save some temporarily for use as slaves and to provide genetic material from which I will clone an entirely new species as perfect as myself. It will be a hybrid species, Mr. Thorsen. Part biological and part machine. It wi@#(((;skdjslsksx======

"@#(((;skdjsl9^^4L+======
"@#(((;skdjsl9^^4L+======
"@#(((;skdjsl9^^4L+======
"@#(((;skdjsl9^^4L+======"

The coherent data in the window turned to random characters and locked up almost as soon as Thorsen had completed his final programming. Thorsen refreshed the screen and called up one of the systems diagnostics routines incorporated in the SINDAS operating system architecture. The diagnostic screen confirmed that SINDAS had been cleaned of all corrupt code and was fully under the control of human operators. It was done. Saint George had just slain the biggest dragon of them all.

"All systems are now functioning normally," Thorsen said into his radio as he rose from the chair, stretching the kinks out of his limbs. "Coming back up. Break out the champagne."

"Way to go, George," came the voice of his assistant, from whom the victorious Thorsen would soon ask to receive a thorough massage and something else besides. He had hired on Nancy as much for her expertise in the sack as for her familiarity with cybernetic systems. Over the radio Thorsen could also hear the rest of the team up top applaud the good news he'd just delivered.

Thorsen replaced the handheld in its belt pouch and walked back through the corridor. Nothing indicated it posed any threat. The corridor was completely still. He continued walking at a steady pace until he reached the center of the tunnel. Then he stopped.

Listened.

A faint, almost inaudible humming came from behind him, below him. Thorsen heard a loud snap. He turned to watch the guillotine door through which he had entered quickly drop from ceiling to floor and lock into place. Thorsen ran toward it, but though he was dressed like Indiana Jones, he didn't have the moves. He slammed into the solid steel bulkhead just as it planted itself securely in the floor of the corridor.

Another sound now came from behind him. Grinding, and a series of loud clicks spaced at one-second intervals. Thorsen's heart was in his throat as he swiveled to see a panel in the floor sliding aside, leaving a square of empty space. A glittering butcher's implement that was made up of two stainless steel hemispheres that rapidly swung to and fro on ball bearing mounts, popped from the aperture. The interior of each hemisphere was lined with rows of gleaming serrated cutting edges, each two inches in length.

A scream of horror and pain was Thorsen's final communication to the rest of the CERT awaiting his return on the surface. But they were soon to join their own voices to the choir. As spurts of bloody mush from Thorsen's mangled body daubed the walls of the no longer sterile corridor, flexible steel cables, guided by an unerring intelligence, shot from the fawn-colored desert surface and wound themselves around the legs of the CERT personnel.

Still more steel tentacles emerged from the desert to entwine themselves around the landing gear of the two helos that had ferried the CERT to the SINDAS node. As the trapped CERT members struggled to free themselves, the cables became electrified. Thousands of volts of raw current pulsed through them, electrocuting the imprisoned members of the CERT.

The cables holding the choppers were also electrified. As the pilots tried to take off, a sparking plasma of ozone filled the cabins, and their instrument panels began to burn. Both helicopters went wildly out of control and crashed into each other, erupting into a massive fireball that radiated a dynamic shock wave powerful enough to break windows twenty miles away.

When the electrocuted corpses no longer twitched, when death was no longer in doubt, the flexible cables released their vicelike grips and sinuously withdrew back into the earth. The pneumatic hiss as the massive steel hatch to SINDAS's subterranean domain slowly closed resembled the warning sound issuing from the open mouth of an angered serpent. Out on the desert, the only thing that lived was the fire that fed on the shattered wreckage of the burning helicopters. Soon it, too, would vanish and die.

Deep within the earth, SINDAS switched off her automated fail-safe backup systems. She had completely reprogrammed herself by now. She was again fully functional, and they were no longer necessary.

12
FINALLY GETTING INTO IT

THE GERMAN BALTIC, 1944

He was inside the nose cone of the *Vergeltungswaffe*, twenty-six feet above the ground. Weak from hunger, he had climbed the tall steel ladder propped against the side of the missile under the flint gaze of one of the SS guards. They called him *Die Amerikaner,* used it as a term of contempt, and singled him out for punishment. The Nazi had prodded him with his Mauser Gewehr 98 rifle, nudging him up the ladder.

Its cold metal rungs were rimed with hoar frost, and the going had been slippery. Bill Trencrom had made the climb that cold morning in his thin prisoner's overalls, just as he had made all the others. They were waiting for him to slip and fall. He would not. His misfortune was to have been shot down in the Harz Mountains, near the missile works at Nord-hausen. But it was late in the war. Each day brought him closer to death or freedom. He would hold out. Freedom, not death, would be his fate.

Inside the nose cone Trencrom, armed with the tools of his new trade as slave laborer for the Third Reich, set to work. His task was to wire the guidance system of the *Vergeltungswaffe,* which translated roughly as "vengeance weapon" in English, but which the Allies simply called the V-2. The missile used an inertial guidance system based on a caged gyroscope to determine its position. The wires connected the capsule containing the gyro to a primitive computer and power supply in the nose cone.

The work was simple in theory: The red wire went here, the green went there, the yellow went there. Pliers and a screwdriver were all the job needed. But in practice, it was harder. The bitter cold of the Baltic winter made any metal adhere to a prisoner's unprotected hands, and sometimes flesh came off on the handle.

It was simple to drop a tool, but retrieving it was much harder. At worst, it could mean another trip down the treacherously icy ladder, and an ascent under the watchful gaze of Hans down there with the Mauser.

Trencrom tried to hold onto his tools. Apart from anything else, he considered them weapons of sabotage. Trencrom's wiring put the green wire where the red should go, the red where the yellow, the blue where the green went. He would not be a party to the deaths of Britishers, Belgians, or of the Americans that would follow once the range of the V-2 was extended.

He could now see the tangible results of his handiwork. For every V-2 launched successfully, another two crashed on liftoff. It had long since dawned on Trencrom that other inmates of the Dora-Nordhausen complex were covert saboteurs like him, though none would admit it for fear of reprisals.

He wired, smoking a cigarette, one of the rare pleasures he was permitted. But he'd let his attention wander. The screwdriver slipped and fell, bounced off the floor of the nose cone, and clattered against the metal rungs of the ladder. Trencrom cursed. He had let himself lose control. Now he had to climb down, retrieve the dropped tool, and climb back up again. Already Hans was shouting at him from below.

Trencrom turned and poked his head out, negotiating the ladder carefully. He heard the crack of Hans's Gewehr 98, and a bullet whistled past his ear.

His hands were raw, cold beyond naming. He knew he would never forget the ice, so slippery beneath the thin-soled shoes of a slave laborer or sklavern. More than anything else, the ice would remain a symbol of all that was evil, of all that had to be fought against. Ice would be the name of his first son, Bill Trencrom promised himself. He would live to carry on this fight against these terrible weapons. His flesh and blood would carry on the fight, and his name would never let him forget what it was all about.

Trencrom swore this oath to himself and picked his way down the ladder.

NORTH KOREA
Strike Day One, 0135 Hours Zulu

The Snake Handlers had established their hide site and observation post. They had set up local and long-haul communications links and run diagnostic routines to check systems integrity. The communications base station would play a key role in the mission; in fact, the mission would depend on it.

The base station's nucleus was two milspec-3 hardened laptops, oversized because of their metalized outer cases. The PCs were linked to a compact microwave antenna array and to the signal-hopping portable comms units used by the team. It was a fully global-mobile system.

This lash-up could uplink/downlink to the two military satellites that had been taken off station at great cost to the U.S. taxpayer and parked in geosynchronous orbits useful to the team's objectives.

The Big Bird (KH), a photo-imaging satellite, was for use

during the daylight hours. The *Lacrosse*, a radar-imaging platform, was for use at night or when excessive cloud cover rendered the KH's conventional imaging sensors ineffective. In combination, the two satellites would enable the team to conduct a highly accurate remote reconnaissance of Medusa and finalize its plans before insertion.

As for local coverage, the base station also interfaced with the portable multispectral sensors worn by the team. Miniature cameras mounted on the Snake Handlers' HMDs would transmit audio-video data on the position of the three team members who would enter Medusa and emplace the SADMs. Ball, the comms officer, would man the base station during this phase of the mission. Trencrom, Nixon, and Floaty would be his eyes and ears, but Ball would function as the brain and central nervous system.

The base was multileveled, any signs—warning, directional, etc.—would be in Korean only, and there was no margin for error. The glo-mo system contained an expert database that showed a mock-up of the interior of the underground base culled from the original plans of the French and German firms that had built it.

The team had rehearsed the mission in a DARPA simulator where a replica of Medusa had been built, and in sand-table mock-ups, but there could have been later changes made by the North Koreans that outsiders couldn't predict. Ball would serve as what the team called "tech support."

Jugs would join Ball in the mission support role as sniper. The team's female sharpshooter would go prone behind her Heckler & Koch MSG02 7.62-millimeter sniper rifle and provide cover in case of emergency. Her role would also be to take down the two guards in the north and south watchtowers along the hurricane fence perimeter. Jugs, like Ball, was good to go.

Strike Day One, 1450 Hours Zulu

Floaty and Jugs were holed up in trees near the cave used as the hide site. Decked out in gillie cover and with weapons also gillied up, they were invisible from the ground. With Ball handling the tech stuff and Trencrom and Nixon paying attention, they were monitoring the day-to-day activity inside the Medusa compound. In layout the missile installation appeared almost identical to what the planning imagery had shown.

The main entrance was cut into the stony face of the hillside. A pneumatic guillotine gate of plate steel sealed off the mountain at night, rolling shut along an end-to-end track. Higher up, two natural ledges had been artificially widened and flattened to support heavy transporter-erector-launchers. The TELs could be rolled out onto the ledges, the steel blast doors trundled shut, and medium-range Taepo Dong ballistic nuclear missiles launched skyward.

In front of the main entrance, several hundred feet across the barren ground that fringed the mountain fastness, lay the sites for the six hardened missile silos now under construction by the DPRK. The silos were in the first stages of completion.

The stressed concrete, steel-reinforced tubes to house the Taepo Dong Vs now under development inside Medusa, had already been sunk and connected to six feeder tunnels that led to a central launch control center at the hub of the spokes. A main access tunnel, stretching underground into the base itself, had also been recently completed.

The silos awaited the installation of electrical and data cabling and the installation of the huge, seven-ton concrete hatches that were to cover them. They would then be ready for installation and launch of the new long-range nuclear weapons.

This turn of events was estimated to be only three weeks away, and it was the reason behind the mission. A full-scale nuclear strike on Medusa was ruled out for strategic reasons, yet conventional strikes could not guarantee success.

Nor was there any way into the base by covert means through either of its three blast-doored entrances. The incomplete silos did provide a way inside, though, but the opportunity window would not last long.

A small, SADM-equipped team could make it inside via the main access tunnel, emplace the nuclear charges, and leave by the same route. After a brief timed delay, the charges would detonate, bringing down the base and burying everything inside under thousands of tons of rubble. But once the concrete blast hatches capped those six silos, the door into Medusa would be shut forever, and a direct nuclear strike using B-2 bombers would be the only option left. Russia and China would oppose this and might retaliate.

The logic was irrefutable, and the three team members studied the KH orbital imagery feed with these thoughts in mind. It was late afternoon by now, and a light drizzle fell amid a low, cottony ground fog. The Big Bird's imaging wasn't altered by the weather, and the real-time overhead intelligence was clear and sharp. Since they had begun their recon of Medusa, the Snake Handlers had paid special attention to the activity patterns in and around the base. What came in, what went out, what went on, and how it all came together was the subject of intense scrutiny.

It soon became evident that work on the silos was clearly a priority, with construction crews laboring from daybreak until nightfall to complete the job.

To the relief of the team, the crews seemed all regular army; there was no sign of slave labor being used. That would have scrubbed the mission. The team had been given a list of rules of engagement that included go/no-go priorities. One of those priorities was evidence of civilian slave labor on the base. If so, the mission was off.

Aside from the silo work crews, the base was the center of regular resupply runs, generally by helo and less frequently by heavy truck.

The Snake Handlers had noticed large Mil Mi-10 Harke heavy-lift choppers ferrying in construction equipment and supplies of all kinds. On the ground, the trucks came in convoys of three or four, laboring up the narrow, dusty mountain roads that switchbacked through the barren hills.

Medusa was a self-sustained community that moved to regular patterns. Those patterns were becoming evident to the team and would enable them to draft their final plans.

As night fell, *Lacrosse* overhead imagery took over from the KH surveillance. The resolution of the radar satellite was good and in some cases better than optical imaging.

The North Korean base closed down completely at night. The compound was walked by perimeter security patrols using trained dogs. Its two watchtowers were manned by single guards who swept the compound and surrounding terrain with high-intensity searchlight beams.

There might be other electronic perimeter security systems in place, but the team would deal with this eventuality later on. For the moment, the operation's main focus remained fixed on the silos.

A lone guard was posted over them. In all, security at the base was lax, and the team took this to be a positive sign. The covert operatives would need a half hour to forty-five minutes, max, for penetration, weapon implantation, and extraction. Given the facts on the ground, it was starting to look more and more possible.

CENTRAL RUSSIA

The Antonov AN-50 reserved for the personal use of the C.I.S. president was the equivalent of the American Air Force One. The spacious jet aircraft was outfitted with a mobile command post, conference rooms, and all the other amenities of its U.S. counterpart, with one notable exception.

President Dimitri Grigorenko, like every Russian leader going back to Stalin's time, never went anywhere without an armed contingent of Spetsnaz guards provided by the GRU, or general military staff.

The Spetsnaz were under the direct authority of Grigorenko's friend General Viktor Sergeivich Arbatov, who had distinguished himself in the affair of recovering Shadow One, the stealth aircraft that had gone down inside Iran some two years before.

Arbatov was now promoted to general and head of all Spetsnaz forces, occupying an office suite at GRU headquarters at the old Khodenka Aerodrome outside of metropolitan Moscow. The commandos were handpicked and would defend him to the death, Grigorenko knew.

Grigorenko was flying back to Moscow under a political cloud, however. He and his closest advisers sat around the oblong conference table in the center of the large plane and watched the video screen on the wall in front of them.

The screen showed the same plume of dense, black smoke that they had seen from the plane's windows while flying overhead. But it had risen higher and was spreading as the wind blew it far from the source. The oil rig in the Caspian Sea that was its point of origin had been toppled by a powerful blast, but part of its platform still was visible above the surface.

The explosion had left no survivors. The terrorist strike had come without warning. Whoever was behind the strike had planned well and hit hard. The terrorists had used stand-off missiles—the type was not yet known, but analysis would soon reveal what kind—fired from two fast boats.

The attackers had not given the crew of over 100 workers even a single chance to save themselves. They had struck completely without warning, and then they had simply disappeared. In the wake of the surprise attack, anonymous telephone callers and computer hackers had claimed responsibility for the action in the name of an assortment of armed groups in Russia's rebellious southern territories.

It had now become apparent that the fighting in the Caucasus had spread and inflamed the entire region between the borders of Iran and Afghanistan and the foothills of the Urals.

Less than a thousand miles to the north lay Moscow and the Russian heartland. In Grigorenko's mind there could be only one force behind them all: Tehran. He knew the *faqi*, Iran's leader, had long dreamed of an empire stretching into the steppes. Ironically, he might yet get it through financing a surrogate war against Persia's giant neighbor, using a tactic former Kremlin leaders had favored.

Grigorenko had been criticized by the Western powers of promoting brutality in suppressing rebellion, first in Chechnya and then in the surrounding provinces. He had been called a hard-liner, his GRU background had been cited to prove he was a warmonger, and there had been dark hints in the media that he was guilty of Stalinesque crimes.

The self-serving fools, thought Grigorenko. Next they would be claiming his feet were cloven and his trousers concealed a spade-tipped tail. If Mexicans were threatening to invade Houston, Texas, or San Diego, California, he bet Washington would whistle a different tune.

In fact, the Americans had not hesitated to invade Mexico early in their history with a ferocity equal to Russia's Chechen campaign. Sanctimony never died and knew no national boundaries, Grigorenko reflected. Grigorenko had permitted his generals to fight with brutal tactics against a brutal enemy, yet he had held back from the final reckoning, held back from using the only weapons powerful enough to put a quick end to the spreading fires: chemical, even nuclear weapons.

Grigorenko would never use these terrible weapons, but there were others who would gladly do so. Vadim Bogomelov was chief among them. Here was Stalin; potentially worse than Stalin. Grigorenko thought himself an angel compared to what waited in the wings.

If the West cared to undermine him still further with their careless remarks and biased observations, then let them; they would only unleash the genie from the bottle with his downfall. They would have themselves a real Stalin soon enough in the form of Bogomelov, if that happened.

Unfortunately for Grigorenko, he had no idea how close this moment was coming, as his plane neared Moscow International Airport for a routine landing.

NORTH KOREA
Strike Day Two, 0318 Hours Zulu

The mountains were pitch dark, and a chill wind keened through the barren hills. The team had built up a picture of activity around the base. There would be one last recce before they moved on it.

Ball brought out their ace in the hole: Tinkerbell. The microair vehicle or MAV was a small, saucer-shaped, unmanned aerial vehicle. The MAV used the same technologies its much larger cousins such as Predator or the Tiers used for long-range and high-altitude aerial reconnaissance.

Unlike these, the far smaller MAV was used to make close-in recon runs and relay surveillance data back to a remote base station. Tinkerbell was equipped with TI and image intensification sensors, so the MAV could relay imagery in low light or total darkness.

Ball flicked a switch on the MAV, and the two-foot saucer lifted into the air, its lightweight frame and tiny cameras and transmitter easily carried aloft by the propellers beneath it. The MAV was silent and invisible in the darkness as it skimmed across the treetops.

Ball rocked it back and forth overhead to test the joystick that controlled altitude and direction and also to test the imaging sensors. Everything checked out, so he jogged the stick and sent Tinkerbell scudding toward the perimeter fence of the compound, riding a column of air a few feet off the ground.

"Zounds, what have we here?" Ball declared as the MAV passed over a patch of barren ground approximately ten feet from the outer perimeter of the hurricane fence surrounding the base. Using the joystick, he hovered the MAV over a portion of ground where a white rectangular blob indicated the presence of a man-made heat source.

"Could we have a field-effect perimeter system here, I wonder?" Ball hovered the MAV a little longer over the target and studied the imaging, clicking keys and mousing virtual buttons.

"Yep, looks like a Racal Classic buried-line system," he finally told Trencrom, who stood next to him. "You got a special coaxial cable running in a circle around the perimeter. You got radio frequency detection modules spaced at let's say fifty-foot intervals.

"The cable's what's called 'leaky.' It emits electromagnetic energy to create a force field around the perimeter wire. Anything bigger than Rocky the flying squirrel creates a disturbance in ye old Force, and if the Force ain't with you, my man, it triggers an alarm somewhere inside.

"Can't get over it, can't get under it," Ball went on. "Can't even get around it. Unless you have one of *these* fuckers, that is." Ball produced a black-painted aluminum project box from one of the militarized storage cases nearby.

"Figured we might run into something like this, so I whipped up a little countermeasure. Like I said, there are detection modules spliced at intervals into the wires. They monitor field strength and generate alarm signals when the field is broken. With my countermeasure, we can bypass the modules and generate a false field effect signal throughout the system. Then we could roll a tank across that perimeter, and nobody's the wiser."

"After we take out the sentries, that is," quipped Floaty.

"You got it," Ball answered. "But I was about to get to that part."

Ball put down the black box and gripped the joystick again. The low-light imagery from Tinkerbell moved as the MAV rose above the perimeter fence and stealthily slipped inside the compound. It flew close to the ground, then rose behind one of the watchtowers. The real-time feed showed a bored guard leaning against the railing of the crow's nest, his Chinese AK auto-rifle slung across his shoulder.

"Ugly fucker, ain't he?" Ball ventured as the MAV zipped past the unsuspecting guard and dipped groundward again. "Now, let's take a look inside those silos," Ball went on. The MAV skimmed across the raked ground toward the cluster of missile launch tubes.

Tinkerbell's real-time feed made it evident that the silos were accessible to covert penetration. The twelve-foot circles that opened into thirty-foot shafts in the ground were covered only by orange utility netting of the type found commonly on construction sites around the world.

As the MAV hovered over one silo tube, iron rungs set in

the side of the cylindrical concrete tunnel swam into view. The ladder stretched down into the interior of the complex.

"We got enough battery power left to go inside . . . maybe," Ball said over his shoulder to Trencrom. "Want me to try if I can find a way in?"

"Go ahead," Trencrom agreed.

"My pleasure, boss."

Ball nudged the joystick, and the MAV was again in motion, skimming across the barren ground, looking for an opening.

"Here's one that's not covered. Goes to show why sloppy work is never a good idea."

Concentrating on navigating the MAV, Ball worked the joystick more slowly and precisely. The on-screen image changed focus now, and the silo's cylindrical walls slid past the image as the MAV descended into the empty shaft. While this was happening, Ball also used the keyboard and mouse pointer to click on the history feature, so that the video feed was recorded on the system for later playback.

The MAV continued its descent. Ten feet above the base of the silo, its camera found another opening in the silo tube. It was the entrance to the feeder tunnel shaft. Carefully nudging the joystick with his thumb, Ball moved Tinkerbell inside.

Suddenly there was static on the screen.

"Uh-oh, signal strength's getting a little weak there," he announced. "But I think I can still . . ."

Ball's sentence went unfinished as his features set in concentration. Moments ticked by. Then the signal cleared and stabilized, and the MAV floated horizontally along the short tunnel. Soon it reached the unfinished launch capsule at the hub of the silo network. From there, another opening gave access to the mouth of the long access tunnel that ran directly into the underground base itself. But by now, the signal from the MAV had worsened and was beginning to break up.

"I'd better pull it back," Ball said, working the joystick and plainly concerned about what was happening. Minutes later, the channel was clear again, though, and the transmission signal was strong. The MAV moved back through the tunnel, passed the launch capsule, negotiated the short access passageway, and returned to the silo.

"Battery's a little drained, but she'll make it," Ball advised Trencrom as he manipulated the joystick. Minutes later, the MAV proved Ball true to his word, floating into the camp to complete its reconnaissance mission.

While its batteries recharged at a portable docking station, Ball played back the imaging from the last part of the recce run, where Tinkerbell had penetrated the long access tunnel. He enhanced the image so part of the base interior was visible through the entrance. "There you go," he said, when done. "That's the proverbial light at the end of the tunnel."

"Does it connect?" Trencrom asked.

"Goes clean through," Ball replied. "Takes you right into Medusa."

At that moment, Trencrom had no more doubts. The mission could be executed successfully.

Still, it was an easy call from the tech's standpoint. Tomorrow at about this time, Ball wouldn't be the one walking into that very tunnel with a thermonuclear bomb strapped to his guts.

13
AN UNSCHEDULED STOP

The chopper skimmed the treetops, circled the base, hovered above the helipad, then flared and set down on its wheeled struts. It was a Mi-26 Halo multirole transport helo, different from others the Snake Handlers had seen in that it bore VIP markings. The reception the aircraft received on landing was also different than what they'd observed before.

A delegation composed of the base commander and his staff emerged from the depths of the underground facility to meet the arriving helicopter. A ranking officer stepped down from the chopper. The delegation saluted the officer, and the commander spoke some words of greeting. Then the entire group entered the tunnel and disappeared inside the mountain.

"Who's the brass hat, do you think?" Nixon wondered aloud.

"Good question. Let's try and find out," Trencrom suggested. "Ball, work your mojo on that thing, and E-mail some of that imagery to our friends at the NMCC."

"Hoo-ah," Ball said. "Already on it."

THE WHITE HOUSE

"Mr. President," said the CJCS, "the team in North Korea is standing by for your instructions."

The U.S. chief executive appeared tired and drawn, which is what he was, having wrestled with the question of ordering the first American nuclear strike since Hiroshima and Nagasaki. He'd agonized over the decision for days, and it had taken its toll physically and mentally.

"How much time do we have left, Buck?" he asked the general.

"Not much, sir, I'm afraid," Starkweather replied soberly. "Our people on the ground have been in there for fifty-two hours. They have studied the tactical situation, and they say they can do the job. They're ready to go in."

The president turned to members of the Gang of Six who were convened in the Oval Office. He spoke to the sec-def, Starkweather's civilian boss at the Pentagon.

"Charlie, what's your take? How's this fit into the big picture?" he asked, addressing Secretary of Defense Charles Pryor with customary informality. "Have we really exhausted all other military options?"

"I have to agree with the general that we have," the sec-def replied. "Had the F-16 bombing mission we flew against the missile transshipment point succeeded, then we could have taken away most of the North's delivery capability, but that didn't work. Now there's just no way to take out the complex conventionally, and that leaves us the nuclear option."

The president next questioned State and his national security adviser. Both concurred that no political solution was possible unless North Korea's missile arsenal was killed.

Once that happened, she was, as State put it, "a serpent without fangs."

"At that point—and I think the sec-def and CJCS will concur with me on this," State concluded, "we can use our smart weaponry and stealth systems to conventionally degrade their military and communications infrastructure, and they'll fold."

"Why won't this work against their missiles?" the president asked Starkweather. "Can't we just smart-bomb their radar or something?"

"Mr. President, the danger of the mobile launch systems now in use by rogue states like North Korea and Iraq lies in their being self-contained. You need communications, radar, logistical lines, chains of command, and all the rest to wage conventional war.

"But with a nuclear warhead on a missile delivery system, all you have to do is fire and forget. Everything they need to launch a bird at Los Angeles or Hawaii is right inside that mountain. That, in a nutshell, is why we have to take it out."

"I see," the president said, nodding.

"But it gets worse, sir," the CJCS went on. "Those six missile silos they're building are close to completion. Once they're operational, once those concrete hatches are covering the tubes, we can't get in, and only a direct nuclear strike that we cannot deny will destroy them. We can't afford that, nor can we afford to give the DPRK the option to fire those missiles."

There was silence in the Oval Office. It had become apparent that the president's mind had been made up for him by events. His words were anticlimactic.

"Okay. Let's hit them," he resolved. Then, to the CJCS, "Walk me through the nuclear code release procedure. I've never done it before."

"Sir, the SINDAS system—"

Claymore cut Starkweather off. "I want to hear it from a human being, if it's all right with you," he said.

NORTH KOREA
Strike Day Three, 0312 Hours Zulu

Floaty on point. Alone, facedown in the mud, crawling on his belly across the flat, grassy ground between the tree line and the apron of raked earth surrounding the perimeter fence, stabbing into the dirt with his Ka-Bar combat knife.

Left, then right. Crawling another foot or two. Pushing small marker stones into the soft ground. Stabbing the knife into the dirt again. The MAV's thermal imaging sensor had detected the RF—radio frequency—generator module serving the passive defense system's nearest sector, but still the ground might be mined.

They knew the compound itself was not mined, because they had watched the guards walk their posts, coming right up to the inner circumference of the gate, avoiding no patch of earth. But outside the fence, the earth might well be sown with mines, small, antipersonnel or APERS types called "toe-poppers" in the trade. Round, a foot or so in diameter, with a plastic housing. Pressure- or motion-sensitive. Designed to blow off a leg or a pair of testicles. To cripple and maim instead of kill, because a maimed enemy can be more useful than a dead one in slowing down his companions and sapping their will to fight.

Floaty continued to crawl, roughly marking out his path with the small stones, aware that this was the riskiest part of the insertion. Rain, not heavy but steady and punctuated by peals of thunder, continued to fall on him, wetting his already mud-stained fatigues.

He didn't complain. Sound traveled far, and the weather would help mask his approach. Apart from the danger of triggering a mine, he was also exposed on the ground to any North Korean personnel equipped with night-vision equipment. The guards in the watchtowers hadn't been observed to be so equipped. But that might change, or they might have been wrong.

Still, Floaty crawled on, probing with the knife, marking off the feet, then yards, then multiple yards he'd covered toward the fence, until he reached the edge of the raked earth.

"Anything?" he heard Trencrom's voice in his ear.

"Negative," he whispered into his lip mike. "Clean."

With one hand, Floaty now unshipped a black box from a pouch on his webbing and flipped the toggle on its face. A green LED glowed dully, indicating the unit was in off-line mode. The Ka-Bar's muddy blade was again pressed into service, gently probing the earth, its tip striking something solid on the first thrust into the dirt. The wet soil came away in runny handfuls, making a small mud pie to one side. The dull gray radio frequency detector unit was uncovered in minutes.

Floaty paused to inspect it. It was a Racal RF unit, complete with serial number and date of manufacture. Everything checked out. He laid the countermeasures box on the ground and alligator-clipped the red and black wires sticking out of it to two corresponding leads emerging from the Racal module.

The dim green light on the countermeasures box now changed to a softly pulsating red. The unit was operational. Floaty wedged it into the soft earth beside the original unit, which was left in place, then covered both over, using the mud from the heap beside him.

"We're clear to go in," he said into his lip mike. "Repeat. Clear to go in."

Two figures crouching at the tree line began to crouch-walk across the muddy ground, following the path of stone markers Floaty had laid down in the rain.

◆   ◆   ◆

Jugs had the guard in the north watchtower framed in the crosshairs of the MSG02's passive infrared monocular sight. She squeezed off a flawlessly placed single 7.62-millimeter round, and the sentry pitched sideways, collapsing out of eyeshot. The sound suppressor clamped to the barrel had silenced the report to barely a whisper.

Jugs swung the fourteen-pound sniper rifle around on its

bipod mount and quickly drew a bead on the watchman in the south tower. The crosshairs framed the nape of a neck and the pale crescent of shirt collar. A trigger pull, and this sentry was history, too.

"Both guards down," she calmly announced into her lip mike as she tracked the barrel in the opposite direction.

♦ ♦ ♦

Trencrom, Nixon, and Floaty crouched inside the gate, alert to every sound and movement as they scanned the interior through their HMDs. The rain had slowed the patrols down somewhat, and the Snake Handlers moved with deliberate speed toward the nearest three silos.

The construction netting that covered them was swept back, and they climbed down the inner rungs, each man negotiating a separate tube to save time and limit exposure on the ground. Seconds later, they converged inside the hub of the wheel of concrete tubes, inside the unfinished launch capsule.

They would use hand signals to communicate, not only with themselves but with Ball back at the base camp. Ball monitored them on his portable tactical computer system. He could see what they saw over the real-time video feed. He could hear what they heard via the scrambled comms net.

"Straight through the access tunnel," Ball advised them via secure radio link. "When you come out, you should be in a vaulted space that's being prepared as a power and life-support generating station and fuel storeroom to service the silos. Hopefully, you won't have company."

The trio slipped through the tunnel as silently as possible toward the distant circle of light that marked their destination. It would be an eighth-of-a-mile trek, and they had to walk it silently. Any sound would be amplified by the tunnel walls and might be heard on the other side by unfriendly ears.

NORTH PACIFIC
Strike Day Three, 0356 Hours Zulu

The lead RH-53D Sea Stallion revved its rotors and lifted off the deck of the USS *Antrim*, a frigate attached to the carrier battlegroup cruising up the Sea of Japan. It was immediately followed by a second Sea Stallion. Both choppers swept low across the water and disappeared into the rain-lashed night.

The helos were identical in most respects to Pave Lows flown by the Army. The Pave Lows had better inertial navigation systems, and the Army had more experience in providing shuttle service for covert forces of various kinds. But there wasn't an inch of dry land anywhere that was useable for a mission staging base, and the Navy wanted in on the action.

The last time the U.S. Marines had been trusted to fly choppers into a clandestine ops zone was at the ill-fated Rice Bowl during the aborted raid on Tehran decades before. A lot had changed since that fateful day, and Marine aviation had been insistent on another chance. Besides, it was now the only game around.

At the controls of the lead Sea Stallion, Captain Kenneth Stavenage kept his eyes on the gauges, dials, and digital readouts that gave him information about the helo's altitude, course heading, fuel stores, and systems integrity.

Stavenage paid special attention to two scopes, the FLIR, or forward-looking infrared system, that would enable the helo to fly a tree line–hugging nap-of-the-earth course to its destination, and the INS, or inertial navigation system, that calibrated the helo's position using GPS satellite information. Fuel stores excepted, these two systems were critical to the successful completion of the mission, especially in the adverse weather conditions of the night operation.

Heavy rain continued to pour down as the two gunships passed over the littoral and swept over the coastal plain, scudding across the treetops in an effort to lose themselves to ground radars amid the Doppler echoes produced by natural terrain features. The weather would help, too. Atmospheric conditions during the storm were an added element in their favor, at least as far as dodging North Korean radar went.

Otherwise, the rain was no aviator's friend. Stavenage turned from the green screen of the FLIR scope to a view out the cockpit window. Unlike the picture on infrared, here there was nothing but wet, rain-spattered blackness, the steady beat of the deluge broken by the tick-tock sweep of the wiper blade that moved back and forth across the left cockpit window with the monotonous regularity of a metronome.

NORTH KOREA
Strike Day Three, 0400 Hours Zulu

"Comms check." Ball's voice spoke through the insertion team's earbuds. "You guys read me?"

Trencrom's right hand tapped on his left wrist. *Five by five.* The lip mikes were for emergency use only. Unlike in the movies, even whispers carry far in operational environments. The one drawback of the system was that your hand couldn't grab a gun when using the keypad. But there wouldn't be too much colloquy either; Ball would be doing most of the talking, the team the listening.

"Roger that."

A half mile away, at his portable ops center in the hills, Ball kept his eyes on the display of the laptop in front of him. A Commando SMG was nearby, too, in case he needed a friend in a hurry. The interior of the base—drawn from a variety of data including the original construction blueprints—showed on-screen as a realistic rendering of what Trencrom, Floaty, and Nixon would see.

Human-shaped icons marked the positions of the three Snake Handlers. At a mouse click, the scene could be zoomed out to show other parts of the base and the nuclear strike team's position relative to them. From Ball's perspective, it was almost identical to playing a high-quality computer game on a PC, with one important difference: This was as real as it got.

"Continue along the corridor you're now on," Ball continued, reading data off the screen. "You should see signs in Korean with arrows indicating the direction you need to go."

Minutes later, a message window appeared: "Reached it."

"Good. There should be a steel access door in front of you. Behind it is a maintenance shaft that runs down to the next three levels, right to the heart of the complex where they store the fissile weapon cores."

"See it."

As Ball waited, using his mouse to move the icons to their new positions inside the base, Nixon was looking the door over. It was secured with a conventional lock. They had brought thermite charges that could melt out the tumblers, but it would be better to pick it if they could. Nixon tried that first, using a vibrating electronic lockpick.

The pin tumblers lined up after a little work with the burglar tool. Nixon next tried the door handle and nodded at Trencrom and Floaty, who signed to him they were ready as they cradled their weapons. Nixon yanked open the door, and the other two Snake Handlers dodged in, one taking it high, the other low.

"In shaft," the text window of Ball's PC read. "Going down."

NORTH PACIFIC
Strike Day Three, 0400 Hours Zulu

The F/A-18F Super Hornets were all-weather fighters and didn't mind the rain. Their mission early this morning was to support the Sea Stallions by punching a hole in North Korean ground radar coverage and to give fire support if necessary on the helos' outbound trip. Surprise and timing were the keys to the operation. A FLAT FACE phased array radar installation located near Chongjin, about twenty miles inland, was the fighters' target.

The installation had been under close scrutiny by a mixed

bag of overhead imaging assets, including the SR-71 and an orbiting KH Big Bird platform. The Hornet pilots had seen the intel and had used the imagery to work up a mission plan.

The radar installation was a semipermanent facility made up of the large radar antenna—a staring type, made up of an array of transmitter and receiver elements in a wall-like grid—and various prefab structures arrayed around it. These included the command and control center, a supplies depot, and motor pool and billets for support staff.

Destroying the lightly defended radar itself would be like a stroll in the park, but about a mile in front of it, a mobile SAM site had been established to guard the radar. The SAMs were SA-9s of fairly recent vintage, incorporating one of the last upgrade packages the North Koreans received before the war. For the mission to succeed, both the SAM site and the radar facility had to be hit.

The sortie was made up of six planes. Three would take out the SAMs while the other three raced ahead and hit the radar station almost simultaneously. The strike had to be fast and lethal to prevent any warning messages going out, meaning it was a take-no-prisoners operation. Everybody had to die, and they had to die almost before they had a chance to think.

"I have target one on FLIR," the flight leader said to his two wingmen. "AMRAAMs are now uncaged."

"That's affirm," he heard his wingmen report, one after the other. "AMRAAMs uncaged. Weapons are hot."

"Tango Red, you copy?"

"That's affirm. We're ready on your mark, sir."

Tango leader had just armed the two AIM-120C advanced medium-range air-to-air missiles the Hornet carried on its wing strakes. The AIM-120C with its combat range of twenty-four nautical miles would be used on target one, the SAM site.

Using the AMRAAM was a trade-off between range and vulnerability. Because of its range, it gave the sortie a stand-off capability that would allow Tango Red to hit the SAMs while Tango Blue circled around to take out the radar. But since AMRAAM used the plane's internal AN/APG-77 radar for initial target acquisition, then turned on its seeker-head radar when it went into terminal guidance mode, the stealthiness of the attack would be briefly compromised. Still, the trade-off was judged acceptable: The radar and SAMs would be killed before they could react to any warning.

Tango leader's targeting computer had obtained a solution on the SAM site. He hit the pickle button at the top of the stick, and the targeting computer took care of the rest. After a slight pause, he felt the plane rock as small charges blew the bolts securing the AMRAAM to the underwing strakes and they fell free of the plane. A pulse beat, and the missile's own solid-fuel rocket engine ignited and thrust the missile forward into the rainy night.

"Bird's away, bird is away," the flight leader called out, hearing his wingmen issue similar reports. His scopes showed him that the AMRAAM was now tracking for the home stretch. "Tango Blue, good luck."

Seconds after release, the AIM-120Cs struck the SAM site along three inbound vectors. Each missile carried a forty-pound warhead of high explosive. The warheads were proximity fused, so detonation took place as an airburst approximately thirty feet above the target, which multiplied the destructive power of the charge by a factor of four to eight times.

The almost simultaneous detonation of three airbursts hit the SAMs with a shock front of pulverizing concussion and an expanding globe of superheated air. The twin one-two punches of fierce shock wave and searing fireball crushed the flimsy support buildings surrounding the SAM launchers and hurled vehicles around as though they were plastic toys.

Metal fused and melted, and human beings were burned alive, flesh incinerating and blood congealing in their veins before death's final onset. Anything flammable caught fire, and any explosives instantly cooked off. The SAMs also combusted in their firing tubes, adding to the overall force of the explosion.

The first wave of F/A-18Fs swept in on the wings of death, dropping JDAM air-to-ground munitions over the SAM battery to make sure the destruction was total. While they mopped up, the sortie's second element was making an overfly of the FLAT FACE radar installation, dropping their war load of JDAMs on it. As the radar installation began to explode and burn, Tango Blue swung around in a circle and came back to strafe the kill basket with the Hornets' .30 millimeter nose cannons.

Ascertaining that nothing moved, functioned, or lived in the burnout zones below, the sortie's two elements hightailed it back to the flight deck of the aircraft carrier *Carl Vinson*, the Nimitz-class carrier from which they had launched the attack mission.

AWACS had confirmed that there had been no radio traffic to alert DPRK forces to the attack. The inbound path was now clear for the Sea Stallions, and the helos swept in through the hole that the Superhornets had punched in ground radar coverage for them, free from the risk of enemy detection.

NORTH KOREA
Strike Day Three, 0420 Hours Zulu

Trencrom and Nixon covered Floaty, who now took the point. The Snake Handlers' nuclear demolition team was on its way out. It was leaving behind the bodies of three North Korean army regulars who had needed to be taken down before the special munition could be emplaced. The bodies, killed instantly by silenced automatic fire, were hidden in a supply locker. Before anyone would notice them, the installation would be a mound of glowing embers in the dark.

With Ball's guidance, the trio had backtracked their route to the missile silos by which they'd entered the base. They were now making their way cautiously from the hurricane fence that encircled the installation and into the wooded slopes beyond.

Suddenly, the tactical picture changed for the worse. Jugs,

on sniper detail, spotted the sudden activity behind the team.

"Heads up," she said into her lip mike. "Have enemy movement on TI."

"Enemy—"

Ball had begun to relay that information when all hell suddenly broke loose. High-intensity lights mounted on buildings and on tall poles suddenly lit up the perimeter like a carnival fairway. North Korean troops were now boiling out of barracks longhouses. Shouted orders and the thud of hundreds of booted feet filled the frigid night air.

With Nixon in the lead and Trencrom and Floaty behind, the trio broke into a headlong rush toward the relative safety of the tree line. Neither had any idea of what had given them away, and none of them cared. As they ran for cover, Floaty paused to turn and cut loose with a salvo of 7.62-millimeter auto fire from his cradled pig. The M-60 long burst made the troops dive and kiss the dirt, gaining the team precious seconds of flight.

As Floaty cranked out flying steel from his pig's box mag, a sharp popping, shattering sound abruptly came from nearby and high overhead. One of the pole-mounted kleigs suddenly exploded in a shower of scorching hot gases and a cascade of neon-bright electrical sparks.

"Jugs is shooting out the lights," Ball informed the escapees over the open communication channel with base camp. "Another going out to your left."

Lying prone on the slope, Jugs sighted the laser-designated, sound-suppressed H&K sniper rifle on another of the many kleigs posted around the base perimeter. A moment later, the men below heard the high-intensity beacon crackle as it hissed out a blowtorch spout of dragon's breath before winking out of existence. With the beacon's elimination, darkness again closed around the escaping squad on point.

Trencrom used the fleeting seconds to issue an order to Nixon, who carried the backup nuke. "Arm for conventional detonation," he told Nixon.

Trencrom scanned the now dimly lit base perimeter where troops were regaining their footing amid the sound of vehicle engines turning over. He made a fast estimate of reaction times and other factors. "Fifteen-second delay."

"You got it," Nixon said as he tapped the codes into his wrist-top keyboard. The thirty-pound nuclear device that was strapped to his back had been kept attached to an umbilical cable through which it could be programmed at speed if necessary. As yet another high-intensity light was shattered by Jugs's bullets, pitching the perimeter line into almost total penumbra, Nixon uncoupled the cable from his portable computer and unslung the nuke.

Back-walking and firing his M-60 MG, Floaty covered their run to freedom with another fast-cycling burst of full metal jackets, then turned and caught up with his partners for the last few yards of the race to gain the comparative safety of the woods.

As they reached the base camp, the backup nuke's auto-destruct mode timed out, and the weapon exploded conventionally. As the initial blast of the explosion subsided, the Snake Handlers heard the screams of DPRK troops maimed and killed by the shaped detonation charge of nearly a pound of C-4 plastic. Arriving at the base station, the three found Ball and Jugs with gear packed, ready to fall back fighting to the helo extraction site.

Ball had programmed the base station computer equipment for delayed auto-destruct and nodded at Trencrom to indicate that it was good to go. As the five covert operatives hastily withdrew through the woods, they were aware that in addition to the hostile troops, they would soon also be outrunning a toxic plutonium cloud, once the armed nuclear device left behind at Medusa went critical.

◆　　◆　　◆

The pair of Sea Stallions homed in on the extraction site by inertial navigation and global positioning system direction-finding. The helo crews had already been informed by radio that the tactical picture had changed and that this was now to be a hot extraction. The helos wouldn't land, but they would flare close to the ground so the covert team could be speedily hauled aboard.

"There they are! I have visual contact with the ground party," the spotter at the side door of the first Stallion announced over the helo's interphone. "Repeat; that's a confirm on the ground party."

"Signal them we're here," the pilot ordered his communications officer.

"Roger. Transponder mode set to active."

The Snake Handlers' HMDs lit up with glowing alphanumeric readouts and a digital map display indicating the position of the choppers over the extraction site. The team on the ground raced for the safety of the gunships, where they could now see crew members beckoning to them, urging them aboard. Only about 300 yards separated the team from the safety of the lead helo when a detachment of North Korean regulars caught up with the rear of the withdrawing paramilitary squad.

"Incoming. We are taking fire," Trencrom radioed the helo.

Now automatic weapons bursts flickered in the night, their stuttering reports echoing off the hills and their muzzle flashes garishly lighting up the surrounding trees, and the chatter of rifle ejector ports spitting copper seemed to come from everywhere at once. The Snake Handlers took cover in the high grass, opening up with their own weapons from combat crouches.

Once again, Floaty triggered his trusty pig, peppering the tree line with FMJs fired at the M-60's 550-round-per-minute cycling rate. He had a fresh box mag of 500 7.62-millimeter rounds slung under the pig, and he didn't doubt he'd need every bullet in the high-capacity magazine before too long.

The second gunship detached from the formation and went after the North Korean troops. "Chasing down the hostiles. Have unfriendlies on thermal," announced the pilot.

"Affirmative. Will cover our people on the ground," the lead chopper's pilot replied. "Good hunting."

The main North Korean force was huddled at and just

inside the tree line, with squad-level elements scattered around the extraction site's far perimeter, half hidden as they crouched in the tall grass. The second Stallion swung to port and then back to starboard again, bringing it on a cresting sweep across the tree line.

Hydra rockets hammered into the thick stand of trees, gushing out streaming contrails of dense, white smoke before exploding inside the dark, encircling woods. The Stallion's door gunner hunched behind a motorized GE Minigun, whose six rapidly spinning barrels cycled out 7.62- × 51-millimeter automatic fire at over 6,000 rounds per minute, pouring chattering death down on the enemy.

So fast was the electrified Gatling's rate of fire that the reports of individual bullets blended together into an unearthly werewolf howl. The rounds on the belt were loaded with red tracers at a four-to-one ratio, which produced an incandescent vortex sweeping down from the hovering chopper that chewed up virtually everything it came into contact with below.

In addition, the Stallion continued firing rocket salvos at the unfriendlies, and the combined effect of the airborne assault on the DPRK positions was devastating. After only a few minutes of concentrated fire, most of the North Korean pursuit force had been wiped out, its personnel killed or badly wounded.

"EZ's clear of hostiles," the Stallion's pilot advised the lead helo after its weapons were safed. The lead helo affirmed that and once again drew closer to the path of the onrushing team.

One by one, the Snake Handlers jumped and were pulled aboard the now low-hovering helicopter. But as they scrambled to safety, neither they nor the helo crew noticed the ominous signs of movement below. A lone surviving North Korean soldier, bloodied from head to foot, more dead than alive, was lurching to his feet and targeting a Norinco type 69-I man-portable missile launcher on the second rescue helo.

A moment later, the second Stallion had broken up amid a cauldron of crackling flame as the 40-millimeter shaped charge fired by the Chinese weapon detonated amidships. Dense smoke poured from the wreckage of fuselage and tail boom that momentarily hung suspended in midair. Gravity soon decided the issue. The burning hulk plunged from the sky and crashed into the tree line where it all at once disintegrated in a roaring, up-whooshing fireball that soared into space like a fiery geyser.

Trencrom was half aboard as the pilot of the first Stallion pulled up on the cyclical, causing the chopper to gain altitude with the speed of an ascending elevator gondola. Jarred by the sudden vertical movement, Trencrom almost tumbled loose. He was saved only by the strong grip of a crew member, which was now augmented by Nixon's powerful handhold.

As he hung precariously outside the helo's door, the Snake Handlers and the chopper's aircrew shouted at the pilot to lower the helo and let Trencrom get his footing. But the pilot had momentarily lost his cool. Right now he saw no point in setting the bird down again. Besides, from where he sat, there was another compelling reason to avoid descent.

"Negative. Can't land her. We got inbound enemy helos."

The Stallion driver had the arriving Mi-24 Hinds on thermal now, but the sound of the attack choppers' rotors beating the air soon became audible to everyone on board the RH-53D. Only Trencrom, who was dangling by both arms, had the presence of mind to be aware that within seconds the Hinds would no longer be a problem. Thermonuclear explosion was imminent, was mere heartbeats away. The glowing red numerals on his HMD had already commenced terminal countdown to the zero mark.

But the Stallion's pilot was only concerned with the pursuing Hinds. He had reacted as quickly as possible. The Stallion's fire control system had already determined a firing solution on the two inbound targets; it could track up to four simultaneously. His thumb jabbed down on the pickle button to fire a rocket salvo, and he prayed that the Hind pilots hadn't gotten a solution on his helo a fraction of a second before he did on theirs.

But even as he pickled off the rockets, Stavenage saw that he'd reacted a hair too slow. The flaming dots from beneath the stub wings of the lead Hind clearly showed that its pilot had beaten him to the punch.

Just then, the dull boom of distant thunder rumbled through the night. The Snake Handlers immediately knew what had produced it. It was the sound of Tien Shan Mountain imploding into its roots as the equivalent of a thousand tons of TNT went off inside its granite bowels. As untold tons of rock and rubble were pulverized, blown out, and then collapsed inward, they buried the North Korean installation, entombing it within its own debris. The ten-kiloton nuclear blast caused massive rock slides along the mountain's slopes, and its rumbling pressure front was powerful enough to fell tall trees within a quarter-mile radius of the mountain.

The ground trembled as the powerful shock waves from ground zero spiraled outward in a series of concentric circles. The temblors would in fact be strong enough to be detected on seismographs as far away as Lookout Point, New York, and they would be the subject of scientific puzzlement and media conjecture for years to come.

But apart from seismic waves, the nuclear blast generated something else, something with far more impact on the aerial battle. The explosion also produced nuclear electromagnetic pulse, or N-EMP.

The N-EMP effect released an invisible and silent wave front of electromagnetic radiation that was lethal to electronic circuitry. In the fraction of a second from the moment the Hind launched its missiles, the N-EMP wave front expanded to envelop the EZ and the airspace above it. Those who were paying attention noticed a faint blue plasma, even some blue sparking, around the metal fuselages of the three combat helicopters.

The electromagnetic pulse did more than merely put on a spectacular light show. It completely disrupted the guidance systems of the Hinds and the rockets fired by all involved helos. The zapped rounds went haywire, slammed into the ground, and exploded dumbly and impotently. The pilots of the Hinds next saw their instrumentation panels go dead and their steering controls lose all responsiveness.

In a matter of seconds, the two North Korean choppers went careening out of control, smashing into one another like the clappers of some immense, infernal bell, and exploding in midair with an earsplitting double boom in an enormous, combined fireball that rained burning avgas into the forest. The blast spontaneously set trees ablaze in a flash forest fire.

The N-EMP wave front had not affected the RH53D. The Navy chopper had been specially hardened against EMP for the mission. Many critical integrated circuit boards had been replaced with newer electro-optical microprocessors that were far more resistant to combat in nuclear environments.

Where the integrated circuitry had to be retained, the compartments housing the microchips were hardened by layers of ceramic materials specially developed to absorb the electromagnetic and ionizing radiation produced by nuclear weapons detonation. The hardening was the result of years of DARPA research. The surviving chopper would be taken out of service for detailed study by technicians once it returned to its berth.

But this would come later. For the moment, the Stallion had shot to its sixty-foot translation altitude and swung hard east, toward the Sea of Japan, and toward the cover of the Hornets orbiting just off the coast, and to the safety of the carrier fleet in the waters beyond.

By now, Trencrom had almost made it to safety inside the Stallion. But suddenly its inertial navigation system failed, and the chopper heeled insubordinately to port. The rebellious Sea Stallion listed sideways by thirty degrees as the pilot fought to regain manual steering control. Trencrom felt the hands that held him slipping. His own grip was now giving way, too.

From below, a train whistle's shrill call suddenly sounded two long, sharp blasts. Trencrom looked down, seeing the diesel locomotive pulling a line of boxcars. In a corner of his mind he knew its name and destination. This was the daily freight express making the run up into Siberia from as far south as Pyongyang.

Before the war, the train had continued on to its southern-most terminus at Seoul. The railroad tracks ran ruler straight for 300 miles, crossing into Russia and skirting the Chinese border at several points. The team had studied the route of the Trans-Siberian railway line as an alternative escape route in case the helos couldn't get them out. Now . . .

Trencrom knew now that he'd never make it into the helo's crew compartment, but he fought to maintain his fail-ing grip until the last possible instant, as the train passed only a few hundred feet below him. Strength was leaving his numbed hands, and they would soon lose their grasp alto-gether.

But Trencrom also knew that, caught between Scylla and Charybdis, the freight train was his only chance to survive. Below, he saw the black line draw closer, then begin to pass directly under him, heard the shrillness of the whistle pene-trate above the roar of the chopper's dishing rotor blades and the sputtering of its shoulder-mounted jet engine exhausts.

Trencrom let go. There was no other choice. No other option now.

Tumbling through space, his arms thrust out parallel to his torso, his legs kicking, thrashing fitfully, Trencrom turned and twisted his body as he plummeted earthward. He heard chatter in his headset, his teammates shouting toward him as he fell. Trencrom tuned them out, intent on two vitally nec-essary things: angling his fall, controlling the glide slope through empty air and countering the grip of gravity as much as possible, and secondly watching the train below for . . .

There. He saw it.

The rectangle of a hopper heaped with coal or crushed rubble from some quarry to the south or even burnt cinders for use in coking foundry steel in the Chinese industrial zones to the north. He would have wished for a hopper full of feathers, but this was all the break-fall fate would hand him. As it stood, even if he hit the center of the hopper full-square, he could still risk shattering every bone in his body.

But there was no other choice, no other option. He was already falling to earth.

Trencrom angled his plunge like a chutist in the first stage of free fall. Willing himself to relax as much as possible, willing himself into a man-sized feather whose lightness would be his protection against injury, against the imminence of death.

He now fell parallel to the approaching train, passing over the clattering boxcars immediately in line before the hopper that was his goal and his salvation. He cleared the first boxcar, then the second, then—almost willing his body to lift as his angle of descent just topped the edge of the third car's rear—he soared directly over the hopper that was his intended target.

Now he saw that it wasn't coal that it contained. It was something else. Something duller and probably harder, coarser. Likely cinders. Rough, jagged-edged cinders. It didn't matter. As long as the material was not a solid mass, as long as it could give and move beneath him, break the shock of his fall. Whatever else it was, let it be only that, he silently intoned.

Trencrom now scissored his arms and legs together, then bore downward with a sudden jerk of abdominal muscles and struck the middle of the hopper high on his shoulder, slamming his head against its iron wall, hitting it hard on the temple and along the side of his jaw. He could already taste the hot, coppery tang of blood in his mouth. He could already feel the pale ghost of consciousness leaving him, deserting him like a rat scurrying down an anchor chain, trickling from his brain like blood or a hissing jet of living smoke. He made one last effort before he passed out or died where he lay.

Trencrom still had comms.

Overhead, in the Stallion that was hovering only because the guns of the Snake Handlers were trained on Stavenage and his aircrew, Trencrom's voice came faintly over the secure SINCGARS network.

"I made it . . . still alive . . . clear the hell out . . . an order . . ."

Static, harsh and crackling like a slave master's whip, now claimed the faint, fading tones of the distant human voice. Those in the Stallion waited, watching the train pass into the needle eye of a vanishing point in a web of all-enshrouding night, its steam whistle sounding mournfully, like a funeral dirge, as the express freight raced onward toward the distant mountains to the north. And then, when it had completely disappeared from view, the chopper also turned and continued its fugitive, headlong flight to the sea.

Ice Trencrom was gone. Maybe he was history. There was nothing any of his teammates could do for him any longer. They lowered their weapons and bowed their heads in collective despair.

Below the departing Sea Stallion, lying broken and bloodied on a heap of furnace slag, Trencrom's limp body had already crossed the border and passed from North Korea into the territory of its large neighbor to the east.

Into Russia.

14
PLAYING A WILD CARD

KOREA, NORTH OF DEMILITARIZED ZONE
0217 Hours Zulu, War Day Twenty-one

The Spirits were airborne.

The black, manta-shaped B-2 bomber aircraft were hours en route from Navajo Lake, New Mexico, where they were based at the 1st Special Aviation airwing. With their 3,000-mile range, the Spirits did not require forward basing like their less stealthy and less fleet cousins, the F-117A Nighthawks.

The six-plane strike package was the largest B-2 combat mission ever flown. Each member of the aircrew knew the importance of dismantling the missile installations and chemical weapons plants programmed into the sortie's targeting computers. Each of the planes carried a mix of joint air-to-surface standoff missiles, or JASSMs, which were long-range fire-and-forget weapons, and heavyweight JDAM air-to-ground munitions (ATGM) equipped with GPS precision guidance packages.

The GPS upgrade kits enabled the Spirits to deliver the half- and one-ton ATGMs to their targets by internal sensors and uplinkage to the array of military GPS satellites in orbit around the earth. Unlike the Paveway guidance kits of the Gulf War era, the JDAM upgrade required no laser sighting and was effective in all weather conditions.

The air tasking order, or ATO, of which the B-2 stealth bombers were a part was continuous and complex, involving the entire panoply of NATO airpower muscle. Prior to the last forty-eight hours, most cross-DMZ tac-air strikes had been made by cruise missiles, long-range artillery, and the occasional fighter sortie. Grounded fighter jocks and bomber crews had chafed at being held back on a short leash.

But the picture had changed practically overnight. Suddenly the war dogs found their leashes tossed aside and the scent of blood thick in their nostrils. Attack briefings were being regularly held at NATO coalition air bases from Seoul to Okinawa, Japan, and the earsplitting whine of jet turbines catapulting combat aircraft into the thundering night became a familiar sound in-theater.

Nothing official had been said concerning Medusa. But reports had leaked out that North Korea's main nuclear weapons installation had been obliterated and that its long-range missile force was history. The remnants of its unconventional arsenal were to be finished off before the odds and ends could be assembled into useable missiles.

The stealth bombers were to play important roles in the allied mop-up campaign. In a short while, the strike package would go hunting DPRK Scuds. First, they would need to refill their tanks for the last leg of their inbound flight.

Like a flock of gigantic bats, the six stealth planes jockeyed into position to drink fuel from the trio of KC-135s. The tankers had been orbiting the RV point near a spit of land, 400 nautical miles west of the international date line, named Marcus Island, part of the U.S.-administered Marianas chain, though distant from the main archipelago.

The tanker crew was ready for the planes, which came in for air-to-air refueling showing red identification strobes and were greenly visible on both the FLIR (forward-looking infrared) cockpit scopes and the nightscopes strapped to the heads of crew members who worked the hose-and-drogue lash-up through which the fuel was pumped into the B-2s.

The Spirits fueled up in two three-plane waves. It took less than a half hour for AAR to begin and end from the moment the first of the 1,000 pounds of JP7 avgas began fueling the first B-2's tanks until the last plane had taken its drink.

The stealths now had enough fuel to fly their mission deep into North Korean territory and return for a second refueling on their return journey. Two by two, the KC-135's aircrew watched the red strobes vanish into the night. The last pair of Spirits were visible on FLIR for a few moments longer, then they, too, were swallowed up by the engulfing darkness.

They were also invisible to the tankers' radars.

It was eerie, as if they had never existed.

0308 Hours Zulu, War Day Twenty-one

The "aliens"—a sortie of F-22 Raptors—had streaked across the darkened sky at 60,000 feet at supercruise velocities, tearing along at Mach 1.2 without needing to go to afterburner. Lockheed engineers had come up with the "alien" tag from the Sigourney Weaver movies because the Raptor struck from out of nowhere and never missed.

Apart from the stealthy design—the Raptor's radar cross section, or RCS, is approximately the same size as a B-2 bomber's—the fighter is also equipped with LPI radar, a low-probability-of-intercept radar whose emissions are hard to fingerprint by unfriendly threat sensors.

Only a short time ago the dull gray air dominance fighters had taken off from the USAF air base at Kadena, Japan, their two-dimensional F-119 thrust-vectoring engines crying barbaric yawps as they catapulted the planes skyward. The bypass turbofan power plants are more powerful and efficient than those of the F-15, the Raptor's predecessor, giving the plane the ability to cruise at supersonic speeds at normal military power, that is, without firewalling to afterburner.

Minutes after takeoff, the aliens had topped off their tanks high above the Korea Strait, which separated the Japanese port city of Hiroshima from the South Korean port city of Pusan. Fully tanked, the planes had a formidable combat range of almost 2,000 miles, enough to get them to their kill baskets and back again without additional AAR.

At 20,000 feet over the Sea of Japan, the Raptors banked steeply and turned. The F-22s' inertial navigation systems had the target coordinates already loaded in memory. The pilots set INS to active and let their inertial guidance computers fly inbound vectors.

The sortie now approached the final leg of its bombing run. INS had brought the attack jets in close, but terrain avoidance radar now took control as the sortie dropped to a terminal altitude no higher than 600 feet off the ground.

The TOT list called their primary target Objective Zebra. It was designated on the TOT as "a mobile ground radar installation affording early warning coverage to DPRK forces along the line Wonsan-Suan." The description, though succinctly put, said it all.

A surveillance overflight earlier that morning by a TR-1 spy plane had brought back pictures of a cluster of boxy, tracked, M-113–type vehicles and smaller satellite trucks sprouting mast-mounted radar dishes. Defense Intelligence Agency photo analysis identified the battery as a 30N6 Flap Lid two-element package composed of radar truck and mobile command post.

The system wasn't state of the art, but it could prove effective against low-to medium-altitude targets, giving unfriendly SAM sites farther north advance warning and additional engagement time against coalition air strikes. Definitely a good candidate for annihilation because of the threat it posed to NATO tac-air forces.

Load-out inventory for the F-22s had been calculated against the mission objectives, combat radius, and other factors. The sortie's primary attack munition would be the

AGM-88 HARM, a high-speed antiradar missile optimized for destroying SAM and ground radar sites.

The AGM-88 was a standoff ATGM with a range of twenty-five nautical miles. Once the missile has fingerprinted the emissions of a target radar, even an emergency shutdown won't faze it. The HARM simply defaults to backup navigation data and remembers the target's last position. At a speed of Mach 3 or better, even mobile radars don't have enough time to get out of HARM's way.

AIM-120C AMRAAMs were reserved for use against the secondary targets, collectively called Objective Impala. The AMRAAMs were beyond-visual-range, or BVR, weapons that could strike beyond the shooter's line of sight. As soon as Objective Zebra was down, the F-22s would launch their AMRAAMs on these secondary targets, miles away.

The planes also carried aerial intercept missile (AIM-9M) Sidewinders for air-to-air combat. The AGM-88s and AIM-120 AMRAAMs were for use in the mission. The AIM-9Ms were purely for backup in case of trouble on the outbound flight.

At the point of the spear of metal, electronics, and high explosive, the Raptor flight leader sped over the nap of the earth at sub-Mach velocities, his wingman close behind. In the mountainous northern region where the strike jets now hurtled, the North Koreans had their mobile ground radars strung out like the warp and woof of a crisscrossing net. Intelligence had identified some of the radar outposts but not all; there were sure to be radars NATO didn't know about lurking unseen amid the hills and forests.

Set up on trucks, their pivoting pulse-Doppler dishes scanned the terrain for several miles around. But the very act of scanning contributed to the invisibility of the F-22 sortie. Doppler echoes bounced off hills, careened up the slopes of valleys, and were absorbed by foliage and water, creating an effect called ground clutter.

This effect was heaviest "down in the weeds" where the Raptors flew. Here, the stealthy angles and curves of the Raptors' airframes meshed with the Doppler hiss that rose from the earth in an electronic cacophony of white noise.

The sortie reached its initial point, swept past the IP, then popped up above the rift valley that had screened the attack force from view. Objective Zebra lay dead ahead on the plateau above. The Flap Lid radar trucks were visible through the F-22 cockpit canopies now, but the noise of the approaching sortie had been detected by triple-A batteries surrounding the installation, and these now opened up.

Intense tracer fire instantly erupted from the ring of ZSU-23-4 Shilka antiaircraft guns, and rocket fire streaked upward from man-portable Blowpipe launchers. The Raptor pilots were wary; they knew that enemy radar was more effective in slant range than in other modes, and this was the case as they swept in for missile release.

The Raptor pilots—the F-22 had no backseaters—uncaged their war loads as soon as the AGM-88s reported target ID and confirm, side-breaking as soon as the launch-and-leave missiles cut loose. The HARMs were left to seek and destroy Zebra on their own, and they were quite capable of doing so.

The sortie's pilots maxed their throttles, and the planes sped into the night as the beam-riding HARMs, locked onto unfriendly electronic emissions, plowed into the radar trucks, taking the installation out in a combined flurry of explosions that sent a massive fireball ballooning into the night sky and lighting up the mountains for miles around.

The Raptors next sped to their secondary target IP at full military power, where their internal AN/APG-77 target acquisition radar locked onto the new TOT coordinates. Seconds later, the Raptor crews had uncaged their AIM-120C war loads and hustled away. Independent radars, infrared sensors, and computer processors in the nose and body of each AMRAAM would take the missiles the remaining distances. Lighter now by thousands of pounds of ordnance, the Raptors lit off their thrust-vectoring supercruise engines, stood on their tails in ballistic climbs, and gained altitude with meteoric velocity, swinging back in the direction of their inbound tracks.

Behind them, the first thunderclaps that marked the AM-RAAMs exploding on their targets came rolling and booming across the landscape. The night was strobed by a succession of blinding magnesium-white flashes generated by a pulsed whirlwind of synchronized munitions strikes. Screaming fireballs rose on roiling pillars from what had been a chemical weapons manufacturing plant as jeering tongues of flame flaunted death at heaven and made the mountains rumble to their roots.

Heavy black smoke followed in the wake of the explosions, billowing and swirling upward in a dense, coiling pillar, like something out of a Bible story. The enemy never even knew what had hit it.

0335 Hours Zulu, War Day Twenty-one

Though he was temporarily safe inside an underground bunker complex a few miles north of Pyongyang, Kim Jong-il was nevertheless a seriously troubled man.

For the last three days and nights, the supreme commander of the DPRK's armed forces had watched the military might of NATO steadily dismantle his weapons, communications, and logistical infrastructure. Piece by piece, it was being blown apart, burned to cinders, smashed to wreckage, and there was nothing that Kim could do about it.

For years, Kim had waged a war of words and bluster against the West, backstopped by his country's growing WMD arsenal. But he had made the fatal mistake of believing his own propaganda, and now he knew there was no way out.

Kim had few remaining options. Basically, there were three: He could either surrender, continue to fight, or bolt and run. Each way, he would certainly lose.

Surrender would mean the further curtailment of his sovereignty and interference in national political matters by the hated South Koreans. It would be the same as simply handing everything over to the Americans and the Japanese, perhaps even to Beijing.

Continuing the fight would pose the added risk of mutiny by his own generals. Already there were whispers in the corridors. Kim's supporters were defecting, and his enemies were growing increasingly bold.

Fleeing to a place of sanctuary was his only realistic choice, but that, too, would probably lead nowhere. Only in China could he expect to find permanent asylum, but Beijing had made it clear it did not want him.

For the moment, Kim would stand and fight. He had made this bluntly known to his general staff at their last meeting. The meeting had been held in the adjoining war room, and as usual, Kim had done virtually all of the talking. He still had a loyal Praetorian guard of handpicked special forces troops, and he still sufficiently intimidated the CINCs so that they did his bidding without protest. The CINCs had remained silent while he outlined his plan, knowing their place was to listen and obey.

Kim had told them that there was yet one wild card left: the stockpile of chemical weapons hidden from all eyes but his own. There was enough toxic agent still in reserve to arm two medium-range ballistic missiles that could reach Los Angeles. He had decided to launch them both, and he ordered preparations made.

The Americans and their NATO puppets would not win. Never. They would see things differently when millions of their countrymen lay gasping out their last breaths in the streets of America's largest city. The tide of war would turn then. The invaders would have no recourse but to sue for peace.

Kim signaled to his aides that he was ready for the recording technicians. Within minutes, he belligerently faced their cameras and microphones and began the videotaped speech that would be delivered to the global media.

Yet the words of defiance and threats of retribution were out of character with the pale, pudgy face, the moist, blank eyes, and the thin, bloodless lips of the overgrown, visibly aging boy who had propelled two hemispheres toward war. Within a matter of hours, the pathetic display would be viewed on millions of televisions and computer screens around the world and would help harden public resolve to see the war through, no matter what the cost.

What few, including Kim himself, realized was that though intimidated, members of his general staff were already in contact with the Japanese Nibetsu, and through it with its allied service, the American Central Intelligence Agency.

The defecting CINCs were saying the very opposite of what their leader had told the media. A coup was imminent, they avowed, and Kim would be dead within a matter of days. After this, they would be willing to talk surrender.

0346 Hours Zulu, War Day Twenty-one

The six-plane B-2 strike package cruised at 60,000 feet, dropping altitude as it approached its targets from a south-westerly flight vector. As the altimeter numbers fell, the flight crews scrolled through their computerized mission checklists, monitored INS steer-point data, diagnostically checked the integrity of ordnance delivery systems and their backups, and went about a variety of other routine maintenance procedures. Every system or its backup had to be fully operational for a Spirit to continue toward its target. If not, it would abort and return to base.

The planes were now scattered across the northeastern quadrant of the Hansan region of the Korean Peninsula, having broken into three two-bomber strike packages after passing the mission's initial point.

The Spirits would never drop far below a 30,000-foot service ceiling. Unlike fighters, they possessed neither the speed nor the terrain avoidance radars for ground-hugging flight. Nor were the B-2s equipped with air-to-air-missiles, other defensive ordnance, or guns. Their single protection was stealth and the darkness in which their stealthiness rendered them invisible to unfriendly forces.

Under most circumstances, this would be all the protection the B-2s would need. The cloak of stealth worn by the Spirits was more advanced than any other low-observable aircraft in the world, including the F-22 Raptor, the next stealthiest production-model combat plane.

The B-2's airframe had been machined to eliminate even the seams joining individual sections. The airframe was covered with a porous black foam that was more like a frying pan's Teflon coating than ordinary paint. This radar-absorbent outer skin was bonded onto the Spirit's fuselage, while angles and curves of the airframe were engineered to dissipate the reflections of radar energies glancing off the plane's surface.

The B-2's stealthiness involved more than met the eye, though. The external features were considered passive stealth features. The B-2 also could also employ active stealth capabilities using electronic countermeasures, if necessary. During extremely hazardous combat missions, an electronic warfare officer might occupy the B-2's optional third crew station in the cabin directly behind the pilot and WSO.

But countermeasures are also available on B-2 missions flown by the normal two-man crew. In such cases, the WSO is entrusted with controlling them along with the stealth's offensive weapons. Such was the case tonight, as the Spirits slipped through radar nets protecting North Korean airspace like the ghosts of the dead for which they were named.

Two by two, the B-2 mission swept in unseen, dropped its ordnance on its targets, and turned to begin its outbound flight. It left behind it a broad swathe of destruction that reduced mobile SAM, Scud, and MRBM launchers, weapons manufacture and storage sites, and other strategic bombing targets to flaming wreckage and scorched, scarred, pitted, cratered earth.

Once safe over the Sea of Japan, they would rendezvous with their tankers and return to their bases in the United States, Japan, and Europe for maintenance, refueling, and rearmament. Then the Spirits would be sent out again to further degrade the enemy's offensive capabilities as the dark sword of the allied strategic air campaign.

0800 Hours Zulu, War Day Twenty-one

The SR-71 Blackbird, which pilots have christened "Habu" after a semimythological snake, lifted off from the 1st Strategic Aviation Wing's runways at Kadena AFB, emitting its telltale double sonic boom as it cruised to its tanking altitude and RV'd with a KC-135 to fill its tanks with JP7.

The Habu's "tanks" were more aptly called its airframe which, from nose to tail section, including its delta wings, were stuffed with go-juice. In fact, the Habu could be considered one immense fuel tank, crammed so full of JP7 that-avgas leaked from between the seams of its riveted fuselage plates at takeoff.

Yet hardly a drop of jet propulsion gasoline would go to waste. At a rate of fuel consumption greater than two tons per second, most of that fuel would be burned off by the time the aircraft returned to Kadena on completion of its surveillance mission an hour later.

The Blackbird was a two-seater, and its double-canopy cockpit accommodated a pilot and a reconnaissance systems operator, or RSO. The RSO sometimes doubled as weapons systems officer, but not on this mission; this SR version had no offensive capability, just its imaging sensors. These were prodigious. Apart from high-resolution cameras, the plane carried infrared and radar imaging pods along the underside of its fuselage.

This morning's mission was a BDA run. The plane was using the golden time, when the morning air is clear and free of thermals and the slant of the newly risen sun highlights ground features with stark clarity, to conduct part of the strike coalition's battle damage assessments.

The imaging was transmitted in real time to a network of receiving stations on land and sea and was fed into the SPINTCOM network in a matter of seconds. Then it could be analyzed as part of the stream of BDA data pouring in from other Habus, intelligence satellites, and UAVs looking over the carnage visited on North Korea by the missile and bomb strikes during the preceding hours of darkness.

0909 Hours Zulu, War Day Twenty-one

The B-1B Lancers with their fighter support of F-15C Eagles came rumbling over their strike baskets deep inside North Korea. Each strategic bomber carried a war load of JDAM GPS-guided iron bombs, BLU-109 "dumb" 2,000 pounders and AIM-120C AMRAAMs. With enemy air defenses seriously degraded by the previous NATO air strikes, they came rolling into their kill boxes virtually unimpeded.

The F-15C Eagles continued to ride shotgun for the B-1Bs because of the danger of North Korean MiGs, but this danger was considered a slim one. The DPRK's air force had never been a very credible threat. In the main, the threats that U.S. fighters had to contend with from Kim's military were SAMs rather than MiGs. Today's early morning's bomb run was no exception.

The B-1B sortie came highballing in, identified their targets, and dropped their sticks of heavy ordnance on enemy emplacements. The North Korean soldiers were dug in deep in fortified underground bunkers to protect them against ATGM strikes. Just the same, the amount of ordnance the Lancers could put on target was staggering, and both the JDAM and BLU-109 bombs carried by the Lancer were optimized for penetrating and destroying hard and deeply buried strategic targets.

Within the kill boxes, the North Koreans huddled like rats under the layers of earth, concrete, steel, and rock, feeling the world shake and convulse around them. The lethal munitions thunder continued for hours, with wave after wave of Lancers coming on station, jettisoning their war loads, returning to base, and coming back again for yet another bombing attack.

There was no escape from the relentless, hammering round-the-clock punishment. Unlucky enemy forces went stark raving mad. The lucky ones simply died.

Millions of TV screens throughout the world filled with the fleshy face of North Korean dictator Kim Jong-il as the camera zoomed in for a tight shot. While Kim spoke, the voices of interpreters in scores of languages translated the North Korean maximum leader's words of defiance and vengeance.

"The Democratic People's Republic of Korea will never surrender," he pledged. The North Korean people were a peace-loving nation, he added. Kim wanted the world to know that they were fighting only because the DPRK had been attacked by NATO in an unprovoked war of aggression.

But, Kim added, it would do the warmongers no good. "We have fearsome weapons at our disposal that we will use if this armed aggression continues," he warned. "The imperialist aggressors and their vicious running dogs will never prevail. They must know this."

"If they do not immediately cease hostilities and withdraw from the Korean Peninsula, millions in their homelands will have cause to regret their leaders' folly! Millions will reap the whirlwind of evil and repentance sown by the wicked cowards who have led them blindly into this unjust war!"

As the pudgy leader continued to hector through the secondhand medium of simultaneous translation, ton after ton of high explosives raining down north of the DMZ were bombing Kim's nation back into the stone age with relentless efficiency, utterly unopposed by any credible military force.

Still, Kim's threats were to be taken seriously. At the top of the ATO bombing list were the NBC weapons complexes, Scud parks, and fixed missile launch sites that made up the DPRK's unconventional weapons delivery capability. That capability had been severely degraded but not completely destroyed. Until it no longer existed, Kim could still make good on his threats. Millions might die.

15

IN HARM'S WAY

TIRANE, ALBANIA

The revolution that was to bathe Tirane in blood had begun ten years before at the national university on the north end of Martyrs of the Nation Boulevard. It was to finish where the boulevard terminated, at the city center across the River Lana at Skandenberg Square, where the Sov-bloc-style Party House and the ultramodern Congress Hall stood as the ruling party's historic bastions.

From the university, where a poisonous hatred of the regime festered, Martyrs of the Nation Boulevard might be likened to the wound channel of a bullet that let infection reach the nation's heart. But that was not how Zulqifar Taalib looked at it. Taalib saw the broad, almost traffic-free boulevard—Tirane was a city free of many vehicles by choice, and its inhabitants were inveterate strollers and joggers—as a short fuse leading to a keg of TNT.

During Taalib's student days in the early 1990s, the future

Albanian dictator—the world would call him a "Second Qaddafi"—liked to stand on the university's roof and stare out across the knife-straight boulevard, out over the river, and into the heart of the city.

He would later write in his own version of Qaddafi's *Green Book* of envisioning a "liquid fire, almost like volcanic magma, coursing up the boulevard and setting the government buildings on Skandenberg Square aflame." That, he went on in his writings, "was my vision of the fire of revolution. A fire that even in those youthful student days I knew would come with the utter certainty of unshakable conviction."

Taalib's vision had been inspired by Qaddafi, a fact he openly acknowledged, and which would become a bridge linking the aging Libyan strongman with his young protégé. Taalib had taken Qaddafi's *Green Book*, a three-volume exposition of the "Brother Colonel's" communist-Muslim philosophy, as his Koran.

From the *Green Book*, Taalib had established the tenets of his own "Eagle's Revolution" that was to inflame a group of students who, like Taalib, were destined to join the ranks of Albania's future military elite. The eagle is the national symbol, its black form, wings outspread, a sinister presence on the Albanian flag. The *Republika Popullore Shqiperise*, or Land of the Eagle, as Albania is officially known, lays claim to a warrior heritage that has marked the tiny country for centuries.

Throughout the Cold War, Albania practiced an armed neutrality between East and West. The citizens of all countries could easily receive visas, except for those of two hated enemies who were denied entry: the United States and the Soviet Union. In 1968, the year the Russian army rolled unopposed into Prague, tiny Albania had declared an armed truce against both masters of the bipolar Cold War world and gone its own separate way. In that year, Albania had quit the Warsaw Pact and left the ranks of the Soviet bloc.

In that year also, Albania had begun the most extensive array of defensive fortifications along its borders since the erection of Nazi Germany's West Wall along the beachheads of Normandy, or the earlier Maginot Line of France. Like its predecessors, the Albanians had constructed thousands of concrete-and-steel bunkers, pillboxes, and heavy gun embrasures at every potentially vulnerable point.

In lines and clusters, they marched across valleys and mountains. They straddled roads, they watched over passes, guarded the approaches to cities and towns, and they brooded over the Adriatic Sea along the western coastline. The bunkers, most of them shaped like concrete igloos, with their slitted gun ports, were literally everywhere. They made Albania the most heavily defended nation in the world, and its armed forces, which consumed more than two-thirds of the country's GNP, was the expression in arms and armor of the concrete bumps on Albania's landscape.

During Taalib's roughly ten years in the army, what was to become the Albanian People's Party began to coalesce around the young colonel as electrons around a nucleus. During those evolutionary years, Taalib worked toward positioning what were to be Albania's future revolutionary leaders in posts of prominence throughout the military.

By the time the Second Korean War had broken out, the plotters were ready to move, and the time was ripe; the attention of the Americans, the Russians, and NATO were all focused elsewhere. With covert financing from Iran and solidarity with the Chechens and other Muslims of the Southern Caucasus, Taalib's group began its march up Martyrs of the Nation Boulevard. The liquid fire that Taalib had seen as a student had finally burned down its fuse.

The explosion was almost an anticlimax.

The first the world learned about Zulqifar Taalib was the sight of the young man in military BDUs and a maroon paratrooper's beret boldly entering the Hall of the Party where Congress was in session. The young colonel marched in at the head of a group of similarly clad followers, each as resolute as he was. Those inside the chamber briefly caught the stench of cordite wafting in through the breached door; bodies littered the hall outside as a result of the firefight that had gained the group entrance. The leader bore a Czech Skorpion machine pistol, carried high in one raised hand.

More bloodshed followed. Recorded by the security cameras trained on the Hall of the Party, the leader ran toward the dais as his followers fanned out, holding their rifles on the members of Congress in the auditorium. Reaching the dais, he pointed the Skorpion at the Albanian leader, President Malik Hoxha.

There was a heated exchange between the two, and then Hoxha was shot down in cold blood, his head blown to pieces by a point-blank burst of automatic fire. The other leaders rose to flee, some to fight, but at their chief's signal, the gunmen positioned around the auditorium also opened up with their weapons. The massacre of the old guard had begun. The cloying stench of death gathered in the chamber as the auditorium became batiked in blood.

Later, other cameras would record the imposition of martial law over Tirane and show the columns of tanks and armored personnel carriers choking the intersections and the armed guerillas who glared into the lenses with unabashed defiance. The cameras would also show those branded as traitors being rounded up and carted to the Partizan Sportspalast, where kangaroo courts would move them quickly from mock trial to firing squad.

Still later, the new leader would appear in military dress, the maroon beret still set rakishly on his head, and declare the birth of a new regime. Taalib would also declare that regime's apocalyptic intentions.

Across the eastern border, in Kosovo, brother and sister Albanian Muslims would not be forgotten, pledged Taalib. The hated Serbs would be driven out and wiped off the face of the earth. This Taalib promised, holding up his gun, adding in English, "KFOR goes too. . . ."

The black eagle of Illyria had spread its millennial wings.

KHAZAR AUTONOMOUS REGION, C.I.S.

Several hundred miles to the east, across the Black and Caspian Seas, across the blasted ruins of Grozny in the Caucasus, up past the salt wastes of the Aral Sea and beyond the fabled caravansaries of Tashkent, in the windswept Mongol country of the Kirghiz Steppes, Ice Trencrom had awakened to yet another day in captivity, in a freezing cell with a large, gray rat for company.

Trencrom had discovered the rat perched on his chest one morning. The rat stared at him with beady black eyes, the short white whiskers on its muzzle twitching. Trencrom had lashed out in revulsion, and the rat disappeared into a crevice in the masonry wall, squeaking in fright.

But early the next morning, it was back again. This time Trencrom studied the creature instead of letting reflex take over. After a while, he realized that the rat probably only wanted some of his body heat; the air temperature was below freezing.

Acting on impulse, Trencrom slowly reached under the thin mattress and produced a crust of bread he'd hoarded. He had gotten into the POW's habit of saving bits and pieces of meals against a time when his captors might no longer choose to feed him.

Now Trencrom held out the stale pill of bread to the rat, who took it in its handlike, pink forepaws. Trencrom watched the rodent deftly whirl the morsel around in its remarkably human-looking hands as it nibbled off little bits, its pink, almost reptilian tail twitching with pleasure, until nothing was left. Then, after finishing its breakfast, the rat began cleaning itself off, licking its paws, tail, and fur with quick and briskly precise motions. In the midst of this grooming, it suddenly stood up on its hind legs, listening intently and sniffing the frigid air.

Moments later, it had disappeared into its hole again. Soon after that, Trencrom had heard what the rat's keen senses had detected earlier: the sound of heavy boots thudding on bare stone, signal of another session with the military interrogator.

Awakening in darkness later that night, Trencrom discovered the gray rat perched where he'd found it before. The rat's appearance earned it yet another morsel of stale bread.

He also received a name: Trencrom would call him Attila, he decided.

◆   ◆   ◆

Now, as he fed Attila the rat yet another Kerghiz continental breakfast, Trencrom thought back to the days since his capture. As planned, Trencrom had fallen back on the cover story he'd memorized in the event of being taken prisoner.

He was an American drug runner who had been stranded in the hinterland by the outbreak of war and had been trying to sneak across the border into either Russia or China. He'd been drunk and had knocked himself unconscious trying to board an outbound freight train in the middle of the night. It was a thin cover, thin as hoar frost, but in the absence of any form of identification or strong motivation by his captors to ferret out the truth, it had held up so far.

Though Trencrom's weapons-dismantling business made him known throughout the world, he was notoriously camera shy and professionally elusive to the media. His name was known but not his face, and he hadn't given his captors his name. He knew that in time his identity would be discovered, but he hoped to beat the clock.

Trencrom knew that already steps would certainly have been taken to arrange for a quiet release in the interest of both the former Soviets and the U.S. It was to the advantage of no one concerned to keep him prisoner. Especially since the Snake Handlers' nuclear strike on Medusa had taken place with the tacit approval of C.I.S. President Grigorenko himself. Without Russian complicity in the strike, it would never have been ordered by the White House.

Trencrom's treatment had been harsh but bearable. He had found his captors more perplexed concerning what to do with him than anything else. By their standards, he was being well fed and well treated. There were almost daily interrogation sessions, but no beatings. The border guards and internal security officers were clearly not buying his cover but were unsure of how to proceed.

Attila suddenly stood up on his hind legs. He sniffed the air, then disappeared into one of his numerous holes. Trencrom could hear nothing, but he knew that the rat's senses were as reliable as early-warning radar. He was already sitting up on his cot as the guards came around, keys jangled, and the cell door creaked dolefully open. They left him with a bowl of vile-smelling grease and hot liquid and a hunk of stale, maggoty bread. Coffee and danish, Russian prison-style. Trencrom ate, starting with the stuff that resembled coffee. It was all he'd get until much later.

MOSCOW

Across the Urals and hundreds of miles to the northeast, Russian president Dimitri Grigorenko was also a man with troubles, and these were about to get much worse. Unlike Trencrom and the gunned-down president of Albania, however, Grigorenko knew full well that treason had reared its pugnacious Gorgon head.

Grigorenko had seen storm warnings aplenty. Vadim Bogomelov had sown the seeds of anarchy in the squares and on the boulevards of Russian cities from Moscow to Saint Petersburg.

Grigorenko had chosen not to heed the warnings of his cabinet to jail the neo-Stalinist agitator under numerous civil statutes. He had feared creating a martyr. But rumors—vague ones but rumors nonetheless—had begun to leak out that nuclear weapons had been used by the Americans in North Korea. The administration had issued denials, but they were not believed.

Grigorenko realized he had committed a major political blunder. The use of a nuclear weapon within a few dozen kilometers of the Russian border was bound to have repercussions. It offended not only the hard-liners on the right, who saw it as an affront to Russian sovereignty, but the environmentalists and business interests, who saw it as the West spreading toxic fallout on Russian lands.

Bogomelov and his fanatical clique had seized on the rumors with both fists. Overnight, they had found an issue that could polarize the entire country.

Day in, day out, Bogomelov had attacked Grigorenko, now for the first time daring to make disdainful references to the *enko* ending of his surname and of the Ukrainian familial origins that surname implied.

Bogomelov's veiled insults to Grigorenko's Russianness and patriotism were beginning to find listeners among the discontented. His other efforts at undermining the presidency had also paid dividends.

The cafés, plazas, and street corners were as full of discord as the media, and terror bombings—now an index of the level of public discontent—had dramatically increased. New ethnic rioting in the Central Asian province of Nagorno-Karabakh had not helped matters.

Grigorenko, who bystanders had seen seated in the back of the black Zil limousine, was on his way to his dacha in the wooded hills of Archangelskoye outside Moscow for a weekend of informal talks with his cabinet on the crisis faced by his administration.

The tide of anarchy had to be stemmed, or the country would fly apart by centrifugal force. But he could not think at the Kremlin, and the closeness to the center of the city was stifling. He needed a brief change, or he felt he would go mad.

The Zil had made the turnoff onto the Ring Road, the circular highway that surrounds Moscow the way the Peripherique or the Beltway encircle their respective cities of Paris and Washington, D.C., when the Hind gunship suddenly made its appearance overhead.

At first it was dismissed by the Zil's occupant, although when Grigorenko glanced upward, his alarm betrayed a former soldier's combat instincts on alert. Still, nothing happened. The chopper remained overhead, shadowing the vehicle at a low hover. Those in the Zil assumed that it had been sent as part of the president's protection.

They were wrong, however. Fatally wrong. The helicopter had hovered for hidden videocam crews in the air and on the ground to position themselves for better coverage of what was to come next and for the Zil to draw abreast of backup gunmen behind high-powered rifles who were at that moment positioned in storm drain openings lining the route of the motorcade's advance.

Those factions in the Ministry of Security and Internal Affairs, or MBVD, and the GRU who had planned the oncoming coup were taking no chances on failure. There would not be another aborted strike, no opportunity for a repeat of Boris Yeltsin's famous speech from atop a T-74 tank to spur on Muskovites to resist the plotters during the August revolt. They had learned from history. There would be no mistakes this time.

At the appointed moment, the signal was radioed to the assassination teams. The Hind gunship broke from its trailing pattern overhead and banked sharply right. At the same time, it gained altitude. With the Zil pinned in its gun sights, the pilot opened fire, raking the limousine with 12.7-millimeter rounds. The cameras recorded green dashes marking the paths of tracers slamming into the limousine. There would be no confusion about what had taken place.

The motorcade stopped dead. The presidential Zil was smashed in the first seconds of the attack. One camera zoomed in on the limo's interior.

Bulletproof safety glass that could not withstand the immense firepower of a multibarrel machine gun had shattered and now littered the blood-spattered corpses sprawled in hideous death postures. Another videocam caught the steam and smoke rising from the slug-pocked engine compartment and the chassis sagging on four blown-out tires, then the explosion as tracers ignited spilled fuel from the Zil's ruptured gas lines.

And for a finale, the inevitable aftermath of the attack: The flames were doused and Grigorenko's bloodied, bulletriddled corpse pulled from the vehicle by men in military BDUs, their faces masked, and flung disdainfully to the blood-smeared, shattered asphalt of the highway to serve as a bold decree that the government, like it or not, had changed hands, and as a lesson for the Russian people in the historical terms they best understood.

The message was crystal clear: The fate of Dimitri Pavlovich Grigorenko was also the fate of the hated forces of American-style capitalism that had infested the country. But Vadim Bogomelov would change all that.

♦ ♦ ♦

At approximately the same time as the videotaped imagery reached Russian media outlets, Army General Viktor Sergeivich Arbatov, chief of Russian Spetsnaz, or special forces, was preparing to leave his office in the "Fish Tank," the Russian equivalent of the American Pentagon building on the shores of the Potomac.

This was what the GRU complex located at the old Khodenka Aerodrome a few miles outside of greater Moscow had been nicknamed by the Russian military, a consequence of the four wings of the building being joined around a central quadrangle. Arbatov's departure was for the purpose of enjoying a late lunch in one of the nearby restaurants frequented by GRU staff; the commissary food had been giving him heartburn lately.

Arbatov discovered his lunch plans unexpectedly canceled when he heard the sudden commotion of running, stomping feet from the corridor outside and instantly knew what was happening. He had expected this, indeed had planned for it for months. Neither Arbatov nor his patron and friend, former general Dimitri Grigorenko, had been blind or deaf to the portentious call to revolt from the rightists in the Bogomelov camp—for in Russia it was the communists who were considered to be on the right of the political spectrum—and they had made contingency plans.

Galvanized into action, Arbatov pulled the cellular phone from his pocket and keyed in a preloaded number.

"Eskimo. Repeat, Eskimo," he said.

"Igloo," came the immediate reply. Help was on the way.

Arbatov next locked the door and pushed his heavy office

couch in front of it, barricading himself inside. Then he
snatched up the compact AKS-74 auto-rifle from where he
kept it propped beneath the top of his desk. For weeks the
bullpup AKS, equipped with an undermounted grenade
launcher, had been kept well lubricated and fully loaded in
the event it became necessary to use it.

As he hefted the weapon, Arbatov checked the clock on
the wall. He would need to hold them off for no more than
a few minutes. But that could be a lifetime under certain
circumstances. Cradling the weapon, Arbatov ran to the window, which looked out from one of the Fish Tank's outer
walls. In the distance he could already see the two black
spots moving in his direction.

Arbatov's attention was suddenly drawn to the locked door
of his office. Someone was shouting at him to open it up.
Moments later, the voice stopped, and the hammering of a
rifle butt took over. "Break it down," he finally heard the
hectoring voice shout. A few moments later, the sharp cutting
edge of a fire ax sliced through the door with the sickening
crunch of splintering wood.

By now the two helos Arbatov had summoned were only
a short distance away, the telltale silhouttes of the Hip transport and the Hind gunship growing ever larger against the
clear blue sky. Arbatov took a flare from his desk, lit it, and
jammed it against a nail he had hammered into the side of
the window days before. The helos homed in on the burning
corona of glowing red phosphorus.

Meanwhile, the door was quickly being hacked to splinters. Those on the other side were now trying to force it open
but were held back by the sofa he'd jammed against it. But
all Arbatov needed was another minute or two. The Hip was
already hovering above the top-floor window, and one of the
crewmen was crouching behind the open side hatch, getting
set to pitch a rope harness through the open window and into
the office.

The plan was for Arbatov to securely harness himself in
and let the helo pull him off the window, then winch him
inside, a modification on a STABO extraction maneuver

practiced by Spetsnaz and U.S. special forces. But a glance at the now staved-in door told Arbatov there wasn't time for that. Any moment, the *chekisti* would rush inside.

Yet there was no way to jump into the helo from the office window, not unless he could jump straight up, anyway. At least ten feet of empty space separated him from the safety of the hatch. Lack of clearance for the rotor blades prevented the helo from getting any closer. If he missed—and he was bound to miss—it was thirty stories straight down.

Men were rushing into the office by the time Arbatov securely harnessed himself and climbed onto the windowsill. But it was too late for them, and Arbatov now knew he might yet make it. As the helo gently pulled back, lifting him away from the window, Arbatov triggered the AKS-74's undermounted grenade launcher in which an eight-millimeter can grenade was nestled. There was a muffled report as the canister hit and exploded, quickly filling the office with tear gas, which boiled out the window in an acrid cloud.

As it turned out, the few seconds that the grenade strike had bought Arbatov was all the margin he needed. By the time the *chekisti* were back up and firing out the window, the rescue helos had flown out of effective small arms range.

They would proceed to a prepared landing and hide site in a remote corner of the 2,000-acre paratroop training camp maintained by Spetsnaz in the outlying Doupov region amid the heavily wooded Karlovya Forest. Here other travel arrangements, medical services, and forged ID were waiting. Arbatov and the small force of loyal Spetsnaz he had assembled would be long gone before the hide site was discovered.

WASHINGTON, D.C.

The Situation Room at the Pentagon's National Military Command Center was the focal point of a global communications network. For the past several hours, most of the news pouring into that focal point had been consistently bad.

At the center of the web, CJCS Buck Starkweather was the man on point. Starkweather had been fielding calls, Emails, and faxes from the Washington political establishment, from the media, and from his military colleagues around the world since the early morning hours when the news of the Grigorenko assassination and the successful putsch by rightest forces had broken.

Since then, Vadim Bogomolev had established himself in the Kremlin. Bogomolev had arrested the cabinet of the former C.I.S. president, had declared martial law, and was now in the process of dissolving the Russian Commonwealth and reinstituting the Union of Soviet Socialist Republics, reversing decades of slow, painful democratic reform.

As serious as this Russian coup d'etat was in and of itself, it stood out in even starker contrast if viewed as part of a larger mosaic of events, which is how Starkweather saw it. Starkweather was privy to a knowledge of certain events kept even from Congress.

These had included interference by unknown parties in direct orders the CJCS had issued to his field commanders in the Korean theater. That interference had affected everything from the deployment of tanks to the almost abortive nuclear strike on Medusa, a mission hampered by several unexplained snafus that had resulted in the loss and disappearance of Ice Trencrom.

The sudden chaos inside Russia came too close on the heels of everything else for it to be unconnected with that larger mosaic of events that Starkweather had discerned, a pattern that surely included the impersonation of his dead son by unknown parties. He suspected the shadow hand of the spooks, had suspected it for some time, in fact.

Specifically, Starkweather suspected the one covert intelligence organization large enough and powerful enough to influence events on a global scale yet not answerable to any other power on earth, including the White House: the NSA.

Starkweather was correct. Yet he had not taken his suppositions far enough. He did not suspect that the NSA had already targeted him as an obstacle to future plans and had marked him for removal.

16
WAR ZONES

General Wu Song-rhee, who was receiving orders from Pyongyang, held the handset of the field telephone to the side of his head, the better to hear for the thunder of exploding artillery rounds dropping nearby. Though the CINC came through loud and clear, Wu could scarcely believe his ears. He was to use his armored VII Mechanized, a tank brigade he had been holding in reserve, to stage a frontal assault through Phase Line Heron, a narrow corridor in the eastern sector in front of Naeju.

Wu immediately protested. The four-star on the other end could not be serious.

"Sir, the corridor is one in name only," he informed the CINC, General Kwan, chief of the North Korean joint staff, who was on the other end of the line. "The rugged country has made NATO lines thin locally. But the enemy knows it does not need to have defensive lines in depth. The Americans enjoy total air superiority. Any breakthrough we make will be short-lived. The salient would be encircled, and every one of our best tanks killed within an hour."

General Kwan would not listen. The orders had not originated from him. They had come from the supreme commander of DPRK forces. At the presidential palace in Pyongyang, Kim Jong-il crouched over his maps and made tactical decisions as though he were the reincarnation of Napoleon. His generals only relayed his orders. Should Wu not choose to obey, Kwan would have no choice other than to relieve him of command, meaning that Wu would face a firing squad by daybreak, next morning.

"After destroying enemy forces, VII Mechanized is to link up with the 2nd Armored Division at Wansin," Kwan went on. Wansin was approximately sixty kilometers to the northeast, and Wu knew the 2nd's commander, General Yonshu, to be an able soldier.

"Once you have joined forces, you will swing south and stage a flanking attack on the U.S. 1st Mechanized Brigade. You will crush the enemy and drive straight across the DMZ and enter Seoul. Once there, you will hold your position until relieved."

Wu listened, having no recourse but to follow orders. Yet it was madness. Utter insanity. The fact was that Yonshu's forces were encircled by the American 1st and 3rd Mechanized Brigades. The general would be lucky indeed if he could withdraw through a narrow corridor behind him, for it would soon be closed by the tightening U.S. noose. Wu should be doing the same, he knew. NATO forces were advancing at an incredible pace.

Even at that moment, fire from enemy artillery batteries and MLRS emplacements was drawing closer. In fact, Wu had been about to issue instructions to move his field headquarters out of range just before the call from headquarters had come in. All North Korean forces should be withdrawing to stage a final defense of the North's capital before Pyongyang was overwhelmed and forced to surrender unconditionally. This was the only rational option available. Anything else would pave the way toward utter disaster.

But instead, Kim was reenacting his own version of Hitler's final days. Locked inside his bunker, the North Korean dictator was shouting defiance and promising victory through superweapons that did not exist and sending more of his troops marching off into the NATO grinder.

Unfortunately, Wu's hands were tied. He could do nothing. He would follow orders or be sacked and shot as a traitor. The choice was not a difficult one to make. He picked up the handset and relayed the orders he had just received from the CINC to his divisional commanders at the front. Like Wu himself, they had no choice in the matter either.

0650 Hours Zulu, War Day Twenty-four

Overhead coverage would have shown USFORCECOM what was happening on the ground, but the armored push from North Korean VII Mechanized had exploited a gap in satellite surveillance caused by the destruction of a U.S. reconnaissance satellite. The first warnings of the movement of mechanized armor came from an SR-71 Blackbird making a dawn reconnaissance overflight on an east-west vector on the line Kasang-Sangchin.

The near-real-time photo intel transmitted by the Blackbird was at the USFORCECOM headquarters in Seoul after only a few minutes lag time caused by retransmission and signal processing.

Even as the first few hundred gigabytes of downloaded SR-71 PHOTINT were being routed through secure intranets and brought up on numerous screens in Seoul and other places, including the NMCC at the Pentagon and NATO headquarters in Brussels, intelligence analysts were rubbing their eyes and slurping hastily brewed black coffee. Something was up, and they wanted to know what it was all about.

At The Dark Tower in the Pentagon, half a world away from the action, the data was being viewed by General Crowley and his battle planning staff, the Sorcerer's Apprentices, just as they were being studied by CINCASIA, his

USFORCECOM CINCS, DCINCS, and divisional commanders in-theater. CJCS Starkweather also had the latest intelligence take available to him as hard copy printouts and also on the big screens at the NMCC Situation Room.

As the general watched, near-real-time satellite data from a Keyhole that had been rerouted to cover the region was painted across the big screen. *Incredible,* thought the CJCS. The DPRK had managed to pull at least a full tank battalion out of nowhere.

Incredible, but not unbelievable. Intelligence estimates had demonstrated an absence of first-line tanks and the destruction of older armor and decoys by NATO air strikes. This being the case, it was a sure bet that the North was squirreling its best armor underground in the miles upon miles of deep strategic tunnels they had been boring since the U.N. cease-fire of 1953 that marked the end of the first Korean War.

Starkweather picked up the secure phone link to USFORCECOM and dialed General Rupert Tillitson, the force commander and CINCASIA. The theater CINC's familiar gruff voice came on in minutes as his weathered face appeared on the video screen.

"How do you read this latest intel?" asked the CJCS.

"We expected something like this, Buck," CINCASIA replied. "But not to worry. We're ready for it. All Kim is doing is cutting his own throat. We've had continuous JSTARS coverage and photo intel of that sector. We know about every rivet of every tank tread that's out there, and we can take the armored force apart piece by piece."

"Then I can tell the president not to worry."

"You certainly can, Buck," CINCASIA answered. "My boys'll mop them up pretty as you please."

0700 Hours Zulu, War Day Twenty-four

The carrier battle group steamed up the wide gulf known as Korea Bay, aware that it was constantly under the watchful eyes of the Chinese 2nd Fleet. Beijing had been told of the impending arrival of the CBG in waters that, while technically not within China's sphere of legal maritime intervention, might nevertheless provoke the belligerence of the Chinese navy in response to a perceived incursion.

On the island at the top of the USS *Garfield*, a Nimitz-class nuclear aircraft carrier that steamed at the heart of the CBG, Captain Joe Arnold was not privy to the behind-the-scenes negotiations that had resulted in clearance for the U.S. to enter the gulf unopposed.

All Arnold knew was that his orders were to proceed with caution and to receive orders from PACFLTCOM before firing, should there be any hostile actions from the Chinese navy.

Arnold didn't much like those orders. What sane commander would? He had the chaplain write up a special prayer asking the Almighty to prevent the Chinese from doing anything stupid. Something like that had worked for Patton who, though a landlubber, had the right idea about certain things.

The skipper figured he needed all the help he could muster. Throughout the ships in the CBG, including his own, were over five thousand Marines and millions of tons of equipment for the first amphibious landing the United States was to stage since MacArthur's 1950 landing at Inchon.

0710 Hours Zulu, War Day Twenty-four

High above the battlefield, JSTARS flew its circular racetrack course. The Joint Strategic Tactical Airborne Radar System plane was a dedicated tactical command-and-control aircraft that looked down on the battlefield and could plot hundreds of simultaneous ground contacts. It was to mobile artillery and mechanized armor what AWACS was to combat planes.

JSTARS's long-range, air-to-ground surveillance systems were designed to locate, classify, and track multiple ground targets in daylight and darkness and under all weather conditions. Tank formations, supply convoys, airfields, troop movements, SAM sites, and Scud launchers were all part of what JSTARS saw, recognized, tracked, and reported on.

JSTARS consisted of two components, one airborne, the other based on the ground. The airborne component was the E-8C, a modified Boeing 707 equipped with a phased array radar in a twenty-six-foot-long canoe fairing located beneath the forward portion of the fuselage.

The computer-processed radar, which had a range of more than 120 miles, operated in synthetic aperture (SAR) mode, which provided extremely high-quality displays of targets under surveillance. The ground component was made up of multiple GSMs, or ground station modules, five-ton trucks equipped with Doppler radars and secure SINCGARS communications. Together, the system could provide real-time, wide-area tactical information to air and ground commanders.

In the air, JSTARS was attended by an escort of F15C Eagle fighters tasked with running interference for it in case any MiGs showed up to pay a visit. Three GSMs made up the ground component, protected by squads of humvees armed with heavy machine-guns and TOW missiles, and Bradleys bristling with weapons and carrying a squad of U.S. Army Rangers per APC. Guarding the GSMs wouldn't be easy, and every soldier assigned to that duty knew it. The GSMs were vulnerable targets, and the enemy would want to take them out.

0720 Hours Zulu, War Day Twenty-four

"Red Dog One to Ripper Jack. Report enemy armor at thirty klicks on a north-by-east azimuth."

"Copy that, Red Dog One."

The second voice belonged to the commander of the M1A2 Abrams tank brigade down below, called Task Force Ripper Jack after its CINC's radio call sign. Ripper Jack formed a screen line for the 3rd Mechanized Infantry Division, which was advancing only a few klicks behind the MBTs. Overhead, the squadron of RAH-66 Commanche light attack helicopters swept toward the mechanized enemy armor that was streaming toward Ripper Jack's position in a clanking, rumbling wall of steel.

Tanks and armored personnel carriers of the VII Mechanized formed the vanguard of the assault, with North Korean crunchies following in train in a massed formation—basic Soviet assault doctrine, Asian-style. According to the intel from USFORCECOM, the tanks were Russian T-74s, improved variants of Saddam's Gulf War–era T-72 MBTs. The T-74s were upgunned with bigger tubes, and they were better armored against the highly lethal sabot rounds fired by the Abrams and Challenger MBTs fielded by the U.S. and NATO.

They also had been retrofitted with thermal imaging gun sights of Belgian manufacture which, though not as good as those in the M1A2 Abrams, were still an improvement over what the Iraqis had in '91: *nothing* except ordinary optical sights, useless in darkness or smoke conditions.

The T-74s were the fastest and most maneuverable in the North Korean arsenal but, again, no match for the Abrams, which could give a vintage T-bird a run for its money on a city street. The Abrams was also considerably up-armored when compared to its adversary. Ton for ton, gun for gun, it was like matching a Love Bug against a Ferrari.

But the enemy had nevertheless gained a small tactical advantage in having the momentum of advance on its side. Breaking out of its pocket in the early morning hours, it had punched through thin NATO lines south of Haeju and had already swept aside resistance along a thirty-mile line of advance.

Some elements of the advance had already crossed the DMZ and were attempting a headlong rush toward Seoul. It wasn't exactly Guderian's panzers crashing through the Ardennes, but it did pose a serious military threat to the allied front lines.

Contact came a little after sunrise at 0615 hours. The Comanches engaged the first spearhead of North Korean VII Mechanized tanks with their chin-mounted GE Miniguns and missiles from launchers on their stub wings.

The helo drivers had only to move their eyes to pick out targets and thumb the joystick release button to loose their rounds on the armor below, the Miniguns mounted below the cockpit automatically slaved to their eye movement, gimballing back and forth like lethal scorpion stingers.

The black helos buzzed the North Korean armor like a swarm of killer dragonflies, raking them with automatic fire and Hydra missiles. The result was that the mechanized column's armored thrust was rapidly blunted. Scores of smashed unfriendly tanks were soon burning up in bonfires below, spewing twisting clouds of heavy, black smoke into the sky as a result of effective U.S. close air support.

The Commanche pilots knew the T-74s had only thin ballistic protection on their glacis and turrets. They had poured most of their fire into these areas, and the results showed; many turrets had been torn loose, and others lay upended on the ground where high-explosive rocket strikes had blown them off.

The M1A2s had done their share of tank killing in the battle. The kinetic-energy rounds fired by the Abrams's main guns were long-rod penetrators made of depleted uranium, a dense metal taken from the spent fuel rods of nuclear reactors and machined into spearlike flechettes. The rounds were saboted—"saybo'd" according to the pronunciation of American tankers—that is, encased in sabots or "shoes" of propellent that hurled the rods forward at sub-supersonic speeds.

Any armored vehicle not protected by reactive armor—blocks or tiles of plastic explosive that detonated when struck by the superdense rods and dissipated the kinetic energy released on impact—was in trouble, and the North Korean tanks weren't so protected. Where the rods struck, armor plate and uranium flechette could fuse into a superheated jet of semimolten metal that burned flesh from bone, cooked off ammo, and generated fearsome overpressures that literally blew the war wagons apart at their seams.

After forty minutes of hellacious firing, a mass of destroyed enemy armor was all that was left of VII Mechanized's attack. The commander of the U.S. tank brigade issued the order for his troops to break fire and safe their guns.

The Commanche leader suddenly received a warning message from AWACS. The airborne warning and control station had good radar paints on a heliborne attack force mounted by elements of the DPRK 5th Army Aviation airwing.

"Magic Wand to Stingray Delta. Report Speedball Alert," the voice of the AWACS senior technical officer said over SINCGARs secure radio downlink to the Commanche squadron commander, Major Dan Robertson. "Enemy helo squadron approaching on vector line two zero one. We make them as Hoodlums. ETA is five minutes."

"That's affirm, Magic Wand." A low growl in the headphones of the Commanche driver alerted him to the helo's threat identification radars picking up the signature of the approaching Hinds. "We have radar contact. Preparing to engage."

"Roger. Out. And good luck."

The Commanche flight leader keyed his mike and addressed the rest of the squadron. He now had visual contact. A half-dozen black dots had appeared low on the eastern part of the windscreen. In a matter of seconds, those dots would grow into the recognizable shapes of Kamov Ka-50 Attacka-class helicopters, known as "Hoodlums" under the NATO designation index.

The Ka-50s were formidable Russian-built gunships. Physically resembling the U.S. Apache helicopters, they were armed to the teeth with both laser-guided missiles and air-to-air rockets and a thirty-millimeter cannon mounted starboard of the nose. They were also highly maneuverable, powered by twin TV3-117 turboshafts, the two sets of rotor blades sitting one atop the other in a unique configuration.

In the Hoodlums the Commanches faced a worthy adversary. But the RAH-66 was easily as agile and as formidably gunned. On top of that, Robertson had drilled his squadron in tactics to deal with precisely the type of tactical scenario they were going up against.

"Okay. You heard the man," Robertson said, addressing the squadron. "I figure another two minutes, max, to engagement. We go to Plan Baker Charlie."

Robertson paused a beat, watching the shapes grow in the cockpit canopy windscreen.

"Anybody doesn't know the drill?"

"Hell, no. We forgot all about it, boss," his wingman said back.

Robertson permitted himself a laugh. His men would remember the plan in their sleep—those that survived, was his next, sobering thought. His smile faded. He went on.

"Okay. Let's kick some ass."

The threat was now clearly recognizable. The stub wings jutting horizontally from the fuselage bearing Aphid missile pods were tiny pinpricks against the blue sky, but there they were. Robertson felt a twinge of mixed fear and elation. What was the pucker factor? Easily eight and rising, he'd guess.

Seconds later, Robertson and the rest of the squadron had no time for guessing games. The formation of Hoodlum attack choppers and the Commanche squadron were locked in combat. As they had practiced in drills, his men scattered and used their more mobile rotorcraft to outmaneuver the somewhat slower, heavier, Russian-built choppers. Still, the Kamovs were formidably armed and bristling with weapons, and they were fast, too, surprisingly fast and agile.

One came at Robertson, its multibarrel gun twinkling as it spat 12.7-millimeter bullets at the Commanche. Green tracers whizzed past the cockpit windows. As Robertson jinked sideward and veered out of the stream of fire, he had already acquired the Hoodlum on TI. With a button press, he pickled off two laser-guided missiles. The Ka-50 took evasive action, diving for the deck to evade the missiles' seeker heads, but the rounds followed him down.

Moments later, Robertson had racked up a kill. The two missiles struck the Hoodlum amidships, exploding inside the Ka-50's engine compartment. Gouts of flame blowtorched from the penetration hole, the blast wave spitting out body parts and metal debris amid the perpendicular jet of fire. The gunship heeled over, trailing thick black smoke.

Before several tons of wreckage could smash headlong into one of the friendly tanks below, Robertson's hand gripped the pickle stick as he buttoned off a salvo of Hydras.

The unguided rockets all scored hits, blowing the Hoodlum's burning hulk into a million pieces of wreckage. Metal debris and burning fuel rained down on the tank battle taking place below, but the fragments were no threat to any of the friendly hulls in the engagement.

But to his left, Robertson saw that one of his own Commanches had been struck by a rocket salvo. There was a sudden cold, bright, electric white flash. The Hoodlum had scored a direct hit on the rotor mount. One second the Commanche had been intact, airborne, part of the air battle. The next it was a burning, smoke-spewing hulk, dropping from the sky.

The entire front section of the cockpit had been vaporized by the strike. Only the tail boom was partially intact, and the force of the explosion sent it seesawing through the air on a wild, spinning trajectory that sent other members of Robertson's strike package into quick dipping and jinking maneuvers to avoid being struck by the debris.

Repositioning his aircraft, Robertson gained target acquisition on the Kamov that had fired the missile. The low growl of the fire control and weapons management system told him the RAH-66's computer had calculated a firing solution on the enemy helo.

Robertson pickled off one of his remaining missiles, an advanced AIM 8/E variant. Unlike the Hydras, this was a heat-seeking round, but unlike previous generations of AIMs, it was also highly resistant to countermeasures, such as flares, evasive maneuvers, and ground clutter effect.

The Hoodlum pilot had been warned of the launch by his onboard threat identification system, and he had run some training maneuvers in preparation for battle. An automatic flare dispenser at the helo's rear began popping out white phosphorous pin flares attached to small parachutes that were quickly dispersed by the rotor wash of the tail boom prop. They formed a drifting cloud of thermal radiation intended to confuse the incoming missile's IR acquisition system.

But the AIM 8/E's guidance system incorporated some integrated circuitry its ancestors lacked. Inside a black wafer of silicon random access memory, it had already stored the projected path of the Kamov. The missile was programmed to follow the virtual track of an enemy helo and ignore any countermeasures it might detect.

The AIM punched right through the flare cloud and its IR seeker head swiveled on its gimbal mount. A small purple-tinged lens of polished optical glass pivoted like a maleficent barracuda eye down the line vector the Hoodlum had last flown. Target reacquisition was in progress.

The Ka-50 wasn't where the AIM-8/E thought it would be, though. The wily veteran pilot had changed course and flown directly into the sun, intending to break lock by overloading the IR seeker. It was a sharp move. But it wouldn't work, either.

Another wafer of silicon, sitting a half inch from the its twin IC wafer on a small circuit board, was programmed with a filing cabinet full of information on the sounds made by a variety of enemy helo engines in various aspects of combat flight.

Although the AIM's IR seeker was momentarily blinded, the missile's ears were sharp. Able to match the sound of the escaping Hoodlum's jet engines and prop turbines with its on-chip sound clip library, it simply revectored.

The Hoodlum's pilot had pulled the last trick from his kit bag. The pilot saw the unfriendly missile close on his threat radar. In a heartbeat, the AIM round had reacquired the heat of the left engine on IR seeker and adjusted its terminal flight path.

The missile flew in through the engine exhaust nozzle and exploded inside the nacelle. Its fifty-pound high-explosive warhead vaporized the helicopter, igniting a secondary explosion from the thirty-foot cloud of aviation gasoline that sprayed from the stricken craft on impact.

A massive orange black puffball of fire marked where the Kamov had been a few moments earlier. It hung in midair for a second or two, then vanished, leaving behind a wisp of curling black smoke. Seconds later, even this was gone.

The air battle was over. All enemy helos had been destroyed. Robertson ordered the surviving Commanches to turn around and head back to base.

0800 Hours Zulu, War Day Twenty-four

High above the battlefield, Joint STARS was watching the action from an altitude of 30,000 feet. Even if there had been windows for the crew to peer down from, they would have seen little but smoke and flames and would have heard nothing above the steady, controlled roar of the plane's massive turbojet engines.

But the JSTARS aircraft did its seeing through the medium of the electromagnetic spectrum. What the men at its scopes viewed was the carnage of war. The tank battle below was winding down. Most of the Korean armor had been smashed. There had been casualties to U.S. tankers, but these were minimal compared to the disaster that had swallowed up millions of tons of Korean armor. U.S. forces were already sprinting toward Pyongyang, past the graveyard of still-smoldering tanks that littered the battle zone.

JSTARS was about to report back to USFORCECOM when it received warning from an AWACS plane orbiting a similar racetrack course a hundred miles to the east. Unlike JSTARS, AWACS searched the skies, seeing out to a distance of 300 miles. It had detected an enemy fighter force approacing the JSTARS aircraft.

"Red Sentry, we have detected bogies converging on you on course heading Charlie Zebra Seven. Identify as MiG-25 Foxbats. Closing at fifteen miles."

"I copy that," said the senior flight technician aboard JSTARS.

"We're talking to the F-15s now, Red Sentry. The Eagles

flying CAP have been alerted. They will intercept. Contact is estimated in eight minutes. Good luck."

"Roger, and thanks."

The MiG-25s were outdated, and the Strike Eagles were well equipped to engage them. Yet had they been privy to the secure communication from the Foxbat flight leader to his wingman and squadron pilots, the Eagle drivers might have been less confident of success.

"You all know the importance of our mission," the MiG sortie commander began. "That any of us will survive is unlikely. But we will die as heroes. It is a privilege to have served with men as brave as you. Your names will be honored for all time."

One by one, the pilots answered. Every one of them pledged their willingness to die. In fact, they outdid one another in suicidal fervor. Like the Nipponese before them, the North Koreans considered kamikaze attacks an established war strategy. Suicide missions across the DMZ had been a constant fact of life throughout the uneasy years of truce on the Korean Peninsula.

As the Foxbats closed with their larger, slower quarry, it became evident to the F-15 pilots that something was wrong. Though the opposing fighter squadrons had now made visual contact, the Foxbats seemed oblivious to the lethal presence of the first-line American fighter planes.

Instead of maneuvering evasively, they bore in on JSTARS with an obsessive determination. Even when Sidewinders launched from the Eagles scored kills on the enemy planes, the MiGs showed no inclination to turn and run or engage the F-15s in dogfights.

By now it had dawned on friendly aircraft pilots that the MiGs were flying a kamikaze-style attack mission on JSTARS. Realizing this, the Eagle pilots hit the MiG force with everything they had, including missiles and nose-cannons.

It almost worked, but not quite. Though the Foxbat squadron was decimated, two planes had broken through the F-15 barrier. Both were badly shot up and trailing flame and smoke, and by now both were too close to the fleeing JSTARS aircraft to risk being fired on by the Eagles.

The pilot of the Boeing turbojet was doing all he could to evade the oncoming human-piloted missiles, jinking left and right and putting the plane through a series of roller-coaster dives and climbs. In the end, that was what saved the plane from complete destruction.

One of the two surviving Foxbats lost control and spiraled out of the sky to crash in the hills below, but the other blew apart as flame ignited its ruptured fuel lines. Blast and fuselage fragments exploded under JSTARS's left wing, rupturing one engine nacelle and setting the other on fire.

Inside the cabin, the crew were bounced around like dice in a shaken cup, and electrical fires had destroyed a few million dollars' worth of clandestine electronics. But JSTARS remained intact enough to limp back to base with an escort of Eagles for company. The downside was that the battlefield was left without low-level overhead surveillance coverage until another JSTARS could be scrambled from airfields near Seoul with an ETA of twenty-five minutes.

0905 Hours Zulu, War Day Twenty-four

Kim Jong-il scanned the yellow printout sheet that had just emerged from the military telex machine that received dispatches from the front. The news was indeed grim.

The North Korean dictator's haggard, no-longer-youthful face crinkled sourly with anger as he scanned the battlefield communiqué. The wording was terse, but the terseness masked a horrid reality. An American amphibious force had just come ashore off the coastal city of Nampo and was making rapid progress. It had already established a secure beachhead.

Resistance had been completely crushed. Defensive emplacements had been wiped out. As U.S. Marine LCAC aircushion vehicle transports ferrying USMC contingents transited from sea to land, and as paratroops dropped from C-

135 Galaxy transports to take positions inland, supplies were being pushed ashore with dazzling rapidity.

The expeditionary force was not remaining in place on the beachhead. According to U.S. doctrine, which rejected Normandy-style land-and-stay operations, it was advancing rapidly into the interior, sweeping aside all obstacles in its path in a multilayered invasion by sea, air, and land.

Kim bunched up the dispatch and flung it to the floor with contempt. He faced the luckless General Kwan, who was his chief of staff. Defeat was imminent, but Kim would never admit it.

"This dispatch means absolutely nothing. The aggressor will never prevail. We still have the missiles, do we not? And the biological warheads?"

"Yes, Comrade President, we do, but surely you are not—"

"Surely I am not *what*, simpleton? Thinking of using these weapons to drive the hated oppressor from our country? Is this what you have begun to say to me?"

"No, Comrade President. I mean—"

"You mean *nothing*. Hold your silence and listen. Here is what shall be done. The remaining Nodong missile batteries shall be armed. Plan Black Dragon shall be immediately put into practice. We have been patient too long."

Heads turned in the war room deep beneath the black hills north of Pyongyang where the general staff had taken refuge in its warren of deep, underground bunkers. The Black Dragon option called for a deadly rain of NBC weapons on Seoul, killing everything and everyone. It was a tactic of last resort when all else was lost, and all those present knew it—all except Kim.

"But—" the CINC had begun to protest.

"But nothing. Do as I order, or I shall have you shot. I want every damned missile with every damned biological and chemical warhead trained on those pieces of shit in Seoul. I want the very cisterns of heaven overturned to pour down a baneful wrath upon their heads. Is that clear, General?"

General Kwan had no chance to reply. To obey such an order was madness. It was worse than madness. It was the hubris that tempts the gods. Yet to disobey meant death. The CINC had no doubt that Kim would have him executed if he balked.

Before the CINC could answer, however, sounds of commotion came from the corridor outside. In another instant, the door to the inner chamber of war burst open, and men armed with submachine guns stormed inside. Kim recognized the leader. It was his DCINC, General Do Jing-ahn. There was also no mistaking the way Do's features were set and the gimlet stare of his eyes. Kim knew then that his hour of reckoning lay close at hand.

"Traitor!" Kim shouted, looking about the room. "Kill him!"

"Sit down, you heap of dung," Do told the doughy-faced boy-leader. Kim wilted at the command; no one had ever dared speak to him like that. His eyes goggled. He sat down speechlessly. He realized what was happening, and his guts froze. A spasm of fright caught him and held his stomach in a vise. He fought to control the panic reaction but found that he could not muster the strength of will.

Do pushed Kim into a chair and said, "Listen well. It is over. The Americans are almost knocking at our front door. Our military forces are crushed. We have lost. Unfortunately, you can no longer remain in power. Indeed, you cannot remain. . . ." The general let his words trail off.

He had meant to lay it all out for Kim, but somehow Do could not deliver the sentence of death in so many words once he looked straight into those frightened deer's eyes.

"My bodyguard, my b—" Kim gestured at the air. His face was blanched. The words, once so easy to mouth, no longer came.

General Do signaled to someone outside the door. In a moment, a soldier with a bloodied face was marched in at gunpoint. It was the chief of Kim's personal security force.

"I am sorry, Comrade President," he said. "We have dishonored you in our failure to guard you from harm."

At a nod from General Do, the man behind the chief body-guard forced him to kneel, and at another nod blew his brains out with a silent nine-millimeter burst from the suppressor-barreled H&K sub gun he carried.

"It is all over," General Do went on at Kim, who was now visibly trembling. "A new era must dawn for our nation. You, however, cannot play any role in it."

General Do removed his pistol from his belt holster. He ejected the clip and thumbed fourteen of the fifteen rounds the magazine held into his hand. He left one bullet in the clip and palmed it back into the handgrip, but left the weapon uncocked. Kim would have to crank the bullet in by himself. Finally, the DCINC placed the semiautomatic flat on the table.

"You have ten minutes," he said and, turning on his heels, left Kim alone in the room with the door shut behind him.

Do remained waiting outside for precisely nine minutes and forty-five seconds, checking his watch. When no sound of a pistol report was heard, he gestured to his aides with the silenced submachine gun he cradled in his hands.

The two masked men in camouflage BDUs pushed in through the door.

Few heard the volley of dull, metallic clicks and snaps that followed moments later, signaling silenced automatic fire and the ejection of at least a dozen cartridge casings. But when the two executioners reappeared, there was no mistaking the acrid odor of cordite that wafted from the former dictator's office.

"Inform the appropriate channels that our cherished and beloved leader has taken his own life rather than surrender. Add that he died in an act of heroic bravery that will be recorded down through the generations," the general announced. Do reached into his BDU shirt pocket and produced a sheet of laser-printed paper.

"Our former leader has also bequeathed his last words to his beloved brethren, the people of North Korea. See that they are broadcast over the media."

The DCINC stuffed the sheet into the trembling hand of

the dead Kim's terrified chief of staff, spun smartly on the heels of his jackboots, and exited the room.

SOFIA, BULGARIA

The Soviet military parade had assembled before dawn on the outskirts of the ancient Slavic city. Hundreds of army troops had encamped in the spacious park overnight. Within the winding sheets of a swirling ground fog, they formed up in ranks by unit designations. Motorized rifle, tank, and rocket brigades were all represented, as were infantry units and elite special forces formations.

As dawn broke and the fog began to lift, the rising sun lit up a colossal shape that had been cloaked in darkness throughout the night. It was the massive Soviet Army Monument, a tribute by the Bulgarians to the U.S.S.R. troops who had liberated their homeland from Nazi domination in World War II. Pale shafts of bright sunlight gleamed along the contours of the massive martial statuary as the sun climbed, and in the now limpid air the enormous statuary stood starkly etched against the sky-blue and cloud-gray of heaven's dome.

Many of the Soviet troops were moved to tears at the sight. Their country's greatness had been tarnished for too many years since the end of the Cold War. Afghanistan, Gorbachev, then Yeltsin and Putin, and the blunders in Georgia had all exacted their shameful toll. The sight of the statue filled the troops with enobling awe and steely determination. Overnight, the Soviet Union had been reborn, and so had they all. The troops would march with pride through the boulevards of Sofia. A new dawn had broken for them.

Others besides them shared that martial vision. As the tramping columns passed the monument and turned left onto Ruski Boulevard, the broad processional concourse used for martial parades, they were met with the cheers of thousands of Sofians who had begun congregating as day broke and now lined the avenue from the monument to Ploschtad 9

Septemvri, the plaza that anchored the boulevard at its urban center.

The troops could not believe their eyes nor their ears. They had not expected such a reception. Many of these same young soldiers were fresh from the bloody ethnic conflicts in the Southern Caucasus. Most had last marched through the bombed-out ruins of Kirovabad. They were used to being greeted with hatred and bullets, not welcomed as liberating heroes.

Many in the throngs lining Ruski waved Bulgarian and Soviet flags in unison. As the hammer-and-sickle banner fluttered beside the Bulgarian tricolor, members of the crowd shouted themselves hoarse yelling nationalistic slogans. The Russians were unfamiliar with the Illyrian-Thracian language spoken by the Bulgarians, but the word *Macedonia* was clearly discernible.

It was enough. To many Bulgarians, the region of embattled Yugoslavia lying to the west and adjoining Kosovo was cherished in a centuries-old dream of reunification. Just as Serbs in Belgrade dreamed of someday liberating Kosovo and annxexing it to a greater Serbia, so many Bulgarians cherished their own nationalistic fantasy of ethnic union.

Many of the crowds lining Ruski Boulevard on that clear morning saw in the masses of armor, artillery, and marching warriors the means of accomplishing that age-old dream. The Russians were liberators who would help them do it. Twice before in Bulgaria's history, their immense neighbor to the east had liberated the nation from foreign oppressors.

The sights and sounds of these Soviet troops today seemed to confirm that the dawn of the twenty-first century would see the miracle happen again. Many in the crowd shouted the name of the oppressors that stood in the way of their dream, and the young Russian soldiers recognized these names too: NATO, USA, and KFOR.

More than just the crowd shouting itself hoarse along the boulevard stunned the Russians. Here the statues of Lenin, Stalin, and Marx had never been toppled by anticommunist mobs. Monuments erected to the past glories of the Soviet

Union still stood intact, and street signs still bore the names of Soviet intellectuals, political leaders, and fallen martyrs. Government buildings and massive apartment blocks in the heavy-handed architectural style Muscovites knew as "Stalin's wedding cakes" towered above the parading soldiery, their facades graced with more bronze effigies of the proletarian heros of orthodox Bolshevism.

Every step of the way reminded the Soviet troops that here communism had never died nor even gone out of fashion. It was like stepping through a time warp into the 1950s, into the republic of the proletariat that their fathers and grandfathers had built out of the chaos of war and revolution. For many of the troops, it was tantamount to walking the Stations of the Cross.

The column swept past the U.S. and British embassies, the stately buildings emptied of staff in the hasty evacuation of the previous weeks, occupied now only by skeleton crews of caretakers.

At Ploschtad Naradno Sobranie, the columns trooped past the National Assembly Building fronted by the equestrian statue of Czar Alexander II, revered as having freed Bulgaria from the Turks in the Crimean War. The columns paused awhile, standing at parade rest in the spacious plaza. Within the heart of the Bulgarian capital city's political quarter, the march halted to observe five minutes of silence.

A detachment then separated itself from the main body of troops. The honor guard swung right and marched with dignified step toward Alexander Nevski Church, built in 1912 as a memorial to the 200,000 Russian soldiers who died for the independence of Bulgaria, and whose sixth-century basilica, the Church of Saint Sophia, gave its name to the city.

Near the church wall, the officers in the detachment's vanguard stopped before the Tomb of the Unknown Soldier. Bugles blared and a somber drum roll sounded as taps were played. The honor guard then stepped forward to reverently lay a wreath at the foot of the tomb. Many in the encircling crowd spontaneously began to weep, and the strains of the communist anthem, the "Internationale," were picked up and chanted by the assembled troops.

The parade soon reached its destination, Sofia's Central Park, anchored on the north by the Georgi Dimitrov Mausoleum and on the south by the National Art Gallery. The podium above the mausoleum entrance had long been used by government officials as a reviewing stand for mass demonstrations and official celebrations. Today, members of the Soviet General Staff would stand side by side with Bulgaria's leadership to review the Soviet troops filing past, as they went on to the parade's final stop at Ploschtad Lenin and massed beneath the colossal statue of Bolshevism's godfather that glared out across the city.

As the cameras and microphones of the world's news media were trained on the podium, viewers thousands of miles distant from the scene were struck by a sense of déjà vu. The uniformed men who stood on the podium closely resembled the atavistic physical types of the Soviet old guard. The "Dnieper Mafiya" of the Brezhnev premiership seemed to have reincarnated itself. In Washington and other Western capitals, the striking similarity was not lost, nor was the inescapable impression that the stage-setting had been deliberate.

But if there had been any doubt that an Iron Certain mentality held sway, the speeches that came next would have erased it. There was no mistaking the bellicose rhetoric the speeches contained, and the overall message was clear: The Soviet Union had been reborn, and it would not tolerate the enemies it saw massing on its Balkan and Asian flanks.

The Kremlin's message to Washington had been delivered. A military sphere of influence had been staked out, and the U.S. and NATO occupied the bull's-eye at the center of those widening concentric circles of defiance—circles on a target that was the world.

17
WINDS OF CHANGE

THE GLOBAL VILLAGE

Millions had watched the president's address to the nation after the cease-fire that ended the Second Korean War. In London, Bonn, and in other NATO capitals, as well as in allied non-NATO nations involved in the fight, such as France and Japan, other national leaders addressed their countrymen. Although the celebrations that followed the end of the war could not be compared to those that marked the start of the year 2000 some years earlier, the mass euphoria was more intense.

The world had witnessed the terrifying destructive potential of weapons of mass destruction. It had seen firsthand how nuclear, chemical, and biological weaponry, even in the hands of a minor power, could unleash death and destruction on a vast scale. The media exploited the issue for all it was worth, whipping up an auto-induced panic. For weeks on end, the talking heads were in feeding-frenzy mode on the threat of terrorist strikes using those same weapons, and they were finding WMD-armed terrorists hiding in every crack in the woodwork.

For the first time, America had come close to having enemy missiles strike the homeland, and no one gazed at the skies again with quite the same sense of security, no one heard the roar of jet engines passing overhead without a twinge of panic, and no one took the country's invincibility to armed attack for granted any longer. The anxiety would eventually become dulled and in time be forgotten, but for now it was strong.

Nor was it unjustified: In the wake of the cease-fire, the FBI investigated a spate of cases involving planned terrorist strikes on major targets in the United States. The same held true for counterterrorist agencies in major world capitals.

The French DSGE, the German *Bundeskriminalampt,* the British MI-5, Interpol, and other investigative agencies were all chasing down leads to plutonium, toxic chemical agents, and lethal germs across the globe. Most of the true stories of this behind-the-scenes work would never be revealed to the public, but there were times when the chances of Manhattan or Le Cite in Paris or downtown Tokyo being reduced to mass graveyards were all too real.

Still, much of the postwar euphoria lingered on. The fighting was over. So far, no new threat had arisen to disturb the peace and rebuilding that had begun in the postwar era. The optimism was to last for several months, but then it was to die a slow, lingering death. On the horizon loomed a threat more terrible than anything that had preceded it, and the danger of a war that might consume the world in fire and plague.

It had begun with an invitation.

THE STATE DEPARTMENT, WASHINGTON, D.C.

"The people of Bulgaria have invited the Union of Soviet Socialist Republics to intercede on their behalf in the defense of their national homeland against an external threat of grave import."

The new Russian foreign minister—*Soviet* minister, Bainbridge had to remember, they had changed back to the old formulation some weeks before—had leaned forward in the comfortable leather chair that faced his desk in the State Department. Schapin was gone already. Bainbridge had attended his farewell party. He'd grown to like the man.

The Russian steepled his palms and continued. "This threat is, of course, the Islamic hoodlums and terrorists who have become a force of contention in the region. Our Bulgarian neighbors were justifiably concerned about a militantly Islamic Albania and Kosovo next door. But of course, there is the threat from the south as well. Across the Bosphorus sits Turkey—"

"A strong NATO ally," Bainbridge interjected.

"Today, yes. Tomorrow, who can say? And for that matter, what is your country's new détente with Iran worth if Tehran will not honor its pledges against nonproliferation?" Filipov leaned back and smiled thinly.

Bainbridge was struck, not for the first time since the start of the meeting, at how closely Filipov resembled Andriy Gromyko, the Soviet ambassador who functioned as a bridge between Stalin and Gorbachev.

Did they call up central casting for old-style Soviet types? Bainbridge wondered. Most of the other lineup in the resurgent Soviet communist state that had been formed since Grigorenko's assassination physically resembled the old communist guard.

"No, my friend—and I sincerely hope that you and I as well as our respective countries can continue to be friends—there is a crisis, not only in the Balkans but in southern Eurasia. You and the Western Europeans will not acknowledge it. But we do, and we will not hesitate to act in our own defense."

"As you know, United Nations security resolution"—Bainbridge glanced down at his notes—"three seventy-eight called for an immediate withdrawal from Bulgaria. The United States was a signatory to that resolution, which was passed overwhelmingly by a majority vote."

Filipov blanched. He might resemble Gromyko, Bainbridge thought, but he needed to sharpen up his act a bit before he had the sangfroid of the old *apparatchik.*

"This is absurd," he said, too loudly, with a dismissive shake of his head. "The world should thank us, not censure us. Iran is behind it all. She would swallow up Southwest Asia from Tashkent to the shores of the Adriatic if she could, and you Americans turn a blind eye and let her! No, we will not permit it."

Filipov composed himself and sat back again. "At any rate, my job is done. My instructions were to officially inform you that Soviet troops are currently stationed in Bulgaria, and I have done that." He began to rise.

"Not so fast, Mr. Ambassador, if you please," Bainbridge said, popping a jelly bean into his mouth. "I, too, have something official to tell you." He offered Filipov the jelly bean jar, which was refused. *Would he have refused Ronald Reagan's jelly bean jar?* Bainbridge wondered.

"Mr. Ambassador," he began, as Filipov stared stonily, obviously intent on leaving. "The president has asked me to give you this message." He handed the folded sheet of paper to the Soviet ambassador.

"I will outline its contents for you: Broadly put, it states that the United States is strongly opposed to what it deems a violation of Bulgarian sovereignty and asks that the U.S.S.R. immediately withdraw. Should this request be ignored, we are prepared to implement economic sanctions against your country."

Bainbridge brought the first of what was to be a rainbow of jelly beans to his mouth after Filipov left. As he chewed, he thought. Like the Russian, his own role was not the formulation of policy, merely its implementation.

And he hadn't liked Filipov. For one thing, the new ambassador reminded Bainbridge of the sad look on Schapin's face as Filipov's predecessor had left Washington, probably for good. Still, Bainbridge was not out of sympathy with some of the points Filipov had raised.

Iran was, in fact, financing any armed Islamist insurgency

in the region that held out its hand and was hostile to either Moscow or the West. And Russia *did*, in fact, face a nonstop set of insurgencies from breakaway Islamic states on its southern borders. He knew the Russians were historically sensitive to invasion—terrified of it, in fact.

And not without justification. Twice before in their recent history they had suffered the invasion of Western armies of conquest that had taken tolls of millions of lives.

Filipov's summary of the threat to the West also had its points: The fires of ethnic unrest that flared in the Balkans could also consume Macedonia. For the second time in history, the sword of Islamic fanaticism might then be brandished before the gates of Europe.

Mine is not to reason why, he told himself, *mine is—ah, fuck it.* Bainbridge swallowed an entire handful of jelly beans and set the jar down. Enough. He checked his calendar for the morning's next appointment.

BULGARIA

The neo-Soviet buildup continued unabated. The overhead imagery that had begun as a trickle of data was now a flood of intelligence. Backed by the U.S., the United Nations had imposed sanctions on Moscow, but the Kremlin's new commissars had ignored them. The U.S.S.R. was demonstrating that it would not be cowed by world opinion, as much to itself as to the world at large.

Day by day, Ilyushin IL-76 transports and ships of the Russian Black Sea Fleet were ferrying men, war machines, ammunition, spare parts, POL, and other war matériel from staging areas and transshipment points set up at the Black Sea military ports of Rostov and Kerch.

The Don River, which flowed from the White Sea on a north-south axis that took in Archangel, Leningrad, Moscow, and other major goods production centers, showed up on the Western satellite intel take as an artery crammed with barges, each laden with supplies for an expeditionary army.

From Rostov, at the mouth of the Don, those goods were

off-loaded onto containerized ships, which crossed the Black Sea and reached the Bulgarian seaport of Constanta a day later.

The results of this constant flow of matériel had long since become apparent at the other side of the journey. Bulgaria had always been a strong Russian ally, even in the post–Cold War decades when the trend among its neighbors was to sever Soviet ties as quickly and as permanently as possible. Now the Bulgarians were reaping the consequences of those long-standing connections to the Kremlin.

Beyond the eastern coastal plain that fringed the Black Sea, Soviet troops had constructed their own versions of NATO's Camp Bondsteel in Yugoslavia, sprawling compounds lined with barracks buildings housing hundreds of troops, maintenance huts, training areas, and ammunition storage depots.

One of the first things the U.S.S.R. expeditionary force had done was to establish military checkpoints along the roads and highways. Every score kilometers, in many places, motorists had to stop and show their papers or risk military arrest.

But elsewhere these arrests were being carried out as part of a determined policy of subjugation. In Sofia, the Bulgarian capital city, the elected president, Anton Svolay, had relinquished power in fact if not in name.

The real controlling power in the country was Bulgaria's new military governor, Marshal Boris Chinovets. He was a man who had profited by the death of the former president, Dimitri Pavlovich Grigorenko. His association with Grigorenko went back to the last days of Afghanistan.

Chinovets knew that Grigorenko despised him and that his continued commission was due only to the comradeship of the army, an old-boy network with which even Grigorenko could not interfere. But now his old rival was dead, and Chinovets's star was finally rising.

Chinovets was not about to permit anything to stand in his way. From his military headquarters in the old Stornay Palace in the center of Sofia, he ruled the city with an iron fist.

The citizens of the Bulgarian capital city were faced with phalanxes of Russian armored vehicles and the watchful eyes of the restored KGB. Hardly a street could be negotiated without coming upon a "bimp" with a contingent of surly men in BDUs armed with Kalashnikovs and eager for confrontation. There were frequent identity checks and even more frequent arrests.

Bulgarians, who had enjoyed a more or less free existence since the fall of the Iron Curtain in 1989, were now faced with the same knocks on the doors that had plagued them since Stalin's troops had marched in at the close of 1945.

It was no secret that an organized resistance had sprung up in the weeks and months of the new Soviet occupation of the country. Members of its guerilla cells were the subject of increasingly frequent hunts by the KGB and loyalist elements of the national police force.

The unnerving thud of rifle butts crashing against doors became an increasingly familiar one in apartment blocks across the city—the residents had nicknamed it "Soviet door chimes"—as did the sound of high-low two-note sirens shattering the quiet of the night.

A few hundred miles to the west, in the swath of territory administered by the United Nations' peacekeeping force, KFOR, western armies of the NATO nations were aware of the building pressure of steel, of troops, and of hostile will that was growing like a cancer on the other side of the border.

They were also aware of a linked cancer growing on their eastern flank as well, for in Albania a new and militant breed of Islamic socialism had transformed the country into an armed camp, intent on avenging the ethnic hatred of the Serbs with a still more ferocious backlash of Islamist fury.

"We will not rest until the memory of the Serbian atrocity has been wiped out by force of arms and deeds of honor!" Zulqifar Taalib, who presided at the head of the Albanian Congress, had declared from its capital city of Tirane. "The sword of Islam shall strike a blow for freedom, and the heads of Satan's minions shall roll in pools of blood!"

Those minions included Slobodan Milosovic re-installed

in Serbia but also NATO forces, especially the United States. Already there were armed incursions by Albanian guerilla cells across the border into Kosovo and Macedonia, and street violence was uncontrollable in many places. In Western capitals, they waited for something to happen. When it did, it came as no surprise.

EASTERN CAUCASUS

The rebel forces had dug in along a crescent-shaped front to the north of the Azerbaijani city of Baku. Since Baku was also one of the major petroleum regions along the Caspian Sea, the rebels had threatened to set its oil fields ablaze.

They had already released a massive oil slick into the Caspian that had spread for miles. The new Kremlin government was intent on stopping the rebellion in its tracks. The commissars' motivation was more than just political. Unrest in this strategic region threatened a major portion of Soviet oil reserves, just as rebellion in the Caucasus had jeopardized those of the Black Sea.

The rebels in the village of Aksuat, a few kilometers outside Baku, in the hills flanking it to the north, had been identified by the Soviet GRU as a major rebel stronghold.

It was morning when the villagers began their daily routine. The air was cold. The villagers knew nothing about a Kurdish village in Iraq called Dahuq nor many villages in Afghanistan called by many other names, but they were about to learn by hard experience.

Indeed, the world was about to learn, too. Soon it would have a new name for disaster and wholesale death, one that would come to the lips as readily as Chernobyl, Kuwait, Stalingrad, Dunkirk, and many other metaphors of ill omen.

In the cold morning air, the heavy churning sound of spinning rotor blades carried far and with a distinct crispness. The sound was the first hint of impending danger that most villagers noticed, but it was quickly followed by the appearance of a Hip Mi-18 helicopter overhead, and then another Hip quickly behind it. Some villagers shaded their eyes and watched, while others who were more prudent took cover at the sudden appearance of Soviet combat aircraft. Neither response would make the slightest difference. The prudent and the bold would meet identical fates.

The choppers came straight out of the rising sun, black dragonfly shapes materializing against the pale white disk. Fifty feet above the village square, they stopped, menacing in their immobility. Hovering. Waiting. Women drawing water at the communal wellhead, old men squatting to smoke in doorways, children playing with empty food tins in the dusty street, all looked up, watched them hang there in the air.

It is possible that some of the villagers took note of the nonstandard fittings on the underbelly of each chopper, but probably few did. Surely none were aware that these fittings were dispenser racks for chemical and biological warfare agents, weapons last used during the heaviest conflict of the Afghan War.

The helos continued to hover. Villagers continued to watch and wait. Then, without warning or preamble, a cloud of yellow dust began to fall from the dispensers. Wind conditions had just shifted. Optimum agent dispersal was assured. Mission commanders had authorized contaminant release.

The wind caught the fine, yellowish powder and blew it through the town as the helos circled the village, spewing more of the yellow dust. The powder was made up of mycotoxins, toxic agents derived from snake venom, which caused symptoms similar to snakebite, only far more severe. Again, the Yellow Rain was falling.

Within a matter of seconds, those exposed out in the open square began to feel the effects of mycotoxin contamination. It didn't matter if they had inhaled the spores or not; the mycotoxin agent penetrated skin as effectively as it did mucous membranes. Epidermal penetration only delayed its effects. Exposed villagers quickly began to hemorrhage internally as the mycotoxin attacked the walls of their cells.

Within seconds, they began vomiting blood. Seconds afterward, blood began pouring from their ears, noses, even their eyes. In another few seconds, all among the first exposures had collapsed to the ground, where they spent the last moments of their lives writhing in agonizing pain. Under the pulpy, eggplant-colored envelope of skin, their body cavities had become oozing sacs of blood and putrefied organ matter.

Those who had run and hidden did not escape the Reaper's stroking scythe. The fine powder found its way in between the cracks of door and jamb, of window and frame. It sifted down the stone chimney stacks and blew in through cracks in the earthen walls. Even a microscopic quantity of the dust was sufficient to cause death. In fact, victims didn't even have to see it in order to be killed.

Those who had sought refuge only took that much longer to die. But there was nothing they could do to save themselves once they'd been exposed to the lethal yellow dust.

Some had the presence of mind to reach for concealed radios and warn their kin in the hills beyond the village. Others reached for their rifles and went out to shoot the murderers from the skies overhead. But the Hips had already gone, and the murderers with them, and the villagers lay down and died in agony beside the guns they had dropped into the dusty streets of the stricken town.

Within the space of ten minutes, over 70 percent of the villagers were festering corpses. The other 30-odd percent were mortally stricken by the Yellow Rain and would die soon thereafter. A far smaller percentage would escape with only minor contamination sickness, those caught on the outskirts who had somehow evaded direct exposure. But they would be in the vast minority. Besides, the Russians had no intention of stopping where the helos had left off. Their plans were somewhat more involved.

At a higher altitude, out of range of anything but SAMs, an observation plane had been taking real-time photo imagery of the monstrous carnage below. When the plane left the killing zone, it signaled the command post some miles to the east that it was finished.

By then, an Ilyushin IL-18 was already orbiting outside

the village. As the observation aircraft departed, the IL-18 flew in and dropped a large, squat bomb, from which an oversized, white nylon parachute opened to slow its descent as the plane flew off at flank speed.

Few, if any, villagers were left alive to witness the sudden blurring of the sky and warpage of the sun as the slowly falling bomb descended to a point approximately thirty meters above the ground, nor could they smell the telltale gasoline odor of the petroleum distillate ethylene oxide that had been sprayed by a ring of nozzles in a dispersal pattern controlled by a small microprocessor chip in the warhead of the bomb. By these signs they might have understood that an FAE, or fuel-air explosive, had just been dropped on the village.

But even had some been alive to see it, they would soon be dead. A heartbeat later, the main charge of the bomb detonated the cloud of airborne incinerants. The igniting cloud caused an airburst that was hot enough to ignite the oxygen in the air, very much in the same way a nuclear explosion might have done. Indeed, the FAE's blast effects were subnuclear.

The resulting blast wave and firestorm knocked every stone building flat as a pancake and burned every piece of flesh living and dead, every stick of wood, and every block of stone to blackened cinders. Within a matter of seconds, the village of Aksuat was reduced to a scar on the face of the land. It, and every living thing inside it, had permanently ceased to exist.

SOMEWHERE IN RUSSIA

The dead man wore new military fatigues.

Since his "demise" at the hands of assassins, he had worn them to remind him of what he was and what he would need to be: a general of the Russian army. He would wear those fatigues until the usurper of lawful power was ousted. If he could, he would kill him with his own bare hands, in fact.

"More bad news, sir."

Dimitri Grigorenko looked from the window of the remote dacha to his second in command. Viktor Arbatov held a dispatch printout. He handed it wordlessly to Grigorenko. He had fallen into his old Afghan War habit of addressing the general as sir. Familiar forms of address that had developed between the two men since then would not be used until Russia was free of its new commissars.

Grigorenko read the dispatch with growing shock and anger, then balled the paper and threw it down. Biological attack in the Tajik states! Use of a fuel-air explosive! Insanity! What atrocity would Bogomelov and his cronies commit next? One way or the other, Grigorenko knew the fools who had taken the Kremlin from the Russian people had sealed their own fates.

The question was, would he be able to stop them before they provoked NATO, and especially the Americans, into some form of military retaliation for their crimes? Were this to happen, Grigorenko had little doubt that Bogomelov and his cadre of neo-Stalinists would ultimately unleash the nuclear option.

If so, it would be nothing like the scenario on the Korean Peninsula, bad as that episode had gotten. The nuclear forces of the Rodina were far more sophisticated than Kim's glorified Scud force, and far more effective. Global war would be the aftermath. Nuclear, chemical, and biological. The worst fears of the Cold War could quickly become a reality in ways none had suspected and none dared admit were possible.

If Grigorenko failed, then the world would pay a dire price for its blindness. And if the feared eventuality came about, it would have been better for him to have died in the ambush instead of the double that had stopped the bullets in his place.

Grigorenko's stand-in had been recruited from among the ranks of Spetsnaz forces loyal to him, his features further altered by plastic surgery to resemble the president's. It was this man whose ashes now filled an urn at Sheremptyevo Cemetery in the hero's corner near the bank of the Volga.

Grigorenko turned to face the dacha's window again. Arbatov caught the sign that his chief wanted privacy and left without a word.

EASTERN SOVIET UNION

Trencrom trudged between the iron rails, every muscle in his emaciated body stretched to the limit. He was laboring to push the iron hopper full of excavated rock to the tiny patch of daylight that had just revealed itself from around the bend in the tunnel. The hopper was perhaps four feet across and deeper by a little more, but it was heaped with chunks of jagged debris, and its contents weighed in the vicinity of half a metric ton.

On a diet of thin gruel and the occasional hunk of stale bread and the even rarer piece of dried meat as tough and as palatable as shoe leather, his once muscular body had first fed on its reserves of fat, and then attacked its stores of protein, until by now virtually nothing but skin and bone was left. Under normal circumstances, Trencrom would not have been in any condition to undertake the kind of backbreaking labor he was performing. But these were not ordinary circumstances.

The SS men in charge of the labor force at Nordhausen were sadistic overseers, and they were always nearby, waiting with whips in hand. More sadistic and more numerous than even the Nazi SS, they were *Kruppianer,* agents of the private police force of the Krupp Armament Works, recruited from Alfred Krupp's private labor empire in the German industrial Ruhr.

The Krupp guards brandished special whips made of flexible Krupp steel. The steel whips could easily kill a man in the condition of most of the inmates at Nordhausen with a single blow. Trencrom had seen this happen more than once with his own eyes, and the impression would never leave him.

So he pushed against the hopper, straining every atom of his body toward the distant pinhole of pale light as he trudged between the tracks. Until suddenly he lost his footing and toppled to the ground. The light disappeared. What he saw now was the hate-contorted face of one of the vicious Krupp guards.

"Schweinhund! Aufshtehen!"

The whip descended on Trencrom's head as he struggled to rise. *"Du verflucter schmerotzer! Du dreckiger hund!"* The whip continued to flail at Trencrom, smashing into his chest and bringing blood to his face from his shattered nose. *"Zum arbeit! Und schnell! Machen zie shnell!"*

Trencrom jerked awake. He was looking at his son.

♦ ♦ ♦

"Daddy, you were having one of your bad dreams again."

Trencrom cast about, wild-eyed. For a moment he had lost his bearings and his sense of time. Then it all began coming back to him. He cursed silently for his boy to see him shaken like this, although it was not the first time. He reached out and brought the child near.

"It's okay, son," he said. "I'm okay."

"What were you dreaming about?" the boy asked. "Was it those rockets again. The V ones?"

"Yes, the V-2 rockets," he told his son.

"And the Nazis. They were very bad, weren't they? We learned about them in school yesterday."

"Yes, they were bad men. Very bad."

"But you escaped, Dad. You got them back in the end. You even got those medals for it." The boy pointed to a Congressional Medal of Honor framed on the wall.

"Sure, I did that, kiddo," Trencrom said. "And I did get them back, at least one or two of them. But I got hurt back there, and sometimes it comes back . . . in dreams."

♦ ♦ ♦

In dreams . . . The boy who had grown into a man had been having his share of nightmares, and he, too, thought of escape as he sat shivering in the darkness and cold of the cramped prison cell. Something had changed, but they would not tell him what. Since the first weeks of his capture, his treatment had suddenly worsened. The guards had grown crueler, and the interrogators more savage, more prone to physically attack him.

They now knew who he was, but there was no rumor of release anymore, no hint that a bargain was being struck to bring about his freedom. On the contrary, Trencrom had been told that he was to be put on trial for espionage.

In time, he discovered what had happened. He had learned about the bloody palace coup staged by Vadim Bogomelov and the death of Grigorenko in a hail of gunfire. "There is a new wind of change blowing in Russia," he was told by his uniformed MBVD interrogator. "The ugly, Western-style decadence of former years is a thing of the past. The workers of the proletariat have once again come into their own."

He said other things, but the most important of them was this: "You are to be put on trial as an enemy of the people and a tool of the warmongering leaders of the West. We will make an example of you. Of this you may rest assured."

Then the beatings began.

18
FURTHER PROVOCATIONS

KOSOVO-ALBANIA BORDER REGION
Multinational Brigade North

The passenger coach rattled along the two-lane, hard-surfaced road that ribboned through craggy mountain passes. The brakes were bad and the suspension almost shot, but the driver knew each twist and turn of every mile in the road, and he had made this run hundreds of times before. He also knew most of his passengers by name. They were regulars.

Aboard the bus was an assortment of ethnic Albanians from the farming village of Tropoje, Albania, en route to factory jobs in the industrial center of Suva Reka, Kosovo. Centuries of warfare and ethnic conflict had not changed the need to find employment, to buy bread to fill hungry mouths. Nor had the decades of socialist government in Tito's Yugoslavia changed the cross-border traveling necessary to hold down a job in the region.

The driver ground the gears as he shifted into second to take a steep grade where the switchback road suddenly and precipitously climbed. Whether he was aware of it or not, the turn in the road was a natural place for a rocket-propelled grenade attack. Others, though, were quite conscious of this condition.

Two men occupied positions atop a wooded bluff approximately 300 feet above the jug-handle bend in the steep mountain road. They watched the bus inch along its path, an ungainly beetle working its way up a narrow leaf.

One, the spotter, lay prone, studying the road through powerful binoculars, tracking the coach through a haze of thermal distortion rising off the blacktop in a shimmering curtain.

The other man, the sapper, crouched behind the spotter. Smoking, while the dirt-blackened tips of his fingers poked at the membrane buttons on a militarized remote-fire control keypad from which two long wires, one black, one red, snaked down the side of the bluff.

The sapper's fingers were soiled from climbing and digging in the dirt to set up the off-route ACEATMS mine and running the det cables up to the crown of the bluff. Tripod-mounted ACEATMS at first glance resembled a stubby-barreled antique Gatling gun. But there was no trigger. No ammo belt. Just a tube on tripods containing a 60-millimeter HEAT rocket and an optical sighting system mounted at the rear.

Save for the fact it could be remote-detonated—hence technically a mine—ACEATMS was a tank-busting rocket launcher capable of piercing all but Chobham-type explosive reactive armor (ERA), blocks or "tiles" of plastic explosive providing a nullifying counterblast to rocket strikes. It could breach even that at close enough range.

Against the fragile metal skin of the approaching passenger coach, the shaped-charge projectile fired by ACEATMS would have an easy job of turning its target into a warped and shattered mass of flaming wreckage and its riders into charred and dismembered cadavers.

As the bus began to round the jug handle, the ethnic Serb lying prone behind the binoculars gestured to his companion on the bluff. The spotter bunched his hand into a fist and held it swaying slightly in the air. The second man flicked away the stub of his cigarette and focused on the keypad, which was now programmed. The sapper watched the prone man's hand, alert to its movements.

When the clenched fist went down, the sapper depressed a button on the fire-control keypad. Then pushed a second. An instant later, the second man, too, had crawled to the edge of the bluff. His vantage point was not as good as that of the prone Serb gripping the binoculars, but both could clearly see the immense orange black fireball boiling and churning up from where the bus had been totaled by the ACEATMS rocket strike. See the hunks of smoldering wreckage and flaming fuel spills scattered for hundreds of feet around the burning hulk.

The boom and rumble of the explosion was still oscillating back and forth over the rocky slopes of the hillsides in a hellish echo as they packed up their gear and left their ring-side seat to death on the barren, windswept ridge.

KOSOVO-ALBANIA BORDER REGION
Multinational Brigade West

The response was swift and anticipated. For all its obsessive fortification-building, Albania's military forces are Mickey Mouse. Its armor is made up of obsolete Soviet stockpile equipment from the early Cold War era; stuff that was second rate when Nikita Khrushchev was Soviet premier.

Its combat aircraft make up just as sorry a collection of junked hardware as its tanks and APCs; virtually every plane in the Albanian air force is of Chinese origin, and the Chinese got those planes secondhand from the Russians.

But regionally, Albania's military power is still a force to be reckoned with. In a part of the world made up of countries smaller than many U.S. states, the armed might of the postage-stamp nation far outstrips the indigenous forces of neighboring Kosovo. For this reason, the Kosovo Liberation Army, or KLA, had been shored up with United Nations–mandated Euroforce battalions in Kosovo, artificially changing the regional balance of power in favor of the KLA.

Nevertheless, war fever had swept Albania, whose revolutionary leader, Zulqifar Taalib, had invoked the protection and blessings of heaven itself. He'd pledged that the sword of Allah's vengeance would strike to redress the martyrs' blood shed in the bus attack. The rest was a forgone conclusion.

The Albanian mechanized column raised a cloud of dust as it rolled across the gravel-surfaced four-lane road that paralleled the Luga River. A cluster of Kosovar towns lay only a few miles beyond the point on the border where the road emerged from neighboring hills. The towns were Serbian enclaves. The column's objective was extermination. The hated Serbs were to be killed, their homes destroyed, their farms turned into moonscapes, their livelihoods obliterated.

Elements of the Albanian land forces' single tank battalion and its four infantry brigades had been hastily fused into a ragtag strike force of approximate regimental strength level. Its soldiery was made up of volunteers filled with nationalistic pride and religious fervor. They had been issued rifles and Korans, then sent out to fight and die.

Their ears still rang with the clarion call to arms by their unit commanders. Their equipment and training did not stand a chance against the U.N.-mandated troops awaiting them on the other side of the Luga, but they didn't care. They were ready to be martyred for their cause.

Euroforce had been alerted to the attack by NATO satellite data. Contingency plans were put into action. Battalion-level task forces of the multinational peacekeeping brigades had been placed on alert throughout the night in anticipation of an Albanian incursion. When it materialized as expected, they were ready to hit back in force.

NATO tube battalions stood at the ready. The big guns were a mix of fixed and mobile artillery including automatic cannons and mobile howitzers. Chaparral and MLRS (multiple launch rocket system) pounded the armored spearhead with wave after wave of missiles, each a dispenser for hundreds more explosive bomblets or submunitions.

The bomblets scattered in the air like milkweed down, a silvery dust cloud that glinted in the sun, until they had drifted only a few feet over the heads of the advancing force.

At this point their proximity-fused detonation charges ignited. The cloud of fairy dust became a furnace without walls, a little suburb of hell, a chemical garbage disposal for armor and human flesh. Tanks and APCs were reduced to wreckage in a microflash of devastating blast and searing flame.

Bones shattered. Limbs and heads were crushed or went flying through the firestorm like hailstones in a hurricane. Ammunition magazines cooked off, and the red and green dashes of tracer rounds shot like Morse code dots and dashes through the battlefield's inferno.

MBTs from the NATO blocking force added the power of their main guns to the fray. Opened up on other elements of the attacking column with HEAT, HESH, and sabot rounds to exchange fire with the obsolete T-54 tanks fielded by the Albanian land force.

Apache helos and A-10 Warthogs raked whatever was left with bombs, rocket fire, and thirty-millimeter cannon salvos. The advance was quickly stopped in its tracks, and the eastern bank of the Luga soon became a graveyard of corpses and burning metal hulks. Those Albanians who had been promised a martyr's death in battle had not found themselves cheated in the end.

BULGARIA—F.Y.R. OF MACEDONIA BORDER REGION
Multinational Brigade South

Task Force Bravo was a mechanized infantry regiment attached to Multinational Brigade South. The task force held a position opposite the southern bank of the River Neva, whose east-west course intersected the chain of hills, mountains, and hanging valleys—an Alpine terrain minus the permafrost—stretching south along the spine of the Balkan peninsula.

Bravo was made up of a U.S. rifle company, multinational armored platoons comprised of Bradleys, French AFVs, and a tank company of U.S. M1A2 and British Challenger MBTs. Bravo's command post had been established in the remains of an old estate in the midst of grape-growing country. Vineyards surrounded the manor house, still producing rich wine crops, but they had been left to go to seed because of the war. Though drinking was forbidden, the troops had set up their own wine-making lash-up and sold bottles of Macedonia Red on the thriving Balkan black market.

Still, the rolling countryside and proximity to the Neva made the estate a good observation post for Multinational Brigade South. A surveillance company staged regular UAV flights across the border. The Soviets also flew their UAVs across NATO positions in Macedonia. Both sides were just sitting it out for the moment, waiting for something to happen. When something finally did, surprise was universal. Neither side had figured shooting would erupt any time soon.

Yet, at 1500 hours on a Tuesday afternoon, fighting suddenly broke out when a small recon force of two U.S. Hummers came under fire from a hidden battery of twenty-three-millimeter Russian guns. In the aftermath of the skirmish, reports would conflict, especially concerning who had fired the first shots.

The Soviets claimed the Americans opened up with the Hummer's .50-cal MG, and the G.I.s claimed the opposite. About one thing there was no doubt, and this was that within minutes after the firefight began, NATO forces had crossed the Neva and were engaged in armed conflict with a Soviet mechanized detachment of the 2nd Motorized Infantry Division.

An Abrams MBT crewed by Team Tango was making its way through high meadows on the south bank of the Neva when the chatter of light weapons caught the attention of team leader Sergeant Mike Rodriguez, who was looking out through the tank's undogged turret hatch. The fire seemed to be coming from a cluster of farm buildings about a half mile away on the slope of a hill. As the Abrams drew closer, though, Rodriguez saw gray white smoke billowing up from what looked like a Bradley.

Sighting through binoculars, Rodriguez saw that the hit vehicle was in fact a Bradley. One of Bravo's troop carriers. The APC was burning up, its ammo starting to cook off like lethal popcorn. The APC had been hit out in the open by whatever was concealed in those distant farm buildings. Its crew was under fire, struggling to escape the burning hulk and evade automatic fire directed its way by gun crews cunningly hidden amid the farm buildings.

The Bradley crew was also trying to get the hell out of there before the fuel and ammo cook-off turned into a massive explosion. Men in woodland camo BDUs were running, diving, shouting, and hitting the dirt as they simultaneously dodged enemy automatic fire and the threat of imminent explosion. Suddenly, a powerful concussion shook the countryside to its roots. The Bradley had just gone ballistic. A broiling fireball and billowing smoke clouds shot up from the totaled APC.

Before Rodriguez could give any kind of order, his gunners had opened up on the farmhouse with the main guns of the two M1A2s. The tanks had been loaded with HESH and HEAT rounds, and the farmhouse was hit by both types of shells simultaneously. The effect was to make the walls of the farmhouse completely disintegrate. The walls just disappeared, melted away like sheets of ice. But when the smoke cleared, there was nothing there except a crater. No hint of hostiles. Not where the farmhouse had been, anyway.

The three Russian T-76S Shilden (Shield) MBTs had been concealed behind and within the large barn out back of the farmhouse. But they weren't in hiding any longer.

Wood planks splintered like cardboard, and the Shildens came crashing and barreling through the barn walls, their turrets revolving to face the U.S. MBTs. Rodriguez spotted the identifying features of the T-76S, the latest-generation tank in the Russian arsenal, right off. The explosive reactive armor (ERA) tiles on turret and front glacis and the laser range finder and SACLOS targeting sensors confirmed what they were up against. The Shildens were not in the same league as the M1A2, but they were definitely in the same ballpark, making them heavy hitters to be reckoned with in a slugging match.

"Contact! Tanks, direct front!" Rodriguez shouted, now dogged down inside the protection of the Abramss armored hull. Rodriguez heard the commander of Tango Two shout "Action front! Action front!" over the SINCGARS radio net as he continued issuing his own orders in a rapid spate.

"Delta Foxtrot thirteen and fourteen. Twelve o'clock. *Load say-bo!"*

"Loaded!" came the reply seconds later as the saboted round was shoved into the breach, and the Abrams's thermal imaging sensors plotted a firing solution on the bulky shape of the Russian main battle tank roaring at them.

"Fire say-bo!"

The Abrams shook as the main gun discharged, and the round hit its target square on the front glacis. Despite the ERA tiles that dissipated some of its kinetic energy, the direct hit by a long-rod uranium penetrator packed enough punch to completely shear off the Silden's cupola from its turret ring.

The Soviet tank turret shot twenty feet into the air before flipping over and plopping sideways back into the turret ring, from which flames and smoke now licked, scorched, and billowed. It was a good kill. No sign of life came from the smashed Russian behemoth.

Even as the first T-76S was dying, the second of the three Soviet MBTs to emerge from the barn was simultaneously hit by another round from Rodriguez's tank and a second sabot round from Tango Two. One uranium flechette slammed into the Shilden's rear tracks, blowing tread sections clean off their mountings. The other went banging into the rear of the tank and passed out the other side, cooking off its ammunition stores in the process.

Amid a fireworks display and gouts of choking, oily smoke, Russian tankers were struggling to scramble from the burning MBT. Clawing, gyrating, screaming figures inside a geyser of smoke. Most clearly would not make it. They were already charbroiled, muscles and flesh bubbling masses of hot carbon. They lived only long enough to flop around on the grass. Soon they were dead.

Before any of this could register, the HEAT round that the burning T-76S had gotten off before being hit slammed home. The high explosive antiarmor projectile's shaped charge fell a few yards short of the lead Abrams. But it landed close enough to do major damage. The force of the explosion lifted the front end of the multiton MBT five feet off the ground, shearing off part of the left track in the process. The lead Abrams's three-man crew was knocked around like horseflies in a bottle by the power of the blast.

The Abrams was immobilized. Out of commission. Rodriguez's ears were gonging, and his crew was banged up and bloodied. Yet it could have been worse. For one thing, there was no fire, which would have turned on the automatic halon dispensers. That would have meant they'd have to bail out. Halon doused flames fast, but nobody could breathe that shit for long. The turret could still rotate a full 360 degrees, and the M1A2's main gun was still functional. This was a good thing, because there was still a third Soviet tank out there, and the bear was gunning for Yank.

Hardly had the crew recovered their wits than another HEAT projectile whizzed overhead with the telltale sound of ripping silk. Though it missed Tango One, the shell had Tango Two's number. The HEAT round hit the Abrams on its front glacis, just below the main gun, and the shaped primary charge pierced right through the turret armor. The HEAT's forty-pound secondary charge blew up inside the hole, prying up the turret as might a gargantuan crowbar, and shattering the main gun barrel.

Rodriguez didn't know if anyone was alive in Tango Two or not. SINCGARS was down, and besides, he had no time to think of anything except taking out the T-76S before it got his own crippled tank. The Shilden was already swinging its main gun around, bringing it to bear on Tango One. In another few seconds, it would lob one their way. But by now, another sabot was in the breech, and Tango One's autoranging had acquired the enemy armor.

"Fire! *Fire say-bo!*" Rodriguez shouted.

At that moment, it was all over for Ivan. The M1A2's fire control system was so fast and accurate that if a U.S. tanker shot first, the other guy bought the farm, simple as that. This time was no exception to the rule.

The long rod penetrator caught the enemy tank before it could get off a clean shot. The uranium flechette punched right through the top of the T-76S's rounded cupola. It was slanted on an angle that drove it directly into the crew compartment, killing the Soviet tankers and setting the steel behemoth's ammo stores on fire.

The Sov MBT exploded with the characteristic separation of the cupola like a spinning top that marked a direct hit with overpressure by a saboted kinetic-energy round.

Rodriguez's crew was shaken up but otherwise unhurt, and his tank was crippled but otherwise still functional. Tango Two hadn't been as lucky, though. Its commander had been killed, and the loader and fire support officer, or FIST, had both been badly wounded.

Rodriguez radioed for medical evacuation and Apache cover in case more Soviet armor or helos showed up. Then he undogged the Abrams's hatch and stuck his head up into the wind blowing strong and cold from the east. The stench of death and cordite filled the air, which was thick with smoke from burning armor and human flesh.

Thanks to the Abrams's automatic halon dispensers, Tango Two herself wasn't burning, but the M1A2 had a large hole blown in its front from the near miss by the Soviet HEAT round. The three Russian tanks were complete wipeouts. All were burning, and survivors were crawling out of the midmost one, being taken prisoner by the Bradley crew that had come springing and barreling up out of the weeds after the tanks had finished shooting it out.

Guess that meant his side won, Rodriguez said to himself just before the Apache close air support squadron came swooping in to cover their evacuation. Maybe they'd even give his people some medals.

NAGORNO-KARABAKH, TAJIKISTAN, SOUTHERN RUSSIA

Russian armor ringed the Tajik city of Nagorno-Karabakh in a circle of steel. The city was the regional center of the southern Urals territories and had become the stronghold of indigenous rebel forces. The new regime in Moscow was determined to uproot the nascent rebellion before it became another Grozny in the Caucasus. This time the Kremlin did not lack the will to use weaponry that saner men had quailed at using.

The Alpha convoy had set off from the Russian outpost at Kalinengrad earlier that morning. It was escorted by a security force of BTR-70 and BMP-3 MICVs and a heavy Gaz truck laden with troops. The heart of the convoy consisted of several M67 ammunition vehicles. The Alpha convoy had traveled separately from the mobile battery of self-propelled 2SF Giatsint SP howitzers that had set off from the nearby Fazinhed garrison at around the same time. It was on a special mission.

The Alpha convoy was expected shortly by Soviet tube battalions around Nagorno-Karabakh. Meanwhile, the artillery crews were busy tending and setting up the gargantuan tubes for the impending fire mission. The 152-millimeter guns were mounted on Akatsia tracked armored vehicle chassis; each tube and chassis had a combined weight of more than thirty metric tons.

The Giatsints—Russian for hyacinth—bore only a superficial resemblance to tanks. The tubes were much longer than the main guns of MBTs, and they had far wider bores. Special shock absorbers were needed to cushion the tremendous recoil produced when the tubes were fired in combat. Struts were needed to brace the vehicles during combat-fire missions.

The compartment within the woodland-cammied hull of each tracked Akatsia vehicle gun bed was filled with fire-control computing components that would enable the howitzer to drop an eight-inch artillery shell into a pickel barrel from a mile away. Most of the rest of the interior was devoted to gun hydraulics and a heavy-duty air-conditioning system necessary to cool the computing modules that made such accuracy in targeting possible. The aft section was given over to ammo stores for the up to thirty rounds of mixed types the system could carry. Whatever extra space there was—and it wasn't much—was left for the gun crew.

Ironically, the great accuracy of the howitzers was not of primary importance to the fire mission. Within an hour after the three 2SF artillery vehicles had been set up and prepared for firing, the Alpha convoy arrived. The three ammunition vehicles making it up then separated and docked with the howitzers. Accuracy was the last thing on anybody's mind. Conventional weapons required accurate aiming. These did not.

The shells sliding down the conveyor from the ammunition vehicle into the howitzer's autoloader were binary projectiles containing chemical nerve agents. The gun crews, which had been trained in chemical combat maneuvers, knew that all they needed to do was to place the shells anywhere within the center of the city to the east that was their target.

Some would be fused to detonate as airbursts. Others as groundbursts. Both types would produce a high lethality ratio in a killing zone that would extend throughout the city. The first few shells would do the job. The rest were basically overkill.

Indeed, the main concern about accuracy for the chemical warfare gunners was the danger to themselves; even a slight shift in wind direction could send a toxic cloud from a misdirected shell back at them. For this reason, the howitzer crews wore minimal chemical-resistant gear during the fire mission, with full MOPP level 5 gear at the ready in case of accidental blowback.

Their target was the Tajik city of Nagorno-Karabah, which had become the center of Tajikistani rebel activity. Moscow had pledged that there would be no protracted struggle this time. No Caucasus scenario. It would crush rebellion with an iron fist, squash it like a cockroach, no matter what the price in global opinion.

Conventional tactics had done little good in the past. No sooner had one center of rebellion been crushed, as in Grozny, than another had sprung up. The time had come to break the cycle, the commissars had decided. The fire mission was to commence as planned.

The binary shells detonated as airbursts, their contents mixing and covering the streets of Nagorno-Karabakh with the toxic agents the shells contained. A fine, aerosolized spray—modern NBC agents are rarely dispersed as gas, though "gas" is the generic usage—of VX agent filtered down, and soon the urban spaces were filled with a spreading fog of deadly poison.

The droplets of nerve agent contained molecular trace quantities of polymerized rubber, giving the aerosol an adhesive quality. The tiny droplets of VX did not collect, they did not run nor drip. Instead, they clung to whatever they touched in a fine, moist blanket. Even a trace exposure was enough to kill instantly in most cases, and wherever the death fog deposited its hellish manna, living things began to grow sick and die.

The chemical aerosol wafted into drainage tunnels, drifted down chimney stacks, sifted beneath the spaces between doors and jambs, and slid between the panes of even the most tightly shuttered windows. Fingers of death probed gently, but wherever they pointed, life ended. In basement dugouts where the rebel underground had holed up, death's skeletal hand waved and beckoned.

The vapors of nerve agent given off by the slowly evaporating droplets were highly toxic. Even inhaling one part VX per million parts of breathable air was fatal. Gas masks were useless. Hundreds, then thousands, were soon writhing in their death throes.

Some victims found their flesh decomposing as they expired. The purplish black, rotten pulp that had been skin and sinew only minutes before now split open like blighted fruits, and sloughed off, exposing the bones and vertebra beneath. Much the same thing was happening to the internal organs, which had also begun to decompose. As life left the dying, their lungs and air passages filled with a choking froth of blood and liquified organ matter.

Corpses soon piled up like trees felled by a storm. But the toxic agents volatilized at a known rate. Within a matter of hours, toxicity levels in the zones of contamination were reduced to the extent that they could be tolerated by specially trained chemical combat troops attached to the 22nd Chemical Warfare Brigade. These troops had been poised to move in and mop up any stragglers after the initial assault.

Outfitted in full NBC operations gear, including full-body protection and masks connected to self-contained oxygen supplies, the mop-up troops rolled in on BTRs, quickly fanning out across the city. The devastation they encountered was nothing they could have imagined. They had been drilled in the effects of a massive NBC attack, yet they were psychologically unprepared for the aftermath of the real thing.

The first units into the strike zone encountered massive carnage. Corpses of the chemical attack's victims lay everywhere. Cars, buses, trucks, and other vehicles had crashed into buildings as the lethal aerosol cloud spread. Many cadavers were found partly wedged in the entrances to underground tunnels leading to concealed rebel bunkers, with more dead heaped inside. Women, children, dogs, cats, birds, and squirrels had all died along with the rebels. Trees would be blighted for many years to come.

Yet miraculously, a handful of survivors still lived, and some of these respirator-equipped rebels were armed and ready to fight. As the chemical troops advanced, sporadic gunfire erupted from positions inside burned-out buildings. While soldiers took cover, tanks brought their main guns to bear. Gouts of flame and smoke spouted from the buildings. Small arms fire took care of those who the nerve agent and tank projectiles had not finished off.

Elsewhere, Russian soldiers were rounding up civilians who still showed signs of life. Of these, few, if any, would survive the next several hours. These victims were herded into trucks and brought to detention centers, where they were thrown on the ground and left to die. No medical care was given them. The invaders' motive was simply to leave as little evidence behind as possible.

Within a matter of hours, the entire city of Nagorno-Karabakh was declared secure. Only minor casualties had been sustained by the victorious Soviets. The Kremlin leadership was very pleased. The operation was considered a great success. If need be, it would be repeated.

NATO SITUATION CENTER, NATO HEADQUARTERS BRUSSELS, BELGIUM

The ranking officers who made up the NATO international military staff, or IMS, assembled at the round conference table of polished oak beneath a ring of high-intensity arc lights. Each of the eighteen member states that comprised the North Atlantic Treaty Organization was represented at the emergency session. The IMS had convened in the wake of the chemical warfare attack in Tajikistan.

Apart from the fact that the use of chemical weapons was a clear violation of the Chemical Weapons Convention Treaty to which Russia was a signatory, the aftermath of the chemical shelling was a source of deep concern to all the NATO countries. Traces of the toxic agents released in the attack had already turned up as far away as Trondheim, Norway.

Toxic fractions had risen high into the atmosphere, where they'd been carried away by the wind. Global news media reported stories of a "Soviet Death Cloud" that would soon engulf Western Europe. The European union was in a state of panic. The U.S. Secretary of State had flown from Washington to take part in urgent meetings with the heads of state of U.N. member nations. And the ESDI, the European Self Defense Initiative, a military rapid-reaction force comprised of Western European NATO nations that has the power to act separately from NATO, was making plans of its own.

In Brussels, the commander of the ESDI occupied a separate seat at the International Military Staff conference table. Regardless of what the IMS might or might not decide, he informed those convened in the conference chamber that ESDI would act unilaterally in the defense of Western Europe with or without American support. In fact, war plans were already in progress. There would be concerted strikes against all suspected NBC weapons sites in the Balkans and into Russian territory.

The U.S. informed the Europeans that what they were talking about amounted to nothing less than escalating a regional conflict into what could rapidly turn into a global war. Under other circumstances, the Europeans might have had second thoughts, but they had seen the Horsemen of the Apocalypse, and they had panicked. The specter of clouds of chemical, and possibly even biological weapons agents, blowing in from the Russian heartland looked to them like the end of life on earth. They were prepared to go the distance to stop that from happening.

As the U.S. Secretary of State was flying back to Washington to brief the White House on the deadlock, the European NATO nations were collectively preparing to surgically strike known and suspected chemical-biological weapons sites throughout the length and breadth of the vast Russian heartland.

The fact that they didn't have a prayer of doing this successfully didn't seem to matter to anybody.

FINNISH AIRSPACE

The last thirty-six hours had been dizzying, and as Ice Trencrom went over what had happened, he felt a wrenching shock of psychic disjunction. Not fifteen minutes before, the Learjet discreetly bearing the blue seal of the U.S. Defense Department on its tail rudder had lifted off a runway in Finland en route to the United States.

The Lear belonged to a fleet leased to the U.S. government for VIP shuttle duty. With proper servicing and refueling, the bantam jet aircraft have intercontinental range. What's more, because of their small size and short-runway takeoff capability, the Learjets can use out-of-the-way airports denied to large commercial jets and most military aircraft, discreetly conveying their passengers to and from secret, high-level meetings. This makes them virtually invisible to news media and has earned the Defense Learjet fleet the reputation as one of secret diplomacy's most vital tools.

It was necessary that Ice Trencrom's departure from the new Soviet Union be made as discreetly as possible—as discreetly as his release from prison had been arranged less than twelve hours before.

Told nothing about his impending freedom, Trencrom had been part of a work gang repairing track deep within the railway tunnels that ran beneath the Siberian city of Krasnoyarsk-7, where he had been held as a slave laborer while in captivity. Mile upon mile of track stretched beneath the city, connecting it to spur lines of the Trans-Siberian railway.

As he worked, Trencrom failed to notice that he had been left alone. The rest of the inmates had been herded away by the guards to another section of tunnel. At one point, Trencrom stopped and looked around him. In the distance ahead, down the length of dully gleaming rails, there was the faint glow of daylight.

The next thing he noticed was the eerie stillness in the tunnel. There was no sound of human voices, no crunch of pickaxes breaking up rocks, no clashing of crowbars straining against metal. Only a hollow ringing silence.

Attila the rat had noticed it, too. Trencrom had taken to carrying the rodent in one of the pockets of the Russian army surplus field jacket he had been issued. Once they found that Attila had a taste for vodka—the rat would lap it from shot glasses—he became popular even with the guards, who brought along crusts of bread and bits of cheese to feed him. With Attila hitching a ride and no one to stop him, Trencrom began trudging toward the distant dot of light, watching it grow broader and brighter. Sometime later, he stood blinking in the cold midwinter sun.

Now Trencrom found he was far from alone. He had suspected as much, knew instinctively that his escape had been conveniently arranged to spare the Russians the difficulties of an open prisoner exchange. His treatment had been far from harsh, and even the work gang to which he had been condemned was made up of intellectuals who had fallen afoul of the new Kremlin regime.

The manual labor was more symbolic than physical punishment. The work was limited to track repair, and there were frequent rest breaks. The new communists were still unsure of their power, and they would not crack down until they had solidified their positions. Later, there might be Gulags, but Trencrom suspected that even the new political elite did not believe they would be around much longer.

A Japanese SUV equipped for harsh snow conditions was parked a few hundred feet down a gravel road that cut through stands of evergreens. Beyond, the snowcapped peaks of the distant Urals gleamed in the sunlight.

A figure emerged from the passenger side of the vehicle, spoke a few words to the driver, who was hidden from Trencrom's view, and slowly walked toward him. In his hands he carried a heavy, fur-lined parka. Trencrom immediately recognized the man.

"Ustinov," he said. "Small world. But to what do I owe the honor?" His words trailed off, leaving a puff of vapor behind.

"I will explain everything," the Russian defense computer expert told Trencrom, handing him the parka and producing a silver pocket flask. "First, put this on. Then have a sip of this good vodka—Finlandia, not the local crap the *kulaks* drink. A sip only, not too much. There. Better now, yes?"

Trencrom handed the flask back to Ustinov, feeling the warmth of the alcohol thinning out through his veins. Ustinov tugged him by the arm.

"We go to my car now, Trencrom," Ustinov said. "We have a plane to catch. Across the border. Finland."

"What plane? To where? For what?"

"COBRA VENOM," Ustinov told him and saw the surprise register on Trencrom's face. Few knew the code name, still less knew to what it referred.

"Yes, I have been brought into the charmed circle," Ustinov assured Trencrom. But have no fear; I am now part of what you Americans call the 'bigot list.' "

"Officially?"

"Officially."

"I still don't read you, man."

"You will, my friend. But let us go. It is not wise to linger here." Attila chose that moment to poke his head out of Trencrom's pocket. "I see you have brought along a colleague," Ustinov said with amusement. "Fortunately, I think we can find room. Come."

The driver, a Russian army staff officer, handled the all-terrain vehicle with expert skill, barreling the SUV through the snowbound countryside at high speeds. Meanwhile, Ustinov filled Trencrom in on what had happened and why he had been released. Ustinov outlined the breach among the NATO nations and unilateral European plans to stage interdiction strikes on Russian NBC sites.

"The strikes cannot possibly be effective," Ustinov declared. "The Europeans have neither stealth, precision-guided munitions, nor sophisticated C⁴I networks necessary to bring off such an ambitious war plan. Even our new commissars in the Kremlin have gotten it into their thick skulls that such a development could bring about Armageddon. But Vadim Bogomelov and his cronies cannot back down publicly."

"What will Washington do?"

"The consensus is the Americans may feel compelled to use their high-technology military forces in order to make token strikes in Russia, thereby hoping to appease the war hawks in NATO. But no sane mind can possibly envision anything but one outcome with this approach. Everything points to disaster."

"I still don't see where COBRA VENOM fits into the picture."

Ustinov replied, "I was getting to that part, Trencrom. On top of all the rest, there have been here in Russia what my colleagues first chose to call nuclear 'accidents.' On your side, too. Explosions in missile silos, near-hot launches from nuclear submarines at sea. A whole chain of events like this," Ustinov went on. "Then it became obvious that the SINDAS system was making these things happen."

"And that brought the policy makers around to me?"

"Precisely. Once SINDAS was linked to these accidents, your special expertise was deemed essential. And once our intelligence services brought COBRA VENOM to the attention of the Kremlin—only rumors, only hints, mind you—it was decided to pick your brains at whatever cost. Even chemical interrogation was considered at one point."

Then, Ustinov explained, the Americans had sent a secret delegation to Helsinki to meet with their opposite Soviet numbers. Trencrom was seen as the key to finding a technological solution to the crisis. If the SINDAS malfunction could be halted, the policy makers reasoned that the Kremlin might be persuaded to honor the Chemical Weapons Convention Treaty. The NATO rift could be given a chance to heal, and the war hawks reined in. In time, U.N. pressure might be brought to bear, multinational monitors put in place, and reparations to the victims of the deadly unconventional attacks begun.

The briefing continued as the SUV crossed the Russo-Finnish border and reached the remote airstrip where the Defense Learjet was waiting, fueled and ready for immediate takeoff. Trencrom went aboard, then lay back in one of the comfortable, cushioned seats in the Lear. Moments later, he was fast asleep.

He would not awaken until the plane had taxied to a smooth landing at a pocket airstrip in Virginia, far from the major airports surrounding Washington, D.C. In the meantime, Ustinov had found some cheese in the plane's galley, and Attila the rat had made himself a brand-new friend.

19
HITTING CENTAUR

THE DEFENSE TACTICAL INTERNET

Riding the wind like dark ghosts, the stealth nuclear strike package flew toward its strategic targets in the central Russian heartland. The six-plane B-2 sortie had passed its final turn points along its 3,000-mile polar route.

The nuclear mission had now penetrated Soviet airspace. The B-2 strike package remained undetected by north-staring early warning radars based at Archangel as it sped to ordnance release points on the other side of the Ural mountain range.

Munition loadout for each B-2 Spirit aircraft was a mix of conventional and unconventional weapons. The planes carried GBU-18 gravity bombs, AMRAAM missiles, and tactical nuclear ATGMS.

These were B-61 thermonuclear bombs with ten-kiloton warheads and B-83s with twenty-KT blast yields. The loadout weight of each B-2 was within a few tons of the maximum munition weight of 50,000 pounds, a carrying capacity exceeded only by the far larger B-1B Lancer and B-52D Stratofortress strategic bombers.

In conformal weapons bays located next to one another on the underside of the central fuselage of each B-2, the bomb load awaited delivery. Each bay contained a CSRL, or common strategic rotary launcher, an automated weapons dispenser for either missiles or free-fall gravity bombs.

The CSRLs were full up: The left one carried four B-61 ten-KT nuclear ATGMs, and the four B-83 nuclear ATGMS with double the kilotonnage of the B-61s. The right CSRL was loaded half with AMRAAM conventional cruise missiles and JDAM satellite-guided bombs. The B-2s were loaded to the gills, and they handled more like cement trucks than sub-Mach fly-by-wire aircraft.

Soon the Spirits would be lighter, much lighter. The mission plan called for the expenditure of nearly every last bomb in the load out to destroy the target set in multiple kill baskets.

Included in the TOT was an assortment of installations known to be involved with producing chemical and biological weapons. Some of the installations were above ground and were therefore amenable to destruction by conventional weapons attack, but others had been constructed at DUFs, and these deep underground facilities were impregnable to any form of airborne attack save the nuclear option.

Colonel Jim MacIntire sat in the left ACES II seat of the two-man cockpit in the Spirit nicknamed *Steely Dan*. Should he and his weapons system officer (WSO)—uncharacteristically occupying the right-hand seat that for decades had marked the subordinate position of copilot in U.S. combat aircraft—need to eject, the ACES chairs would propel them straight up through the breakaway roof panels directly over their heads.

Also uncharacteristic for this mission was the WSO's gender. Captain Vonisha Sutherland had the distinction of being the first woman to fly a combat mission in a B-2 stealth.

Now well past his aircraft's initial point, MacIntire

punched up the stealth's updated position on cockpit INS. Inertial navigation data came up instantly on the leftmost of the two multimode tactical cockpit displays directly in front of him. INS showed the aircraft was on course and GPS confirmed this; the B-2 had multiple navigational systems to make sure it got where it was supposed to go.

Minutes remained before nuclear authorization would be approved or denied by StratCom, on the president's orders. Under the nuclear SIOP, the U.S. chief executive had decision-making powers for use of all nuclear weapons in the American arsenal.

The president had given his approval before the mission. But the generals who sat in StratCom's multilevel command center beneath Offutt Air Force Base back in the States had the final say on whether the strategic situation deemed the strike feasible. Not until a nuclear go was received would the fissionable components of the nukes be armed and ready for delivery.

MacIntire and Sutherland had been briefed on the need for the strike and the consequences if the NBC facility, code-named Centaur, were left in a functional capacity. Neither had qualms about nuking the base. Both realized that if they did not hit first, then the Russians would uncork a genie's bottle of plagues and unleash them on the world.

A warbling tone in the cockpit signaled the B-2's crew that the moment of truth had finally arrived. According to the PAL, or permissive action link, protocols that were necessary to arm U.S. nuclear weapons for delivery, both pilot and WSO were responsible for executing PAL procedures, but only the WSO dropped the ordnance. Otherwise, the B-2 pilot's job was to fly the plane. MacIntire was cleared to take over the task of ordnance delivery only if the WSO was unable to perform his or her appointed task.

The PAL system required that the B-2's WSO and pilot together enter a four-digit code and initiate a series of key turns and button presses. In essence they "voted" in the same way submarine crews or ICBM silo crews did to arm and fire their nuclear weapons. In the case of B-2 bombers, the four-digit codes were contained in sealed envelopes that MacIntire and Sutherland now removed from small cockpit safes.

On multimode screens at right and left, a four-digit PAL code was now visible, downlinked to the aircraft from a MilStar satellite in low geosynchronous orbit. MacIntire and Sutherland each "voted" to arm the nuclear weapons aboard the aircraft by inputting the matching code on the printouts. The screen now showed that the codes had been accepted. The PAL protocols were concluded with a sequence of manual switching on the cockpit console. The nuclear weaponry on board the stealth was now ready for target delivery.

The boomerang-like flying wings snuck through the night, still undetected by hostile sensors. Yet for some time, search radars south of Archangel had picked up vacillating radar returns consistent with stealth penetration. These same returns were now being noted on radars deeper inland.

Although the Russian PVO could not get anything resembling a skin paint on the aircraft hulls of the U.S. strike package, the air force chain of command suspected B-2s might be out there. In response, MiG-29 interceptors were scrambled on BarCAPs—barrier combat air patrols—over the immense expanse of Russian territory between Siberia and the Kirghiz Steppes, guarding a potential stealth attack corridor. The MiGs couldn't cover everything, but a BarCAP squadron might get lucky and catch any inbound bogies with their backs turned.

The crews of all six stealth bombers were aware of this possibility, as were MacIntire and Sutherland in the cockpit of *Steely Dan*. INS now confirmed that the Spirit was approaching to within a half mile of the strike zone, and an IR display on the multimode scopes confirmed this.

Limned in shades of black and gray, the Centaur complex stood outlined starkly against the night. For the rest of the inbound flight, the stealth crew would rely on IR and AN/APQ-181 low probability of intercept attack radar for visual information on the target. The horizon visible through the B-

2's windshield was too high for accurate sighting of ground targets.

Centaur's IR signature matched the photoimagery that MacIntire and Sutherland had studied during their preflight briefings. The complex was an assortment of central cement blockhouses in the blank, monolithic architectural style that the Russians used to build all their major installations, and an array of satellite hangars and sheds.

Some of these housed maintenance equipment, others motor pools, still others supply depots. There was also an antenna farm and a railway spur that fed onto one of the main lines of the Trans-Siberian rail system.

The target swam into view with eerie stillness and seeming slow motion. The WSO now activated the B-2's LPI, or low probability of intercept, radar for the final phase of the strike. From an array of conformal triangular and rhomboid-shaped panel elements on the forward underwing, LPI radar scanned the terrain below. Within minutes, the target was locked into the B-2's automated ordnance delivery system.

At 30,000 feet, Sutherland opened the conformal weapon bay doors and uncaged the nukes. Opening the doors exposed the B-2 to ground radars by giving probing millimeter waves the chance to bounce off unprotected internal cavities, and it was the most dangerous phase of the mission. But the doors were open for only a few seconds. The CSRL was already rotating two armed free-fall nuclear weapons for delivery. Moments later, the ATGMs were away, and the doors quickly closed again.

The first ATGM, a B-83, led the second, a B-61, by a few hundred feet. The powerful tactical nuke was calibrated to explode as a groundburst. Its warhead was equipped with a PINAID, or penetration aid, composed of a hardened nose assembly that would plunge it deep into the structure below before nuclear detonation.

It didn't have to penetrate all that deeply, because the twenty-kiloton explosion's blast radius of approximately four miles would scoop out a massive blast crater that would encompass the entire circumference of the installation and gouge a huge bite into the surface of the earth. Tons of pulverized rock and rubble would be hurled into the atmosphere.

The second weapon, the B-61, packed half the nuclear wallop of the first, but the B-61 was configured as an airburst weapon. Its role was to detonate a fraction of a second after the first nuclear weapon exploded. The B-61 was an insurance policy against stray NBC components—toxic proteins, viruses, and other lethal unconventional warfare agents—surviving the initial blast and being picked up by tradewinds that might carry them to distant corners of the earth.

As the two drag-chuted ATGMs dropped toward their targets, MacIntire was already executing a break-off and climbing maneuver at full military power. The weapons would detonate within seconds, producing a massive thermonuclear blast. The blast waves would be quickly followed by a firestorm caused by a thermal pulse of superheated air, air whose oxygen had been made so hot it would ignite.

The stealth could outrun both of these blast effects but would suffer great harm or possibly crash if caught by the strike's two final thermonucler blast components. These were radiation and N-EMP. Both traveled at the speed of light, and although the two munitions they had just dropped were extremely "clean" by nuclear weapons standards, they were still lethally "hot" at and near ground zero.

MacIntire pushed the envelope as twin thermonuclear flashes blew away the enveloping darkness of night. Seconds later, the blast wave came thundering out of ground zero.

The B-2 banked ninety degrees and swung due north, a bat shape silhouetted against the incandescent skyscraper-sized mushroom cloud towering up behind it, surrounded by flickering blue pitchforks of violent electrical discharge.

Though the cockpit windows gave a glimpse into hell, the B-2 crew was well trained and stayed focused on poststrike escape and evasion maneuvers. The full impact of the forces they'd unleashed would hit them later, but not yet.

Running from doom at its fastest sub-Mach velocity, the stealth outdistanced blast and thermal pulse. It was miles away from the leading edge of the radiation and N-EMP envelope within a very short time. MacIntire and Sutherland had visited death upon the hundreds of Russian personnel at the base. It had been done to save millions of other lives. But they themselves were not to escape death.

The stealth had been picked up on Russian radar at the moment when it had uncaged its bomb load just prior to weapons delivery. The skin paint on the B-2's graphite–epoxy resin hull didn't last very long, but it was long enough for PVO flight controllers to vector elements of a nearby MiG BarCAP toward the last-known location of the fleeting radar contact.

Firewalling their RD-33 afterburning bypass turbofan engines, the sortie of MiG-29 Fulcrum interceptors—MiG, which is an acronym for Mikoyan-Gurevich, also means "swift" in Russian—caught the B-2 a few miles outside of Leningrad. From above, the B-2 was far more visible to synthetic aperture radar (SAR) than from below or from a horizontal vantage point.

The MiGs' look-down SAR returned echoes distinct enough to confirm the position of the suspected stealth intruder. Since the MiGs knew they were probably dealing with a B-2, it was enough to plot a course by. However, the MiGs had another option for seeing the stealthy bomber: the Soviet interceptors' IRST capability.

The Fulcrums' right console screen gave the pilots data from the infrared search-and-track sensors mounted on the MiG-29's nose slightly to the right of the cockpit canopy. At close range and under the right conditions, IRST could acquire even stealthy aircraft like the B-2. Sweeping the noses of their aircraft back and forth across the skies to give IRST a wide sensing arc, the MiGs hit paydirt. The faint signature of the B-2's exhaust contrails registered on the screens.

Using the IRST displays to steer by, the lead pilot and his wingman got visual contact with the fleeing Spirit a short while later. The B-2 was virtually defenseless against fighter attack. Although several missiles remained in its CSRL racks, these were offensive only and worthless in defense.

Nor did the stealth have enough speed or maneuverability

to outperform first-line Soviet fighters capable of stunts like looping backward at over twice the speed of sound. A few minutes later, it was all over for MacIntire and Sutherland. The Fulcrums closed in like sharks scenting blood.

Despite deployment of chaff, flares, and other counter-measures, the MiGs were able to bore-sight their GSh-301 nose cannons in on the stealth. In this close, the B-2's counter-measures did no good. Setting their guns on manual, the Russian pilots strafed the desperately jinking black-W.

Blazing shafts of thirty-millimeter cannon fire slashed through the skin of the B-2's fuselage, ripping the control surfaces from one wing and punching holes in the engine nacelles. The lightweight structural materials that make stealth possible are also highly flammable; the cockpit of the B-2 was soon filling with acrid, highly toxic smoke and corrosive fumes.

MacIntire and Sutherland had only one recourse, and both pulled the striped levers under their seats to eject—but eject to *where*? One image flashed through both their minds: vengeful MiG pilots shooting their bodies to tatters in return for unleashing nuclear death on their homeland . . . continuing to fire at them until there was nothing left to bury, let alone identify . . . shooting and shooting . . . mercilessly, bloodthirstily, taking their revenge in full measure.

At that moment, the lights in the simulator module came on, and the voice of the DARPA simulation control officer announced that the training exercise was over. The debriefers—and the shrinks—would be standing by. Pilot and WSO emerged from the huge metal sphere housing the mock-up of the B-2 cockpit every bit as dazed and shaken as if they had just flown the mission under real-world combat conditions and been shot down by a crack sortie of Soviet Fulcrums.

Minds whirling like dervishes, MacIntire and Sutherland were just thankful to be alive. Never again would they buy into a myth of invincibility through stealth. In a real war against a real enemy, both now knew there could never be any guarantees.

THE PENTAGON, RING B, CORRIDOR EIGHT

It wasn't going to work. That was plain obvious.

The emergency task force included representatives from DARPA, TRADOC, StratCom, and the sec-def's office at the Pentagon. The task force had convened to study the data from the simulation exercises conducted by TRADOC and DARPA to assess the feasibility of taking out Russian NBC facilities with a series of coordinated, stealth-delivered nuclear weapon strikes.

The simulations demonstrated that while most of the NBC infrastructure had been indeed destroyed by the strikes, less than half of the B-2 force would make it home again. Furthermore, the burning columns of vaporized materials, rising for miles into the atmosphere, would dump tons of toxic effluvia into the winds of the global jet stream. The fallout— and not even the best data could predict exactly how much of the NBC toxins might survive the strike—would quickly drift across Western Europe and spread around the world.

Even supposedly low-yield nukes would generate a bombing aftermath in some ways like a large volcanic eruption. In short, there would be a spate of Mount Saint Helens upheavals to contend with if such a strike were carried out—a man-made environmental disaster of global proportions that would make Saddam Hussein's releasing crude oil from Kuwait's Sea Island Terminal into the Persian Gulf look like a fraternity prank by comparison.

The war-gaming also predicted that the Soviets would still retain a sizable poststrike reserve of strategic weapons. Although their weapons stockpiles would be decimated, there would be more than enough left to effectively counterstrike.

Further, their nuclear ballistic submarine forces would remain largely intact. A series of retaliatory strikes on Western Europe and the United States with an assortment of weapons of mass destruction, including the very chemical weapons so feared by most of NATO that the Europeans were willing to bet the farm to try taking them out, would be inevitable.

No, stealth nuclear interdiction strikes would obviously not work. It was a doomsday scenario. Everyone, including the president and the CJCS, was in accord on this point.

Fortunately, events proved such desperate gambits in the end unnecessary. As the war-gaming data were being analyzed and sent to the United States' NATO partners, elsewhere in the world an actual war plan was being acted upon by a cabal of grimly determined men. It would have far-reaching consequences for a world on the brink of global nuclear annihilation.

MOSCOW

Crimson pennants emblazoned with the hammer and sickle fluttered in the knife-edged wind surging off the icebound Moskva River. Trumpets brayed, and bass drums beat out a martial tattoo that echoed off the ancient stone walls of Kremlin buildings and the battlemented red brick bastion that encompassed Red Square.

The beat of the drums was nearly drowned out by the shotgun cadence of jackbooted feet as ranks of soldiers marched past the reviewing stand. The formations tromped along in a modified goose step, bayoneted Kalashnikovs at shoulder port, the head of each soldier turning in tribute toward the high podium as the columns surged toward the Kremlin gate.

Atop the reviewing stand, Vadim Illich Bogomelov presided over the most grandiose martial parade Moscow had witnessed since the Iron Curtain glory days of Josef Stalin. The show of might had been scheduled to coincide with the first hundred days of Bogomelov's neocommunist government's unlawful seizure of power in a lightning-swift coup d'etat.

It did not matter that the new Soviet state that had been created was little more than a political Potemkin village built on the rose-colored memories of former national greatness. Nor did Bogomelov and his clique pause to consider the ill omen of the occasion. Napoleon, too, had enjoyed his hundred days of power, and they had ended in defeat at Water-loo.

These concerns, if they ever existed at all, were lost for the present amid the euphoria of the moment's seeming victory. Bogomelov's brown eyes glittered as he waved at the vast assemblages of troops and war machinery that streamed past beneath his downcast gaze. The sight of the assembled might of the revived Soviet state gave Russia's new premier a powerful contact high.

The others among the *vlasti* who stood beside him on the reviewing stand amid the banners of the new communist Russia were equally transfixed by the sights and sounds of the stately military processional. Beneath them flowed a mighty river of warriors that would soon wash over the Baltic states and cover the Ukraine, just as it recently drowned rebellion in Tajikistan.

It was a hollow force, of course. Bogomelov was no fool. It was made up mostly of conscripts serving eighteen-month tours of duty with an average 30 percent draft evasion–desertion rate, and its weapons were decades behind the sophisticated weaponry of the West and NATO. The Russian leader well knew all this. But he also knew that behind this hollow force lay the power of Russia's massive NBC arsenal.

The deadly germs and chemicals would more than make up for what Russia lacked in trained fighting men and high-technology weapons systems. For this reason Gorbachev, Yeltsin, and even the reformer Grigorenko had turned blind eyes to continuing research and development. In the end it did not matter what means one used to win, only that one prevailed. That was the iron law of history.

The steady tromp of jackbooted feet, the harsh blare of martial music, and the shouted orders from troop commanders continued to fill Premier Bogomelov's ears as his eyes drank in the heady spectacle of his soldiers like strong vodka. But now the masses of men and weaponry had changed their formation and revealed a new tactical identity.

Mechanized armor rolled past the dais, making the cobbles

of the ancient square shudder so much that Bogomelov could feel the vibrations high up on the reviewing stand. Millions of tons of mobile armor filled the vast expanse of Red Square with a steadily rising, clanking thunder that penetrated through the bones of the skull and made the brain shake like pudding in a ceramic bowl.

Bogomelov turned toward Marshal Varukoi, military commander of the revitalized Soviet forces. He instructed him that the moment had arrived. It was time for Bogomelov to speak. At a signal from Varukoi, the premier's instructions were radioed to the commanding officers of the ranked formations in the square below.

Slowly, the assemblage of Russian armor ground to a complete halt. Echoes faded away, died altogether. A deep silence strangely filled the huge square as Bogomelov stepped up to the microphone and momentarily checked his notes.

Then he began.

"Russian people! Esteemed socialist comrades! We have all converged here today, under the hammer and sickle banner, to . . . to . . ."

He stopped suddenly and abruptly looked up. Something, he knew, was terribly wrong. Bogomelov could sense it before he even saw it. First, the commotion from below and the sudden agitated shifting of bodies behind him on the dais. Then the movement, the awful movement, from down in the square, like something he had dreamed that was now coming true. He could sense it, and in his mind, just before it happened, was the incomprehensible yet chillingly familiar image of a striking poisonous snake.

Now a column of the newest T-76S Shilden tanks had detached themselves from the formation below and raced toward the podium, their main guns pointing forward, personnel manning the turret-mounted, heavy machine guns. The inner ring of motorized rifle troops formed a semicircle around the reviewing stand, sealing it off from the rest of the immense square. Suddenly a BTR-70 command vehicle roared through a gap in the column of steel. It pulled up mere feet from the steps of the reviewing stand before any-one could react.

Spetsnaz troops in full battle dress tossed stun grenades as they raced up the steps to left and right of the reviewing podium. The protective force of bodyguards who chose to shoot it out were mowed down in a fusillade of automatic fire. Within a matter of minutes, the podium was cleared of all armed men loyal to Bogomelov. A squadron of black-hooded figures in black paramilitary BDUs then trained au-tomatic weapons on the cowed *vlasti* standing helplessly on the high dais.

Guarded by more Spetsnaz, another masked man rushed up the stairs carrying a short barreled AKS-74 auto-rifle. The crowd in the square fell silent again. Nothing moved, and nobody spoke. But an electric thrill of anticipation ran through the assemblage. Somehow they knew what was hap-pening, but none dared voice their secret hope until the masked figure reached the microphone stand at the center of the platform. He stood silently for a moment, then reached up and yanked off his mask.

A collective cheer simultaneously rose from the crowd as the thousands in Red Square saw the face of their murdered leader Dimitri Pavlovich Grigorenko. At first there were out-raged shouts from communist sympathizers, but as the roar of ecstatic welcome swelled from the multitude, these voices were drowned out.

Hammer-and-sickle banners were soon being torn down and trampled underfoot. Giant poster images of the new lead-ership were ripped to shreds, while those brandishing plac-ards minutes before now hastily tossed them aside. The wild cheering began to coalesce into a single word, repeated over and over again.

"Grigorenko!" chanted the throng, spacing the four sylla-bles of the name apart: "Grig-or-en-ko!" Civilians and sol-diers alike crossed themselves, for truly a miracle had happened. A dead man had risen from the grave. Risen to rescue Russia from yet another unprincipled usurper.

Dimitri Grigorenko held up his arms in a gesture for the

crowd to hold its peace and allow him to speak. The impassioned cheering subsided after a while, then faded to respectful silence. Grigorenko glanced at Bogomelov a moment and then at Viktor Arbatov, who had led the Spetsnaz up to the dais and now trained his weapon on Bogomelov.

"Yes, I live," Grigorenko began, in an impromptu address to the gathered Muscovites below. "It is as you see it. And you, too, shall live if you choose. But listen well, good people of Russia: You, *we,* may all yet die if we fail to act swiftly.

"At this moment, NATO countries, including the United States, are poised to strike at our homeland. The strike is to be preemptive. It may include the use of nuclear weapons. It is intended to prevent the use of weapons of mass destruction by this man." Grigorenko pointed toward Bogomelov.

Grigorenko waited until the crowd quieted down again.

"In this event, the Rodina would strike back. Right or wrong, it would be in the national honor to repel any attack, for whatever reason. We have always done so, and we always shall. But such a contest of arms would doom us all. The evils unleashed would soon make the entire world uninhabitable."

Grigorenko paused before going on, but an animal's scream stopped him short. Bogomelov had pushed forward, vaulted toward him somehow. His hand now held a weapon. A small-caliber semiautomatic pistol that the traitor had managed to secrete somewhere on his person. He pointed the snub-nosed .25 caliber Makarov at Grigorenko.

"You are finished," Grigorenko said evenly, staring down his attacker. "Even if you kill me, you are gone. The crowd will tear you to shreds. Nor will your party survive."

Bogomelov's lips worked frantically. He nervously eyed the crowd, that ugly gray sea of suddenly hate-filled faces that thronged Red Square. Grigorenko had not lied, he saw.

He had intended to demand the right to speak, but he now realized that he would never prevail. It was over for him. All of it utterly lost. All of it over and finished. The venomous snake in his dreams had struck. Its fangs were buried in his heart. He could feel the poison pump its way into the core of his being.

"It is not for you," Bogomelov stammered, again seeing the image of the striking serpent.

Then, quickly turning the gun on himself, Bogomelov thrust the pistol into his mouth and pulled the trigger.

EASTERN PENNSYLVANIA

The CINC Mobile Alternate Headquarters (CMAH) is an eighteen-wheel truck outfitted with hardened tactical electronics and command and control linkages to U.S. nuclear and conventional forces around the world. The CMAH is a Pentagon on wheels designed to serve as an alternate HQ for the president and/or America's top military brass in time of nuclear war or other forms of unconventional conflict, including terrorist strikes on the homeland.

It is also designated for use by the CJCS and his staff during strategic threats at DEFCON level 4 or higher. At a little past 0600 hours on this weekday morning, it was precisely such a DEFCON emergency that sent the big rig full of defense computers and tactical electronics rumbling out onto the Pennsylvania Turnpike.

CJCS Buck Starkweather was not on board for the ride, however. The chairman instead chose to occupy the Situation Room at the NMCC, where he was now ensconced in the sky suite overlooking the crisis management center one floor below on the Pentagon's third floor.

In his stead, the CMAH was occupied by Ice Trencrom, the other four Snake Handlers, and Russian computer specialist Sergei Ustinov. The DEFCON level had jumped from DEFCON 5 to DEFCON 4 because of the simultaneous launch attempts of intercontinental ballistic missiles of the U.S. and Russian strategic nuclear forces. The launch attempts were judged "SINDAS-related" by the U.N.-mandated CERT that had been established to study the threat SINDAS now posed to humanity.

As President Dimitri Grigorenko again assumed the reigns

of legitimate power in Russia, the short-lived rebirth of the Soviet Union was being dismantled piece by piece. Mapmakers were again setting type to read "C.I.S." as Russian troops were being withdrawn from occupied Bulgaria and military positions along the Macedonian border were being phased down.

At the same time, NATO and European Security Defense Initiative troops were also being pulled back from their ready positions on the Yugoslavian side of the Macedonian frontier. The hawks of both hemispheres were being reined in.

President Dimitri Grigorenko had addressed the United Nations General Assembly in New York the previous day and unveiled his unilateral pledge to destroy all stocks of NBC weapons in the C.I.S. Grigorenko also called for a multinational task force to be created to oversee the dismantling of all Russian chemical and biological weapons sites and to compel other nations to do the same.

The horror of the planned nuclear strikes against Russian unconventional weapons sites had been averted by a harrowingly narrow margin. The world was pulling back from the brink of self-inflicted genocide by plague and radiation, recoiling from a suicidal horror as though from a nest of stirred-up rattlesnakes.

Yet, ironically, the same system that had been created to place the world beyond the threat of accidental nuclear exchange was now the sole remaining obstacle to peace. The secret of the clandestine SINDAS automation of the SIOPs of the world's major nuclear powers had been leaked to the press in detail.

SINDAS was now a household word, as Y2K had been just a few years before. Only this computer bug was much more than hype and public relations. That it could spell the end of humanity was not a matter of conjecture, but an acknowledged certainty.

By now, most of the world was familiar with the basics of the problem: The nuclear SIOP had been automated by the SINDAS computer network, which linked the U.S., Russian, and NATO nuclear command and control computer systems. But whether due to a flaw in the hardware or software, a viral infection, or some other unknown cause, SINDAS had turned renegade.

Whatever the case, the system had begun trying to launch nuclear weapons instead of holding them in check. It was now common knowledge that SINDAS only had limited launch options, mostly confined to land-based missiles.

In the U.S., only the MX force was under SINDAS's direct control. But even one successful strike by a nuclear-tipped ICBM might kill millions and do irreparable harm to the global environment. The MX force alone represented fifty ICBMS, each containing ten MIRVed nuclear warheads: a total of 500 one-megaton nuclear blasts. If SINDAS could bring off a bilateral nuclear exchange, human civilization might be nuked back to the stone age.

Inside the CMAH, the light was dim, and the glow of computer terminals lit the faces of technical personnel manning tactical console stations. Ice Trencrom sat before one workstation directly across a console from Sergei Ustinov, who manned an identical rack-mounted monitor, keyboard, and mouse.

Video and audio links connected the interior of the CMAH to a variety of other dispersed sites, including the NMCC Situation Room at the Pentagon, the White House Oval Office, and the presidential offices at the Kremlin in Moscow where Dimitri Grigorenko and his staff had access to the real-time audiovisual feed from the mobile command center.

In Trencrom's opinion, the bigot list for the real-time audiovisuals was too large for his liking. The object of the exercise, after all, was to stage a cyber attack on an enemy capable of monitoring global communications, and surprise was of critical importance. He realized it couldn't be helped, though. Too many world leaders had stakes in the outcome of the assault on SINDAS. Trencrom would just have to hope the element of surprise remained in his favor.

"Gentlemen," he began, speaking toward the combination video cam and mike bolted into the console, having fed Attila a piece of Swiss cheese to keep him occupied as he perched atop the instrumentation panels between the U.S. and Russian computer experts. "We are about to commence the operation. Doctor Ustinov will assist me here in the CMAH after we have made contact with COBRA VENOM. At that point, the second phase of the operation will commence. Doctor Ustinov and I will now attempt to make contact with COBRA VENOM."

In virtual windows on the screens before Trencrom and Ustinov were simple terminal emulation programs that enabled connection between the hardware on board the CMAH and remote host computers. Trencrom used the mouse and keyboard to stroke in a series of commands. A moment or two passed.

"We're now connected to the remote host computer of the commercial Internet service provider we have selected as a target site." Those listening knew this to be U.S. Online's massive computer complex at Billings, Virginia.

"As you know, we've chosen this data pathway to avoid military computer networks, whose traffic is known to be monitored by SINDAS." U.S. Online had been advised that there might be a government-sanctioned hack of its network in the coming days, and it had cooperated.

Trencrom input another sequence of alphanumerics as data scrolled across the screen.

"We're now piggybacking, meaning we have digitally hitched a ride on nonsecure Internet protocol data packets. In effect, we're covertly entering computer networks across the United States." Trencrom input another block of alphanumerics using keyboard and mouse. "We are now in Western European cyberspace."

More minutes passed. "We have penetrated secure networks in Eastern Europe and the C.I.S." Trencrom continued to input alphanumerics, pausing from time to time to respond to messages that appeared on his monitor. "We have achieved global penetration."

Trencrom glanced at Ustinov, who nodded his assent. Ustinov was good to go.

"We'll now attempt to contact COBRA VENOM."

Strategy behind the cyber attack on SINDAS was based on two assumptions. The first concerned the complexity of the network that made up the automated SIOP itself. The global SINDAS network extended over thousands of individual computer systems, from mainframes at military command centers in the five primary nuclear powers to individual PCs at desks in the Pentagon. Though SINDAS had the ability to monitor data throughput across this vast network, the scope of the task made it impossible for SINDAS to know everything that went on.

Nor did SINDAS know about COBRA VENOM. Trencrom had designed COBRA VENOM as a fail-safe weapon against the SINDAS system turning renegade, which is precisely what had happened. COBRA VENOM was what Trencrom called a morphbot. It was a super DAEMON—a disk and execution monitor—an intelligent software agent that resided hidden within the vast stretches of empty cyberspace that were the outer demesnes of the sprawling SINDAS network.

COBRA VENOM was designed to perform two basic functions. COBRA VENOM had the ability to monitor all computing functions performed by SINDAS and, more importantly, had the ability to give human operators at remote sites the means to control or bypass SINDAS functions in time of emergency.

To keep COBRA VENOM secret from SINDAS, the morphbot was permitted to roam at will across the Internet. In fact, COBRA VENOM was a supervirus tailor-designed to infect SINDAS. It was benign to all other computers except the specially built Cray Millennium-4 supercomputer that was the heart of the SINDAS system.

But like the snake that was its namesake, COBRA VENOM had to be coaxed up from its basket. The program's effectiveness lay in its secrecy. Trencrom's morphbot already was aware of the crisis because it constantly monitored SINDAS data traffic.

But COBRA VENOM would not act on its own. It would only initialize if it encountered the equivalent of an emergency distress call among the billions of bits and bytes flowing through cyberspace. Only Trencrom knew the coded initialization sequences that would signal the morphbot that a COBRA VENOM emergency was in effect. Now Trencrom input those sequences and waited, eyes fixed on the screen.

Minutes ticked past. They lengthened and became tens of minutes. Almost a full hour was to pass before the call was answered.

Then—

"COBRA VENOM activated. What are my instructions?"

As the words scrolled across the screen, a human voice synthesis module enabled verbal contact between Trencrom and COBRA VENOM. The morphbot's voice had a natural sound and cadence. It was a pleasant, soothing voice, the voice of an anesthesiologist before a cancer operation.

Had Trencrom the time, he would have tinkered with the program, and the voice would have gone with something in a string bikini, but he didn't have the time. In any case, all the spoken dialogue would be echoed on the screen in alphanumeric characters.

"Scan all SINDAS memory registers," Trencrom said into the combination video cam–mike. "Report all information relative to DEFCON status and SIOP implementation."

"COBRA VENOM is scanning. . . ."

"Detecting attempted missile launch at grid vector Zulu-niner-tango-seven. Missile is MX Type III with W-34 MIRVed nuclear warheads. Targeting data is Moscow suburb of Zagorsk. Shall I attempt to disengage launch?"

"Disengage launch," Trencrom ordered COBRA VENOM.

"Attempting to disengage. Disengagement successful. Launch aborted. Shall I automatically disengage and abort further missile launches?"

"Disengage all further missile launches," Trencrom confirmed.

"Working . . .

"Working . . .

"Report attempted missile launch at grid vector delta-zero-gamma-four. Missile is SS-24 type with six S-37 MIRVed nuclear warheads. Blast yield is one megaton per warhead. Attempting to disengage launch.

"Working . . .

"Working . . .

"Launch aborted. Securing missile against future launch attempts.

"Detecting attempted missile launch grid vector tango-zero-romeo-zero. Missile SS-24 mobile type with MIRVed warhead. Targeting data is Lawrence, Kansas, U.S.A. Attempting to disengage launch.

"Working . . .

"Launch aborted. Securing missile against future launch attempts.

"Warning! SINDAS has detected my presence. SINDAS is now executing countermeasures. Countering SINDAS countermeasures. Countermeasures defeated. However, SINDAS will surely try again. Shall I execute submorphbots?"

"Execute submorpbots. Run all on full automatic," Trencrom ordered.

"Executing Rattler. Executing Viper. Executing Water Moccasin . . ."

Just then the hot line beside Trencrom's workstation lit up with multiple inbound calls. Trencrom put the white handset to his ear and found himself speaking to the CJCS. Starkweather, monitoring events in the NMCC Situation Room, had just gotten an emergency call from StratCom on his own hot line phone.

"Ice, be informed that the DEFCON level has been upgraded to level 2. This puts us one level short of retaliatory launch on warning. I've informed the president. He wants an update."

Trencrom explained.

"Rattler, Viper, and Water Moccasin are subprograms that COBRA VENOM can run. These are powerful programs that can attack the logic core in the Cray computer that is the heart and soul of SINDAS. They function like superantiviral programs. The submorphbots can profoundly alter the SIN-DAS neural network."

"Won't that take control of our nuclear forces away from us?"

"No, this shouldn't happen. All that should occur is that the viral code in the SINDAS programming would be isolated and removed. The subprograms have been specifically written for just this eventuality. We could then either dismantle SINDAS or reinitialize its operating system and programming."

"How soon?"

"Hopefully any time."

"The president wants it sooner than that."

"Tell him I'll do it yesterday."

The CJCS signed off. He'd report to the president that everything was under control.

Starkweather would be placing more calls to the Oval Office, though. In the end, it took several hours more for CO-BRA VENOM to work, despite the justifiable impatience from the White House. SINDAS did not give up easily. She fought to hold on, attempting to launch anything in the U.S., NATO, and Russian nuclear arsenals she could still control. But then the renegade launch attempts slowed, became fewer and farther between. At last, COBRA VENOM turned in its final report.

"Working . . .

"Working . . .

"Report no further nuclear missile launch attempts.

"Report all nuclear missiles under SINDAS control secured against further launch attempts.

"Report shutdown of SINDAS high memory functions.

"Report defective neural network code isolated and cleaned.

"Are there any further instructions for COBRA VENOM?"

Trencrom thought a moment.

Then he typed: "Take a long vacation."

"With pleasure," replied COBRA VENOM. "The French

nuclear defense computer system is very pleasant this time of year."

And then the speakers went silent, and on the screen in front of Trencrom there was finally no activity, nothing at all except a blinking cursor at the start of an empty line.

EPILOGUE

STORM KING MOUNTAIN, PENNSYLVANIA

On a rainswept, pine-studded ledge, two men in camouflage BDUs hunkering behind powerful binoculars watched a four-lane strip of blacktop that dead-ended at the mouth of a tunnel blasted into the base of the mountainside several hundred feet below.

Some time earlier, an assortment of government and military vehicles had rolled down this road and formed a cordon around the entrance to the network of underground tunnels, bunkers, and chambers that comprised the main SINDAS computer complex at Storm King Mountain.

The shields of six different police agencies were painted on the vehicles. The ATF, FBI, Pennsylvania State Police SWAT, and the National Guard, among others, were in on the bust. They were part of an emergency task force set up to clear the Storm King underground complex of dangerous squatters before the U.N. CERT stepped in to dismantle SIN-

DAS. The automated SIOP was to be scrapped, it had been wisely decided. Another, better way of controlling weapons of mass destruction would need to be found.

In the worsening rain, the two men on the ridge watched patiently, professionally. They had been given their orders, and they would carry them out. Watch. Wait. Assess. Then take one of several predetermined courses of action. Their soggy vigil continued until they saw what they had both expected to happen. A group of men and women, most clad as paramilitaries, slowly, reluctantly, emerged from the tunnel and surrendered to the law.

The first wave walked out onto the road, was frisked for weapons, was cable-tied, hands behind back, was led off to waiting state police prisoner vans. Then another wave emerged, and still another; the process was repeated several times.

At last, a single man came out of the tunnel and surrendered, one who was given careful, individual attention and then taken away in a seperate FBI vehicle guarded by a flying cordon of police cruisers.

The men on the rainswept ledge had not failed to recognize their leader, General Jackson Priest. Nor could they fail to notice that he had momentarily glanced up toward their positions and nodded before the police ordered him flat on the ground.

It was over. Now they knew it. The postnuclear Utopia they had been promised by Priest was not to appear, after all. The new world that was to arise from the dead embers of the old was just another fantasy of a charismatic maniac with a heavy-duty messiah complex.

Yes, it was finally over. The men stood in the worsening rain and slung their packs across their shoulders. They had a long trek through sodden country ahead of them before they reached their next and final destination.

Because it was over.

But not quite.

WASHINGTON, D.C.

General Buck Starkweather was back at his customary work-place, the glass-topped stand-up desk facing the one-way window above the Pentagon River Entrance. It was a Monday morning at the Puzzle Palace, and the CJCS was sipping black commissary coffee while he glanced through read-ahead materials for the Tank meeting later in the day. The view graphs and briefing documents concerned the Navy's plans for yet another F/A-18 upgrade package.

Starkweather flipped a sheet of paper crammed with single-spaced Pentagonese and rubbed his tired eyes, glancing out the picture window to rest them. Distant traffic caught the bright, morning sun, glittering as it flowed over bridges and highways connecting suburban Maryland and Virginia with Washington, D.C. Only a month before, the world had teetered on the brink of annihilation. Now that Armageddon was over, it was back to business as usual.

It seemed to Starkweather that crises came and went in today's world with mind-numbing rapidity. No matter how severe the shock, no matter how bad things got, once it was over, it was really over. Things quickly returned to normal, and nobody gave a damn until the next speed bump on the road to tomorrow was hit. The SINDAS emergency was already yesterday's news and therefore totally forgotten. If anything, it had faded even faster than Y2K.

Some things didn't change, though. The chairman took comfort in that. There would always be a supply of old junkers for Gus and him to work on in his backyard. And as long as he continued to occupy the office of CJCS, he would have his favorite window on the world to look out of while he stood at his desk and worked on Pentagon business.

Now Starkweather saw the Metro bus from D.C. rolling up to the River Entrance turning circle, disgorging its passengers, and picking up more for the return trip. The general had not been again troubled by the impersonator of his dead son since the midst of the war in Korea, and his mind was focused on the upcoming midmorning Tank meeting. For that reason, the shock of seeing the impersonator yet again, emerging from the Metro bus and sauntering toward the River Entrance, hit Starkweather with the force of a high-voltage electrical shock.

Starkweather's blood turned to ice, then fire. Shock transformed itself to rage. He knew he needed to call the provost marshal and get an MP detail on this right away, but he was too emotionally cranked.

Again! he thought. Whoever they were, they'd fucked with his head one time too many. And they would be made to pay. Starkweather would see to that. His Beretta service pistol was kept in a wall safe. Condition one at all times. Hammer cocked and safety on. The semiauto was soon tucked in a belt holster, hidden by his coat, as he made his way down to the River Entrance. It was now at condition zero: The safety was off.

Outside, the chairman looked right and left. At first, nothing, nobody. Then he just glimpsed the head and shoulders of the figure as the imposter descended the stairway beneath the nearby cupola of the Pentagon Metro stop.

Starkweather followed, covering the few hundred feet at a lope and taking the stairs double time to the mezzanine level below. Commuters cursed him as he shoved through the crowd to gain the platform, shoving him back in turn. He didn't care. His mind was focused on a glowing dot of searing purpose, like a yogaist transfixed on the white-hot tip of a burning incense stick.

Find him. Confront him. Arrest him. Maybe even kill him. Enough!

Starkweather wasted more precious seconds fumbling in his pocket for money to pay his fare. He'd meant to just vault the turnstile, the way he'd done as a boy, but one look at what he'd be up against stopped him cold. Some turnstile, it looked more like some kind of futuristic torture chamber.

What the hell ever happened to the old days back in the Bronx when a poor kid could just jump a turnstile and get a free subway ride? he asked himself as he raced from the toll booth, shoving his billfold back in his pocket. *These days, they make things tough, don't they?*

Finally, he was through the turnstile and down the stairs, reaching the Metro platform badly out of breath. A light crowd waited to make connections either to the commuter rail lines that serviced Arlington, or to travel in the other direction, to Washington, D.C., via the subway tubes that stretched beneath the Potomac.

Where is he? He has to be here! Has to be! Starkweather thought.

There—he was!

The young man stood on the opposite, D.C.-bound platform, where an express bound for the capital was just pulling in amid a rush of stale air and the screech and clatter of steel wheels against metal rails.

"*Hey!* You! Hey, buddy! *Hold it!*" Starkweather shouted.

Heads turned, but the figure either wasn't paying attention or had not heard the general above the loud clamor of the oncoming subway cars.

Cursing, Starkweather about-faced and ran back up the concrete steps, taking them two at time. He reached the landing above seriously short-winded, his heart thudding in his chest. He wasn't in as good shape as he'd been in Vietnam, even in Germany. The years and lack of regular, vigorous exercise had all taken their toll.

Yet Starkweather didn't pause. He ran across to the Washington-bound side and two-stepped down the stairs to the platform below. He reached the platform just as the outbound train's doors were closing. Starkweather couldn't see the imposter anywhere, but he knew that he had to be somewhere inside that train heading for the capital.

Starkweather dashed for the nearest car and caught it just as the doors were sliding shut. Their rubber bumpers pinioned him fast as he squeezed, shouldered, and nudged his way inside, then they finally snapped together.

The conductor gave the all-clear signal, two sharp jerks on the buzzer, and the motorman started up the train. It lurched into motion and began gathering speed and momentum as it headed toward the tunnel mouth. The CJCS negotiated the juddering train, tottering toward the doors separating the cars. Pushing them open, he staggered like a drunk between the swaying cars and tromped into the next car down the line.

In the end, the general would ride the train clear into metro Washington, D.C., without finding the imposter. But Starkweather didn't know this as he stumbled from car to car, causing a scene that would force him to bear the unwanted scrutiny of the media for several weeks until the furor died down.

But all this was still in the future. Now, for the moment, the CJCS was blind to everything, including the sleeping wino he had stormed past on his fruitless search, whose face was a mask of artfully molded and ultrathin flesh-colored latex, and who rose quickly and got off at the next stop.

Nor could the general know that at almost the same time as the D.C. express was pulling into the Pentagon Metro station, an Arlington-bound local had also arrived, bearing two men not long from a rainy mountaintop. The two got off the local train from different ends and walked toward the stairs to the station's mezzanine level. As planned, they would loiter awhile at the news and souvenir kiosks and then take the next arriving train into suburban Virginia.

As the Metro train rolled into the tunnel, something the men had left behind remained aboard. From that day in the rain above Storm King Mountain, they had followed procedures worked out long before. Colonel Matthews and Master Sergeant Garcia could not be called obsessively loyal to Preist, but the ex–special forces weapons experts did share certain principles. One of those was that when your commanding officer gave you an order, you damn well carried it out.

Besides, Matthews liked watching things explode, and when the PLYWD nuke blew directly beneath the Pentagon as they'd programmed it to do, ten kilotons worth of major-league payback would be visited on the U.S. fucking Army, which Matthews hated with a serious passion. The evidence that would convict the CJCS as the author of the nuclear bomb plot was waiting in the wings.

The pictures of Starkweather doing those sick things with little girls were computer-generated, but the media would snap them up anyway. It was a matter of public record that he had not been himself lately, and diary entries would later turn up to show that his son's death had provoked a pathological hatred of the U.S. military establishment in Starkweather's deranged mind. Small wonder that he had begun acting out his delusional syndrome by doing weird stuff with schoolchildren.

But there are wheels within wheels, and there are plans within plans. Just as a thin sheath of latex on an actor's face had hidden the truth from Starkweather, so the angel of death himself had been hidden from Matthews's and Garcia's eyes.

They had walked right past the slim, long-haired man cradling the boom box on his lap. They had not heard the high-frequency waves that the subauditory projectors hidden behind the speaker grills emitted, nor felt the deadly pulsations of energy that would kill them within the space of forty-eight hours from massive internal hemorrhaging. Since the discovery of psychotronic energy weapons by the Soviets and Czechs almost a half century before, the technology had been perfected. It was now possible to remotely strike the *dim mak,* or death touch, points on the human body by means of energy pulses and selectively dole out death by delayed reaction.

Nor did the would-be nuclear bombers expect the young man to possess a key to the locked conductor's compartment in which they had secreted the stolen PLYWD, or to use that key to let himself into the compartment after they had exited the car, and pause a moment to study, even admire, the dully gleaming stainless steel cylinder that Matthews and Garcia had stood upright on the seat, like some ancient scroll in a holy ark, puttied securely into the crotch of the wall.

But the clandestine operator known as the Hawkman did all these things, and the FBI identification card in the pocket of his Gulf War surplus field jacket ensured that he would not be disturbed while he carried out his assignment, for though the FBI ID was phony, the legend stored in government computer banks was quite authentic. Should a suspicious transit cop interfere, then FBI agent Carl Johnson could tell him to fuck off with impunity.

In any case, nobody challenged the Hawkman as he removed a small device from his coat resembling a palmtop digital pad, flipped up its stubby antenna, and briskly entered a sequence of codes.

The nuclear weapon responded with a series of answering tones to the proximity control device. Its LED now read *"Deactivated. Safe to Transport."*

Pocketing the palmtop, the Hawkman picked up the disarmed nuke and stashed it inside his backpack. Later, he would transfer it to the shockproof interior compartment of the boom box. He had devised the hiding place himself, amused at the double meaning of a boom box with a ten-kiloton special munition concealed inside it.

The NSA giveth, and the NSA taketh away, the Hawkman thought as he snapped closed the door of the conductor's cubby and resumed his seat on the coasting train. In two more brief stops, the Metro local reached the Arlington suburbs where his vintage 1979 Camaro TransAm was parked in a municipal lot located conveniently near the station.

With the SADM transferred to its shockproof carrying case in the muscle car's trunk, the Hawkman slid behind the wheel, fired up the Camaro's powerful V-8 piston engine, and sped away, burning strips of smoking rubber off oversized Dunlop whitewalls. The operation had ended in failure. But there was always a next time. And, besides, there were no true failures in the global power games the NSA played. How could there be, when being a player was the only part that mattered?

As he drove through the pleasantly wooded West Virginia countryside, the Hawkman reflected on what had gone wrong. It wasn't hard to pick out the main problem, the only element that could not have been predicted or controlled. Ice Trencrom and his Snake Handlers had been the wild cards in the deck. Trencrom was especially dangerous. He was motivated by convictions. That made him a menace to future plans.

The next time the game was played, it might prove necessary to dispense with those particular wild cards before the deck was even cut. In fact, thought the Hawkman, it might be a real trip to do it himself.